Praise for *Shadowed by Grace*

Cara Putman's *Shadowed by Grace* is an amazing story of a young female photographer who goes into a war zone to seek the truth and to possibly save her dying mother. When Rachel Justice is assigned to the care of Lt. Scott Lindstrom, she is already fighting her own internal war. Scott is trying to save sacred treasures but soon he sees that Rachel is the real treasure. Set against the backdrop of World War II, this book is action packed and fast paced but hugely romantic. Well researched and tightly written, *Shadowed by Grace* takes us right into the fray and doesn't let go until the last kiss. Beautiful!

> Lenora Worth, *New York Times* best-selling author
> of *Bayou Sweetheart*

My heart pounded with excitement from the first chapter to the last of *Shadowed by Grace*. With an authentic knowledge of World War II history, a gentle hand of artistry, and a heart for true love, Cara Putman draws in readers until they feel they've traveled through time to watch a story unfold of heroes and the women they love.

> Cindy Woodsmall, *New York Times* best-selling author
> of *The Winnowing Season*

The World War II era is my favorite period to read and write about. It's a good thing for readers that it's Cara Putman's favorite time too. *Shadowed by Grace* is a delightful book drawn from a little-known sidebar of World War II history. If you enjoy this fascinating era, reading great love stories, and journeying through the Italian countryside, you will love this novel.

> Dan Walsh, best-selling author of *The Unfinished Gift*,
> *The Discovery*, and *The Dance*

Steeped in rich historical detail, *Shadowed by Grace* is a fresh and fascinating foray into the annals of World War II, capturing the

reader with a plot as turbulent as the war that raged across Europe
. . . and as breathless as the love story that burgeons within its
midst.

Julie Lessman, award-winning author of
The Daughters of Boston and Winds of Change series

Against the backdrop of Italy, the little-known efforts of the
Monuments Men in World War II come to life in the pages of
Shadowed by Grace. A rich blend of the search for a father,
the hunt for lost treasures, and the desire for a lasting love told
through unforgettable characters. It's a story written by one passionate about the time period. This story will sweep readers into
the journey for lost art, a father, and love!

Tricia Goyer, best-selling author of thirty-five books,
including *The Promise Box*

From colorful Naples to magnificent Florence, Cara Putman's
Shadowed by Grace takes the reader on a tour of wartime Italy, as
Monuments Man Lt. Scott Lindstrom rushes to save priceless art
while photojournalist Rachel Justice chases after a missing piece
of her past. Soaring language, deep characters, engrossing history,
a riveting plot, and a heart-pounding romance . . . do not miss this
story!

Sarah Sundin, award-winning author of *On Distant Shores*

I literally devoured *Shadowed By Grace* and was unable to think
of anything else until I finished it. Full of intriguing characters and
bursting with engrossing details of World War II and the Monument
Men, the novel revealed history I knew nothing about. Everyone
should read this book and understand this unique part of our history.

Colleen Coble, author of *Butterfly Palace*
and the Hope Beach series

Readers may be familiar with the Monument Men from the movie
of the same name, but never will a story of their antics be told

with greater depth and emotion than in *Shadowed by Grace*. Cara Putman's tale of love, intrigue, and purposes higher than our own is a book not to be missed!

Kathleen Y'Barbo, best-selling author
of The Secret Life of Will Tucker series

Cara Putman does an incredible job of transporting readers to war-torn Italy. The historical details add depth and authenticity that readers of historical fiction clamor for. I was swept up in Rachel and Scott's story, their plight, their hopes and dreams, and when their dreams collided, I rooted for them to find their way back to each other. For anyone wanting to learn more about the Monuments Men and their important mission during World War II and the role women played on the front, this is a must read.

Cindy Thomson, author of *Grace's Pictures* and
Annie's Stories, the Ellis Island Series

With characters that will steal your heart, set against the active backdrop of World War II, *Shadowed by Grace* exhibits why Cara Putman is an award-winning author. This is one story not to be missed.

Robin Caroll, author of the Justice Seekers series

In *Shadowed by Grace*, Cara Putman exhibits a gracious and impactful understanding of the greatest generation. Her passion for these characters, and this time in our nation's history, shines through this story.

Marybeth Whalen, author of *The Mailbox*,
The Guest Book, and *The Wishing Tree*,
cofounder of the online women's book club, She Reads

Shadowed by Grace transports you into a story that will captivate you from the start. A masterful blend of history, fiction, and thrilling romance.

Jenny B. Jones, award-winning author of *Save the Date*

Putman delivers an exciting, well-told tale drawn from true-life war crimes. While her hero and heroine work to recover some of Europe's most precious art, they discover love and the mysteries of their own past. Well done! An interesting read.

Rachel Hauck, best-selling author
of *The Wedding Dress* and *Once Upon a Prince*

I've watched development of this Monuments Men story from its conception to its birth, but I had no idea how powerful the story would ultimately be. Putman artfully weaves themes of grief and loss with bright lights of hope and faith, against the desperate backdrop of World War II. You won't put this book down, and these characters will be a part of you forever.

Nicole O'Dell, author of twenty-three books
and founder of Choose NOW Ministries

A World War II love story at its absolute best! Cara Putman artfully weaves real history and fiction with a deft pen, taking her readers on a journey not soon forgotten.

Tamera Alexander, best-selling author
of *To Whisper Her Name* and *A Lasting Impression*

Shadowed
by
Grace

CARA C. PUTMAN

I'll be Seeing You

in Italy

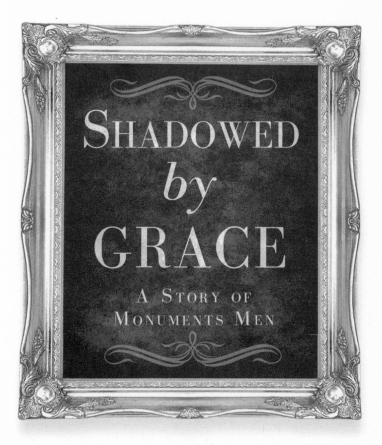

SHADOWED

by

GRACE

A STORY OF MONUMENTS MEN

B&H
PUBLISHING GROUP

Nashville, Tennessee

978-1-4336-8178-3

Published by B&H Publishing Group,
Nashville, Tennessee

Dewey Decimal Classification: F
Subject Heading: ROMANTIC SUSPENSE NOVELS \ FATHER-
DAUGHTER RELATIONSHIP—FICTION \ WORLD WAR,
1939-1945—FICTION

Publisher's Note: The characters and events in this book are fictional,
and any resemblance to actual persons or events is coincidental.

Scripture quotations are taken from
the Holy Bible, King James Version.

1 2 3 4 5 6 7 8 • 18 17 16 15 14

In my life I have been graced to know great men—my grand-fathers, father, and husband. All have been heroes as they live lives dedicated to country, family, and the women they love. As I finished this book, one of those men—one who lived in the Greatest Generation—graduated to heaven on January 27, 2013, after ninety-three years of a life well lived.

This book is a fitting tribute to my Grandpa K. You may not have served—even though you were drafted four times—but you were a symbol of all that was right with your generation. My prayer is that my sons will live lives that build on the legacy you and Grandpa C. left. If they do, they will be heroes in the stories God writes in their lives.

I miss you, Grandpa. Be sure to tell Jesus "Hi" for me.

Chapter 1

Philadelphia, Pennsylvania
March 1944

"YOU HAVE ONE CHANCE to make this fly." Bobby Hamilton leaned across his broad desk and stared her down. "I had to pull more strings than I knew I had to get the brass to bite on sending a woman to Italy. Who sends a woman to a war-torn country? Getting credentials? What a mess." The man waved his beefy hands down in a dismissive gesture. "Then getting you on the *Queen Mary*?" He chomped hard on his cigar.

Rachel perched on the chair in his crowded office as the Andrews Sisters belted out "Boogie Woogie Bugle Boy" on the small Kadette radio sitting atop a stack of papers on Bobby's overloaded credenza. She kept her back so straight her men's-style tailored blazer pulled her shoulders back.

She didn't blink, couldn't give a single sign of weakness. Her editor may have taken all those steps, but she'd had to convince him first, all while watching her mother waste away day by day.

"I hope you know what you're doing, Justice."

"I *do*." She put as much force behind the word as she could without shouting.

He leaned back in his chair, unlit cigar poised to punctuate a thought. "You've got talent. A way with that camera."

She stroked the case, feeling as if it naturally extended from her.

"Don't let me down. Send back photos that will wow readers." He didn't have to mention his bosses.

"Yes, sir." Rachel lurched to her feet and straightened her skirt's front pleat as she hurried from the room before he could call her back.

There was so much to do. Too much before she could join the mass of soldiers and handful of civilians who would cross the Atlantic aboard the HMS *Queen Mary*. If she hurried, she could finish cleaning the apartment and still make it to the hospital before visiting hours ended. It was a stop Rachel had to make, yet dreaded. How could she explain to her mother what she was doing while hiding her secondary purpose?

Rachel climbed the stairs to the small flat she'd shared with her mother for as many years as she could remember. With her coming absence and her mother's declining health, Rachel had let the lease lapse. A friend already had the few boxes filled with Rachel's lifetime of mementos and memories while another friend held her mother's things. The furniture never belonged to them, so it would stay. All that remained was to clean what she could, leaving it in reasonable condition for the landlord.

As she tackled the small bedroom with a bucket of water and a rag, Rachel reached as far as she could under the bed. Her cloth-covered fingers groped against a surface . . . a book? She dropped the rag, then stretched farther, inching her head partway under the bed to reach the item. She grasped an edge and pulled it free.

The volume had a spiral-wire binding with heavy cardboard covers. Between those were thick pages covered with charcoal drawings. As she flipped through it, some of the images looked like different sketches of the same scene. Over and over. From different angles. Varying perspectives. Alternating attempts at techniques. Some were quite good, others pedestrian. All contained one woman, a large hat obscuring her features as she stared across a meadow at a field of some sort. Another hill appeared to be terraced, its steep edges softened by the drop-offs.

Rachel flipped through the book but did not see a name, a year, even a location. Nothing indicated who the artist was or when he worked. The book might contain preliminary sketches of a larger work. She'd often seen her mother use the same technique on the rare occasions they had enough extra money to allow her to create an oil painting. Because supplies were so precious, her mother labored over each painting, testing visions until she had one that pleased her.

It had grieved Rachel to sell her mother's paintings. But with their limited income, the paintings were what she could sell to keep her mother in the hospital. Now those were gone.

She scanned the pages one more time. One drawing held initials in the right-hand corner: RMA. Initials that weren't her mother's. Rachel slipped the book in her knapsack next to her mother's diary she'd found while cleaning out the closet, then returned to her work.

An hour later she closed the apartment door, leaving the key with the super on the first floor. As she walked the streets to the hospital, she slipped between those walking home from work or heading out for the evening. A GI wrapped his arm around a pretty girl bundled in a rich velvet turban and heavy coat. A mother guided an energetic son in his zigzagging pattern up the sidewalk.

Who would miss her if something happened? Her mother? A handful of others? But there was no one to wrap an arm around her and pull her close, whether to ward off the chill or because he couldn't get close enough. She'd poured her energy into proving she could handle a career as a journalist. The last year her remaining time had been poured into nursing her mother, trying to coax life into her.

The brick hospital loomed in front of her. Rachel stepped inside, nodded to the volunteer at the desk, then wound her way through the too-bright halls to the back of the third floor where her mother waited in a ward. The faint scent of disinfectant almost covered the distinct hospital aroma that surrounded Rachel. She sipped the air through her mouth as her gaze bounced around the ward.

She crept toward her mother's narrow bed but couldn't force herself to look into her mother's eyes, not when the woman had read her every thought with a glance from the moment Rachel had first breathed.

"Tell me."

"What?" Her gaze strayed, anywhere but Momma's knowing eyes.

"You have news. Something big. Earth changing."

"All of that happens across an ocean." One of which she would cross. Soon. A chill skittered down her spine. She wanted this, didn't she? In fact, she'd pushed so hard for it, her editor couldn't ignore her a moment longer. She'd won. But when she looked at her mother, lying there pale and emaciated, Rachel feared she'd lost.

A harsh cough rattled from her mother. She tensed as if a vise squeezed the very air from her lungs. When Rachel knew her mother couldn't sustain another breath, she relaxed.

Rachel laced and unlaced her fingers. "You okay, Momma?"

"As okay as I can be." A wan smile tipped her mouth as her mother dabbed a handkerchief against her lips. Rachel exhaled when no blood dotted it. "So . . ."

"I've been assigned to Europe. I leave on the next boat."

Her mother frowned, the edges of youthful grace slipping

from her in the motion. "You got your way. Proved you were ready?"

"Yes, ma'am."

"I see." The words sounded harsh like leaves crunching against an autumn sidewalk.

"I want to do something that matters. Bring the war home to people who can't imagine it. To those who are weary of the news we aren't winning. Somewhere there are stories that show the progress we're making. I want to share those."

"I suppose you talked your way to Italy in the bargain."

"Yes." There was no way Rachel would stop before she reached her goal. It didn't matter what she had to prove to whom—she'd do it. All to find the man who'd abandoned her before her birth . . . but the man who might have the money to get Momma the treatment she so desperately needed.

"I don't want you looking for him." Steel undergirded the words, the kind that if Momma had her strength, Rachel wouldn't dare to cross. Instead, this time she'd be half a world away.

Half a world.

The prospect could scare the spit right out of her or force Rachel to find the courage the war required.

Another cough called Rachel back to her purpose. Without a miracle the tuberculosis would call Momma home soon. Her mother reached across the blanket for a handkerchief, her fingers knocking it to the floor. Rachel rummaged through her purse for a handkerchief, anything that would ease Momma's suffering. Her hands brushed the book, then a handkerchief. She handed the soft cloth to Momma, then retrieved the book.

"What do you have?" Momma's voice was a weak whisper.

"I found this under the bed."

"You should have left it there."

"What is it?"

"A trinket from the past." A cough shook Momma's frame, daring to pull her under and never let go.

"Momma?" Rachel tucked the book in her bag and scrambled to ease her mother. She had to stop it before the cough robbed Momma of her life.

The doctors said there was nothing more they could do, but Rachel knew it was a lie. They needed money before they'd try another treatment. Now she had the vehicle to make more money—she had to board the boat in New York City. Then Momma wouldn't rely on the kindness of old family friends. Not when the hospital couldn't keep her much longer without writing *paid in full* across the bill.

"Maybe I should stay, . . ." Rachel's words trailed off.

Momma shook her head. "Why stay here and watch me waste away? Get out there. Take that camera and shoot the best pictures. You've got more talent than anyone over there."

"You need me here."

"Not as much as I want to know you're making something of yourself." Her momma squeezed out another smile. "Give me a hug and drop me a line every now and again. Ruth will make sure I get them."

Rachel nodded, fighting the tears that crowded her vision. "Yes, ma'am." She had to do this. For Momma. And for herself. She needed to prove to the rest of the world she could create art with her camera that mattered. That she could make a difference in the war effort. That her past did not control her future.

But if Momma died while she was gone . . .

Her mother struggled to rise off the hospital cot. She fumbled with the silver necklace she'd worn every day Rachel could remember. "Here, take this. I want you to have it."

"Momma . . ." Rachel's fear escalated. "You shouldn't give that to me."

"I received it in Italy. You should take it back." Momma shoved it at her, then started coughing.

Rachel took it and slipped it into her pocket. "Here, take a sip of water."

"Good afternoon, Miss Justice." The nurse handed Momma a small cup filled with water. "Ready for your afternoon nap?"

Momma fought to catch her breath. "If you stop this coughing."

"You been at it?"

Momma frowned. "You couldn't hear me at your station?"

"No, ma'am."

"I guess it's not as bad as I thought." Momma closed her eyes, fatigue that never used to plague her pulling down the muscles in her face.

"I'll send postcards, Momma." Rachel leaned down and kissed her cheek.

"See that you do. You know I've always loved getting mail." She opened her eyes, the icy blueness standing in stark contrast to her pale skin. "And Rachel?"

"Yes, ma'am?"

"You leave your father alone."

Chapter 2

Naples, Italy
May 15, 1944

NOTHING WAS GOING AS advertised.

Lieutenant Scott Lindstrom's spine locked into place where he stood. He couldn't have heard the man right. "You want me to do what, sir?"

"You heard me. I'm attaching that photographer to you. We need the good press. And you need the work."

Scott fought back a retort. He didn't need a job. His parents and fiancée had told him he didn't need this one, but he needed to come. Needed the assignment as an officer with the Monuments, Fine Arts, and Archives Division, where he could do something meaningful in the war. The problem was, even those in the brass who thought he added value to the army weren't organized enough to let him do anything outside Naples. The rest thought his mission a waste of time.

Millennium of priceless art waited outside the walls of head-quarters, and he had to cool his heels because he had no supplies and no transport. Everything was complicated by the immense needs present in a city that had been all but destroyed as the Allies

battled the German army for control. Refugees due to the erup-
tion flooded what was left of the infrastructure. The last thing
he needed was responsibility for some dame who wasn't smart
enough to stay home.

He knew why he'd come, why he'd accepted the risk.

Why would she understand?

He hadn't come only to shore up classic buildings that had
stood since the Roman Empire that aerial bombings destroyed. Or
locate priceless pieces of art created by masters in the thirteenth
century to ensure the fighting hadn't destroyed them. Or plan for
the restoration of those that had been touched by the war. The
tales that art disappeared behind the lines made it more important
than ever that he leave the city for the locations where the sculptures, paintings, and altarpieces were housed.

He couldn't do that with a tagalong.

"Sir, I'm not a babysitter." No, he'd come to Italy to save
the history of Western civilization. At least the masterpieces and
sculptures he could find.

The officer stared him down. "Do you want me to attach
her to a unit headed to the front lines? How do you think that
would play if she got injured or killed? This way you can keep
her safe."

"She's a woman, sir."

"Of course. This is a new war." The man leaned back and
crossed his arms over his chest.

Scott sighed. "How long?"

"A week. Bore her. Bring her back ready to take the next boat
home. You have orders. Now get to it." The general turned to a
pile of papers on his desk.

Scott snapped a salute and double-timed it out of the office
back into the crazed maze that made up headquarters. His art
degrees from Harvard combined with his post as curator of a

small museum in Philadelphia hadn't prepared him to ferry a woman around a war zone.

When he hit the foyer, Scott stopped. The general had left out a few key details. Like how to find this reporter. He couldn't expect to stumble upon her. He stopped at one of the desks outside the office. "Hey, I'm supposed to squire Rachel Justice around. Any idea how I find her?"

"Check the public relations division. It's a couple buildings over."

"Thanks." Scott slapped his garrison cap on and then made his way to the hallway.

Soldiers marched up and down the narrow walkway in the old hotel the army had requisitioned. He waited for a gap, then thrust his way into the flow until he wound his way outside. A jeep zipping by kicked a barrage of rocks and clods of dirt against his uniform. One more layer of grime to add to countless others. What he wouldn't give for a hot, steaming shower. The destroyed sewer system was one of many gifts the Germans left when they destroyed Naples and pulled back.

The air overflowed with the sounds of a war machine gearing up for action. Yet he stood in place waiting to fulfill his assignment of saving masterpieces.

So far the Fifth Army command hadn't cleared him to do anything but wait . . . now with a guest. Guess he'd better find her. He headed in the general direction of the press offices. He sidestepped a child, cheeks gaunt and eyes hollow, as the boy sifted through the rubble of what had been a home. Maybe a day ago, a week ago, even a month ago. It didn't matter now. The stone structure sat shattered along the sidewalk. Many of the villages surrounding Naples bore the same look. Shelled remnants stood next to intact apartments, victims of the tug-of-war between the Allied forces and the Germans. The bombs fell with little perceivable discretion. Killing here. Sparing there.

In the face of the brutal realities of war, not the war correspondent's black-and-white version but the living-color kind that plastered images he couldn't shake, he understood the arguments that monuments and fine art didn't matter. What mattered was ending the war.

Even the bombing of Monte Cassino began to make sense, though it had provided the perfect propaganda for the German war machine—reinforcing their image that the Allies had no understanding of the value of historic sites. That Americans were the barbarians intent on destroying rather than saving.

Scott stopped and watched the boy a moment, then reached into his shirt pocket and pulled out a Hershey's D-ration chocolate bar. "Boy."

The child ignored him, moving as if by an unstoppable force, building small piles of rubble as he worked.

Scott slipped into rusty but improving Italian. "You must be hungry." The thin face bore testament to the hunger that must claw at his belly. Scott might not appreciate the culinary delights of K rations, but it ensured a full stomach. The Germans had taken much of the produce and livestock in their retreat, leaving the peasants with little to live on.

Scott waved the bar in front of the boy's eyes. "Here. A gift for you."

The boy turned to him, the bleakness in his eyes not shifting at the sight of the candy.

Scott tucked the bar in the youngster's pocket and then patted it. "Eat it when you like."

The wind ruffled the kid's hair, and Scott watched another moment before resuming his march. Scenes like that were best abandoned. There was only so much he could do to affect the suffering surrounding him. Even that little bit pulled at him, whispering, *What difference would one candy bar make to a child*

who may have lost father and mother and have no place to live, let
alone to get real, healthy food?

He shook his thoughts loose. Straightening, he stepped
around the demolished building. Despite the massive needs duty
beckoned, along with a certain Rachel Justice.

⟡

The soldier bent near the boy with a candy bar. Light brown hair
waved beneath the edge of his helmet, and his smile caught her,
the warmth genuine even from a distance. What would it be like
to have those eyes focused on her?

Rachel tightened her scarf, then reached for the camera that
hung around her neck. Pressing down on the small button tucked
next to the winding knob, she opened the front of the camera
and drew down the bed until it locked. She looked through the
viewfinder and framed the shot. Holding her breath, she flipped
the shutter and prayed the photo developed the way she imagined.
Could this be the one that brought the large price of the war
home to people whose own houses were under no threat of enemy
bombs?

Her heart broke at the emptiness in the little boy's eyes as he
stood there in tattered rags with bleeding hands.

What pain had he experienced?

Had that been his home?

Rachel snapped two more shots, then paused. She'd save film
for the next image that grabbed her attention. She might have a
bag full of film, but who knew when she'd find more in Naples.

"You there. What are you doing?" The soldier's raised voice
chased her back to the moment. His gray eyes sparked as he stepped
between her and the boy. A head taller than her, he formed an
intimidating figure, but she'd seen the tenderness he displayed a
moment earlier.

She held her hands up, grateful for the neck strap that kept the camera from dropping to the ground. "Taking photos." He edged closer and she stilled. "Lieutenant."

"Ma'am." His controlled voice didn't match the fire in his eyes. He reached toward her camera, but she sidestepped out of his way and stumbled over a chunk of debris.

"No, you don't. I'm credentialed." She forced her lips to curve into a smile she didn't feel.

"That's no reason for you to take this child's photo."

"Every reason."

"Like what?"

"Making people back home understand."

"This?" He swept an arm across the shattered scene. "They'll never understand from their warm, dry homes." He almost vibrated with energy, a simmering passion that drew her.

She stood straighter. "Not if we don't communicate reality through images."

"You must be an idealist if you think a few pictures will make an impact."

His words caught Rachel off guard as she studied his solid frame. Was she? If so she should be back home telling the propaganda the army spoon-fed journalists instead of risking her life in a place where a bomb was as likely to land on her head as she was to arrive back home in one piece.

She eased back as she shook her head. "No."

"Then you might have a chance."

"To change minds?"

He shook his head. "To survive."

The drone of planes flying across the sky had her ducking, a reflex that had become second nature in the weeks since arriving.

The lieutenant stood tall as if the planes didn't bother him. "They're ours."

Okay, so she needed to spend more time with the flash cards the army handed out. "How can you tell?"

"The shape of the body." He glanced behind him, then stiffened. "The boy's gone."

"He's smarter than we are."

"Maybe." He checked his watch, then tipped the brim of his hat toward her. "Good-day."

He sauntered away, at ease in a world that threatened to spiral out of control in an instant. Her heart stuttered right along with the plane's engine. She watched the plane, praying it would find its way out of the city before it landed. When it disappeared from sight, she released a breath. Still her heart raced.

Nothing inspired her attention after he left. It was like a dirty lens clouded her vision. Might as well head back to the press office and demand—again—they assign her to anyone heading north.

She needed to find her father. Somehow. And fast. That wouldn't happen in Naples, not when the lone clue she had was that Momma had spent her time in Tuscany and Florence. Each day in Naples delayed her efforts to find him. And save her momma.

❧

After a few wrong turns, Scott spied a paper sign that flapped in the breeze created by all the uniforms walking past. Public Relations Division. Scott straightened his shoulders, ready to do battle and convince whoever waited on the other side that his mission mattered. He rapped on the door, then opened it and walked in.

The fiery beauty from the street stood in front of the battered desk that looked like it had taken collateral damage in the bombings. Dark curls escaped the containment of her captain's cap with its small, circular war correspondent patch. Her pale skin emphasized high cheekbones and soft chocolate eyes that gave him the impression she saw deeply. The top of her head reached the edge of his shoulder, yet she stood as if trying to look taller. Somehow she'd slipped around him and beat him to the office. When he'd talked to her about the child's photo, he wondered if she might be Rachel Justice but hadn't asked. Looked like he'd find out soon.

"Can't you see? I've got my press credentials." She thumped a piece of paper on the sergeant's desk.

The man stared at her impassively. "I can't help you, Miss Justice."

So he'd guessed right. The way she stood straight and stared at the sergeant telegraphed she knew how to handle herself, and he found himself rooting for her even as he dreaded the idea of baby-sitting her. Scott might not receive much respect from his peers, but it looked like she got less.

"You won't help me. And it's *Captain* Justice." Air hissed through her teeth, her shoulders so stiff it looked painful.

"Ma'am."

Scott stepped forward. "Miss Justice? I'm sorry, Captain Justice."

Her spine tightened and she didn't bother to turn his direction. All righty. "I've been assigned to assist you."

Sergeant Bowers, at least that's what his name tag stated, looked his way. "You gonna help this dame?"

"I. Am. Not. A. Dame. I'm a captain in the United States Army." Her fists clenched and released as she leaned toward the desk.

"It's an honorary classification and you know it, miss." Sergeant Bowers rolled his eyes and thumped his desk. "It's to keep you from getting harassed if you're a prisoner of war."

Miss Justice sputtered like an engine running low on gasoline. He had to save her from her righteous indignation. "Sergeant Bowers, seems Captain Justice has been assigned to travel with me. You should have those orders somewhere."

"She's assigned to you?"

"Or me to her."

She turned his direction, and the fire in Rachel's eyes didn't do much to give him any hope she approved. Well, he didn't much like it either, but orders were orders.

Her gaze narrowed. "Did you follow me here, Lieutenant?"

"No, ma'am. Should have asked your name out there and saved us both time."

She studied him, enough to make him wonder what she saw and whether he passed her inspection. "That was a kind thing you did."

"Thank you." He turned back to the desk as the sergeant har-rumphed. Captain Justice spoke before he could.

"Look, Sergeant. I worked long and hard to get my employer on board. Then it took United Press an interminable amount of time to get the application completed and even longer for the intelligence section to investigate me. I believe they know everything about me right down to my shoe size." A tinge of color climbed her neck. "Then I had to travel on the *Queen Mary* to England. From there hitch a ride to the boot of Italy. All of this took months. *Months.*"

"Welcome to the army, miss." The beefy sergeant crossed his arms and stared her down.

She stood even taller. Maybe she'd reach the bottom of his jaw now. How could he stop her before she alienated the man who would give her the access she craved? "Now, Miss Justice . . ."

His words didn't slow her down. "Now I'm here and you won't even look at my credentials." Her jaws seemed screwed together under her tension. "That's not acceptable."

Bowers snorted. "Take a number. There's a lot about war people find unacceptable."

Scott pulled the orders from his pocket. "Here's the general's signature. See?" He pointed but the lout didn't budge. "I've got her for a few days. Maybe you can find her assignments after that."

"You sure you want her?"

What could he say? That he thought it was a fool idea? That the general was getting both of them out of his way? Or grin and act like it was brilliant? Seemed that was the remaining option. "Give me access to a jeep, and we'll clear out."

"How do I do that? Snap my fingers? Whistle up the requisitions genie? Your wish is my command?"

"Something like that."

The man rolled his eyes, then reached in his desk and pulled out a blank sheet of paper. He scribbled something on it, stamped it, and thrust it at Scott. "Good luck." Then he grabbed another sheet, this one pretyped, and filled in a few blanks, stamped it, and slid it across to Rachel. "Ma'am, you are here at the pleasure of the United States Army. It can revoke your credentials faster than it granted them. You might keep that in mind."

Rachel narrowed her eyes as she scooped up her credentials and the piece of paper. Before she could say anything else, Scott tugged her toward the door. Sometimes you had to know when to leave so you could fight another day. Guess Rachel hadn't learned that.

She would soon enough.

He hustled her outside. "What should I do with you?"

"Nothing. Stick me in a corner. That's what the rest of them do." She huffed, sending up a spurt of air that puffed a dark curl from her forehead.

He laughed but still didn't know what to do with her. It was fine and dandy to say he was responsible for her. He didn't even have a real office. He traveled with the Monuments' list in his rucksack and commandeered open desks whenever he could. Ernest DeWald was working on acquiring a designated office for the Monuments Men, but the primary effort remained repairing Naples and pushing the front north.

In the meantime should he walk her around Naples? Reinforce the devastation that haunted the area—a direct result of the bombing both sides had inflicted on the city? Illustrate the devastation in people terms? She'd already captured his interaction with that boy. Should he have done more for the child? Did someone notice when he was late coming home? Or had this war left him alone?

"Where'd you go, soldier?" In another setting her words could tease. Here they had a hard edge.

"Wondering how this works."

"What's there to make work? You're the unlucky soldier who's been tasked with babysitting me." A shadow of something . . . defeat maybe . . . darkened her features. "And I'm the unlucky journalist who won't see the war and will never get close to Tuscany."

"Hey now. This isn't a holiday. And that's not a very flattering depiction."

"Didn't know your ego needed inflating."

Ouch. What had he done or said to earn that? She might be cute, but she knew how to jab. Fine, he'd do his job and then send her to the next unlucky soldier tasked with one Rachel Justice.

Chapter 3

RACHEL FELL ONTO THE bed, ignoring the sounds of laughter and conversation that drifted into her hotel room. When she'd returned earlier that evening, the lobby had overflowed with soldiers intent on forgetting the front they'd left behind and would return to. The walls seemed thin, like the bombing had left a network of spider cracks that sound penetrated, but at least this hotel remained in one piece. Thanks to the benevolence of the war office, she had a room she shared with only one roommate, and it had a sink and cold water. Down the hall she shared a bathroom with others.

She should count her blessings. She should, but she couldn't.

The military hadn't extended a warm welcome, but then neither had her editor, Dick Forsythe, in the United Press Naples office. He didn't appreciate having a woman in his office . . . thought she was too distracting, so she stayed away. As long as she brought in a roll of film a day, Dick was happy.

With each new day she was no closer to finding her father. That meant she was no closer to saving her momma. Mail hadn't caught up with her yet. The postcards Rachel mailed the family watching her mother couldn't say much. But at least the Troxels could tell her momma she was alive. How she longed for someone to tell her the same about Momma.

She wanted to believe, had to believe, or all of this was in vain.

Why did she long to meet the man who had never cared about her? Not even enough to send her a simple postcard, let alone a few dollars to help? Maybe if Momma hadn't worked two jobs most of Rachel's life, Momma wouldn't be so sick now.

Couldas, wouldas, shouldas didn't change reality.

The clock ticked on. Time slipped through her fingers while she waited for the army to give her permission to head north where her heart whispered she'd find answers if any existed.

If only she knew where to start.

Traveling to Italy had seemed like a good plan. After all this was where Momma met her father and fell in love. Yet after scouring her momma's small apartment, she'd found little to point her to the man. A cryptic diary and a sketchbook that might not be connected at all. She'd brought them with her, scouring their contents on the trans-Atlantic passage.

She pulled her momma's diary from her musette bag, stroking the emerald leather cover. Tonight she didn't want to look at the sketches. She wanted to see her momma's spidery writing and doodles that filled the pages. After opening the cover, a tear slipped out at the sight of her momma's words. She brushed it off her cheek, lest it fall and smear the fading ink.

Touching the book, she could almost imagine Momma sitting next to her on the bed. What would she tell Rachel about her father?

Other than leave him alone? Nothing.

Rachel sighed and set the diary with the sketchbook. She'd examine them later. Much had changed in twenty-four years, not the least of which was the war. Maybe someone with United Press or another news agency could help her, but for the next few days, she'd travel with the mysterious soldier.

He'd acted with such care toward the little boy, then defended her to the sergeant. Warmth flooded her at the memory of his care, something she'd never experienced in a home without a father or grandfather. Even the memory of the lieutenant's efforts to redirect her when she'd wanted to let the grunt behind the desk know what she thought of his tone made her smile. Lieutenant Lindstrom didn't know her, but he'd cared enough to keep her from foolish actions.

In the morning she woke, the diary clutched to her chest. Her roommate's bed looked like no one had slept in it, a distinct possibility with the odd hours Dottie kept as a nurse.

Lord, help me. Give me wisdom. Keep me safe.

Her thoughts wandered to Psalm 4. *"Hear me when I call, O God."* Strange how she'd heard that psalm in Sunday school, and even when she wasn't sure she believed God cared about her, the urge to pray sprang to her lips.

How she needed that assurance in a land she didn't know with a people she struggled to understand. She needed somebody to hear her. To see her. Could that be God?

She stood and dressed in her uniform, opting for khaki trousers instead of a skirt. Adding a shirt and tie, then the dark-olive dress jacket and garrison cap, and she looked like she belonged.

If she could believe it.

After grabbing her camera, she pulled her musette bag over her shoulder and headed downstairs. She'd arrive downstairs to meet Scott before the assigned time.

When she reached the lobby, Lieutenant Lindstrom sat in an oversized chair, an Italian newspaper across his lap.

"Planning to read that?"

He startled from wherever his thoughts had carried him. "Pardon?"

She gestured toward the paper. "Do you read Italian?"

"Passable knowledge. I spent a year at the American Academy in Rome before returning to the States to work in a museum."

"That sounds more than passable."

"I'm trying to make it better. My job requires some fluency if I want to be effective."

She eased onto the chair next to him. "Why?"

"Have you been to Rome, ma'am?"

"No." Only in her dreams carried on the wings of her momma's remembrances.

"There's an ancient beauty to that city. To Italy. It collides with modern realities. It blends into a mix unique to this country. One moment you walk across stones laid by Romans centuries before Christ's birth. The next you're on asphalt squeezed across the narrow roads designed when horses were the main transport."

"You love it."

He inclined his chin. "I do. To help preserve its culture, I'll need to connect with local art officials. There is value to the places. Buildings. Art. We are defined by what we love and respect."

"So what aspect will you show me today?"

"I'm not sure." He shrugged. "My mission exists in theory. The army believes there are more important duties at the moment. It's hard to blame them. But with every day more is lost or destroyed."

Rachel pondered his words. He believed what he said. It was clear he valued his job, but it wasn't fully formed yet. Was this why the general had thrust her off on him? Both of them lost in a sea of war without a real role?

Her warm chocolate-colored eyes sparkled as she stroked her camera. Hard to imagine how such a small machine captured such vivid photos. Scott pulled the *New York Herald Tribune* from beneath the Naples daily rag. "Have you seen this?"

"No. I don't get much American news unless I'm in the press office."

"Turn to page A7."

She accepted the paper with a curious gleam. "Anything in particular I'm looking for?"

"You'll know it."

The pages rustled and then she straightened. The photo sat in the middle of the page of war news. A simple image that captured a soldier interacting with a child amid rubble. The photo conveyed how war had aged the child.

One child.

Her photo.

His image.

He wasn't identified, but somehow the photo had made it back to the States and was already in print. He could imagine how many other papers had picked it up from the United Press or other photo wire service. The image captured so many nuances and realities in one frame.

"Oh my." She breathed the words, lifting one hand to her throat.

"It's a powerful image."

She nodded. "I knew it was special when I snapped it. But seeing it in print . . ."

"How did it manage to land in the paper already?"

"The editor picks a few photos to be wired immediately. The others are flown on military transports." The pages trembled as she looked at him. "I dreamed it would be picked up."

Her enthusiasm charmed him, even as he knew he needed to quell it. "It's not a good idea to have you join me, Captain Justice."

"You won't take me?"

He ran a hand along his neck trying to ease the tightness creeping into the muscles.

She sat on the edge of a chair, her posture so perfect it looked painful as she waited for his decision. He had strict orders to take her, yet he couldn't imagine a worse idea than traveling alone with a beautiful woman into an area the Germans might hold.

She was flustered and he'd caused it. She'd come to life when he showed her the photo in the paper and now sparkled with excitement. If they were thrust together for the crawl north, then he'd focus on keeping her safe.

Some soldier wolf whistled as he walked across the lobby, and faint color stained her cheeks. Scott glared at the soldier who then winked at her. If this was how the soldiers treated Captain Justice when they weren't telling her to go home, then he was glad she'd been assigned to him. He'd treat her like a kid sister and restrain his thoughts from straying to the piece of hair that kept falling across her eyes, begging him to brush it to the side.

No, when Elaine had given back his grandmother's ring, he'd had all the reminder he needed that war was not the time to plan the future. He'd keep Captain Justice safe, then hand her off to her next guardian.

"Let's find some more images for you to snap."

She pulled her gaze from the page, and her grin blinded him. "Let's."

Scott led Rachel outside to the ramshackle excuse for a jeep the sergeant had assigned him. "Hop on in."

"Really? Are you sure it will make it around the block?"

"It's the best transportation I've had so far. If we're lucky, we won't break down before we return." After they hopped in, he double-checked the extra can of petrol in the back. The vehicle grumbled to a start, and then he drove through the streets of Naples and out of town.

"Where are we headed?"

"A village at the foot of Mount Vesuvius near Sant'anastasia." He could check the church and the art it should hold. Connect with local people. Practice his Italian and maybe perform first aid on damaged structures. Rachel could follow along and capture images to bring the war home.

"I didn't realize Vesuvius was so close to Naples. For some reason I've always pictured it off the mainland." Rachel shaded her eyes as she scanned the horizon. "Wish I'd been here in March when it blew."

"I missed it by a few days, but other soldiers said it was surreal to see the explosion from Naples. There's nothing like that on the East Coast."

Clouds roiled across the sky, painting the hills with craggy shadows. The hills looked like crumpled scrap paper arranged in clusters. He imagined an artist like Monet painting with frantic strokes as he tried to capture the nuances the light created. Now to find some of the masterpieces Renaissance artists had created centuries ago. A bird dipped toward the jeep, a worm clasped in its beak.

Rachel shifted against the seat. "Where are you from?"

"Philly."

"Me too."

Scott studied her, then squeezed the steering wheel as he cleared his thoughts of this dark-haired beauty. Philadelphia was a major city. He shouldn't expect to know her. "Worked for a small museum there, bringing in special exhibits. Grew up near Valley Forge and returned after getting a degree at Harvard."

"Wow. That's a prestigious college."

He paused. She didn't offer anything about herself and where she'd lived. Interesting. "God opened a door. I knew I wanted to pursue art after so many weekends at the Philly museums. I had no idea how my family could pay for it, but He made a way."

"God hasn't done much of that for me. At one time I thought he might, but now he's forgotten me." Rachel shuddered, then hunched her shoulders. She looked like a turtle pulling its head in its shell as she burrowed deeper into her jacket.

"So are you going to reciprocate?"

She looked at him with a cute, wrinkled-nose expression. "What?"

"Share some of your facts and history."

"Not on the first day."

Okay. He could honor that, though the drive might get long if she didn't want to talk. The clouds overhead indicated it could be another day tainted with cold rain. For spring the rain kept the roads mired in mud. Just one nice day. That's all he wanted. One day to get out of Naples. Do something important. If they got turned back by rugged roads or roadblocks, he'd go crazy.

"You okay?"

"Yeah. Fine." He relaxed his hold on the steering wheel. "Can you grab the map in my bag? I think we go about five miles out of town before turning."

"Kilometers?"

"Sure. Check the map."

Rachel bit her lower lip as she pawed through his bag, but he still saw her grin. "This it?" She held up a crumpled piece of paper.

"Looks right." He worked to keep his attention on the heavily rutted road rather than on the woman next to him.

She spread the map across her lap and frowned. "Guess I should have taken Italian. My momma did. She studied here in the twenties."

Scott glanced at her in time to catch the shadow that fell on her features. "You didn't study it?"

"Not enough. If my mom wanted me to, then I didn't have the desire." She turned the map from side to side. "I'll have to work hard to say more than *grazie*."

"Not many Americans care to do that." Today would be his first real test. He hoped he was up to the challenge, especially with an audience.

Chapter 4

May 16

THE HILL THEY DROVE stood like a multilayered terrace, each level lined with the remnants of vines. Grapes maybe? Rachel fingered Momma's silver locket as she searched the landscape. She'd never seen anything like it in Philadelphia. She hadn't grown up in an agricultural center. Now she wished she'd asked her mom more questions and made her talk about Italy.

The GI seated next to her drove the jeep with confidence, but what did he see? The silence that settled over them said he didn't need to entertain her. Yet the longer the silence stretched, the more curious she became. Then she'd catch him looking at her. The kind of glance that telegraphed he saw her, really saw her, and wanted to know more.

Her cheeks warmed and her palms sweated. He'd given her openings to share some of her story, but the words failed. They'd just met, and she couldn't let him see the turmoil roiling inside. No, she needed to affix a look of composure and strength and never let it slip. One word from him and she'd spend her time in Naples fighting with Sergeant Bowers for another assignment.

"Do you think we should stop?" She held up the map. "We should have arrived by now."

He glanced at her, his brows merging in a frown. A crater in the road almost yanked the steering wheel from his hands, and he fought the car back into position. "A couple more minutes. We can't go fast, so it's still ahead of us."

"All right." She turned back to the map. The lines zigged and zagged across the page without making much sense. Guess this wasn't the time to mention she'd never had occasion to drive or use foreign maps.

They approached a crossroads. "Which way, Justice?"

She stilled as her name sounded like a caress. "I'm not sure. Sorry."

He pulled the jeep to the side of the roadway and gestured for the map, which she handed over with a smile. After a minute studying it, he eased back onto the road. "We'll try left."

"Try? Aren't we in a war zone? Trying doesn't sound safe."

Did he just growl?

He was driving her into the unknown and growled at her. Rachel crossed her arms and leaned against the bench seat. Her gaze darted back and forth. Far behind them the dust of a vehicle rose in a cloud. What if they drove into Germans? Or partisan Fascist troops? Would her rank as a captain protect her in the event she became a prisoner of war, or would they know it was a sham?

"I'll get us there and back."

She nodded but refused to comment, not sure her voice would cooperate. She turned to look at the cloud but couldn't tell if it drew closer.

"What are you looking at?"

Rachel shrugged. "I can't tell. Is someone following us?"

Scott shook his head. "As far as I know we're alone out here. But there are a lot of men in the army."

"You're right." Rachel turned around and tried to focus on what was ahead of them. She'd anticipated many things when she asked for a war assignment. She tried to weigh the costs, and compared to her momma's life, this seemed small—when she was half a world away reading the stories and watching newsreels. Now that a shell could explode next to the jeep or a bullet could pierce her, it seemed real. Too real.

She longed to excel at her assignment, to see her name grace the byline for photos that filled newspaper and magazine pages next to Therese Bonney's photos. Maybe Rachel's photos could impact breakfast conversations around the States. Then she would belong with the elite photojournalists who could tell an entire story in fewer column inches than their typing brethren. That was an important purpose. One that gave meaning to her time in Italy even if she never found her father. Even more important, with each photo that found its way into the papers, she'd earn the extra money needed to keep her momma alive until she could finance a miracle.

A formation of planes flew overhead, and Scott jerked the jeep to a stop at the side of the road under a tree. She hunched down reflexively and startled when Scott pushed her down, then placed his body over hers. She felt him move, then ease away, and she fought the urge to pull him back down. She felt safe with him between her and danger.

"They're ours."

Relief surged through her veins, making its way to her brain even as she missed the security his arms around her generated. She tried to relax her muscles but felt locked in place.

"Village should be over the next hill."

"All right." It was all she could squeak out. *Please help me find my father. Fast.* Then she could leave on the next ship headed home. To safety. To her momma.

The gears ground as Scott restarted the jeep and shifted to force it up a steep hill. The vehicle slowed, chugged, lurched, and then grunted over the crest. Rachel breathed out. "Guess we don't have to push."

"Not yet." Scott pointed ahead of them. "If I read the map right, that's it. You wouldn't think much is there, but according to my list, we should find an interesting altarpiece in the local cathedral."

As they approached the town, a couple young boys kicked a small bucket back and forth. Their clothes hung in tatters from their filthy bodies, their hair long enough to braid. Rachel longed to scoop them up, take them to the creek for a good scrubbing, and then somehow find clothes and shoes for them. The boys stepped from the road as the jeep eased by. She could imagine the pain of nothing to protect their feet from the sharp rocks and ruins.

"Slow down!" She scrambled for her camera. If she could capture their image—children playing in the aftermath of war. All the mothers back home could imagine their children caught in the same situation and pray for an end to this war. Maybe they'd even send money to the relief organizations that began to infiltrate southern Italy.

Scott waited while she snapped a shot. "Got it?"

"I hope so."

"All right. In that bag I've got a stash of chocolate bars. Grab a couple?"

Rachel nodded and found a few.

"*Buono giorno. Cioccolato?*"

The boys eyed them then each other, leaned toward the vehicle, then away. The taller one cocked his head. "*Sì?*"

Scott waved the bars at them. "*Per tu.*"

The boy nodded, dashed to the jeep, grabbed the bars, then stepped back. "Grazie."

Scott drove to the town square.

Rachel glanced around. Other than the two boys, no one was about. "It's so quiet."

Scott nodded. "It is. But we know someone is here. The boys can't be alone."

Rachel hoped he was right. She couldn't imagine what their lives were like now, let alone if they'd been abandoned. Movement caught her attention. "Over there."

The road circled around a plaza with a broken fountain, the church standing on the far side of the open space. The statue that graced the fountain had lost an arm and bore a series of cracks. Rachel tugged her camera out and framed the shot against the cross on the tip of the cathedral's modest facade. Roof tiles scattered across the courtyard, dotting the plaza with clay shrapnel.

A bird sang a song, its trilling whistle piercing Rachel. Could it warble a hymn of praise among the destruction?

"Village doesn't look too bad."

"Tell that to those who live here." How could she convey the devastation in a way that reached Americans? To show how the ongoing crawl up the boot of Italy left little behind. "What the Germans don't take, we destroy."

"It's war." Scott voice fell soft between them.

He was right. She knew that. "We see it. What about those back home?"

"You mean the moms hanging blue flags in their front windows? They care deeply. Everybody knows someone over here. That gives them an interest in what's happening."

The clouds parted and a beam of light fell across the cathedral. The cross almost glowed in the rays. Rachel stepped farther from the jeep and snapped a shot, then framed another including the broken fountain and crushed building next to the church. Out of the destruction the church seemed to whisper there was still hope. She longed to believe it. That hope waited to be grasped with both hands and yanked to her heart. That life, this country, could be salvaged before everything in the path of two armies was destroyed.

A man in priest's robes exited the back of the church. Rachel stepped back, not wanting to distract the man but wishing she'd opted for the standard-issue WAC skirt rather than the more practical trousers.

"Buono giorno." Scott exited the jeep and made a small bow in the direction of the priest.

"May I help you?" The words hung in the air, heavy from the Italian accent. The priest eyed them, not unpleasantly, yet he didn't extend his hand or offer his name.

"I'm Lieutenant Scott Lindstrom, United States Army. I'm here to check your church and artwork."

"Why?"

"We want to help you protect them."

"Like the Germans?" The man's placid features transformed into a frozen mask.

"No." Scott looked at Rachel. What did he think she could do? "We want to help you protect your treasures."

A formation of planes buzzed overhead, and the father ducked. "My name is Father Guilliamo. Come in, come in. Is not safe out in open."

A few minutes later he placed a plate of hard biscuit cookies and a pot of tea on a battered kitchen table. "We have little."

"We expect less," Rachel assured him.

"Hardship . . . it is our companion. But nothing compared to the suffering of our Christ." He poured, then offered the cup to Rachel. "All day we wait. For what we are not sure. But we wait."

"Waiting is hard." Scott shifted against the hard-backed chair.

The counter stood empty. The kitchen itself clean but spare. Even with rationing, Americans experienced abundance. The parish kitchen reinforced just how little one could survive on.

The priest poured weak tea into two more cups, and they all sipped. What would Scott do? Sitting in uncomfortable closeness, wondering what they should do next, seemed counterproductive.

Scott gulped his tea—had he even tasted it?—then pulled a small booklet from his jacket pocket. "Father, I'm here to offer the assistance of the U.S. Army to your church."

"I need no help." The priest swept a hand around the room. "I have a roof. End the war. That would help most."

End the war. If they could do that. But with soldiers continuing to slog in the valleys around Cassino, that seemed unlikely . . . laughable even.

"We do what we can."

"Stop gunning down civilians."

"I'm sorry?" Rachel couldn't help the words that erupted from her soul. Machine-gunning?

The father made like he had two hands clenched around something and vibrated them, the way a gunner in a plane would. "Innocents are killed while Germans and Fascists fight."

A sick feeling rose against the cookie she'd choked down. "We don't do things like that."

"These old eyes have seen."

Scott swallowed and then straightened in his chair. "Please accept my apologies on behalf of the United States." He looked down at his hands. "War causes great tragedies. This is one. I am here to help avoid another tragedy. Father, is your altarpiece safe? Did it stay behind or did the Germans take it?"

The man eyed him, wariness and skepticism casting shadows. "Why should I trust you?"

"Because I value the great treasures of Italy. Because the things we value speak volumes about the country and the world we will have after the war. Because the things that were created in Italy should stay here, in the land of their birth. And because the Allies have created a team to help you protect what is yours."

Rachel stared at him, soaking in the passion of his words. He leaned forward under the weight of his beliefs. A fervor in his gaze matched the intensity of his words. His passion drew her like a child to a stream on a warm day.

The father matched his posture.

"What of Monte Cassino's monastery? If you value the old things, the ancient treasures, why destroy that?"

The distance shortened between the men. The passion on their faces caused Rachel's breath to catch in her throat.

Chapter 5

SCOTT BREATHED FOR A moment, then exhaled a whoosh. "Sometimes we have to value human life more than monuments." He choked out the words he knew were true. Would the father respect the position or show him outside?

"Still they fight. In the same positions."

The words settled across Scott like a heavy shroud. Yes, three months after the Monte Cassino bombing, the Allied forces remained bogged down, but this last assault might work. It had to for the troops to move forward. He prayed the irreplaceable library had been moved, its archives protected, but feared it hadn't since all there would have assumed the abbey would never feel the thrust of bombs. Until the battle was over, the extent of the damage couldn't be known. Anything they heard was German propaganda. The priest studied him as if reading his thoughts. What could he say to make the priest trust him? Probably nothing, so he held his silence.

If the father didn't believe him, wouldn't entrust him with the information about the altarpiece, then what? If he couldn't make the local priests, archbishops, and art officials trust him, his mission would fail. That prospect haunted Scott.

The man jerked his chin down. "Follow me. We take your vehicle."

Warmth rushed through Scott. He could finally do something for the art, but he tamped it down. Nothing to celebrate until he knew for sure where the priest planned to take him. Maybe on a wild-goose chase or straight to the local Fascists.

The ride passed in silence other than occasional directions from the priest as he sent them on roads that wound ever back from the village and main road.

Scott felt Rachel's gaze but stayed focused ahead. He had to, because if he looked back, he'd see everything he'd left behind in Philadelphia. He'd spent his education and career developing expertise in Italian Medieval and Renaissance art. Now he could help preserve it from the devastation of a war. He felt destined to help protect it; otherwise, he'd let Elaine walk away in vain.

That day on the pier seemed so long ago, more so when this beauty sat next to him, turning his thoughts homeward. Yet it wasn't that long ago because he carried his grandmother's wedding ring in the bottom of his duffel in a sealed envelope. A constant reminder that when he'd boarded the ship to Europe, he had abandoned his dreams for the future. He and Elaine could have been married by now, happily starting life together in a brownstone her parents bought them. Instead he bounced over rutted roads in a dilapidated jeep with an Italian priest and an intriguing photographer.

Thirty minutes later Scott stopped to refill the petrol from a can.

"Do we have enough to get back?" Rachel whispered as he set the empty container in the narrow space beside her.

"We'll make it."

"Over the next hill and down a narrow road." The priest pointed toward the coast. "I hid the pieces where I felt certain they would survive. Vesuvius, she gave me sleepless nights with her eruptions. I have worried the Germans found them. But the telephone lines are down, and it is impossible to know. Maybe God sent you to answer my prayer to know the altarpiece's fate."

Scott wanted to be an answered prayer.

"Do you believe God can use you? Answer prayers through you?"

"I hope so, Father." Though it seemed doubtful.

"In a kilometer we shall find out. You already are an answer to the prayer resonating in this old heart."

Scott hoped he still felt that way when he steered the jeep from the village.

─────※─────

Rachel braced herself as Scott maneuvered the jeep around potholes and craters. She'd glanced back a few times but hadn't seen any vehicles trailing them. If the priest sent the altarpiece here to hide it, she couldn't imagine there'd be a good outcome. Not based on the state of the road. Heavy fighting must have pounded the area. She hoped, no prayed, the battle was long over.

Could she be an answer to prayer? The words lingered in her soul. She'd never considered being part of an answer. Instead, she tended to focus on the answers she needed, like finding her father before it was too late. Only as the armies battered through the Purple Heart Valley could she hope to follow them into Tuscany and beyond.

Her camera bounced against her and she clutched it. If it broke, she'd get a quick ticket home. That couldn't happen.

"Turn here."

Lieutenant Lindstrom followed the instruction. The jeep jarred and Rachel's teeth clicked together. She ran her tongue over them, grateful none had chipped.

"Down this road and off another sits a small village. My brother once served as its priest."

"Where is he now?" Rachel leaned toward the front seat.

The man shrugged, a gesture both weary and heavy. "I cannot say. He disappeared on a dark night in December. The villagers think the Gestapo took him."

"I'm sorry."

He shrugged again. "It is all in God's hands. We all are." He turned and pointed into the woods. "Now we walk."

Fifteen minutes later he led them to a network of caves. "At different times Italians have hidden here. Avoiding German demands to transport to labor camps. The Germans demand too much." He pulled out a flashlight and flicked on the light.

Scott waited for Rachel to enter. Did she want him ahead or behind? Either felt dangerous, but she entered the dim reaches of the cave and followed the father through its twists and turns. When the flashlight's beam flickered, the priest pointed to the left. "In that hollow."

Scott slipped past her and reached into the darkness. "Nothing's here."

The priest pushed forward. "You missed it. It is in pieces. We dismantled the altarpiece."

Scott reached back into the darkness. "I'm sorry. I don't feel anything."

The priest groaned, a sound that seemed to reach from the depths of his being. "It must be here. No one knew I hid it here. No one but my brother."

Rachel tried to stay out of the way in the confined space as the priest brushed past her. The torch's light wavered again, and he thrust it into her grasp. "Steady it."

Scott groped in the darkness but shook his head. Rachel's heart sank. Whatever had been hidden here was gone, or Father Guilliamo led them to the wrong place.

Scott and the father huddled in front of the place where the painting was supposed to hide, and Rachel reached for her camera. The lighting failed to reach far enough, but she had to try. She hesitated, then snapped the shot.

"Where could the altarpiece be?" The father's soft words filtered to Rachel.

Scott shook his head. "I don't know. Are you certain no one else knew it was here?"

"Yes." The priest's shoulders slumped, and he seemed to age before Rachel's eyes. "I am at a loss."

"Was anything else here?"

The father paused for a moment. "Our village held little of value, just the altarpiece. You must find it."

"I can't make any promises, Father."

The man of the cloth pulled himself straight. "Then you may leave and I will search. Now back to the village."

With sure steps the priest led the way from the cave. The sky darkened as they rode back to the village in silence, the jeep jerking and sputtering. Scott stopped on the square and turned to the father. "Thank you for trusting us with the altarpiece's hiding place. I will do all I can to find it."

The man studied him in the gloom. "I believe you. Grazie." The man paused, almost invisible in his black cassock. The men clasped hands, the man's trust causing Scott to stand taller, then the priest turned to Rachel. "*Signorina.*" He climbed out and disappeared into the parsonage behind the church.

Rachel slipped into the front seat, settling in as Scott popped the jeep into gear. The vehicle jerked then shimmied across the road and out of the village. After several minutes of silence, searching the area along the road for signs of anything, Rachel swallowed when she saw a flicker.

"Do you see that?"

"What?" Scott's voice had a strangled edge.

"There was a flicker of light in that field." Rachel's gaze roved across the darkness. "We should have left earlier."

Keep us safe, Lord! The jeep felt like a tiny island in the midst of a hostile world. They'd been behind enemy lines since they left Naples, and that reality hadn't changed while they explored the cave with the father. The jeep launched into a hole and then jarred to a stop.

"Come on, come on." Scott muttered in low tones as he pushed against the gas. The wheels spun, but the vehicle remained trapped. "Can you drive?"

Rachel shook her head. "I'm from the city. Never learned."

"You get to now. Unless you'd like to spend the night out here."

As a distant drone of planes rumbled across the cloud-covered sky, Rachel shuddered. "I'll try anything."

He gave her a quick primer, but the levers and pedals blurred in her mind. Right for gas, left for brakes? But which one for shifting gears? "I can't do this."

"I've got to push."

"Can't we both do that?"

"Not if you want to keep the vehicle on the road."

"Okay." Rachel closed her eyes. She had to do this. "Tell me when you're ready."

"Whatever you do, don't go in reverse."

"Great." She gritted her teeth. "You didn't tell me how to find it anyway."

Scott disappeared behind the vehicle. A deep breath. She could do this or they'd be stuck. Out here. She couldn't spend the night on an isolated Italian road with a stranger. "Now."

At the terse word Rachel shoved the stick forward and put her left foot on one lever and her right foot on the other. The engine ground and chugged as it tried to rock forward. "What should I do?"

Scott groaned.

"Are you okay?"

"As fine as I can be shoving this monstrosity out of a crater. Keep revving the gas."

Right pedal. At least she hoped that was the correct one. She pushed it to the floor, and the vehicle squealed as it launched from the hole. "What do I do?"

"Push on the middle pedal."

She shoved it down and the vehicle stopped, throwing her forward like a rag doll. Her chest slammed into the steering wheel, and she moaned. "I don't want to drive."

Scott hurried toward her. "You okay?"

Should she tell him it felt like the steering wheel was imbedded in her? There wasn't anything he could do about it. "Umhmm."

"Slide on over, and let's get back to Naples."

Rachel nodded and eased across the seat. Her neck felt like she'd spun around a ride at a fair too many times. If she kept her head steady and didn't turn, maybe she'd be okay. Then she'd crawl in her bed and not move until her ribs quit aching and her head stopped throbbing.

Captain Justice didn't look good. He hadn't expected the vehicle to lurch from the pit with her foot pressed against the gas. She'd been game to learn something new, and now she shifted like an eighty-year-old woman who'd experienced a beating. What else could he have done? Asked her to push?

He didn't like being this far from other soldiers. At this time of night, there was no guarantee their own guys would welcome them if they stumbled across a patrol. He hadn't meant to spend so much time searching for the missing altarpiece. Now he didn't know the safest course of action. Find a place to hide along the road and risk running into partisans or Germans? Or push back without headlights to Naples?

The road was littered with craters left from bombs and possible mines. If he wasn't careful, they'd get stuck again or worse. On the open road they were the perfect target for some flyboy who couldn't tell if they were friend or foe in the dark of night.

He edged the vehicle forward, trying to spot the deeper darkness of the craters. At this rate it would be daybreak before they returned to Naples. The front left tire sagged into a pit, then bounced ahead. Rachel gasped.

"How bad are you hurt?"

"I'm fine." The words were tight, as if pushed through a straw.

"Not buying it."

"Too bad." Rachel looked away and he waited. "There's nothing you can do. Just get us back to Naples."

"That's the problem."

"I don't like the sound of that."

"We can't return in the dark. The best option is to find a place to pull off and wait for dawn when we can see the road."

"No."

"This isn't a debate."

"I can't spend the night out here with you." She shrank away from him on the seat.

"Ma'am, I want to return you in one piece." He inched the car forward as she gazed out, her body angled away from him. They inched along. Had the Germans seeded the road with mines as they retreated? He hadn't seen any earlier, so it should be safe. Still, should he risk it when he had company?

Nothing the army had given him laid out a procedure for situations like this. By himself he'd find a place to hole up. Today he had a passenger. A beautiful one. One he needed to protect in body and reputation. He needed someplace she'd know she was safe.

He'd heard stories of reporters and soldiers becoming more than friends. That wasn't his plan. She was his assignment for a few days. Nothing more. Elaine had made it clear when she broke their engagement the day he boarded the *Queen Mary* that military life and love didn't mix. He had no reason to think Rachel, no Captain Justice, felt any different. And with the nature of war, chances were strong he'd never see her again.

It felt like the road inched beneath them as he scoured for danger. "Help me find a place to pull over."

Rachel shifted but didn't look at him. "What do you think I'm doing?"

Scott bit down to keep from snapping back. He could imagine what cycled through her mind. How could he make her feel safe instead of stuck between unknown armies and him? Returning to the village wasn't safe now. It sat behind them, and the road to Naples lay in front, both lost in darkness.

Chapter 6

May 17

SHE COULDN'T ALTER THE fact she'd spent the night with the handsome Lieutenant Lindstrom without anyone to verify nothing happened. Who would believe searching for an altarpiece in an isolated cave had made it impossible to return? It sounded weak even to her, and she'd participated in the search. It wasn't like she could find a cab or another way home.

She couldn't deny he made her feel safe, unlike some of the GIs who leered at her like they hadn't seen an American woman in months. He evoked images of strength and honesty with the way he treated others, qualities that drew her. But did she trust Lieutenant Lindstrom?

She didn't know.

That didn't matter. She had to rely on her instincts and work with him. Especially if she wanted to make it back to Naples. "I haven't seen anything that looks like a lane."

Scott huffed out a breath. "Me either. Doesn't make sense though. I remember seeing several on the drive."

"Maybe we haven't gotten close enough to Naples yet."

"Possibly."

Rachel searched her side of the vehicle. Somewhere she'd find safety. She refused to consider the alternative. After several interminable minutes she saw something to the right. "Lieutenant, stop!"

He eased the car to a stop. "What?"

"Can you see through there? I think it's a path."

Scott leaned forward and she eased back against the seat to give him more space. "I don't know. Let me scout down it a bit." He pulled the vehicle under a stand of trees, then turned to the back, slapped a helmet on his head, and grabbed a rifle of some sort. "Stay in the jeep. Grab a C ration to eat. There's a can opener in my bag. Wouldn't hurt to slap your helmet on too. If anything makes you nervous, head for that tree. Then I'll know where to find you."

"Sure." Sprinting into the unknown darkness sounded like a perfect nighttime war activity.

He stepped from the jeep and melted into the darkness. Every so often, she caught a glint of moonlight off his helmet before he disappeared from view.

The darkness squeezed her, almost as real as a person. Her skin felt clammy as her mind groped for safety.

They'd seen an occasional cottage or farm off the road. But she'd heard rumors of the Italian men who lived in the woods, avoiding being pressed into service by the German army. Were any of them watching her?

~~~❦~~~

Scott worked his way down the path. He tried to pick his steps for maximum stealth, but it was hard to avoid twigs when the sliver of moon kept hiding behind the clouds. He hated leaving Rachel behind but couldn't see an alternative. The uncertainty by the road seemed safer than the unknown off the road on a narrow path leading deeper into darkness.

As he neared the end of the path and a clearing, he edged back into the trees. A cottage. No lights shone from it, but he needed to proceed with caution. Who knew what waited inside? A small structure to the left looked like it was used to shelter animals, though he didn't see or smell any.

How best to proceed?

He didn't want anyone in the dwelling shooting before he could explain his presence. Yet he hadn't seen much to indicate whether anyone still called this place home.

Guess there was one thing to do. *God, keep me safe.* He aimed his gun high and then moved. He didn't want to leave Rachel alone one moment more than necessary.

"Ciao?" Scott cleared his throat and tried again. "Hello? I'm a friend."

Well, he could hope the words were true. Pray this wasn't the home of a partisan who'd decided Mussolini and Hitler were the right men to lead Italy into the future.

The door eased open and a capped head appeared. *"Sì?"*

Great. Now he knew someone was here, but what should he say next? His Italian still came out rusty, and he didn't want to speak the wrong phrase. How to make the man understand he just needed a place to stay?

"We're . . ." Not lost. He knew where they were. He just didn't like where that was. "My friend and I need . . . rest."

The man cracked the door farther. *"Americano?"*

"Sì."

"Come."

After some Italian mixed with sign language and pointing, they arrived at an understanding. They could stay until daybreak and get off the main road. "Grazie."

He hustled toward the road. Time to get Rachel to shelter. He reached the curve and slowed his pace. Time to be deliberate and make sure no one had joined her. As he eased up to the jeep, he tensed. He couldn't see Rachel.

Should he head to the tree? *No, examine the jeep first, then head to the rendezvous point.* He crept toward the jeep. "Captain Justice?" The word rasped into the silence.

"Lieutenant?"

"Everything okay?"

She uncurled from the tight ball she'd coiled into. No wonder he had missed her. "We'll spend the night down the path. There's a farmhouse and a place for us."

She nodded. "Are we walking?"

"No, I'll move the jeep. Can't leave it here."

Even though he'd checked the house and barn, Scott inched down the lane. He almost backed in so they could leave in a hurry but decided to turn it around as soon as they reached the house.

When they pulled up to the farmhouse, the farmer waited with a dim lantern casting shadows along the walls. A pallet of blankets rested against the wall. He pointed at it. "You . . ." He folded his hands along his head as if sleeping. "I . . ." He tapped his forehead, as if he would watch.

Scott nodded. "Grazie." He turned to Rachel. "You take the blankets. I'll stick with the jeep."

"Are you sure this is safe?" Her gaze darted around the small room.

Then a woman in a nightgown, blanket clutched around her shoulders, entered the room. "My wife." The man beamed as he touched his wife's shoulder. "She . . ." He whipped his hand as if stirring something.

Rachel's shoulders relaxed. Did the presence of the woman make her feel safer? "You all right here?"

"I will be. Thanks." She climbed over to the blankets and eased down onto them. Her eyes closed, and she fell asleep in an instant.

"I sleep." He pointed outside, then bowed a bit toward the couple and slipped away. It wouldn't be comfortable, but when he returned to Naples, he could say with full honesty a couple and a door stood between them.

That was the best he could do. It had to be enough.

The couple whispered, their melodic Italian wrapping around Rachel as she tried to relax. As soon as she heard Scott leave, her body seemed determined to stay awake.

She'd come to Italy to find her father.

A man she knew so little about. When she got back to her hotel room, she needed to dig deeper through the journal and diary to find any clue that identified him. If today was any indication, she couldn't count on what the next day would bring.

Rachel tried to draw in a deep breath, but her ribs protested. She'd hit the steering wheel hard. While she hadn't wanted to worry the lieutenant, she'd feel sore for a while.

Was this even a shadow of how her momma felt as she battled tuberculosis? Rachel hadn't received any letters from her mother in the month since she'd left the States. Worry kept pricking her. Was Momma still alive? The alternative crimped her heart.

Someone touched her shoulder, and she opened her eyes. Maybe she'd dozed after all.

"Signorina?"

Rachel rubbed her hair from her face, her thoughts foggy and her torso battered. Where was she? A farmhouse somewhere in Italy. A rumble sounded outside, vibrations snaking through the floor and into her body.

"Lieutenant? Is he here?" Her voice croaked as the wife helped her to her feet and directed her out back, not seeming to understand her question. Rachel searched for him but didn't see him on her way to the outhouse. When Rachel returned, the woman shoved a package in her hand.

"*Cibo.*"

"Thank you for the food." Rachel hurried out the front door. Where was Scott? If he left her, she didn't know what she'd do. Another explosion rumbled somewhere. It was close enough to curdle her blood.

"Miss Justice, are you ready?" Scott moved with efficient, hurried movements as he readied the jeep.

"Yes."

"Then let's be off. There's a battle raging somewhere near here I'd like to avoid."

Rachel clambered into the jeep. Almost the moment she touched the inside, Scott had it lurching forward. She winced at a flash of pain as her head lashed forward.

"Sorry."

"Just get me back to Naples in one piece."

"That's the aim."

The ride was quiet, punctuated by the rush of planes sweeping overhead. "Those are ours."

Rachel vowed to spend some time with those flash cards. The lieutenant kept his gaze bouncing between the road and the sky, and his attentiveness helped her relax.

After a long morning they entered the outskirts of Naples. She had never been so delighted to see the battered and demolished city. After working through checkpoints and worming around rubble, Scott pulled in front of the hotel.

"Here you go."

"Thank you." She sat in the jeep, unable to move as the reality hit her. They'd made it back.

"Do you need help?" He looked at her in a way she couldn't quite decipher. It wasn't the look most men would have used. It felt like he didn't want to overstep and wasn't sure how to help.

She pushed against the dash and winced against the flash of pain. "I'm fine. Thank you again for getting me home." Well, the closest thing she had to home in this devastated place. "See you later today?"

"Let's plan on tomorrow morning. Check in with your editor and get some real rest."

His protective words made her smile. "Yes, sir."

He flashed a salute with a smile, then waited until she entered the hotel's front doors before pulling the jeep into traffic. She watched until he disappeared. She'd been assigned to him for several more days, but maybe she'd stay in Naples. She made her way to her room and sank onto her twin bed.

"Rachel Justice. Where did you keep yourself last night?" Barbara Skiles looked elegant in her standard-issue uniform as she sashayed through the door and across the small hotel room.

"Nowhere important." She softened her words with a smile at her fellow journalist.

"Uh-huh. Spill the beans, girl. There's not enough excitement around here so I need you to liven things up." Barbara brushed the front of her jacket, then smirked at Rachel. "And if he was tall, dark, and handsome, all the better."

No, light brown hair, gray eyes, and a few inches taller than her was best.

"Do tell us you're okay." Dottie Winchester slipped around Barbara and looked like she couldn't decide whether to be scandalized or grateful to see Rachel. "I've been frantic."

Rachel could imagine her roommate worrying and bringing others into the party as the hours dragged by. War or no, Dottie seemed determined to keep everyone safe and together. "I'm sorry. If I'd had a way to get word to you, I would have. My army escort and I got stuck after dark on a mine-laced, cratered road. He found a safe place for us to wait for daybreak."

"Your escort?" Barbara waggled her eyebrows. "I knew this would be good. Tell us more."

"There's nothing to tell." Rachel sighed as she tried to think of a way to distract Barbara. To explain the care he had taken of her without once threatening to slip over a boundary. "I slept in a small farmhouse on a pile of blankets chaperoned by a sweet, older Italian couple, while he spent the night in the jeep."

Dottie twisted her hands together. "Were you safe?"

"I made it back."

"I'm glad." Dottie winked. "I'd hate to think my remaining roommate option is Barbara."

"Good news, toots." Barbara linked arms with Rachel, and she brushed down the stab of pain. "After you get cleaned up, we're headed to the press office. The buzz is some of us will be assigned to specific divisions. That means we're headed out."

"I've got orders for next week." Though moving ahead couldn't be any more dangerous than the adventure she'd just had.

"You know how it is. When the army says move, . . ."

Dottie joined Rachel on the other side, and they spoke in unison. "We move."

Chapter 7

May 22

AS THE DAYS PASSED, Scott couldn't wait for action. He took what other officers called jaunts around the countryside when he could, but when Miss Justice disappeared from her hotel with an assignment to a unit, he lost his guaranteed access to a jeep. Without her he had fewer tools to complete his mission. The inactivity made his days drag when he couldn't talk his way out of Naples. He tried to contact her at the press office, but whatever they had her working on left her no time to respond because he never heard from her. For now the army needed her on another assignment.

As May drew to a close, he was left to his own devices. He rested in a netherworld between the "real" army, all of whom had dozens of tasks, and the occupation government, busy rebuilding Naples. They treated him like a civilian and resented his presence.

"What's happening?" DeWald's voice startled Scott from his depressed thoughts at his makeshift desk.

"Didn't hear you."

The man chuckled wryly. "Finishing work on your next assignment? There are a few details to organize."

"So I hear." Could he help the slight edge to his words? Not if he languished in the office another day.

"Snap out of it, Lindstrom, and get your head back in your task." DeWald's stare bored through Scott. "Lucky for you here comes the solution to your problems." The head of the MFAA's small band of men in Italy inclined his head toward a private on the other side of the room.

The man saluted when he reached them. "Rumor has it you need wheels, Lieutenant."

Scott eyed the soldier in front of him. "I do."

"And I have a jeep and orders to transport you."

"Why?"

"Someone wants to keep your sorry carcass alive. Maybe they're tired of your bellyaching. All I know is I have orders and the keys." The man's posture matched the arrogant tone of his words. DeWald hid a smirk behind his hand.

"Have a name, soldier?"

"Private Tyler Salmon. Sir."

With the attitude and sneer, Scott could understand why DeWald would think it a great idea to dump a problem soldier in his lap. Scott couldn't turn down a jeep when days could pass before another came his way. He hadn't seen even a spare carburetor floating around, let alone a full vehicle. Supplies hadn't been too happy after the one he'd used came back with dents and squirrelly alignment thanks to his foray into the countryside. "Your orders?"

The man eyed him from beneath overlong chestnut hair and reached into his inside jacket pocket, yanked them out, and plopped them on the desk.

Scott scanned them. Looked authentic. "All right. We'll leave first thing in the morning."

"What do you want me to do now?"

"Roust up extra petrol. Once we're out of Naples, getting more is next to impossible. I'd like to make it back."

"Unlike last time?"

Scott stifled the urge to throttle Private Salmon. For all the ribbing he took, Scott wished he'd never let Captain Justice in his jeep. Sure he'd enjoyed the company, and she seemed to enjoy his—until the sun set and they got detained—but that had been out of his control . . . mostly. "It's complicated."

"War is." The private retrieved his papers. "See ya in the a.m."

"Be here at six." He'd make sure they didn't get caught at night.

"Yes, sir." The man sauntered away.

Scott grabbed a few of the Frick maps the Army Air Force had prepared for the bombers. The maps were overloaded with landmarks but could help him identify where they needed to go. Reports had it streamlined maps were on the way, but he'd yet to see them. Navigators struggled to use the overcrowded maps as they sought to avoid monuments while hitting war targets. The current maps were bloated like everything else in the occupation forces. If something could be done in an hour, why not make it a week? With a jeep he'd make each day work for him.

After Scott spread a Frick map in front of him, he and DeWald spent the next hours comparing it to one of the Harvard Lists for the region and plotting the best approach.

Scott stood. "You want to join us? There's room for more in the jeep."

DeWald shook his head. "I've got to get this outfit appreci-ated. Build plans for the move north. You get out there while I get the framework in place."

"All right." Scott worked until his back ached from bending over the maps. The lines blurred in front of him. If he studied the pages more, he wouldn't be able to make sense of what he saw.

He stopped by Rachel's hotel on his way to his quarters. It was late, but he wanted to try one more time. Now that he had a jeep and a plan, he'd like her to rejoin him. He wandered around the lobby and small restaurant. He just decided he'd wasted enough time when he spotted her dark hair topped with her military cap. An oversized book sat in her lap, and she looked a thousand miles away.

"You're alive."

Rachel jerked to attention, the book sliding on her skirt before she caught it. "Lieutenant."

He'd hoped for a bit more warmth in her voice. "I haven't seen you in days. You disappeared."

She brushed a hand across the cover and sighed. "It wasn't my intent. I got a new assignment when we returned. Taking photos of refugees." She shrugged as she looked at him for the first time. "I thought the press office would inform you."

"They didn't." He let a small smile crack his face. "I'm headed out tomorrow. Would you like to join us?"

She bit her lower lip in an appealing gesture. "I'd like to, but . . ."

"You have an assignment."

"I do. One I'm to keep to myself."

"Ah, one of those." He nodded.

"Yes."

"I enjoyed our day together."

Her gaze searched his face as if she weighed the truth of his statement. He met her gaze and hoped she read his sincerity.

"I did too. Thank you for showing me your job. One of the photos was picked up by the wire service."

"That's great!"

"It is." Her smile had a shy edge to it, and then she shifted as she stifled a yawn.

"I'll leave you to whatever you were doing."

She stood and extended her hand. "Good night, Lieutenant."

He took her hand. What would she do if he pulled her into an embrace? He shook the impulsive thought away and raised her hand to kiss it instead, then turned to leave before he did anything more ridiculous and impulsive.

The next morning Scott paced outside his office. Would Private Salmon grace him with his presence? Vehicles roared along the street despite the predawn hour. If the private didn't show up fast, the early start Scott wanted would evaporate.

Someone laid on a horn, enough that it pierced the racket of other traffic. A few moments later, a jeep slid in front of Scott. "Ready, Lieutenant?"

Scott hopped into the vehicle and nodded. "Let's go."

"Where to?"

"Salerno."

The next days passed as they worked their way up and down streets, trails, and bomb-pitted roads. The devastation extended in each direction. Scott made notes as they drove, looking for landmarks listed in the brochures. In the late thirties his time in Rome had extended to Naples but not many villages—each of which had a treasure. Now his assignment from DeWald was to get to as many of the sixty-five Neapolitan churches damaged by recent battles. By June each should have repair work underway until restoration could be attempted.

What would Rachel think of the countryside, small towns, and churches? Would she sense the loss he felt as they traveled the countryside and worked with local Italian art superintendents to reinforce churches? Churches stood with roofs bombed off. Stained glass created centuries before by renowned artists—shattered. Frescoes incinerated by fire. Roofs could be rebuilt, but salvaging frescoes and stained glass was a different matter altogether.

At the end of long days, he wished for dozens more men trained in repairing and shoring up the great edifices. Then there were the paintings, altarpieces, and sculptures that begged for the careful, cautious hands and skill of restorers. His work as a curator hadn't prepared him for those kinds of challenges. He applied what he'd learned from watching others and talking to the Monuments and Fine Arts Administration officers in Naples.

While trapped in Naples, Scott and the other MFAA soldiers found a sort of stasis, a place of tolerated assignments while restlessness built. Tyler Salmon appeared day after day, and Scott worked with the man, but he wasn't a good fit with the MFAA since he showed no interest in the mission.

One morning Tyler leaned against a pillar pitted with bullet holes as Scott walked around a neighborhood church, evaluating the local Italian workers' progress. Watching him lounge day after day ate at Scott. His pulse throbbed until he could hardly move. He marched toward the man. "Get up and do something."

"What do you want me to do, Lieutenant?"

Scott pointed at a broom. "At least sweep up debris. Make yourself useful."

Tyler shifted until his chest puffed out like a rooster's. "You don't have authority. Someone else gives me orders to babysit you."

Scott clenched his jaw to the point he had to relax or crack a tooth. Not what he needed in the decimated city. "I suggest you wait with the jeep. I'd hate to have it disappear while you support a column."

"Sure. I can do that." Tyler grinned, and Scott wanted to knock the cockiness from him.

What gave Tyler the idea he was untouchable? Maybe reality. Scott had less authority than most lieutenants and less training than the rest. His art knowledge was what got his commission enhanced, not his prowess on the battlefield. Though if he were a wagering sort of man, he'd say odds were good Tyler didn't have a lick more battle sense than he had.

───※───

Rachel's new assignment with the Fifth Division didn't move her closer to Tuscany. She'd spent several days waiting for the Fifth to move. Her editor, Dick, kept her busy at the United Press offices as he mumbled about not liking her moving into the unknown with the division, as if to convince her to decline and stay in the office. But she needed to do something more than stay in place.

She'd wandered the city when she could, but Naples was old news. No more photos would be published until she left the city behind. After Scott found her in the hotel, she wondered where he'd spent his days. She'd asked to be reassigned to him while she waited, but the request was denied. Any moment the Fifth would move, but it evolved into the longest moment of her life. She couldn't do a thing to move the war forward. With each wave of mail and no letter from home, the noose of worry tightened around her heart.

Waiting. What a horrid word when she knew the tuberculosis wouldn't wait as it ravaged her momma's body. It might slide to the side, but it wouldn't disappear without aggressive treatment.

She had to find a way north to Tuscany. Since that's where her mother spent most of her time in Italy, it seemed the best place to search for her father.

One night when the other girls had gone to dinner with a few officers, Rachel stayed behind and pulled out her momma's diary. She closed her eyes and imagined her mom in Italy. A young woman, soul full of dreams, heart filled with ideas of love as she learned all she could about art.

> *The opportunity to study abroad could launch my artistic career. After a year of studying in Florence, I could take a place next to Mary Cassatt. Paint and teach. Instead the romance of Italy, the very word vibrates with beauty*

and love, distracted me. Now I return to the States with a
steamer trunk filled with canvasses and shattered dreams.
My womb filled with a child. A child that will cause my
parents to disown me.

   Even now I love my Italian passionately. My whole
heart is consumed with him. My thoughts constantly return
to him, even as the boat carries me ever farther away. At
least I will have my child, since I will never open my heart
or arms to another man. Italy will be a chapter of my past.
A page I will turn and forget as much as I can. I must turn
my face to the future with its uncertainty. Somehow I will
make a way for us. Us . . . not the way I envisioned my life.

Reading the words shook Rachel. She'd been the reason
Momma abandoned her life's ambitions. Somehow her momma
had survived those days of disillusionment and uncertainty when
her family turned their back.

Rachel leaned back against the headboard. What would she
do in a similar position? Abandon all she knew to run back to
the arms of the man she loved? Maybe someday she'd know.
But as she sat in the small hotel room in a battered city, the possibility of finding a love to cherish for a lifetime seemed beyond
infinitesimal.

It was impossible.

Chapter 8

May 24

RACHEL HAD SEEN ONE painting and the preparatory photos her momma took while in Italy. On a rare visit to her grandmother's, Rachel had noticed a framed photo, dotted and faded by time. She'd studied the composition of the piece, armed with new knowledge from her college art-appreciation class, and knew she would have framed the scene the same way. Her grandmother had smiled, sadness tingeing her eyes. "Your momma took that in Italy. It became the basis for her painting."

Rachel clutched the diary close to her chest. Her momma's paintings had the late Impressionist feel of Mary Cassatt's paintings. Tears flowed at the thought that her momma had given up so much to provide for her, and now Rachel was failing in her attempt to find her father. She swiped at the dampness that trailed down her skin. She had to slog forward, step-by-step, through the muck of war.

Maybe if luck and heaven smiled on her, she'd find her father. Maybe he'd believe her. Maybe he'd have the resources and willingness to help Momma. And maybe Momma would still live.

All Rachel could control was her search.

If her father was an artist, would Lieutenant Lindstrom interact with him? If she had a name, she could solicit his help. Sketches
alone couldn't be enough.

She opened the diary to Momma's earlier entries, rubbing a
hand along Momma's spidery writing, unchanged in loops and
formalness to this day. So much like Momma's personality. A stiff,
almost foreboding exterior walling off the slight silliness tinged
with flair.

> *The nights have a depth, a richness, I can't see in New
> York City. Yes, Florence is a city, but travel a few kilome-
> ters . . . only a few . . . and I find myself thrust deep into
> a velvet sky dotted with diamonds. I search them for the
> formations, the lore of old hidden in its vastness. Then my
> guide arrives and weaves stories of passion and war. I find
> myself swept away by the art and romance.*

What would Momma's life have been like if she'd stood
strong? Vastly different, nothing like her present. Instead, in the
next pages her momma outlined what Rachel saw as a web of
seduction. Gifts and poetry all delivered with a delightful Italian
accent. What could Momma do but fall in love? At least that's how
the diary painted the situation.

Maybe knowing her momma's story prompted Rachel to keep
her walls high, never letting anyone into her soul. She'd spent
weeks in Naples, and yet Dottie remained an acquaintance despite
her roommate's continued attempts to get her to join the girls
when they went out after long days of work. The girls had even
tapered off on teasing her about her night with Scott.

Someday they'd realize they teased about nothing because
nothing had happened. Scott had treated her with complete
respect. Did that mean he didn't find her the least bit appealing?
She shouldn't care, yet no matter how many times she told herself

that, she still wondered why he hadn't been even a little interested. Yet he'd sought her out. That had to mean something.

What did she want?

To lock her heart away and keep it safe?

Or a man who would scale the barriers and wariness to penetrate her heart?

Rachel couldn't risk meeting someone who would seduce her with an imitation of love. The starkness of her thoughts scared her. She couldn't live her life with barriers surrounding her heart.

The room's door banged open, and Rachel shoved the diary under her pillow. Dottie bounced in, her blonde curls swirling about her pixie face. "You missed the most divine night."

"I'm glad you had a good time."

"You must come next time. It's unhealthy to spend so much time cooped up in this small space. You have to get out and do something."

"Dancing?"

"It is exercise." Dottie's grin sparked an answering one in Rachel. "And nice to forget for a bit where we are." She lay back against her pillow. "I always wanted to see Naples. It seemed so romantic." She propped up on her elbow and wrinkled her nose. "This is not."

Rachel stifled a smile. It could be . . . if she spent more time with a certain lieutenant.

The next morning Rachel roamed the streets of Naples, her camera in hand. The breath of approaching summer filled her as she saw rosebushes pushing to life through a mound of rubble that must have been a home before the battle. She opened her camera and framed the shot. This wasn't an image her boss would use, but it spoke to her. Somehow in the rose finding the strength to bud, she imagined the Italian people doing the same. Yes, it would take time. It wouldn't happen overnight, but the country would rebuild.

After snapping a frame, she moved on. This portion of road stood almost clear of debris. She glanced down occasionally to keep from tripping or falling into a hole. Strains of an opera turned her gaze up. She paused when she noticed a Victrola phonograph standing in the glassless window of a second-story apartment. The building looked intact, if one didn't need windows. Maybe that's why the high contralto floated unhindered to Rachel's ears. A bass undertone vibrated with it. Rachel closed her eyes, tilting her face toward the warmth of the sun as the song played.

The moment felt touched by grace. Kissed by heaven with the resonance that life would go on. Despite the destruction.

As the last notes warbled on the air, Rachel opened her eyes and sighed. The warmth of the music penetrated her, and she longed to savor the moment. After raising her Argus C3, she took another photo, trying to capture the contrasting grace of the beautiful phonograph against the broken shards in the window's corners.

A woman stepped next to the phonograph. Rachel pointed at the camera, then the woman. The woman frowned then seemed to understand. She posed, one hand resting on the horn of the phonograph, the other on the window ledge. Her solemn gaze never flinched from the camera until Rachel pulled it from her face and smiled. "Grazie."

"*Certamente.*" The woman waved a birdlike hand and then restarted the phonograph.

Rachel resumed her pace, then turned once when her senses stood at attention. She felt like someone was watching her. She turned to examine the sidewalk for someone, then shrugged and resumed her wandering when she saw no one.

Since coming to Naples, that's all she'd done. Like the stories she'd heard in Sunday school of the Israelites. The problem was, she couldn't afford to wander for forty days, let alone forty years.

She slowed as she reached a battered stone building. In the States it would qualify as a small church, one that would house a small, tightly connected congregation. As Rachel stood in front of this one, she wondered how many of its faithful lived. Did any remain to worship in its battered facade?

The ping of something striking stone mixed with voices carried from inside the structure. Curiosity propelled her to the steps. At the bottom she hesitated, then worked her way up the path someone had cleared. With each step her thoughts turned to her day bouncing across the countryside looking for the altarpiece, but this time Scott wouldn't work inside.

Too many churches dotted Naples and the surrounding countryside to think she'd find the handsome lieutenant inside. If he was, would his smoky gray eyes meet her gaze? What then? He was one of thousands in town, all in uniform, stranded far from home with the threat of death never far from their minds.

She froze, her hand poised over the doorknob. She closed her eyes and sucked in a bracing breath. This was ridiculous. Lieutenant Lindstrom was not in there. Even if he was, he wouldn't notice her. The army had assigned her elsewhere, and their paths would never cross again.

※

Scott brushed the layer of dust and dirt that coated the front of his uniform. "If we shore up that wall, it will support the roof."

Anatole Origo nodded as he studied Scott's sketch, but agreement didn't enter his eyes.

Scott puffed out a breath and tried to relax his shoulders. The man was polite but didn't hide his distrust of the American who told him how to fix his church. They'd worked together for a couple days. By now he should trust Scott, yet his posture remained wary.

"It will work." Scott pointed to the sketch and explained again.

"I see." Anatole gave the barest nod. "We make happen."

The man knew his business—construction of Italian churches—but retained the ability to accept input. He might suggest alternatives but accepted Scott's opinions on how to proceed. The allure of American dollars to finance the renovations and rebuilding didn't hurt. Anatole spoke in rapid Italian to one of the laborers, and Scott turned his attention to the tiny prayer chapel. Nothing less than a miracle had protected the magnificent fresco in the alcove. Scott could imagine God's hand outstretched to protect the image of what occurred during creation. The colors remained vivid as if the artist had dabbed the paint into the wet plaster mere months earlier rather than centuries in the past.

The screech of the doorknob caused Scott to turn toward the small foyer. Whoever had opened the door stood framed in shadows the faint light filtering through the cracked door couldn't pierce.

Scott took a step toward the foyer, then thought again. What if it was a partisan? He wouldn't see anything in time to protect himself or the workers. Anatole's men didn't need the distraction of what could go wrong. Neither did they have anyone to protect them. Maybe that was something Scott should request. With the priceless paintings, altarpieces, and relics many of these churches held, he should have someone secure them.

"Hello, Scott."

The soft words drifted to him. He squinted and she stepped closer. Rachel Justice, a welcome sight in her army-issued skirt and jacket. Her dark hair brushed her shoulders in soft waves he longed to touch. "Captain Justice, Naples is treating you well."

She studied him. "Thank you." She glanced around the interior, then stepped closer. "Reports continue the Fifth will leave soon."

"That's what you want?"

"Yes." She paused as if considering how much to share. "I can't stay in Naples."

"The water's running, and there's a working sewer system now."

"I'm not a delicate flower."

Could have fooled him. Her features carried the light gracefulness of a rose opening from its tight bud to embrace the sun.

"Will you stay?" Her words startled him.

"I'm at the mercy of the army." He motioned to the activity around them in the nave of the church. "There is still much to do here. I'll shore up these broken beauties until the army orders me to move."

She stepped closer as her gaze swept the activity, then returned to him. "Do you mind?"

Did he? Wherever the troops moved, there would be damage. It was a collateral aspect of war that would continue as the army slogged from the Anzio beachhead and across the mountain passes that trapped the Allied armies in a slugfest with the German army.

"I see." Her soft smile suggested she'd read his thoughts. How could she when she'd known him days? He felt exposed. Vulnerable. Uncomfortable yet intrigued.

The silence stretched between them like the long brushstrokes that covered a virgin canvas, conditioning it for the layers of paint to come. Could he risk sharing his thoughts? He had to if he wanted to take their friendship to a deeper place. "Life doesn't always give me what I desire."

"Or hope for." She stepped deeper into the space pocked with open sky. "What are you doing here?"

"The ceiling has to be reinforced."

"Why not start over? There's not much left."

"It's an issue of supplies and resources. These men must be paid, and there are so many buildings with few materials."

"But all those Liberty ships that fill the harbor . . ."

"Saturated with troop supplies." He led her toward a fresco that showed a scene from the Sermon on the Mount. Jesus—modeled on some Italian nobleman from the thirteenth century, maybe the patron—teaching a multitude on a hill, with olive trees in the background. The scene could be from the Italian countryside rather than the Holy Land. "This is why I'm here."

Rachel tilted her head to the side as she examined the painting. "Can you salvage it?"

Could he? Or were his efforts wasted? "I believe I can."

"I know you can." She trailed a finger along an edge of broken plaster that held the outline of a child in colorful robes. No one had told the artist peasants didn't wear such expensive colors in Jesus' time. "It's beautiful, even broken."

"Yes."

"I wish I saw what you see."

He studied her. What caused the lingering air of sadness that cloaked her? "Is that why you're here?"

"What?" She turned her attention from the fresco to him. "I didn't know you were here."

"I know. But why come here, to this church?"

She pivoted and pulled her camera up. She wore it like some women wore a necklace of pearls. "May I? Take some photos?"

He considered pushing, learning why she redirected his question. Yet he wanted her to stay. Whatever motivated her ran deep and seemed more than a desire to take photos, to propel her into a war zone.

"It's fine with me. Just keep me out of them unless you warn me."

She grinned, raised the camera, and snapped a quick shot. "Like that?"

Imp, that's what she was. He smiled back. "My mom doesn't need to see a photo of me in her newspaper."

He'd meant the words to be light, almost a joke, but Rachel's smile slipped.

"I'm sorry, Lieutenant. I'll make sure the photo isn't published." She walked toward a group of workmen surrounding a ladder and never looked back. She studied the workmen, watching the man at the top nail a tarp in place over the apse. Others worked from the roof, all of it an effort to keep rain from penetrating the building.

He walked over and stood next to her, shoulder to shoulder. "They'll cover the openings with tarp."

"Is it enough?"

"It has to be."

They spent fifteen minutes exploring the periphery, then one of the men asked for direction. Scott walked over, but the directions took long minutes to convey. Rachel waited awhile, then waved and slipped from the church. Scott hurried after her, wanting a minute to say good-bye, but when he reached the door, she'd disappeared.

Chapter 9

RACHEL'S THOUGHTS SWIRLED AFTER she left the church. Scott had charmed her, but heat flooded her cheeks as she remembered his reaction to her photo. He'd meant to tease. She knew that. But all she could hear was the voice of her photography teacher and yearbook editor correcting every photo she took.

Even with photos printed in the U.S.'s best papers, she still felt like she'd never take the right kind.

Tomorrow she'd leave Naples if the Fifth left as scheduled. At least that's what the public relations officer had promised her editor. She had much to accomplish before morning. When she left, her hopes that mail would find her lessened. If mail hadn't connected with her in Naples, how could it find her on the move? It was a miracle the public relations officers had agreed to let her leave the city.

What should she expect?

With the stories of mud knee-deep on some mountain passes, Rachel needed to find more trousers that fit. Chances were low the Liberty ships had carried any, but she'd check.

After walking awhile, Rachel made her way to the harbor. The army engineers had done an amazing job cleaning the wreckage of scuttled ships, one type of debris the Germans left when they evacuated. On a clear day, if she looked into the water just right, she could see the ghost ships lying on the bottom that hadn't been tugged from the harbor. She'd failed to capture the haunting images. The buildings along the harbor hadn't fared well either. Some had been hastily rebuilt. Others stood as shells, forms broken, walls sheared off exposing furniture and more.

After a couple of requests for directions, Rachel found the building that warehoused uniforms and refitting supplies. The closer she came to the building, the more uniforms strolled around.

"What's this dame doing here?" The private didn't bother to lower his voice.

"Couldn't find a guy at home?"

Someone laughed, a low, cruel sound. "I bet she'd entertain us."

Rachel kept her back straight and didn't allow herself to react. If she kept her attention in front of her and her pace steady, maybe they'd get the message she didn't care what they said.

"Don't know why they let girls wear uniforms."

"Make them feel important?"

She yanked open the warehouse door and slipped inside. Her shoulders sank as the doors closed, locking out the soldiers' words. She must forget the words and innuendos.

A chorus of whistles reached her.

"Quiet, guys." A private that reminded her of Mickey Rooney rushed to her side. "Can I help you, miss?"

"Captain."

"Sorry." He stepped back. "What brings you to our humble building?"

"I need some trousers. I move out tomorrow."

"Orders?"

"Right here." She tugged them from her rucksack that held extra film, a bit of money, credentials, and orders. "You'll see all is in order."

"Except the detail of women's clothing. Don't get much of that."

She could only imagine. The military wasn't prepped for women. Even though she wasn't strictly part of the army, they sanctioned her arrival and provided her supplies. And she needed pants. "You must have short soldiers."

"A few. But not many as short as you. No offense."

"None taken."

He led her to a stack of rickety shelves that reached much higher than her head. "The smaller sizes are usually on the bottom. We haven't organized since the last group went through, but you should start there."

"Thank you. May I have my orders back?"

He handed them to her with a toothy grin. "Whatever you find, you can take two pairs. I'd recommend a pair of boots and some rain protection. We're hearing it's a mess. Good luck." He headed back toward the front while Rachel stared at the overwhelming piles.

Even though he'd suggested an area to start, she couldn't imagine how she'd find anything in the piles of government-issued clothing. After she'd sorted awhile, a rowdy noise reached her. Must be soldiers ready to be fitted before they moved out. Before long, soldiers made their way into the cavernous area she was in, their loud voices betraying their fear. They might not have reached the front, but Naples was much closer than Kansas.

Rachel dug deeper into the pile. Maybe they wouldn't see her. A shrill whistle canceled that thought.

"Looky here. A pretty lady." A scarecrow, tall, scrawny, and dressed in uniform, sauntered toward Rachel. "How may I be of service?"

She eased to her feet and plastered on a carefree smile. "I'm quite fine. Thank you. Wouldn't want to keep you from finding boots. You'll need them where you're going."

"So they tell me. But I won't find a bee-u-ti-ful woman where I'm going." While his words wheedled, his eyes held something else. A darkness. Fear mixed with the reality of what waited? Desire forced to the surface by the racing future? He stepped closer, his hot breath hitting her cheek. "Join me for dinner."

"Wish I could, but I ship out tomorrow." She grasped Momma's necklace as she tried to remain calm. "Can't keep the officers waiting."

"I'll get you home . . . eventually." He took another step toward her, and her back rammed against the shelves.

Bile rose in her throat, and she felt along the shelves for anything she could use as a weapon. All she felt was fabric. Piles and piles of soft, nonthreatening fabric.

"What do you say?" The brute shoved against her until his frame lined up with hers. She bit down on her lip to keep from whimpering. Where was everyone?

"Bates? Where'd you go?"

Rachel opened her mouth, but the soldier pressed his sweaty hand over her mouth. "Shh, little lady."

"Did you find the boots?" The voice sounded nearer, but the warehouse was so big.

A shudder coursed through Rachel. She needed to get away, but with her arms pinned to her sides, she stood trapped. She clamped her teeth on his hand.

"You—" The man's shrill word cut the air.

A soldier hurried around the corner. "There you are." Then he skidded to a stop. "What are you doing?"

Bates growled and stepped back. "Just talking."

The soldier raised an eyebrow, the one movement communicating disbelief and censure. "I think you should check over there for boots." He crossed his arms and waited.

"Fine." A storm gathered on Bates's face. "You shouldn't have interfered."

"Sure, tough guy." The soldier waited until Bates left. He might be beefier than the one who'd assaulted Rachel, but kindness cloaked him. "Sorry, ma'am. I'll keep him away, but you might want to make your business fast."

Rachel watched until he disappeared and she was alone again, then she scrambled through several piles, determined to find something serviceable before the next wave of soldiers arrived. That escape had been too close.

With two pairs of longish pants in hand, she raced back to find the helpful private. She held the pants and a belt to him. "These will do."

He eyed them with a frown. "You sure, Captain?"

"Unless you have other suggestions."

He shrugged. "I found some boots and rain gear for you." He filled out a couple forms, then slid them toward her. "Sign here and here." He pointed with a pen. "Then you can call those your own. Do you need needle and thread?"

"I've got some, thanks."

She curved her way through the streets back to the hotel in the waning daylight. It was almost dusk when she reached the building's protective embrace. Dottie paced a tiny circle in the lobby. She raced to Rachel.

"Where have you been?"

Rachel held up the pants. "Trying to find anything that comes halfway close to fitting me."

"How'd that work?"

"Not too well."

"The army ain't Macy's."

Rachel smiled at the comparison to the great department store. The warehouse at the wharf didn't compare. "Good thing I'm not picky."

Dottie tugged her up the stairs to their room. "Barbara and I are taking you out tonight. Who knows when we'll see you again."

The girl's eyes clouded as she took the reams of fabric from Rachel and threw them on one of the twin beds. "So we're going to make merry and have fun while we can."

"All right."

"Really?" Dottie blinked as if she didn't believe the ease with which Rachel had agreed.

"Really. I'd like that. . . ."

"Then get ready. Here's a party dress."

"Where did you find that?"

"A girl has her ways, and the blue will be beautiful on you. We leave in five. I'll let Babs know."

Rachel stared at the dress. It was elegant with a full tea-length skirt. How Dottie got it to Naples, she couldn't imagine, but Rachel couldn't wait to try it on and feel the caress of the fabric. When would she have the opportunity to experience feminine companionship and silk? It could be a long time, so she determined to enjoy tonight.

⁓⁓⁓

Scott straightened his tie and garrison cap as he looked in the mirror.

"Come on, Lindstrom. The officers' club will fill by the time we get you away from here." Blake Erikson crossed his arms as Scott stared in the mirror. The man was an addition to the Monuments team, recently arrived from Alabama. Scott liked him, . . . but that didn't stop him from slowing down his actions. Blake frowned but couldn't hold it. "All right, you look good, man."

Scott grinned. He didn't often join the others when they went out, but tonight he wanted to forget the devastation. Instead, he'd sit back and enjoy the USO show. Pretend he was in Philadelphia. "Let's go."

"My turn to join the best-dressed club." Blake slicked down his dark hair with a swipe of his hand and then turned. "There, all set. The others are downstairs."

In a few minutes the group of soldiers joined the others pouring out of the barracks and toward the different rest areas the army had established.

After waiting in line awhile, they entered the officers' club. A festive air filled the building with a band playing swing tunes. Most of the men headed to one of the bars while Scott decided to find a place to sit. Blake joined him a bit later with two Cokes. "Thanks."

"No problem. I figure you'll earn it showing me the ropes."

Scott rubbed his jaw and sighed. "There isn't much to show."

"Nah. I've watched. You've got a can-do attitude I need." Blake took a swig from the glass bottle, then wiped his mouth. "This isn't Oxford."

"You can say that." The band switched from a Dorsey tune to something he'd heard Bing Crosby sing on Armed Forces Radio.

The man studied the room, then turned back to Scott. "It may not be Oxford, but I've always wanted to see Italy. Now I get my chance. Looky there." Blake tipped his bottle toward a table across the way. "You see what I see?"

Scott looked around, taking in the large room filled with well-dressed officers. There were a few women, some in uniform, some in dresses. They looked like hummingbirds flitting around the room, surrounded by men or dancing on the floor. "You'll have to narrow it down a bit."

"Over there. By that fake palm." Blake gestured. "I see a couple fine-looking women."

Scott laughed because most of the soldiers described every woman that way, even the half-starved Neapolitans. He'd heard terrible stories of some soldiers paying them with Monopoly money and kept his distance. "I'm not interested."

"Sure." Blake grinned and tapped his half-empty bottle against Scott's. "I'll get another bottle while you're not interested."

Erikson wormed his way through the crowds, and Scott monitored his progress. Despite his claims, he was curious about the women who had captured the man's attention. A small pixie of a woman leaned against the wall, a bright smile on her face as she listened to the band play Benny Goodman's "Sing, Sing, Sing." A tall Amazon stood next to her, long legs highlighted by the skirt she wore. A third member of the group disappeared in the fake fronds.

Blake approached the group and talked to the gals for a few minutes, his attention focused on the tall gal. She almost matched him inch for inch, not an easy task since Blake was a bear of a man. But the pixie nodded too. In no time Blake had them following him across the floor. "Scott, let me introduce Babs, Dottie, and . . ."

"Lieutenant Lindstrom." Rachel's voice taunted his ears through the band and background conversations.

"Captain Justice." He stood straighter and felt the room telescope around her.

Blake helped the women into chairs. "Can I get y'all something to drink?"

After accepting orders, he moved to a bar, leaving Scott with the ladies. The other soldiers' glares burned Scott's back. Here he sat with an abundance of women when he wanted to focus on one.

The gal named Dottie chatted with Rachel while Babs waited for Blake's return. A couple soldiers drifted past their table with loud voices and pointed looks, but Rachel ignored them while Dottie smiled and shook her head. "I'm quite fine, thank you."

Rachel shook her head as she watched her friend. "You dragged me out here so you could smile and say no?"

"Well, I came to spend time with you." Dottie grinned. "Besides, the right one hasn't walked by."

Scott couldn't help himself. "You mean I'm not him?"

Dottie froze, then gave him an apologetic frown. "Why, no. You certainly aren't. My momma told me I would know the moment I laid eyes on my true love. I must not have met him yet."

"Dottie, you are one of a kind." Babs rolled her eyes and then smiled when Blake returned with a Coke. "I thought you might bring something stronger, soldier."

"Not this one, ma'am." Something in the way he said it seemed to charm the girl.

The military band took off with "In the Mood," and Rachel swayed in her seat.

"Would you like to dance?" Scott stood and offered her his hand.

Her chocolate doe eyes considered him, then she slipped her hand in his. As she did, he stood straighter with the knowledge the most beautiful woman in the room had chosen him. Even if for one moment.

Chapter 10

THIS WAS A MISTAKE.

The thought raced through her mind as Rachel accepted Scott's offered hand.

As he adjusted her hold and tightened his fingers around hers, she could feel it to the depths of her toes. This man was a mystery. Yes, they'd spent moments together, but she didn't know him. Not really. Yet as she'd watched him with the priest, seen him with the various children they'd come across, his heart peeked out. She saw a passion for protecting what he valued. What would it be like to be the object of that attention? Did he worry anyone who caught a glimpse of the real man, the one who cared deeply, would walk away?

This was a mistake.

If he probed, she wasn't sure she could keep her heart hidden from him. His gaze seemed to penetrate to her heart, and if he could see through her, it would be simple for him to penetrate her walls. She couldn't afford to let a man distract her from her two-fold purpose in coming to Italy.

A distraction would cost her precious time. Time she didn't have to save her mom.

Her thoughts flitted to the way a man had woven Italy into a magical land that led to heartbreak. She couldn't let that happen. Not to her.

Rachel fought the sudden desire to yank her hand from Scott's grip before he had her on the dance floor. Before he could encircle her in his arms and she relaxed into his embrace.

One thing she knew to her core: Scott Lindstrom, enigma extraordinaire, could demolish her reasons in a heartbeat.

"I can't do this." The words whispered from her mouth.

Scott hesitated a moment in the path to the center of the hall. He cocked his head toward her. "I'm sorry?"

Dottie waved her fingers at Rachel over a soldier's shoulder as he whirled her around the floor. She looked so relaxed, so contained with a hint of joy that Rachel longed for a breath of that. One dance. One moment of forgetting she was in bombed-out Naples. She could close her eyes and imagine instead she was here during the same time as her momma. The 1920s. A carefree time when the world couldn't imagine a war as all encompassing and devastating as the one crossing the globe.

"Do you need something to drink? Water? Punch?" The concern in Scott's voice led Rachel to shake her head.

"One dance."

He smiled, slow and confident. "That's all it takes."

She tucked her head against his shoulder, unsure how to take his words. Maybe for a few moments she'd forget everything. Instead of wondering or worrying, she'd imagine what her momma had felt the first time she'd danced with her father. Maybe she'd begin to understand the love and passion that convinced her momma to live her life alone since Italy.

That's all it takes? Scott wanted to stop the dance, march out of the officers' club, and straight to the nearest bucket of water. Maybe if he dumped it over his head, he'd regain his senses.

What was it about this petite, brown-eyed woman that turned him into an absolute idiot?

It had to qualify as a miracle that she'd accepted his request for a dance. The band started up with a rendition of "A String of Pearls." Not swinging music; neither was it a hold-the-girl-close-and-snuggle-up-for-three-minutes tune. Perfect for their current relationship. Who was he kidding? Were they even friends? He shouldn't count on spending any more moments with Miss Justice. He enjoyed the pockets of normalcy he imagined with her. He could forget they were here. Maybe they'd run into each other at a dance in Philadelphia.

He swung her lithe frame away from him and then tugged her back. She floated with a grace that made him think she'd had lots of lessons or opportunities to perfect her dancing.

As he maneuvered through the couples on the floor, he noticed several soldiers looking at Rachel rather than enjoying the gals they swung around the floor. "Is your dance card full?"

She startled and looked up at him.

He leaned closer to her ear. "Dance card full?"

"No. It never is." Her eyes twinkled. "I came for the refreshments."

"I doubt the guys give you a chance to sit down."

She shrugged. "I wouldn't know. This is the first one I've attended. A girl can only hide so long."

"Why?"

"Dottie can be persuasive. And I couldn't tell her no since I leave tomorrow."

"Tomorrow?"

She nodded, her hair brushing his chin in a whisper-soft motion.

He swallowed. "Think you'll miss her?"

"Absolutely. She doesn't get in my things, and she's so kind."

Rachel faltered a step and her eyes filled. "She's almost like I imagine a sister."

"Bet you left a couple of those behind."

"No. Only my mom." Tears collected in the corners of her eyes. What had he said now?

The song ended, and Rachel turned toward the band to applaud with the rest. Before the band started another song, she edged from Scott and the dance floor. She didn't make it far before a couple of officers surrounded her, acting like high school kids. If her tight posture was any clue, she didn't relish the attention. Still, he wasn't sure she wanted him to intervene. Maybe he should watch from a distance for a few minutes. Get a better read on how she liked the attention. Then he could come to her assistance the moment she looked like she'd welcome help.

The music made it impossible to listen to the conversation around Rachel, Though her face looked relaxed, the skin around her mouth was tight, and it wasn't from the smile she'd painted on.

Scott elbowed his way through the crowd. "Excuse me, gents." He turned to Rachel. "I believe you saved me this dance."

Her eyes widened and then her smile broadened. "There you are. I wondered where you'd disappeared. I was about to head out with one of these fine men. No sense wasting the night."

"I'm here now." He extended his hand, wondering if she'd accept.

"Yes, you are." She turned toward those assembled around her, looking a bit like Scarlett O'Hara in that movie Elaine had dragged him to while they dated. "I'm sorry to disappoint, gentlemen." Then she accepted his hand, and he led her toward the floor.

The music swept around them as they danced, and he would swear she snuggled close as the music wrapped around them. The others faded into an impressionist surrounding, details washed out by the moment of holding her. Of feeling how well she fit next to him. The music eased to an end, but Rachel remained where she was, so he continued to sway from side to side. What song did she hear? The bandleader announced a fifteen-minute break, and Scott tipped her chin up.

"Rachel, we should get off the floor."

"Hmmm?" She kept her eyes closed, and the longing to lean an inch closer and kiss her overwhelmed him.

"Rachel, honey?"

"Yes?" Her chocolate eyes opened and she startled. "I'm so sorry."

With a swirl of her peacock-blue skirt, she tugged her hand from his and slipped out a side door.

⁘

Her heart pounded as Rachel slipped outside. She needed air and distance. Thanks to the Fifth Division, she'd have plenty of space inserted between Lieutenant Lindstrom and herself starting in the morning. Right now, though, he edged perilously close. As they danced, she'd longed to have him hold her forever. She felt like she'd found her home, and she never imagined that would be with a person. The way he'd marched into the middle of the flood of uniforms and swept her away spoke to her. She'd felt alone and trapped in an unwelcome sea of admiration. Then he freed her.

He'd seen her. And he cared enough to step into the fray.

She liked to stand on the side, camera poised to snap pictures, but never of her. Always of what she saw, the way she experienced the world.

She closed her eyes, then tilted her chin toward the sky. The world around her was dark, but an array of stars filled the sky, almost as vast as those she'd seen from the road that fate-filled day she toured with the lieutenant.

The uncountable nature of the stars made her feel so small, so insignificant.

A tear threatened to escape as she tilted her face further to the sky.

"There you are." Lieutenant Lindstrom's voice sounded tense.

She swiped under her eye, then lowered her face, still not looking at him.

"It's the middle of the night in Naples. You don't want to be out here alone."

He was right. Rachel knew it was foolish to leave the building. Yet had he sensed she didn't want to remain alone? How much her heart cried for someone to see her?

"Can you take me home?" She turned toward him and forced a small smile. "I have so much to do before morning."

Scott studied her a moment, his gray eyes laced with concern and awareness.

Please don't say it. She couldn't bear to hear him acknowledge her pathetic excuse.

"Should you say something to your roommate? Dottie, right?"

"Yes, we can go back long enough to find her. Then I'm ready to leave." If they could find Dottie. Was it even possible in that crush?

"You'll be all right." He placed his hands on her shoulders, staring into her face through the shadows.

What did he see? What kept him looking at her, an ordinary girl far from home? For just a moment she wanted to see the world from his perspective. See herself the way he did.

His hands slid down her arms until he caught her hands, a trail of goose bumps following his touch. He tugged her a step closer, until they were standing with mere inches between them. Her breath hitched in her lungs, and she felt time still. She tried to read his eyes, but the shadows made it impossible.

His hands found her waist and pulled her closer still. "I wish you could see the woman I see, Rachel."

"I do too."

A slow grin spread on his face, and she felt it to her core. "Let me show you."

His head tipped down until their lips were a breath apart. He paused as if giving her the opportunity to back away. When she didn't, he closed the distance, and she felt as if the stars exploded around them.

In that moment she knew how her mother could give her all to another, and it terrified Rachel even as she wanted to prolong the moment. Scott must have sensed her moment of panic because he eased back and touched his forehead to hers. She felt emptied yet honored by that small whisper of distance. She leaned toward him and he groaned.

"Let's get you home." The words were ragged as if it took everything in him to say them.

They found Dottie, and her eyes widened as she glanced at Rachel, but in a moment they were walking the streets of Naples. Rachel's thoughts spiraled. She could not get attached to Scott. She'd leave in the morning and he'd stay here. The chance they'd see each other again diminished to miniscule odds the moment she left Naples.

Where would he be when she left? She'd be on her own and couldn't imagine finding him again. And in that moment all she wanted to do was beg him to follow her. He saw her and didn't press. He seemed to cherish her as he would a friend yet with a spark of more. The potential for something much more.

~~~

Scott held tight to Rachel's hand as they wove their way through the city back to her hotel. His senses still buzzed from their kiss. He hadn't planned his next step yet knew they could never go back and didn't want to. No, he wanted to beg her to stay in Naples with him. To chuck her plans to travel with the Fifth when they left the next day. Here it was safe and he could watch over her.

As soon as she left, he'd have no way of knowing if she was all right.

Yet he couldn't push the words out.

She had a job to do just as he did. And the army called the shots for both of them. She couldn't stay any more than he could leave.

When they reached the hotel, she paused, and he tugged her against the wall. She fell into his arms and he tightened his hold. What was he doing? Had the war heightened the way he felt about Rachel? Elaine had never felt so much a part of him.

"What?" Her gaze collided with his, sending a jolt through him.

He studied her, wishing they had more time. "You're sure you ship out tomorrow?"

She shrugged, and still he didn't let go. "As sure as I can be with the army."

"Remember me?"

"What a crazy thing to say."

If there was even a chance they could reconnect, explore what could happen after the war, then he had to take it. "Look for me in Rome."

"Rome?"

"You'll be there next. And I'll be behind you." He tipped her chin up, memorizing every feature on her perfect face. "I will find you."

Chapter 11

June 3

DEWALD AND THE OTHER Venus Fixers sat grumbling as Scott entered the office. Here he belonged and shared a purpose with men of learning and drive. It should be enough. The drumbeat to do more filled him, and the grumbling only stirred that urge. He'd come with orders to save Western civilization. The longer he sat in Naples, the less likely he'd fulfill that mission.

He bit back words that would add to the cacophony of discontent.

Rumor had it the army would enter Rome in the next day or two. The knowledge left Scott ready to abandon Naples with or without orders. If Rachel was in Rome, then he wanted to be there.

These days without her had threatened to drive him to distraction. He'd done his job, but his mind kept wondering where she was and if she was okay. The idea of a woman running around in an army on the move seemed worse with each passing day. It wasn't like she was a nurse surrounded by other women. No, she was on her own when he wanted her with him.

Keller looked up and nodded at Scott. "Morning."

"Morning, Dean."

"You've got orders, Lindstrom. General Marshall wants someone liaising with the Vatican posthaste." DeWald shoved an envelope at him. "This time it's you. Next time I might send Keller. Or Anthony. Maybe even Blake. Take that jeep of yours and get to Rome. You might make it ahead of some troops. Get a place established. The rest of us will follow as soon as we can talk our way out of Naples."

"Why aren't you going first, sir?" It made sense to send the man who headed up the Italian effort rather than Scott. He'd enjoy returning to the city, more if it stood undamaged if the tales and reports were accurate.

"I get to figure out who stays here and what the priorities are in Rome. So you go first. Figure out what's damaged. Connect with the local art superintendents. You've got a decent jeep and a driver. Make use of it. Besides, you've spent time in Rome. I want you to hit the ground fast. Make sure things are as good as they sound." He glanced at the others. "We've accomplished a lot here, but Naples still has work."

Keller sat back, his hands clasped across his stomach. "Give us a week and we'll be there. Then you can chase the Fifth up to Tuscany while I chase the Eighth."

All right. He wouldn't turn down the chance to check the status of the great city. And if things opened up now that the armies were moving, the rush to Tuscany and then Germany would be rapid. He should figure out the best approach for those future advances. When he'd arrived in Naples, things had been a mess, but the occupation government had been in place. In Rome he'd be there as the Allies arrived. Adrenaline pressed through him followed by the sense he could succeed or fail.

Failure wasn't an option.

It might have been eight years since he'd seen Rome, but some of his art friends and mentors should remain. "When do I leave?"

"With the next convoy. Grab your bag. Anything else you need. Don't assume Rome will have everything. It's unknown what we'll find there."

"We're good at improvisation."

DeWald grinned. "Yes. That'll serve you well."

He hoped so. Because Scott was ready to dig in and locate missing art. "Thank you, sir."

Within hours Scott was sitting in the jeep next to Private Tyler Salmon. They were sandwiched between two half-track trucks as they worked their way north.

"Ready for the big show?" Salmon chewed a wad of gum as he tapped the steering wheel.

"I'm eager to see Rome again."

"Ah, ya been there before?"

"It's been a while." But he remembered his year at the American Academy with fondness.

The tarp on the back of the truck in front of them was rolled back and out of the way. Soldiers looked out, each with a weapon at the ready. Scott hoped it was an unnecessary precaution. The Germans should be on the north side of Rome. Still that didn't stop the planes from trailing south over them.

The closer they got to the city, the more battle-hardened troops he saw on the road from Anzio to Rome. Dust coated their uniforms in contrast to his. Naples hadn't been an easy post, but compared to what these men had seen, it looked like a rest-and-relaxation area. After all, he'd spent time at the Royal Palace of Caserta while they'd slogged their way up and down mountains through mud and artillery shells.

He caught a couple looks as the men examined him. What did they see? A soft office worker? Someone who'd never handled a gun in battle? His pistol wouldn't do much good in the battles these soldiers had experienced. And telling them he'd completed training would be a waste of breath next to men who'd watched comrades in arms die.

No, he hadn't experienced the same war.

Scott pulled his helmet lower over his eyes and prayed for each man on the road and those who grabbed shut-eye in the back of trucks. As they continued toward the Holy City, soldiers hopped on and off the jeep for a reprieve in the hike.

They camped outside Rome overnight. "Tomorrow, first light, we go in."

"You sure? There's still fighting."

"I've got my orders. If you want to wait, fine." Scott stared Tyler down. Would the private gut it out and join him? "But I'm getting as close as I can." After all the Germans couldn't be everywhere if they were retreating. And the sooner he reached the city and started making the key connections with the Italians and Vatican, the earlier they could start the important work of determining what remained.

He hoped the stories that the Germans had taken art were rumors. Then his thoughts turned to the altarpiece that had disappeared from the cave near Naples. Maybe thieves had found it. Or the Germans had removed it. Either was unacceptable. What if the same thing happened around Rome? Many art officials had moved art from smaller towns to Rome's safety. Hopefully, that hadn't been a mistake. Based on the destruction many of the villages around Naples experienced, it seemed like a good decision. Nothing could be as terrible as Naples unless the Germans left Rome unharmed but removed her jewels.

As the sun crested the horizon the next morning, Tyler edged the jeep onto the road, grumbling a steady stream as he did. Scott was grateful to have him so he could focus on the destination and the sky while Tyler worried about the road.

"Tell me why we're doing this."

How could he explain to someone in a way that conveyed the need and passion? Scott sighed. "Italy houses art and architecture that goes back more than two millennia."

"So?"

"What we hold dear is built on that foundation. The Greeks and Romans laid the foundation for everything we value as a society." He thought of the Coliseum and *David* by Michelangelo. Different yet both illustrated the amazing creativity and beauty the human mind was capable of while war depicted the opposite. "People swoon when they see Michelangelo's *David* because it is so perfect. It's good we think it's worth preserving. We send a signal that some items transcend cultures and peoples and have value because they exist."

Tyler shook his head. "Sounds nuts to me."

"Hang around, and you'll change your mind."

Once the jeep entered the outskirts of Rome, Scott wondered how far they could drive. "Ready to take a risk?"

"With you?"

"Who else?"

Tyler jerked the jeep to the side of the road, then scanned the buildings behind Scott. "What were your orders?"

"We'll coordinate with Italian art superintendents in Rome and begin the process of securing the museums and other galleries."

"Did those orders happen to have my name on them?"

Scott made a show of pulling the document from his inside pocket and scanning them. "Tyler Salmon?"

"Give me that." Tyler snatched the paper from his hand and made a show of reading them. "When did I get so tied to you?"

"About the time you showed up and decided I had an easy job that kept you from the front lines."

Something dark passed across Tyler's features.

"Are you with me?"

"What do you think you're doing?"

"Getting as far into the city as we can." Scott rubbed his hands over his pant legs. "I'm not saying we should be reckless."

"Just push hard."

"As fast as we can. Look, we need to connect with the art officials, before a bunch of GIs who can't tell the difference between a da Vinci and a Raphael overwhelm the city."

"Hey, I'm one of those GIs."

"Which is why I'm glad you're with me. By the end of your tour, you'll appreciate the finer details of the world's masterpieces."

"I can't wait." The man grumbled under his breath a minute, then gave a slow nod. "Fine. My momma always told me I needed culture. I never thought it would take a war to make her happy."

The next hour slipped by filled with tense moments as they eased the jeep out of the caravan and started using little traveled roads to maneuver into the heart of Rome. People peeked out windows but for the most part stayed sequestered behind closed doors. The silence was punctuated by machine guns and artillery. Eventually, it got too dark to navigate, and Tyler refused to turn on the headlights.

"You looking for a neon sign announcing our presence to the Germans? No thanks."

"Then we spend the night here."

"Yep, you get first watch." With that Tyler climbed in the narrow backseat and made a big show of twisting around, grunting and groaning as he sought a comfortable position.

"You can cut the show. I get your point."

"You'd better get your gun ready."

"Right." The thought of shooting someone unsettled Scott. He could shoot in self-defense, but he'd never force the issue. Shooting targets couldn't be more different than the reality he'd confront if he wasn't careful. He pulled out a C ration and wondered what waited in the can. He tugged the can opener from the accessory pack and used it to open the M-unit. Looked like he'd gotten lucky with spaghetti. Without a fire he'd eat it cold, but it was something. Tomorrow they'd be in Rome and he'd find better food. At least he hadn't lived off C rations like so many soldiers. After he choked down the noodles, he put the opener on the chain next to his dog tags, keeping it ready for the next time.

As he stayed alert, wondering if a German scout or sniper would spot the American jeep, he worked his way through several psalms he had memorized as a child. The familiar words soothed his taunt nerves.

"The angel of the Lord encampeth round about them that fear him, and delivereth them." So many of David's psalms contained promises like that. Promises that comforted Scott as he stood watch, knowing he couldn't see whatever dangers might wait.

Around two he woke Tyler. "Your turn, sleepyhead."

"This mean you didn't get us killed."

"Not yet." Scott stifled a yawn. "That comes in the morning."

"Great. Let me sleep then. Maybe I'll miss your date with the Germans."

"Maybe we'll find some partisans to escort us, Salmon."

"Nope. We'll end up with a Fascist who'll be all too happy to take us to a German who'll ship us somewhere, and we'll never be heard from again."

"What kind of dreams were you having?"

"The kind that tell me I'm not in Kansas anymore. Or Naples." Tyler stretched and groaned. "Give me a minute." When he returned, he shooed Scott to the backseat. "Hope you can curl up smaller than I did. Otherwise you'll find muscles you didn't know you had."

"Just stay awake."

"Sure, Lieutenant. That's what you brought me along for."

Scott ignored the private's other mutterings and fell asleep. What felt like five minutes later, Tyler shook him.

"Wakey, wakey."

Scott groaned. It felt like he'd slept on a field of rocks, and it had been the jeep's backseat. The boys on the battlefields had to feel beat up. "See, we made it through the night."

"Yep." Tyler pointed through the windshield. "Better get cracking if you want to make Rome this morning."

"I thought you didn't want to rush in."

"That's before a pretty little gal on her way to get water told me the Germans declared Rome an open city. Seems that makes it fair game for the Allies. That would be us."

"Yes, it would." Urgency welled inside Scott. "You know where we are?"

"In general. And the gal told me to head that way." He pointed toward a road that intersected with the one they were on.

"You trust her?"

"Sure." He shrugged. "She called us liberators. Why would she do that if she wanted to harm us?"

"Because she wants us ambushed."

"That could have happened last night. One didn't show up, so we're fine."

Scott hoped he was right. "Let's move out."

When they left the parking lot of a main road, their speed improved. Handkerchiefs and small Italian flags appeared in windows like welcoming flags. Still the citizens stayed off the roads, making passage an easy matter.

As they approached Rome, Scott had Tyler deviate from their course. A battered car followed them, then pulled onto a side street. Scott hadn't seen many civilian vehicles on the road to Naples but shook the thought free. He needed to focus on his strategy for Rome. In a city overwhelmed with riches of history, culture, and meaning, a small museum had sat in this quarter of the city when he'd studied there. He often frequented it, and if he was lucky, the curator would be unchanged. If he was, Scott had entrée to the local art community. That would open doors that could be forced open but were best accomplished through friends telling others he was a trustworthy and good man.

If he could form those relationships, then the work of the MFAA in Rome would be easier than after the fact in Naples. And the easier it was, the sooner they could ensure the important pieces and places were preserved.

"Turn here." After Tyler did, Scott hopped out. "Find a place to wait. Stay close enough to come if I whistle."

"How long will you be?"

"I have no idea." If the curator he remembered wasn't here, he could be out in a couple minutes, empty of any connections or direction. If the superintendent was in, then it could be days before he surfaced. It would take at least that long to entice the man to share what he knew.

And Scott didn't have days to accomplish that.

Chapter 12

AN EERIE SILENCE FILLED the street. Rome wasn't a quiet city, at least not unoccupied Rome. Scott remembered a city that vibrated with conversations, laughter—the noise of a city on the move at all hours. The Rome he walked resonated with stillness. The stillness left him unsettled, scanning the rooftops for snipers, each window for a shadow that contained a gun silhouette.

He edged toward the shadowed alcove of the museum's door. It had contained a small gallery years earlier. The kind of gallery that contained an extensive collection from one thin slice of the rich art history of Italy. Mainly Titian and his related workshop. The Venetian artist was celebrated for his rich chromatic schemes, full forms, and balanced compositions, elements identified in the gallery's collection.

Even more interesting during his time was a visiting artist from Tuscany. An artist whose work he had helped sneak from Italy in the guise of an exhibition. That had served as a useful excuse. The validation to slip the work to a safer environment pending the end of hostilities. One more piece of his effort to protect the beauty and creative genius of a nation.

While he needed to connect with the Roman art community, he also hoped to hear word on the whereabouts and well-being of that artist Renaldo Adamo. Maybe his old friend Mario Armati at the museum could help him on both missions: protecting Italy's treasures and learning about Renaldo. Would the man see him as a peer?

If the curator remained anything like he was in 1936, he'd be in the thick of the effort, with or without assistance.

Scott pulled his thoughts back to the present and the need to get inside a building. Even the flimsy protection of the jeep left him less vulnerable than his current state.

With a few more careful steps, he reached the edge of the building and turned the corner for the main door. Just a few more feet . . . though it felt like a mile as he trudged, gaze constantly roving for any hidden danger. His senses tingled as he scanned and slid. Was this what combat felt like? The alert readiness for a shot at any moment? The certainty that someone watched, someone you couldn't see but who had a clear line of sight on you?

He inhaled around the tightness of his lungs once he reached the shelter of the doorway. If he was blessed, the door would be unlocked. He didn't want to edge around the building to a side door, especially when he couldn't be sure anyone waited inside.

His hand gripped the door, pushed down on the latch, but nothing moved. He banged on the door. "*Signor* Armati? Signor? It's Scott Lindstrom. Do you remember me?" He waited then repeated the barrage on the door and his words. "I'm here with the United States Army. I'm helping with the art."

Silence continued to confront him. Fine. Guess he'd better try the side door. As he garnered the courage to move into the open, the door gave way behind his back. He stumbled backward into the foyer. His eyes adjusted to the dark as he regained his balance.

A short man stood before him, gray hair forming a crown around a bald dome. His suit had a sheen that suggested extra wears and washes than the pristine man he remembered would have chosen. Yet it fit him like it had been tailored for him alone. The suit had been selected during better times.

"Signor?"

The man studied him with eyes that looked extra large behind thick glasses. Yet in them rested the same brilliance and wisdom that had caused Scott to spend hours in this small museum studying this thin sliver of art. Others could have the Michelangelos, da Vincis, and Rembrandts. He'd wanted to soak in Signor Armati's wisdom, not just in art but in living well. This man along with Renaldo Adamo had made Scott's year in Rome so pivotal in moving him into art curation as a career.

"I'm so glad to see you well."

"Mr. Lindstrom. You are back."

"Yes, sir. Not in a way I would have chosen."

"Come. We will sit. Brew something we once called tea."

Scott followed the man through the now-empty gallery. He would ask where the art had disappeared. Later. After the signor trusted he still shared a passion.

The slight hitch and hesitance in Armati's greeting signaled he should proceed with care.

"You are with the Americans? Truly?"

"Yes. The army is already here or right behind me." Hopefully not too far. Scott didn't want to think too long about slipping in advance of the fighting troops.

"We are open. What it means, I know not."

"I pray the city will be transferred without violence to the wonderful landmarks."

The man waved a liver-spotted hand in the air, the veins pronounced. Then he filled a kettle with water and placed it on a small burner. "If we have electricity, we have tea." A few moments later the burner turned red, and he sighed. "It is a good day."

"Did the Germans harass you?"

"No more than the rest of Rome. I tried to be a small target." He shrugged stooped shoulders. "Some days more successful than others." Silence except for the building bubbles in the kettle settled between them. Scott let it build. Being comfortable in quiet would signal he hid nothing.

"Sit. Have tea." The man filled a chipped mug with water and placed a used tea bag in it. Color trickled from the bag. Even bobbing it on the string did little to add to the brew. It would be weak, but Scott accepted it with a nod.

"If the army isn't here, why are you?"

"I'm sent ahead to work with the museums to protect your holdings. See what's been damaged, what is missing, and develop a plan to preserve everything."

"I knew a young man, one without a uniform."

"I haven't changed."

The man considered him, searching his face as if to ferret out the truth. "I believe you."

"Can you help me connect with others? Allied troops will arrive soon. We want to protect your treasures, but I can't do that alone."

"I will try." He pushed his mug of hot water away. "We see if the phones operate."

While he listened, Signor Armati called one, then another. "We meet at the Vatican. Two hours. We must leave." The signor led Scott to a back room. He shoved a pair of work clothes to Scott. "Put on."

Scott decided not to argue, keeping his dog tags on and stuffing his uniform in a bruised rucksack he found in a corner. He threw the rucksack over his shoulder, then followed Signor Armati out the door. The man locked it behind him.

"Do you need transportation?" Scott gestured to the jeep that waited across the street beneath a large tree.

"Not in that. Not until the Germans are finally gone."

Scott waved Tyler over. "I'm going with him to a meeting of museum directors. Stay here. If it gets risky, head back to the nearest Allied position. Come each day until we reconnect. Can't be long."

"You're nuts."

"Thanks. Stay safe." Scott refused to look back as he followed the signor through the streets.

The man took him on a circuitous path that took twice as long as the most direct route. Still he seemed to know when to duck down and kept a constant gaze on the skyline. Was it an occupation mentality? Always watching? Always waiting for something to happen?

Vatican City was a separate city-state within the city of Rome. Tucked against the Tiber River, it filled a hundred acres with its garden, villas, museums, and holy sites. To enter they passed through one of five entrances past the Swiss Guards. The yellow and white flag flapped in the breeze as they entered. Walls surrounded much of the city-state, giving it an enclosed, contained feel. Add in the gardens, and the area felt like a sanctuary in the midst of Rome's sprawling mass.

Scott had visited the Vatican's museums but had never been allowed entrance beyond the public spaces. Signor Armati led him to the Museo Pio-Clementino, the first of the Vatican's many museums. Established in the late 1700s, the collection focused on classical sculptures dating back to ancient Greece and Rome. Scott longed for time to explore each of its rooms and see the wealth of artistic treasures housed in this one collection. Instead, he followed Signor Armati through a series of doors.

The man passed through each with barely a word and a nod to the guards and others stationed at the entry points. None challenged the presence of an unknown man in worker's clothing. Lost inside the vast building, Scott moved quicker to keep pace with the man. Though stooped with age, his stride had not altered.

The man stopped in front of a final set of heavy, wooden, intricately carved doors. They towered above Scott making him feel insignificant, not challenging considering where he stood. Even in the areas the public would never see, the walls and ceilings were beautifully frescoed with religious scenes. Mosaics covered the floors in a pattern of colors.

"We have arrived. Say nothing unless asked. Without these men," the man paused, "you accomplish nothing."

Scott nodded, then waited as Armati signaled the man in full Swiss Guard uniform. The man leaned forward and opened the door without looking at them. It struck Scott as eerie how the soldier knew they were there yet never acknowledged their presence.

Inside the room, a long walnut conference table was surrounded by a buzz of men. The walls were as heavily frescoed as the rest of the building. If he had to guess, Scott would place them in the 1500s. The massive tapestries hanging on one wall looked older, maybe medieval. Their melodic conversations stopped as he entered the room, then switched to hurried English.

"This is him? The American?"

"He does not look like a soldier."

"How can he help us?"

"Where are the others?"

"What takes so long?"

Scott couldn't track who said what in the sea of men seated at the table. Many wore suits, other dressed in the red or purple robes of Catholic cardinals and bishops. Signor Armati took charge by switching to rapid Italian. Scott struggled to keep up with how long Signor Armati had known him, the context, and why those in the room should trust him. Considering how little they'd talked at the gallery, Scott was stunned by the endorsement.

"Let him speak." A man in a cardinal's red robe spoke from a throne-like chair at the head of the table.

Scott approached the table and stood at ease. "I'm here with the Monuments and Fine Arts Administration of the United States Army. We desire to work with you to protect Rome's great artistic treasures and to shore up any damaged monuments. If we can help with locating lost art, we will do that as well."

"Will you steal our masterpieces, our heritage, as the Germans?" A man snarled from across the table. An answering murmur rose from the others.

Scott held up his hands, palms out. "No. Our sole hope is to help you protect and preserve what belongs in Rome."

"Your soldiers won't steal from our caches?"

"Not if we can help it." Scott took a moment to collect his thoughts. "I'll admit Allied soldiers haven't always understood the importance of the areas where they bivouacked. The North African campaign highlighted that. But we've learned. That's why I'm here ahead of the troops to work with you to protect what is yours."

"The Germans had pretty words too. But those were empty."

"Mine aren't. I will do all I can, and those who follow will do the same."

The conversation returned to rapid-fire Italian, at a speed Scott could barely translate. He kept his posture deferential and as nonthreatening as he could. He needed these men to cooperate. If they didn't trust him, then he couldn't do his job. He didn't have time to invest in earning their trust. They had to decide.

The debate raged until Scott's back ached from the length of time he'd stood. Still they talked, yelled, and bickered. Signor Armati caught his attention and motioned to a chair in front of a marble fireplace. The chair looked like a Louis XIV and might even have the original upholstery. Still, Scott chose to stand because if he sat, they might forget he remained in the room.

The cardinal gestured toward a man standing near the door. The man bowed slightly, then disappeared. Fifteen minutes later he returned, followed by several other men, each bearing a tray.

"Come, we will refresh ourselves." He spoke the words in accented English and turned toward Scott with a gracious nod. "Our guest must be parched."

The trays were set on the cavernous table near the cardinal. He washed his hands with a warm towel, then nodded to the others. Scott watched as each man was presented with a hand towel and then a small plate laden with crackers and small cakes. Tea and coffee followed next.

Signor Armati approached him. "Things are hard in Rome but improving."

"Do you have word from Florence?"

His old mentor considered him. "It is difficult. More so than here."

Scott leaned forward. "Anything from Renaldo Adamo?"

"Not in recent weeks." The man considered him, then accepted a cup of coffee from one of the servers. "He wrote you helped him."

"I set up an exhibit in Philadelphia."

"It is more than many did."

"It wasn't enough. Too few paintings and only his."

"It was something." Armati sipped the brew.

The cardinal touched the arm of the chair next to his. "Sit by me."

Armati nodded so Scott accepted the empty seat next to the cardinal. As the conversation restarted, with a more restrained air, Scott realized that by gifting him with that position, the cardinal had given his consent to working with the Americans. The rest fell into agreement with that expectation.

In short order they had an understanding to close all the museums pending further notice. In addition they compiled a list of the places the Allies should guard as the army arrived.

"Soon I will have assistance."

The cardinal nodded. "This is good. You will require much."

As Scott considered all those seated at the table and the great museums and repositories of ancient and medieval works they represented, he had to agree. Rome was a multilayered city with strata of history, culture, and art that went back millennia. He couldn't begin to protect it all. He needed help immediately.

The problem came in finding it.

First he had to make his army understand. And right now he didn't know where to find his army.

Chapter 13

June 5

RACHEL HAD ACCOMPANIED THE army into the suburbs surrounding Rome yesterday with a sense of relief at moving. The week of waiting up to the fourth had tormented her with moments when she longed to return to Naples to see if Scott would hold her. Or had they been caught in a night that wove a spell around them distance destroyed? The thought of his soft kiss claiming her terrified her yet left her longing to repeat it.

Rome transferred hands without a battle, largely untouched. All was quiet as the Romans followed instructions leafleted to them from the air ahead of time. She'd picked up a discarded leaflet off the street where it had curled against a building. "Rome is yours! Your job is to save the city; ours is to destroy the enemy."

The Romans had listened and kept the streets empty, allowing the army to sweep in and clear out remaining Germans. As Rachel arrived in Rome on June 4, the celebration of elated citizens slowed the army's progress.

With a smile to the soldiers who'd entertained her, she hopped from the transport vehicle she'd traveled north on. "Keep my bag safe, boys."

They whooped and hollered agreement. She'd need to keep the vehicle in sight or she'd never find her bag again. Still, she couldn't wait in the truck and not capture the jubilation the liberated showed.

She hustled a few steps from the truck before her steps were halted by the crowd. She readied her Argus. The narrow cobblestone road was lined with stone buildings. Italian flags hung from many windows and balconies. Children in their best clothes, many of the girls' dresses short and the boys' shirts a size too small, climbed on the transport in front of her.

A couple clicks and she captured the scene. The relieved smiles on the soldiers' faces. The joy on a boy's as one soldier plopped his helmet on the boy's dark curls.

In sharp contrast to the lingering horrors and destruction Rachel had witnessed in Naples, the Germans had left Rome intact when they evacuated. Still Naples had appeared safe as the Allies raced to rebuild the infrastructure. It had been days later before the time-delayed bombs started detonating. Rachel knew to approach each building with care, hoping there would be no time-delayed explosions to mar the late-spring days.

As the vehicles lurched forward, Rachel hurried to her truck. A soldier reached down and hauled her up. She landed in a heap on the floor and giggled. The soldiers smiled. She soaked in the moment.

They'd made it to Rome. That meant Scott would follow.

The first hours blurred as she hurried from place to place. Finding the UP office in Rome. Then hours at Albergo Città, the press relations office, waiting for orders or an assignment. In between she watched for Scott. Had he reached Rome?

The way the population sought normal routines reflected a city ready to move forward. But look into the eyes of those on the streets, and Rachel saw a people who had lived in the shadow of terror. Stories reached her of random killings, especially after any show of resistance. Even more after Italians of a certain age and army eligibility did not appear for the mass-ordered evacuations to the north.

The celebrations continued to erupt where Allied soldiers appeared, but as Rachel snapped photos, she hoped the lens captured the shadowed look of hope. It was as if deep in their souls the Italians prayed this was the end of occupations, but fear warred with the whisper of assurance. If she dared to look deeply into her heart, would the same emotions war within her soul?

Any time the thought arose, she thrust it aside. During the busy days the task was easy. At night, in the silence and deep darkness behind blackout curtains, she had nothing to occupy her mind. Only the artist's sketchbook, her momma's diary, and her memories of Scott. None provided answers but created more questions to fill her mind and disrupt her dreams.

She escaped deeper behind her lens. When she viewed the people and scenes around her through the prism of her viewfinder, she could distance herself even from the beauty of Rome. Her momma must have spent time in the city, yet her diary was silent on the fact.

Could her father be right here, hidden in the massive city that had developed into its current form over thousands of years? She woke up determined to spend the sixth visiting many of the capital's museums asking curators if they remembered an art student named Melanie Justice. Though the museums were closed, she spoke with many curators who remained to protect their riches. At the end of the day, Rachel had aching feet, sweat stains on her shirt, and no one who remembered her mother.

The next day Rachel filled her knapsack with the artist's sketchbook, her momma's diary, and her camera. Maybe she could get a sense of the artist and whether he'd become famous by showing the sketchbook and its slight clue of three initials at various galleries. Maybe the curators would recognize him where they hadn't remembered her mother. Armed with a plan and the faintest inkling of hope, she set out.

The sun broke through the clouds as she walked the sidewalks. At every café bistro tables and chairs pushed into the space. Steaming cups of coffee sat in front of many sitting at those tables. She'd heard the cafés were open as the Germans streamed out of Rome on stolen motorcycles with flat tires, even in stolen cars without tires.

An air of romance hung in Rome that would float around her if she sat down and enjoyed the ambience, but the man she wanted to explore it with wasn't near. She couldn't shake the impact his tender kiss had on her heart, but the rose of Rome seemed less vivid without him.

Rachel could imagine her momma sitting there on a spindly chair, watching the passersby. Alone, newly arrived from the States, and waiting to begin her life. Rome? Rachel could still imagine her here. With dreams to take the art world by storm after studying in Italy. Look at how those had turned out. Momma had returned home saddled with disgrace and a baby on the way.

Dreams that smoldered in the ashes as much as the Italian countryside did along the front.

Before the sun cleared the horizon on June 6, Rachel sat exhausted in a corner of the Albergo Città that formed a workroom of sorts, trying to stay as far as possible from the men who had rushed in after finding the headquarters, still unwashed from the battlefield. The sounds of typewriters clacking warred with men grunting as they mumbled through their stories. Rachel ignored the din as she reviewed the content of her short dispatch to accompany the rolls of film and developed photos. Another United Press employee, this one a reporter rather than a photographer, would write the prose that accompanied her photos. Still she could write what she'd seen and experienced since arriving.

She wanted the news desk to wire the photo of the children climbing on the jeep. All that mattered was how the photos hit the editor when he saw them.

The door at the end of the cavernous space banged open. "Boys, we're on the back page now." Looked like one of the BBC correspondents, though she couldn't think of his name.

"What do ya mean?" Archie Letterbein asked.

"They've landed in Normandy."

A chorus of groans rose, and a few threw pencils against the nearest wall.

"They couldn't even give us one day?"

"All those miles of mud."

"Slogging with the grunts."

"Now we're here and nobody cares."

Rachel pulled the photo of the children to the top of her stack. Somebody cared. The people they'd liberated cared that they'd finally worked their way up the boot to Rome. Those still under the thumb of the Nazis cared that they hadn't arrived in Florence and Milan.

The room filled with cigarette smoke as men leaned back and placed their feet next to their typewriters. Marti Piper, a reporter on assignment with Reuters, sidled up to her, dark circles under her pretty eyes. "Guess I can feed this story to the trash can." The pages fluttered from her fingers into the circular can.

Rachel picked them up. "It still matters, Marti."

"Guarantee the BBC chum is right. Rome is now back-page copy if it's anywhere."

Rachel shook her head. "The moms and pops of the boys fighting their way across Italy care."

"I'm gonna start calling you Pollyanna."

"Go ahead. I'm still sending my dispatch."

"Good for you, kid. Maybe someone will even look at your photos." Marti sat on the edge of the table where Rachel had set up her space. She grabbed the photos and flipped through them. Her steady movements paused a couple times. "You're good. I'll give you that."

"Thanks." Heat flushed Rachel's face. "I want more than good. I want Pulitzer material."

"Keep looking for shots like these." Marti tapped one of a celebration in front of a small church. "You might make it." She hopped off the desk. "Well, I'm off for shut-eye now that our purpose has been obliterated by the boys in France."

Despite her words the malaise of the room settled over Rachel. The final push into Rome overshadowed by events on the other side of Europe. It didn't seem right. The boys had paid a heavy price to get this far, many of them giving the last full measure. Now their story would be incomplete if attention pivoted to another front.

After finishing the dispatch, she picked up the photos and article and headed to the editor's desk. Dick Forsythe chomped on an unlit cigar, probably the same one he'd had in Naples if its condition was any indication. The thing looked ready to disintegrate as it slumped in his mouth. He looked up with a frown. "What you got, kid?"

"More photos." She slid them onto his desk. "Dispatch is ready, and they can go out immediately."

He groaned. "Might as well save the hassle."

"You can't ignore them, sir. The story still needs to be told. These people are finally liberated."

"Ain't that the sorry truth. Liberated, and no one cares."

Rachel bit her lower lip. "Look at them. That's all I ask. They don't take up much space or weight."

"Always got a comeback."

"I try." She grinned as he waved his arms at her.

"Off with you. Get some shut-eye or something. I'd bet money this unit will move out of Rome faster than you can say, love me momma's cooking."

"Maybe."

"Guarantee it. Wash up, rest, and get ready for whatever the army has next. You're still with the Fifth, long as you don't mess things up."

"Thank you, sir."

"Don't thank me. Who knows when you'll get a chance to relax in a real bed again."

Rachel gathered her things and left the building. After stopping at the neighboring hotel long enough to drop off everything but her camera and knapsack and brush her teeth, she asked the concierge for directions and left. Rest could wait but not the streets of Rome on the day after liberation. She'd explored Rome in her dreams, wondering what it would be like if she ever saved enough to visit. Now she was here and without the hope of returning during times of peace. She'd use her time until the Fifth moved to soak in the mood and find a few more photos to send in the next dispatch.

If Scott were here, maybe she could take photos for him. Help him catalog art. Talk her way into a couple museums.

The contrast between Naples and Rome gave her pause. The people were gaunt with watchful eyes, yet the buildings were intact with little visible damage. After walking a bit, she stopped at a café and ordered a chilled espresso. The brew tasted bitter as she sipped at a sidewalk table.

Soldiers walked by, some alone, others in small clusters. She watched them carefully, looking for a certain soldier. One whose garrison cap would sit slightly off balance on his head, not quite military precision. She didn't see Lieutenant Lindstrom. His six-foot frame wasn't visible above the others.

Quit looking for him. It would take a minor miracle to find one man in the midst of a city overflowing with soldiers. Still her heart looked for that familiar face. She pulled out a postcard she'd bought at the hotel and jotted a few lines to Momma. Enough to let her know she was safe. Then she collected her things, left a few coins on the table, and started walking.

She mixed with those on the sidewalk, her military uniform drawing respectful gazes from the Italians. Grazies followed the soldiers. Beautiful Italian women threw warm hugs and planted kisses on the cheeks of the GIs who stopped. Rachel held back a laugh at some of the reactions. It was clear some of the men weren't used to the European greeting and didn't know how to respond. Others suffered no qualms and dove in with ardent pecks of their own. If anyone slanted a look her direction, she raised her camera and pretended to take a photo or high-stepped it out of the area. She didn't need anyone thinking she'd welcome attention.

The jeep flew up and down the hilly Roman landscape. Tyler didn't slow as he turned corners. Anyone who stepped in front of the jeep did so at their own risk. Tyler didn't seem inclined to slow down for anyone.

"What's got you flying on the road?"

"Eager to get out of here."

Scott eyed the man. Something more was going on. "Care to elaborate?"

"Lots to see, and knowing my luck, I'll be back on the road as soon as these boys head out."

"Maybe you'll get stuck here with me like you did in Naples."

"They'll let some other bloke take over, and I'll march wherever's next. Somewhere north."

"Over hill, over dale."

"Huh?"

"Never mind." The man had become a decent traveling companion, but he kept his sense of humor under wraps and his private details quiet. Scott glanced around. They were near the

Coliseum, as good a place as any for him to get out and start checking monuments. "Let me out here. Go check in at the depot. I'm walking around."

Tyler cocked an eye at him.

"I can find the hotel again."

"Sure you can. If not, shoot a flare."

"I spent a year here compared to your twenty-four hours."

"War makes a quick learner." Tyler yanked the car to the side of the road, almost hitting a dilapidated jalopy that rested on tireless rims. "Don't have too much fun without me."

Scott hopped out and rapped the hood. "See you tonight."

"If you're out too late, don't wait up for me. I plan to find me a pretty young lady. Let her show me her appreciation."

Unfortunately, there would be a line of women willing to entertain the soldiers and convey their thanks in tangible ways. The thought made Scott recoil. That wasn't the impression of Americans he wanted to leave behind.

After Tyler disappeared in a swerve of tires and hustle of pedestrians, Scott scanned the skyline. He remembered where he was, but it had been eight years since he'd lived in the city. It felt good to join the throngs enjoying freedom.

As he walked, he decided experiencing the city again from the sidewalks was the right choice. He could almost taste the joy and excitement of those he passed. The celebrating Italians were exuberant. He joined the flow of people, garrison cap in his back pocket. Along the Via Veneto, the throngs celebrated with huzzahs.

Scott turned his feet toward the Coliseum. Bells pealed in the distance. One of many small churches or Saint Peter's at the Vatican? Other bells took up the song, and soon the harmony of celebration filled the air. Rosaries were kissed and prayers offered as he watched. The gratitude extended with people reaching out to touch him. Didn't they realize he'd never fired a shot in this war? The fact he wore a uniform didn't mean he'd played a role in pushing the Germans from Rome. He battled for the preservation of the nation's culture, but it was a fight most would never realize existed and, if they did, might not value. Elaine certainly hadn't. Rachel, no Captain Justice, might. He'd seen something that looked like respect in her face when she watched him work with the priest.

Even after the great success of his meeting with the art superintendents the prior day, it didn't feel like he'd accomplished much. The curators had agreed to close their museums for a day or two, and most he passed were shut tight. Long enough to get military police into town to help monitor the passing soldiers.

He'd heard rumors that made him think those preparatory steps were unnecessary. General Clark wanted the men through Rome and thrusting the Germans north. While some soldiers enjoyed their moment to bask in appreciation, many Scott passed wore a dazed look. As if they couldn't believe they'd been asked to keep moving. That the battle hadn't stopped. This was not even a pause on the path to Germany.

Scott reached the Coliseum. Round and round he circled as he climbed the interior. He paused on his hike to take in the view. Rome's beauty stole his breath. Its beauty drew art students like magnets drew metal shavings. And it created a deep hunger in those who longed for beauty. Ultimately, though, it begged to be shared. It was the type of beauty that grew as it was divided among people.

If Rachel were here, he'd show her the Coliseum, but he'd also love to show her the unique spots he'd discovered during his year here. She'd understand and appreciate the heart of the city. She'd see beneath the current events to the depths.

Rachel's soft brown eyes would appreciate the ancient beauty Rome offered. She would understand what it meant to experience something of this age and appreciate the perspective it offered.

It was useless to wish for something he couldn't have. He couldn't imagine a worse place to cultivate dreams for the future than in a war zone. Better to stay realistic. Today was all he had.

He'd almost talked himself into believing that when he caught sight of a woman in uniform. She stood out in the Coliseum, and she drew him to her without knowing he was there, watching.

Chapter 14

SCOTT APPROACHED THE WOMAN, and when she turned toward him, her smile almost blinded him. Rachel! "Captain Justice."

"Scott." Her eyes softened, and her shoulders relaxed as she smiled at him.

"I thought you'd have left Rome."

"Not yet." She patted the space next to her, a brilliant smile lighting her face from the inside. "And you're already here?"

"Been here a couple days. I came ahead of the others."

"Have you found what you needed?"

He nodded. "A man who mentored me years ago smoothed the way with others. I've had meetings inside the Vatican."

Her eyes widened. "What was it like?"

"Ornate. Removed. Apart from everything else. Surreal. I never imagined I'd find myself talking with a cardinal inside those walls. How long will you stay?"

"I don't know." She plucked a piece of grass and twined it through her fingers. "With Normandy the enthusiasm has evaporated for Rome. I'm one of a few who thinks it matters."

He frowned at the thought. "Of course it does."

"Can I help you while I wait to see what's next?"

She wanted to spend time with him? The thought sent a shot of pleasure through him. Rachel, the woman whose lithe frame hit him at the right place, a perfect fit beneath his chin. He would find a reason for her to help and spend time together. If nothing else, he could show her why what he did mattered.

From the reports the art superintendents and the other officials had given at yesterday's meeting, the buildings and galleries stood largely undamaged. There was cleanup work, but small compared to what he'd anticipated. Instead, his post in Rome provided the opportunity to build rapport and goodwill with the local officials. He needed to broach the missing art. Still the few stories he'd heard of paintings being placed on a truck and then never arriving gave him pause, feeling too much like the missing altarpiece. The MFAA would work with the locals to create lists and determine what people knew about each piece. Had it been headed north to a villa in Tuscany? Or had it headed east? He expected that most art had headed north, always north to the regions outside the cities. Remote villas in remote regions, and hopefully not to Germany.

"I would love to show you my city."

"Rome is your city?" She smirked at him as they bumped shoulders.

"Today it is." How had Rachel Justice woven herself into his very fiber? She gave every indication that she had no idea what she did to him. He grabbed her hand and pulled her to her feet. "First we'll stop at headquarters, then we'll find a quiet place."

When they reached headquarters, he led Rachel to the corner he'd secured for MFAA loaded with bags and boxes.

"There you are." Blake sidled up to him. "Enjoy your tour of Rome?"

"It's been quick."

"But you found time to bring someone along." He winked at Rachel, and Scott fought back a rush of irritation.

"Blake, you remember Captain Rachel Justice."

"Miss Justice, it's a pleasure to see you again."

"Captain Justice." Rachel's posture straightened and she inched closer to Scott.

Scott stood taller at the thought she wanted to be nearer him.

Blake opened one box and pulled out manuals and requisition forms. "Has the begging started?"

Scott shrugged. "Not bad."

"Yet."

"Yet."

"It'll come. They always want more. Sometimes I want to remind them they partnered with Hitler. They should ask him for recompense."

"Good luck."

"Always fighting the good fight." Blake set a stack of blank forms on the corner of a desk, topped them with a few pens. "Now I'm ready for the masses."

Keller walked in with a couple boxes balanced in his arms.

"You here already?"

Keller dropped the boxes on a chair. "DeWald decided you could use the help since the military is already in and out."

"I wouldn't say they're out." Scott thought of all the soldiers he'd seen while he walked.

"Give them twenty-four hours, and good ole Mack will have them headed up the road again."

Scott nodded. General Clark was pushing hard to get out of Rome.

"These boys won't even get a good night's sleep." Blake slapped a name plaque on the table. Guess he was officially in business now that he had the sign alerting the world to the fact he was the designated requisitions man.

"They've earned some rest."

"Not with the Germans on the run and still around. Gotta kick them all the way back home." Keller turned his back on the other man and focused on Scott. "So where do you need help?"

"I don't have a handle on what's been moved with intent versus disappeared. There are rooms of protected art in the Vatican. Beyond that I don't know much. The attention is on preventing looting as armies move in and out." He headed to the door. "You guys have this under control. I'm giving the press a tour."

"That's what you call it?" Blake chuckled.

"Yep."

Keller stopped him with a hand. "Much to shore up?"

"Not this time. The damage to buildings is minimal."

Keller nodded. "That's a welcome change."

"Agreed. There's nothing critical that I've seen."

"Get on with your tour, but if the army's moving out as fast as it looks, we'll need to double-time."

"Got it." So sleep would be short while he was in the capital. He could live with that.

When he stepped outside, he found Tyler waiting while the sky behind the jeep began to darken into a cascade of colors.

Tyler snapped to attention when he saw Rachel. "Miss, um, Captain Justice."

"Private." Funny how she turned so regal with others yet didn't take those airs with him.

Tyler looked from Scott to Rachel. "Ready for that Vatican meeting, Lieutenant?"

Scott rubbed his forehead. "I forgot about that. Rachel, I'm sorry."

She put a finger to his lips, and his breath caught at the softness of the touch. "Don't apologize. I understand."

"Can you have a late supper?"

"I'd like that. If it doesn't work out, I can always have a C ration." She grimaced. "So hurry, all right? I'm at the hotel across from Albergo Città." She turned and melted into the foot traffic.

"Don't apologize?" Tyler rolled his eyes. "Looks like there's something between you."

"Maybe." He'd sure like there to be.

He pulled his attention from her retreating form to the meeting ahead. This one had been called to discuss plans for storing the art until the hostilities ended. After giving and getting assurances that everybody wanted the art to be returned to the cities, villages, and original owners, he made his way toward the Hotel Excelsior. Maybe he could get a good night's sleep before shipping out. With beds as soft as the hotel's, it seemed a crime not to at least try. It seemed as good a place as any to look for the headquarters. But first, dinner with Rachel.

⚜

Rachel sat on her bed staring at the envelope the front desk clerk had handed her when she arrived. A small note from her editor accompanied it.

> *Know you've awaited word from home. Thought you shouldn't wait any longer.*

Rachel studied the envelope, hands trembling as she realized the return address included her momma's name, but the handwriting wasn't hers. The paper trembled in her hands, evidence of the turmoil in her heart. Dare she open it? After all this time could it be good news?

She hadn't heard from her mom since leaving the States. Was she all right? Rachel couldn't bear to consider the alternative, but the question whether her momma had already died haunted her. She sucked in a steadying breath, then repeated. She might suck all the oxygen from the room before she gathered enough courage to rip the V-mail open. She held the envelope toward the weak sunlight filtering through the curtains in an attempt to decipher the message.

Finally, in one smooth motion, she ripped the seal from the V-mail. As she unfolded the sheet, tears clouded her vision. She blinked them away, then sighed when she saw her momma's beautiful, tiny script filling the page. The quarter page of the reproduced mail made it tricky to read.

May 8. She was still alive as of May 8! Rachel's heart threatened to beat out of her chest as she clutched the sheet of paper and collapsed on the bed, limp with relief. *Thank you!* Rachel rolled onto her pillow, plumping it under her stomach. Once settled, she read the missive.

> *Darling, I hope this finds you well. Sorry for the delay. I haven't been well but feel better. So I write. Are you enjoying Italy? Inane question really. Of course you are. You have Italian blood and my love for art and beauty. Both will serve you well there.*

The letter continued with a few tidbits about neighbors but nothing about her momma. Then in closing:

> *Take care with the sketchbook. I value it. Do not forget my instruction. Leave your father alone. It is best for everyone you not contact him. You must trust me in this. All my love, Mother.*

Rachel read the words again. Why was Momma so adamant that she shouldn't find him? Didn't she know that would push Rachel to do that very thing? Why did Momma still care so deeply? For goodness sake it had been almost twenty-five years since the tête-à-tête.

After rolling over and sitting, Rachel refolded the letter and slid it into the front of the sketchbook. She examined the drawings again. This time they reminded her of art she'd seen somewhere. Was it something she'd seen in one of the villages or a museum in Rome? If she could remember where, it might provide a clue on the elusive artist she could call Father.

She studied her face in the mirror. Why had he never attempted to find her? All she'd wanted growing up was a daddy to take care of her and Momma. Instead, it had always been the two of them. Barely making it yet self-sufficient. She'd watched the years wear Momma out, but in the last few the tuberculosis had afflicted Momma with its ugly symptoms.

Her attempts to find some hint of who he was had failed as she'd showed the sketchbook at the galleries she found open. Even the initials didn't help. They were too obscure. Her feet were sore and her heart burdened when she'd sought refuge at the Coliseum. Hearing Scott call her name had been the one good part of the day.

God, will you help me find him? You know this is about so much more than me.

Maybe God would listen for Momma's sake. She shoved away the thought that the man, if and when she found him, might be moved to care. If this much time had passed without a word, he may have forgotten her momma entirely. Maybe he didn't even know about Rachel. The harsh possibility could steal her drive if she let it, so she punched it to the side and squared her shoulders, determined to find the man who could and would save her momma.

She stood and paced the small room. If she stayed, she'd feel like a caged animal, trapped and frustrated. The clock said she had some time before Scott came for her, assuming he could get away from his meeting for dinner. So she grabbed her camera and bag. The media offices were close. She'd see if Dick had sent any of her photos through the radiophotography machine. Once run through its magic, the photo would be in the States in minutes, faster than the relay of planes that flew photos over the Atlantic. She could slip over and back before Scott finished his meeting at the Vatican.

Rachel waited at the end of the hall for the elevator. After sliding the cage closed, she wished she'd taken the stairs as it inched to the lobby. The seating area was comfortable with worn-around-the-edges Persian rugs scattered across the floor. She wove her way through the tables toward the revolving door when someone called her name.

"Hold up, Rachel."

She turned, trying to place the voice.

"Tell me you aren't going out alone."

"What if I was?"

"Then I'll accompany you." Archie Letterbein strode toward her, his short legs churning through the distance. A reporter with the wire service, he always wore a happy grin. Yet his eyes carried the knowing of war and its terror. "We aren't back in the States. Not a safe place for a woman alone at night."

Rachel wanted to protest, then glanced out the large windows and accepted dusk had fallen. "All right. I was headed to the press office."

"Now? Why would you waste your time there?" He closed the distance separating them. "Let me take you out for a real meal. Get you authentic pasta."

Rachel glanced at his ring finger. She couldn't encourage him if he was married, and it was too hard to know in this war-torn section of the world if a man would honor his wedding vows. She'd heard stories of women reporters thrust into the arms of a soldier. That wasn't why she'd come. "I shouldn't."

"Look, I'll grab someone else so it isn't just the two of us." He studied her intently, and Rachel felt like he could see into her deepest thoughts. "I can't let you venture out there alone."

"But I've got plans."

He stared her down. "Where is he?"

"At the Vatican."

The man snorted. "He won't get out of there anytime soon. It's a quagmire. Come with me."

"Okay."

"You'll go?"

"As long as you grab someone else. We'll make a party of three."

Archie chuckled, a wry baritone sound. "Good enough. Wait here, and I'll be back in two shakes. Take you to this great place around the corner. It doesn't look like much, but the food is so much better than military food."

"I'm sold, Archie. I'll be here."

"Good, or I'll tell Dick to ship you home faster than you can snap your fingers."

She settled on a clean but shabby armchair. The upholstery had turned nubby and one spring pushed at a sharp angle.

She should be grateful Archie had intercepted her. A foolish risk wouldn't serve her purposes, yet as she watched darkness finish its conquest of the street, an air of urgency kept her leg bouncing while she waited.

A few minutes later Archie returned with a familiar man. "You ever met Lieutenant Scott Lindstrom, Rachel?"

Warmth rippled through her as she met Scott's gray gaze. "I've had the pleasure. Traveled with him around Naples."

Archie quirked a brow as he turned to Scott. "You didn't tell me that, Lindstrom."

"Let's just say you didn't give me a chance as you tugged me out here."

Rachel looked between the two of them. "How do you know each other?"

"We shared a room one semester at Harvard." Archie poked Scott in the ribs. "It was all I could stand with this Goody Two-shoes. We bumped into each other at the Vatican. He said he was headed this way so I bummed a ride."

Scott shrugged. "Always good to catch up with another Harvard alum."

Archie smirked. "At least I didn't spend all my time studying canvas and stone."

"No, you studied the girls."

"And an occasional book."

Rachel shook her head. "No wonder you couldn't room together."

Archie pulled a long expression. "Does that mean you like this lout?"

"He's a friend. And I appreciate every friend I have here." Now Scott's face fell. Why on earth? Rachel shook her head slightly. "Each of you promised me dinner. I'm hungry."

"Let's eat." Archie led the way out the door, the men taking up stations on either side of Rachel. Their attentiveness smothered her. They'd just reached the street when Scott touched her elbow, and she glanced at him. The silence stretched, and she took a step to catch Archie, but Scott held her in place.

"I had no idea what Archie was up to when he asked me to come downstairs. I thought we'd go somewhere . . . alone. Why didn't you wait?"

The look in his eyes almost tore her in two. "I was headed to the press office while I waited for you. Archie refused to let me go out alone. I thought you'd gotten caught at the Vatican and we'd find each other later."

Scott's shoulders slumped, but he straightened, and she almost didn't catch it. "If I say I'll be here, I will."

His words settled over her, and she accepted his chiding. "I'm sorry. I should have waited." She bit her lower lip, then touched Archie's arm. "Thanks for wanting to save me from my naïveté. Scott asked me to dinner earlier. Now that he's here, we can follow our plans."

"Sure, I understand the boy wanting to keep you to himself." He nodded at Scott. "There's a restaurant a couple blocks from here you might try. Rachel, we got our assignments after you left. The soldiers aren't loitering around Rome. We move out tomorrow with them."

"Thanks." Interesting Dick didn't mention that in his note with her mother's letter. She'd have to stop by the press office or make sure she got there first thing in the morning.

"See ya." Archie sauntered down the sidewalk while Scott stood in front of Rachel studying her intently.

He rubbed the back of his neck, then took her hand. "I'd like to take you to dinner if you don't need to hurry back and get ready for tomorrow."

Rachel looked at their intertwined hands, then smiled at him. "Since he's walking away from the office, I have time."

She slipped her arm through Scott's and followed him down the street. He pulled her into a small alcove, then through a door that led to a small room that smelled wonderful. They waited while a waitress seated them. Candlelight softened the room, giving it a warm glow and ambience. Scott set his elbows on the table and stared at Rachel with an intensity that left her feeling exposed.

"This feels almost normal."

Scott chuckled. "It does." A waitress arrived and after an exchange of Italian, Scott looked at her. "I ordered for you if that's okay."

"Sure, I certainly couldn't communicate with her."

"Hopefully, they'll let me pay." A few minutes later the waitress placed steaming bowls of pasta doused in a red sauce in front of them. "Do you mind if I pray?"

She hesitated a moment, then nodded. "Please do."

Scott clasped her hand, a gesture that felt natural even as she couldn't remember the last time someone had prayed with her. "Father, thank You for this time. Bless the food and be honored by our conversation. Amen."

"That was beautiful." What would it be like to feel comfortable enough with God to talk to him like that?

"I'd call it simple."

As they ate, she studied the man across the table from her. He had a depth that drew her to him. What if they'd met at a time that allowed them to explore a relationship? She wanted to know more about him, so she led him through a few questions about his family and Harvard.

"I managed to scrape together the money to stay in school until I graduated with my fine arts degree. Not the best choice graduating when I did."

Rachel took a sip of water. "I can't imagine Boston and Harvard. I managed to receive a scholarship to Chestnut Hill College in Philly."

"I thought it was a Catholic institution."

"It is, but a sister at the private school I attended took an interest in me. It was a great education and a gift really. There's no way I could have afforded college otherwise. As it was, Momma scrimped together the money to pay for books and board. My roommate was the one who introduced me to photography."

"Art in another form."

"I suppose."

"What happened to your father?"

"I never knew him." She held her breath. How would he respond?

Scott took her hand and stroked her fingers with his thumb. "I'm glad God is the Father who is always there. He never leaves us even when we walk away."

She glanced at their intertwined hands, noting how natural it looked.

"Promise me when this war ends you'll come find me at Woodmere, assuming they hold my job."

"Is that the museum you worked at?" She tried to hide her relief that he hadn't probed.

"Yes, small and new, but they allowed me to handle exhibits."

"I walked through it the night before I left. It was opening night for an exhibit by an Italian artist."

"My last contribution." He squared his shoulders. "I helped a friend get his art out of Italy before it could be harmed. It took a couple years to get the exhibit ready, but we preserved his art."

In the sweetness of his pride, Rachel felt herself falling for a man who was unlike anyone she'd known. He had a quiet confidence and a genuine interest in others. He'd been a rock when they traveled in danger and yet came alive talking about the art he protected.

He was a good man.

What would have happened if they hadn't found each other during a war that would tear them apart?

Chapter 15

June 7

AT OH DARK HUNDRED, Rachel joined the others hurrying from the hotel to the Albergo Città. She needed to reload her bag. Stuff all the film and processing chemicals in it she could find and that it would hold. Once she joined a unit, she couldn't depend on a place to restock if she ran out. When she reached the office, Dick growled at her. "My office. Now."

She caught Archie's eye, and he shrugged with a frown. Guess she was on her own. One way to find out what had made Forsythe a bear. She straightened her spine and marched to his small office.

"I don't like this." He'd slumped at his makeshift desk, elbows propped on the cluttered surface, hands clasped.

"Sir?"

"Sending a woman to combat. What are the muckety-mucks thinking?"

"That I take good photos?"

"That's a given. Radiophotographed one to the States yesterday. Should have sent it slow boat rather than let them see the full scope of your work." He rubbed his hands back and forth over his balding head. "You can decline the assignment."

Her breath caught. "Decline?"

"Do I have an echo? Yes, decline." He pushed off the table until he leaned over her. "This isn't taking photos for the social column."

"I'm aware of that, . . . sir." He couldn't keep her here. Surely he wouldn't. She needed to move north, somewhere she could show the drawings and prepaintings in the sketchbook and pray someone recognized the artist. Her search in Rome had been fruitless. She had to believe somewhere someone could identify the man. Since receiving Momma's letter, Rachel felt the pressure to find the man while she still had time. Something she couldn't do from here. "I've been assigned to the Fifth for weeks."

"Now they're moving." Forsythe matched her stare, as if daring her to do the right thing, the safe thing. He couldn't know how desperately she needed to leave Rome. Surely he would see that as weakness and demand she stay put. Stay safe. Stay controlled and inside his protection. She couldn't do that.

He blinked. "Well. Seems you're set and the brass back in New York want you moving out. They must think this is some tea party or something. Fools." He cursed and Rachel tried not to flinch. "You're going out with some part of the army I've never heard of. Seems like a waste to me, but maybe you'll get some good photos and stay out of the firefights."

He reached toward his feet and, when he straightened, handed her a satchel. "I had the boys gather extra supplies. Should be enough to keep your camera operational until you return to civilization."

"Thank you, sir."

"It's also got my number and a few others in there. Anything happens, call or radio through the military, and they'll get it to me eventually. We'll try to get you help."

The word *try* made her want to shudder. Instead, she squared her shoulders and raised her chin a fraction. "If I'm with soldiers, I'm sure they'll keep me safe."

"A camera isn't much protection in the real world, Miss Justice. Remember that. It's not a shield. And that WC on your lapels won't do you a lick of good in the event you're captured, so don't let the Germans or Fascists near you." He grabbed a cigar from his desk drawer and chomped down on it without bothering to snip the end or light a match. "Good luck. I'd hate to lose you."

"Sir."

"Quit with all the sir garbage. Just call me Dick and get back here in one piece."

Rachel nodded, then hiked the bag on her shoulder. Enough film to keep her shooting for a couple weeks nestled among other supplies. Looks like she was set to take this next layer of adventure. "Where should I go?"

"Your government-provided ride arrives in ten minutes. Hope you brought everything you'll need. You'll meet him at the curb of your hotel."

"I'll find him." If only it were as easy to find her father.

She hustled toward her desk and threw everything into her bag. She didn't like the idea of leaving her items at the hotel unattended. At least her momma's diary and the art journal were in her musette bag.

Those in the newsroom nodded her direction as she left. A chorus of "stay safes" followed her. When she'd arrived in Naples, the action had already concluded. Now she didn't know what to expect. She'd heard the stories told by those who'd slogged across Anzio and up Purple Heart Valley, but would this journey north carry the same harrowing experiences?

If it did, could she do that?

Would the military allow her?

She paused in the hallway once no one was around. Leaning against the wall, she tried to steady her breathing. Her heart thudded like she'd run a long distance. She had to get her pulse under control before her ride saw her, or he'd assume she wasn't up to the task. She couldn't make that impression, or she'd find herself right back in the newsroom. She had to go north, even if it meant following the Allies into the teeth of the German army and leaving Scott behind.

She pulled in another breath, releasing it in a trickle as she tried to pull her thoughts from their tentative good-bye. She sighed as she remembered his kiss, one that she still felt imprinted on her lips. He'd lingered until she had to step back and disappear into the hotel's lobby or risk begging him to stay.

A door opened, and she straightened, hoping her thoughts weren't conveyed on her face.

She had to do this. She'd get to Tuscany despite the warnings to stay away.

After the war, she'd find Scott.

~⚬~

Tyler strummed on the steering wheel as he wove along the streets of Rome. Scott looked around, trying to enjoy his last day in the city. Now that he'd received full authorization to follow the Fifth Army, he would move out.

"Where'd you say we were picking up our passenger?"

Scott glanced at his companion. "At the Albergo Città. Turn right at the next intersection."

"Do you mean one of the circles?"

Scott laughed. "They really mess you up."

"How am I supposed to know where to get off or which lane to be in? Give me good ole right angles any day."

"Take a right at your next right angle."

Tyler threw him a limp salute, then maneuvered through the traffic circle. Maybe he'd get the hang of 'em before he returned to the States. Just so long as he didn't kill Scott in one. A horn blared, and a driver waved out the window of a truck in excited Italian. Tyler wrenched the wheel to the right and skirted another vehicle.

"Sure you've got a license?"

"Har har." The man's face looked tense as he worked his way onto a straight road. "Whose crazy idea was it to do that, anyway?"

"It had more to do with the landmarks in the way."

Tyler mumbled under his breath, then turned the vehicle and soon pulled up in front of the hotel. "Want me to get whoever's traveling with us?"

"No, you stay with the jeep." Scott hopped out and pushed into the lobby. Maybe he'd catch Rachel before she left. A man could hope, especially when the way she filled his arms made him long for one more hug, no matter how quick.

He glanced around but didn't see anyone who looked ready to leave. There was no one to ask either. Guess he'd wander until he found someone in charge.

"I can do this." At the soft words he turned the direction of the speaker. Rachel? Her shoulders were back, but her eyes held an uncertainty highlighted by the tightness in her face. A faint color raced up her neck into her cheeks.

She touched her neck. "Scott. Are you my ride?" She leaned forward a bit as if hoping he'd say yes.

"Depends on where you're going."

"My editor told me to find my ride."

What were the odds? Astronomical he was sure, but he wouldn't turn down time with the charming lady. Except this meant taking her close to the front, since he'd trail the fighting men.

Maybe he could stall. Use that as a way to talk whoever had the brilliant idea of attaching a woman to the Fifth out of his harebrained idea. He ran a hand along his neck trying to ease the tightness. "Is your editor upstairs?"

"Yes, Dick Forsythe. With UP. You'll find him on the second floor." She shook her head and seemed to gather herself. "I'll take you to him." Rachel led him into a large room, one that must have served as a ballroom in different times. The floors were carpeted over elegant hard wood, a dark color like mahogany. On the walls tapestries still hung. He'd love the time to examine them and place when they were crafted. A quick look made him think mid-fourteenth century.

"He's grabbed a corner for his office."

The room buzzed with activity. That of a couple dozen people with no room trying to work around one another. What looked like a tent stood in a corner of the room. "Is that it?"

She glanced where he pointed and laughed. "No. That's a portable developing lab. Normally, we'd find a room we can black out. In a couple days that will be set up. The tent is a stopgap. It allows us to develop film without shipping it somewhere else first. Then the editors decide if there's anything to radiophotograph rather than relay it via plane back to the States."

"Where's Forsythe?"

"Headed our direction."

"Why are you still here, kid?" A large man approached them. His shirt was no longer white, and his pants looked rumpled enough that he had to have slept in them. His words were gruff, but Scott sensed something more in the man. He looked like a school principal who had dozens of students who bordered on unruly, each headed a different direction, all involving danger, and he was the only one who could keep track of them. Scott didn't envy him the task. "And who's the soldier?"

Rachel smiled at the editor. "Sir, this is Lieutenant Scott Lindstrom. He's assigned to the monuments and fine arts section. He's looking for a reporter who's supposed to join him."

"You didn't think it was you?" He held out a beefy hand. "Lieutenant."

"Mr. Forsythe."

"Okay. I sent you to find your ride."

Rachel nodded.

"He's here looking for a journalist?"

Scott nodded.

"Then what's the problem? You ride with him, and you both have what you need. You get your ride north; he gets his journalist. Right?"

The guy made it sound so matter-of-fact, he almost had Scott going along. "I need her orders." He placed his hands in front of him, trying to placate the storm starting to build on the editor's features. "I was asked to obtain them. My boss's orders."

The editor mumbled under his breath as he turned back into his office. "You want me to find paper in here?" The office sported an explosion of papers, one that showed the man had serious need of someone to organize his life. Still, it wasn't Scott's fault the man lacked structure.

"Yes."

"Then I guess it's a good thing I have them." The man pulled an envelope off the top of his desk. "Lieutenant, Rachel Justice is my employee and my responsibility. While I wouldn't want my daughter headed into the fray, the military and my boss in the States have conspired to send her there. This is what happens when you have a photog who captures the heart of a scene. Therefore, I have no choice but to send her with you." He stepped closer to Scott, and Scott refused to back away. "However, if anything—and I mean anything—happens to her, I will find you. And I will let you know how displeased I am. Are we clear?"

During his speech, Rachel's face drained of color, and then she started biting back a smile. She was enjoying this dressing down.

"I understand."

"Then we won't have any trouble." The man dismissed them with a nod.

Scott shook his head as they left the editor's space. "What was that all about?"

Rachel choked back a laugh, then snorted. She covered her mouth with a hand. "I guess he has a heart."

"I'd call it attitude."

"Whatever you call it, let's get out of here." She glanced around the room, then back at him. "We're garnering an audience."

"First, I have to read these." He pulled the paper from the envelope and saw her name on them. Farther down he found his. All right. So she was his responsibility. A wave of pride and excitement flushed over him. He'd manage it. Somehow he'd separate his growing awareness of her and the hold she'd asserted over his heart from his assignment.

What other choice did he have? He had orders, and he needed to get north as fast as he could and find the Florence art superintendent and the Uffizi's art. With its rich history since the days of the Medicis, untold masters would disappear if anything happened to the Uffizi's collections.

As her shoulder brushed his, he knew he'd enjoy the trip with her beside him. He also knew she'd be a distraction whether or not she intended.

If only he could leave the beautiful brunette behind before something happened to her. Something he couldn't control.

Chapter 16

NOSTRILS FLARED, HEAT ROLLED off Lieutenant Lindstrom as he led her to the hallway, down the stairs, and out the front door. Rachel wanted to make him understand this wasn't her idea though she didn't mind. Actually, she'd rather travel with him than a stranger. Even though he'd gotten her stranded overnight in a farmhouse with an Italian couple that didn't speak a word of English, he'd returned her safely to Naples.

His silence raised a wall between them, one she wasn't sure she could penetrate even as she longed to know his thoughts.

Was he worried about her? Or annoyed by her presence?

After last night she'd hoped something might develop between them . . . something the war couldn't destroy . . . something unlike anything she'd ever felt.

He paused in front of a jeep, this one in slightly better condition than the heap they journeyed in before. The driver snapped to attention and whistled when he saw her. "She's our passenger?"

Rachel rolled her eyes at the high school infatuation that flashed across the driver's face. The annoyance on Scott's face had her biting back a laugh.

"Captain Justice, meet Private Tyler Salmon. Private, you will treat her with respect. We have the privilege of transporting her north." The privilege? Her heart liked the sound of that word and the way he said it. Scott stared at the private until she felt the challenge. Private Salmon must have too because he settled against the seat, creating more distance.

"I read you, Lieutenant." He looked at her. "Where's your stuff? Don't women travel with trunks?"

"I didn't realize I was shipping out immediately. We'll have to stop at my hotel first."

"This'll be interesting." Salmon shook his head and turned to Scott. "Which way, *sir*?" His emphasis of the last word painted it with sarcasm.

Scott ignored the man as he helped her into the narrow space in the backseat. She stilled at the effect that simple touch had on her. In a moment she was back in his arms at the dance, a memory she couldn't embrace now.

When they arrived at the hotel, she hopped out before Scott could help her. "I only need a minute." She'd kept her bag essentially packed since arriving. She could be in and out of the hotel in less time than it took many people to brush their teeth.

"Five minutes."

She didn't respond but hurried into the hotel. She pulled her room key from her bag and took the stairs to her floor. Once in her small room, she cleared the dresser surface into her bag then added her jacket and trousers. Zipped the bag, then grabbed both musette bags and bedroll. On her way out of the hotel, she left the key at the front desk, then returned to the jeep.

Scott nodded from his position next to the vehicle. "Four minutes. Impressive."

"Thank you."

Scott stored her bags, then offered his hand. She hesitated a moment before accepting the assistance. Once she was settled in the back, he climbed into the passenger seat. "Let's move."

Tyler got the vehicle back into traffic. It slipped in between cars like Tyler thought he drove a race car. Rachel held her hat in place and prayed she'd make it wherever they headed in one piece.

Soon the congested roads ended Tyler's race, and the day became a slow relay. As the day wore on, Rachel settled back feeling the heat of the Italian sun. The kilometers clicked off so slowly she could have walked faster. The hum of artillery sounded in the distance, and Tyler finally pulled off the road.

"Why are we stopping?" She leaned between the two men. "I didn't come along for a pleasant drive in the country. I need to take photos."

"Maybe there's an accident." This time there was no question that Tyler was way over the line on the sarcasm scale.

"Uncalled for, Salmon."

The man shrugged and didn't retract his words.

Scott turned to meet her gaze. "There's not much we can do other than follow the fighting. As the Fifth advances, we'll peel off and check towns. Repeat what we did outside Naples. If we're lucky, we'll assess churches, villas, and other important buildings. If you can photograph what we find, that helps too. Then we'll locate the important art housed in each town. If the town was hit hard, we'll slow down and start repairs. While you take pictures and send them wherever you send them, I'll communicate with Rome, informing headquarters about each village's needs."

"And we'll sleep and eat?"

"Wherever the headquarters sets up." Scott pointed to a bag next to hers. "We have a full complement of C rations. We'll save those for emergencies, but if we need them, we'll eat them."

She wrinkled her nose at the thought of eating those day in and day out. "Guess it's part of the adventure."

Tyler snorted. "You could say that."

She liked him less with each moment. "How'd you get stuck with Mr. Sunshine?"

"He comes with transportation, so I keep him around."

"That beats the alternative?"

"Exactly." Scott pulled out a folded paper. When he opened it, she saw a map of Rome and the boot north. He pointed at a spot not far from the city. "This is where they anticipated reaching by nightfall." Scott smoothed out the wrinkles. "We'll stop at these villages as we get the all clear."

Rachel studied the map, memorizing the layout and as many road names and town locations as she could. None of them looked familiar from the diary or journal. She turned and scanned the horizon. Broken and shattered German tanks and vehicles lined the road and fields. Bodies lay alongside many, some looking as if the soldier had lain in the shadow of the metal monsters for a nap. Others looked as broken as if a giant had rampaged through the field tossing them from side to side with no regard for the life these bodies had housed. She looked away as bile rose in her throat.

She sat in a field filled with images she should snap and send home. Yet, if she got closer, she might lose what little she'd eaten that day. She swallowed. If she viewed the scene through the camera, would it give her distance? She raised the camera, focused, and snapped shot after shot.

❧

The color leached from Rachel's cheeks followed by a sickly tint. Her pale skin hid nothing of her reaction to the scene surrounding them. The German retreat had turned into a skirmish here. How could he warn her to prepare when this was as bad as he'd seen? Worse could wait over the next hill, a slice of earth turned into a hellish vista. At some point they'd run across American and other Allied soldiers. How would she react? How would he?

The radio cackled to life, and he grabbed the microphone. "Lieutenant Lindstrom here."

Scott scratched a note on a piece of paper as the operator gave him coordinates for headquarters. "Roger." He straightened the map and hunted for the coordinates, then stabbed the map. "This is where we're headed, Salmon."

The driver edged the map his direction. "All right. Keep your eyes open."

Rachel's head swiveled, and Scott kept his eyes focused ahead for any sign someone waited to destroy the jeep. His chest tightened from the pressure.

"We're a couple klicks away. If we find HQ there, we'll be in easy distance of several villages we can check in the morning."

Tyler sniffed at Scott. "Another wild-goose chase, if you ask me."

"I didn't." The man could shred his last nerve. Best to let most of what Salmon said float in one ear and then blaze out the other, spending as little time as possible in the space in between.

Rachel's attention flipped back and forth between the two. At least their act pulled her from the scene spilling onto the road. "This can't be good."

"What?"

"One of you will get me killed."

He gave her his full attention, sinking into the depths of her chocolate gaze. "I will do all I can to ensure you make it home in one piece."

"Thank you." Some of the tension eased from her face.

"I bet you left a line of broken hearts across the East Coast."

Scott wanted Tyler to shut his trap as he watched Rachel pull into herself. It was clear as the sky she didn't have anyone. The torment in her posture left him wanting to know why, to assure her she had infinite value. Because as he watched her and spent time with her, he sensed she didn't understand that simple fact. He couldn't fathom why. She was as beautiful as the most vibrant sunset and as smart as anyone he'd met in academia. Beyond that she was valued because God created her, yet he sensed she didn't understand any of that.

"I hate to disappoint you, Private Salmon. I didn't leave a solitary lonely heart behind." Her voice faded until Scott had to lean back to hear the next words. "No one would miss me."

"Not even your parents?"

She shrugged. "If my momma survives the war, she would. But I never met my father. I hope to find him in Tuscany." She pulled her legs beneath her, into a pose that looked better suited for a penthouse on Fifth Avenue than the backseat of a jeep in war-ravaged Italy. She leaned against a bag, closed her eyes, and fell asleep. From her even breathing, he decided she trusted him a bit to keep her safe.

"Where next?" Tyler's words had him turning back over the map, splitting his attention between that and the road.

"Follow the truck in front of us as long as it turns at the next left."

⚬⚬⚬

Rachel feigned sleep as she listened to the two in the front seat. Their dialogue made her imagine a bad short involving Abbott and Costello. Constant bickering with a humorous edge. Often a sharp edge, but she had to work to keep her face slack when she wanted to smile. The last thing she needed was to let the handsome lieutenant any deeper into her soul. She'd already told him more than most. Details she shared with no one.

Most people couldn't fathom a good reason for an absent father. Problem was she couldn't either. They all cycled back to not being enough. For whatever reason her momma hadn't been enough to keep him. Rachel hadn't been enough to entice him to form a family. Her heart cried to understand. The realistic portion understood if she found him, all she could hope was to remind him of his love for her momma so he'd part with enough money for Momma's treatments. Anything else was a dream that couldn't come true apart from the pages of a book or the celluloid of a film.

The next time the jeep stopped she'd take photos. The light was still good, but in another hour or so twilight would alter that. The light values would make shooting a waste of film unless bombs streaked across the sky. Maybe she could replicate Margaret Bourke-White's stunning photos of the German bombing of Moscow. Rachel would never forget seeing the streaks and explosions behind the Kremlin. The photo had defined an aerial assault to those in the United States.

Tyler cursed and braked. The momentum threw her against the front seat back, and she groaned.

Scott turned and offered her a hand up. "You okay?"

She reached for his hand from her cramped position trapped between the two seats. "Not sure you can yank me free."

"I'll try." He gripped her forearms, and with a yank she broke free. It felt like someone had poked her ribs hard.

"What's with the stop, Salmon?"

The man shrugged and pulled his cap lower over his eyes. "You'd have to ask the half-track in front of me. And the troop mover in front of him. Then move on up the convoy. Maybe someone knows. At least we aren't sitting ducks out here on the open road. Nothing but fields on either side of us."

Scott scanned the sky in the familiar motion that let Rachel know he was alert to potential dangers.

Rachel rubbed her side and sank lower. The open jeep wouldn't provide protection if Germans waited to ambush the convoy.

"Put your helmet on." Scott thrust it at her. "Leave it on from now on."

"Won't do much for my hair." She tried to smile, but the seriousness of where they were flattened it.

"I'd rather you travel with smashed hair than die."

She didn't want him to believe her petty. She adjusted the helmet, wishing it sat a little snugger on her head. As loose as it was, the first close shell might knock it off.

"Here." Scott reached for it.

She slapped it into his hand. "Why give it to me if you wanted it back?"

"I might not look like a seasoned soldier, but I served in the National Guard before this stint. I can tighten your helmet." In a quick sliding motion he adjusted the chinstrap, then handed it back. "Try that."

"Thanks." She took the helmet, examined where he'd played with it, then slid it back on. "Much better."

"I'm here to tighten the army's sloppy helmets."

The journey north would be long as they snaked between refugees on the road. The people were worn, shoulders hunched, clothes dirty and tattered. Children walked among the adults. One child was dressed in a yellow dress a couple sizes too small as it hung above her knees. She must have sensed Rachel's stare because she turned, and a shy smile softened her face.

Rachel returned the smile, then shuffled through her bag until she found the sketchbook. Might as well take advantage of the fact she had an art expert with time in the vehicle. Maybe he could generate ideas about the artist. It didn't hurt to ask.

She slipped the book toward him. "Would you look at these?"

Chapter 17

ASKING AN ART HISTORIAN for an opinion tasted a bit like throwing Brer Rabbit into the briar patch. As a child, Scott had heard plenty of stories about Brer Rabbit's penchant for trouble. When Rachel tapped his shoulder with the book, Scott accepted.

"Why carry this journal around Italy?"

"I'd like to find the artist. My mother may have acquired it while she studied in Tuscany. She hasn't told me anything about it though."

Space carried a premium with two bags, so something more motivated her to bring it. Scott wanted to dig deeper but would wait until he knew if he could help her. "The artist could have died long ago."

"Possible, but the clothes look like they're from the twenties, so not that old." She sighed as she braced herself against the back of the front seat. "What do you think?"

Scott opened the cover carefully. If it was important enough to drag across an ocean into a war zone, he'd treat it with respect. The heavy cardboard cover appeared undamaged. Someone had treated the book with care. "How long have you had it?"

"I found it right before sailing on the *Queen Mary*."

"Any thought who created the drawings?"

She hesitated, just a second, but enough to make him wonder why she formulated an answer to a simple question. She definitely held something back.

"All I could find was one sketch with initials." She flipped to the page.

Scott glanced at them. "RMA. Any idea who that is?"

"No." Her gaze flicked away before returning to his. "Momma never mentioned anyone who had those initials."

Okay. He scanned several more pages. "These look like concept sketches. Artists use them to map out how a painting will look. They play with perspective, spacing, and other elements without committing them to oils. Let them determine the best arrangement."

"Momma did that when she found the time to paint. Her sketches had repetitive elements like these." She pointed to the woman, the layout of the hill, and the item she held in her hand.

"Could it be your mother's?"

"I don't think so. She would have just said that. The style is wrong too."

Scott pulled the journal closer as he studied the woman. "Who is she?" Rachel's silence caused him to look up and catch her stare. "If you told me, I could narrow down the location."

"I'm not sure. Even if I'm right, she's unknown."

"Your choice, Justice. Keep your secrets." He turned a couple more pages. "I don't see any initials or name."

"I didn't notice them either."

"Then I guess that's that." He handed the book back to her. "Your guess on the time frame is right. There aren't enough details to place it anywhere. Could be Italy, might be Provence. Wish I could be more help."

"Am I crazy to think the artist is Italian?"

"He could be. But he could also be English, French, German, or even American. People traveled in the twenties. It's not hard to travel between the European nations when they're at peace."

A drone began in the distance and built.

"That's a plane, Lieutenant. We've got to get out of here. We're too visible." Tyler stopped the jeep, hurdled out his side, and headed for the ditch at the side of the road.

"Come on, Rachel." Scott offered his hand but withdrew it as she rummaged through her musette bag. The color had drained from her face again, and she looked ready to get sick. He shook her shoulder. "We've got to move."

"Just a second."

Scott eyed the now-visible plane. "We don't have time."

"Got it." She held up a small book and a handful of film canisters. After she shoved both in her shoulder bag, she scurried from the vehicle. The next moment she had her camera open and pointed to the sky. Her movements tracked the motion of the planes.

"In the ditch, Rachel, in the ditch." Didn't she understand she was a sitting duck? Exposed and vulnerable? And the metallic glint of the sunlight off the front of the camera invited the enemy to aim for her. He jumped in and then tugged her after him.

She skidded down the slight embankment, her feet not finding a grip in the soil. She shrieked then fell backward on top of him.

His breath was forced from his lungs as she sat on his stomach. Her camera dangled against his jaw banging into his mouth, yet she seemed frozen in place. She felt so light, he'd need to make sure she ate, or the pace of war might do her in.

A shrill whistle filled the air, overlapping the drone, followed an eternity later by the thunder of explosions he felt through the ground. Dirt and debris towered into the air before cascading back to earth. Men screamed as shrapnel embedded in the men unlucky enough to be close to the detonation.

Rachel shuddered and covered her ears. Scott rolled, placing himself on top of her, sheltering her as best he could.

A second wave of planes flew by dropping more bombs.

Each explosion seemed to roll through him. More screams followed by moans.

How close were they?

He didn't dare look around since moving would be foolhardy and create a target for the pilots.

He felt a vibration as Rachel twisted beneath him, her mouth moving. The words didn't reach him. His ears were filled with the echoing concussions of the detonations.

At synchronized intervals death and destruction rained about them.

He pushed her head down.

Long minutes passed, and then the silence became real enough to touch.

Rachel shuddered, and he eased to the side.

He eased up, then helped her. Her eyes were wide, shock enlarging her pupils, her cheeks slack. He traced his hand down her cheek, then leaned closer to hear her words.

"We're alive?"

"Yes."

She threw her arms around his neck and held on. He memorized the moment. The feel of her tucked next to him, then tipped her chin up and pulled her close. His lips settled on hers, and he deepened the kiss as she matched his fervor. He needed to end this. Put a stop to the kiss before it got out of control. But all he could think was how close he had come to losing her. One misplaced bomb and they'd both have died.

Tyler stumbled toward them, shock pulling down his face.

Scott jerked away from Rachel but not before he noticed her touch her lips.

Several cars were stopped in front of them, a half-track smoldering in flames. He tried not to imagine what had happened to the men who had been in it. The fields on either side of the road were decimated, civilians bloodied and still. Moans filled the air with a mournful wail. Men writhed not ten yards from the jeep, while others lay still . . . too still.

"We have to get out of here." Tyler pointed to the jeep. "What if they come back?"

"He's right."

Rachel nodded and scrambled up the hill to the road before he could stop her. He raced after her scanning the sky. What if the planes weren't done? He collided with her, but she didn't move. Her gaze was locked on a family they had passed only moments before the attack.

She pointed to a girl, her yellow dress soaked with blood from a shrapnel wound. "We have to help her."

Another glance confirmed his first impression. Nothing they did would help that girl or her family. But if they didn't move, they could all be killed.

A lone drone buzzed, and Scott froze, then raced to the jeep. "Get this thing moving, Salmon. We need shelter."

"There's no time."

Tyler was right, so Scott grabbed Rachel's arm. "Back to the ditch."

She jerked next to him, as if in a trance. He tugged her after him. A lone Messerschmitt soared overhead, and Scott thrust Rachel's head down as he edged toward her. He had to shield her from anything that landed near them.

Salmon hurried across the road and slid down next to Scott. The plane got so close he could see the outline of the pilot. "Why isn't he shooting?"

"Maybe he got lost." Salmon kept his head down, his words disappearing into the soil at his face.

Rachel shook her head and then pulled her camera out and aimed it at the sky, tracing its flight with the lens.

The plane circled back around, this time chased by an American P-38. A cheer rose from the men around them, then the convoy launched back to life. Rachel hesitated as she walked toward the child.

Tears streaked down her cheeks. Scott touched one, but she didn't stir.

"She was alive. Just minutes ago."

"Yes."

"Why would God let this happen?"

That was a question he would never be able to answer.

"Time to go, princess." Tyler patted the jeep as he climbed in and started it.

Rachel nodded but didn't move. Scott took her hand, noting how icy her fingers were. He rubbed her hands between his, trying to ignore how delicate they were next to his longer, calloused paws. "Come on. We've got to stay with the convoy."

❦

Rachel stared at the sky, scanning for any other sign that a plane waited to swoop down on the vehicles. Her senses spun with a horrifying mix of adrenaline, the scent of burning rubber, and dread the planes would return. The image of the little girl with the jagged metal sticking from her chest assailed her. One moment the child was alive and smiling. The next impaled by a shell.

She shuddered as the groans and screams of the injured blended in a horrible cacophony with the yells of others to get the convoy moving. Leaving those killed felt like abandonment. Yet Tyler was right, they had to move.

If the planes returned or others took their place, she'd join the soldiers with nowhere to hide. How many times would she find herself in this position . . . risking her life for a series of photos that might land in a newspaper?

No, not just photos. There was much more at stake. Much more that could be destroyed by one bomb.

The German plane had passed so quickly, she'd had a moment to adjust her camera's settings. She prayed she'd selected the best settings in the split second she had.

When Scott had pulled her into the ditch, she wanted to fight but couldn't. Her body had frozen as he held her, then shifted to position himself between her and anything that might rain from the sky.

"Rachel."

She snapped her attention from the sky and back to Scott. "I'm moving."

"Tyler is moving faster." He gestured toward the car, and when she reached him, Tyler had the car moving forward.

She hurried and slipped inside, clutching her camera strap with one hand and her bag with the other. "I'll need to develop the photos when we arrive. See what I captured."

It took all night to push the destroyed vehicles off the road. The next morning the convoy inched forward. Each kilometer took hours as the minesweepers did their job. She wanted to believe the Germans hadn't had time to inflict serious damage, but all around her a different story played out.

She closed her eyes and tried to pray for those injured and the families of those killed. When the image of the girl in the yellow dress filled her mind, she snapped her eyes open to find Tyler watching her over his shoulder. The man's attention unsettled her, maybe magnified by the fact she sensed others watching.

As long as Scott was near, she felt safe. The moment he'd leave, she'd remember she was the lone woman in a caravan of men. A certain edge kept her from wanting to spend any time alone with Tyler. Maybe she just didn't understand men; yet with Scott she didn't mind.

After a couple days the convoy reached a village. Many of the buildings stood like shadowed ruins in the fading daylight. She'd get up early to take dramatic images of the first light falling on them. Right now, she longed for something to eat and a place to lie down and pretend she wasn't in the middle of an advancing army. Funny how one moment she could practically hum like a hummingbird with an enhanced ability to sense things, and the next she felt sedated.

As they traveled, her thoughts returned to Scott's kiss. She had never felt the way she did about Scott. Somehow he reached a place deep inside her she hadn't known existed. Her cheeks flushed with the intense memory.

Tyler stopped the jeep when a group of soldiers hailed them. After examining their orders, the lead soldier motioned Scott out. "Where you headed?"

"Following the Fifth per those orders."

"To do what?"

"Work with headquarters on monuments recovery."

The man snorted, his face hidden in the shadow cast from his helmet. "You expect me to believe that?"

"Check with HQ. They'll verify the orders."

"Love to if I knew where that was."

"Then I guess you have to rely on the orders."

"Those can be forged. Saw some last week. Germans and the Fascists will try anything to get behind the lines and access to officers."

Scott stayed at ease, but his hand slipped toward his hip where his pistol rested. Tyler kept his hands visible on the steering wheel. Lot of good these two did protecting her. At this rate her own army would shoot her.

"Soldier, I'm here on orders too." She pointed to the patch over her left jacket pocket. "See, I'm with the press. Here to take photos of our brave soldiers. Men like you."

"Orders." He held out his hand, and she passed them over. He pointed at Scott. "You're with me. You two keep the others with the vehicle."

His fellow soldiers trained their guns on the jeep, and Rachel tried to ignore the weapons pointed at her. This situation couldn't get much worse unless the Germans decided now would be a good time for another bombing run. She looked at the buildings in the village that were disappearing in the dusk. The church's steeple pierced the sky, but the bell hung as if its last cord would snap any moment, plummeting it to the ground. She didn't want to be underneath when that happened.

Behind the vigilant men soldiers moved in all directions. All wore full combat dress, burdened with their weapons and gear. Based on the way they hurried, she doubted many of them would get a warm meal or a sheltered place to sleep. Instead they kept to the road, chasing the Germans north. She pulled her camera from the top of her knapsack and held it up. "May I?"

The soldiers glanced at each other, then at her. Both looked like they'd just graduated from high school, definitely younger than the man who'd hustled off with Scott.

"I guess."

Rachel chose to believe the permission was because they didn't think she was a spy rather than the more likely scenario that they hadn't thought taking photos of troop movements was something a spy would do. She hoped their naïveté didn't represent the majority of the troops.

She placed the viewfinder to her eye and slowly pivoted. Somewhere the contrast of building, soldier, and sky wouldn't disappear in the gathering dusk.

There.

The church settled into the background, troops moving in front like burdened ants falling into rows by instinct. A mermaid set in a fountain listed to the left off center in the shot. The composition looked right because it wasn't perfect. Instead it told a story in the way everything sat off balance. Then a little girl stumbled into the scene, hair in a long, dark braid, basket over her arm. The child couldn't be more than seven or eight. What in the name of all that is good were her parents thinking?

Rachel snapped the photo, then watched the child's progress. Her printed dress fell a couple inches too short above her knee. The red ribbon at the end of her braid hung limp and frayed. But the girl kept her chin raised, her pace steady. What would be important enough to send her out?

"May I step from the jeep?"

The soldiers startled at her words. The shorter one looked away as if he knew she'd caught him watching her. The other straightened. "You're under our guard, ma'am."

Had he just ma'amed her? He couldn't be more than five or six years younger than her twenty-four. Certainly not enough to earn that moniker. "I need that girl's name. The editors get crazy if we don't try."

"Then why not ask the soldiers?"

"Can't. They all look alike and have moved on. The little girl stands out." How she wished she could emphasize the blast of color from her dress in an otherwise sea of muddy greens and khaki.

"Go with her." The tall one poked the small one in the side.

She flashed a big smile at him. "Thank you."

After slipping from the jeep, she ignored her soldier and hurried toward the little girl. If only she had Italian language skills. Instead she'd mumble and gesture her way through. Try to make out what had happened with sign language.

"Hi."

The girl's steps skipped to a halt before she continued again. Rachel kept pace with her. The basket was worn, a cloth napkin over the top. The girl's dress even more threadbare when viewed up close. "*Ciao, signorina.*"

The girl's lips moved but her voice was silent. The soldiers' steps slowed as they moved around them as around an island blocking a river.

Rachel puffed hair from her eyes. "Where are you going?"

"Can't you see? She isn't gonna talk." The soldier's words were spoken with a tinge of the south.

"Maybe, but I don't like her being by herself." Reminded her too much of the days she'd been sent on errands a child shouldn't make alone. How she'd longed for the protection of a daddy as she trekked to the corner grocery or the drugstore. As an adult she knew the distances weren't long or the errands too much for a nine- or ten-year-old, but as a child she'd sensed her aloneness . . . again. Just like this child. *"Mi scusi."*

The child paused, her brown eyes solemn as she met Rachel's gaze.

"Can I help you?"

Face weary with an expression no child should carry, the girl studied her. What had the child witnessed? What had she been exposed to by the war as it ravaged her village? The emptiness made Rachel want to weep. Her trips to the grocery store were not even dim shadows of what this child had experienced.

Chapter 18

June 10

WHAT KIND OF RECEPTION would he find at headquarters?

Would the brass welcome Scott and his role, or would he have to prove while swimming up river that he had an important job?

Shadows wrapped around Scott as he entered the church that housed headquarters. The roof sagged in places and in other spots threatened to collapse entirely. They needed to stay out of the bell tower since that bell looked less secure on its rope than his grandmother's ring had been on Elaine's finger.

A table had been rigged in front of an altarpiece. Why on earth had the village priest left it exposed? At least move the altarpiece to a basement's shelter. Scott made a mental note to find the priest and move it STAT. His personal guard, sergeant by the stripes on his uniform, stopped a few feet from the table.

"Sir."

The men hunched over the table focused on whatever rested on the surface.

"Sir, I have a man here who says he works for you. Looks like a spy to me."

The one-star beneath the altarpiece glanced up with a sharp, discerning look. His nose arched like a hawk's beak, and he had an intensity that indicated he didn't miss much around him. "What's that?"

"This man says he's with you." The guard stepped to the side and Scott found himself locked in the general's stare.

"You are?"

"Lieutenant Scott Lindstrom, with the Monuments and Fine Arts. He has my orders, sir."

"Hand them over." The sergeant did as ordered, and the general scanned them while activity continued around them.

Lights had been set up, chasing the shadows to the corners, but the drape over the stained glass wouldn't let natural light pierce the space. The benches sat against the walls, and a group was setting up communications equipment in an alcove. From where Scott stood, it looked like one or two stained-glass windows were intact, while other frames held nothing. "These are in order." The general handed the orders to Scott. "Where have you been?"

Scott straightened. "Sir?"

"They told me you'd travel with us."

"We were in the convoy, sir. Got delayed by an air strike."

"Miracle you found us."

"This fine gentleman made sure I did."

The general chuckled. "I like you. Not many men dare crack a smile. Think war is too serious or something. Problem with that is you need humor to keep from losing hope." He pointed around the room. "There are items here that need to be protected, but my men and I aren't experts. We'll leave that to you."

"Sir."

"You have transportation?"

"Yes, sir."

"Good. Check in with me morning and night. The balance of

time do whatever your mission requires. I'll help as I can, but that may not be much. My objective is Germany as fast as I can get my men there." The man turned back to the map when an aide asked a question.

Scott stood there, stunned by the general's words. He'd just received carte blanche to do his job. So different from past interactions. Had the military moved that far in its thinking?

"You need something, Lindstrom?"

"When would you like me back, sir?"

"At 0700. Get you out there ASAP."

"Quarters?"

"Make do with what the sergeant can find you. Dismissed."

"Yes, sir." Scott turned then paused. "Are you aware I'm traveling with a woman, a photojournalist with United Press?"

The general frowned, his mustache dipping down at the edges. "Whose fool idea was that?"

"Not mine, sir, but she's my responsibility. Will she report here as well, sir?"

"As long as we're in this village. Hopefully, we'll move quickly. Don't want to get bogged down in another slog if avoidable."

"Certainly, sir."

"Dismissed."

When they exited the church, the sky was dark. "Where do you suggest we quarter?"

The sergeant looked around. Many of the buildings near the church bore at least some shell damage. Finding one intact could be a challenge. Especially one with room for his crew.

"Traveling with a woman complicates things."

"Yes, it does." Without Rachel, he and Tyler could sleep in the jeep. Now that wasn't his first choice for her sake. "Better to keep her protected while we can."

"Then grab one of these buildings. One with a separate room for her."

Scott nodded and headed to the jeep. Tyler was the only one around when he reached it. "Where's Rachel?"

"Off playing Good Samaritan. A kid caught her attention."

Scott turned and squinted until he spotted Rachel down the road handing something to a little girl. She waved and came back.

Scott helped Rachel back in the vehicle.

Tyler cranked the engine. "Where we headed?"

"You're staying in the jeep after we find a place to bunk down for the night."

Tyler gave a slow nod. "Okay. Better than the guys who're walking."

"What were you doing in the backseat?" Scott tried to keep his tone neutral. There could be many reasons Tyler had been back there.

Rachel glanced at her bags, hand stroking the locket around her neck.

Tyler's gaze hardened as he met Scott's. "Looking for something to eat. We didn't exactly stop for dinner."

"It's war."

"Driving this jeep all day is like having a great big X on my chest, daring some trigger-happy German to hit me."

"Sir, I'd suggest you move out." The sergeant stood legs apart, gun at the ready again.

Scott nodded. "Sorry. We'll head out."

Tyler shifted with more force than necessary but got moving. Progress was slow as they waited for troops walking ever northward. "Head that direction. The sergeant suggested we find a home and hole up inside."

"Good for you." Tyler rolled his neck. "Sorry. It's been a rough day."

"Yeah, it has." Scott accepted the olive branch. "We aren't in Naples anymore."

"I don't want to repeat my experience in North Africa and Sicily. Dodging artillery shells ain't my idea of fun."

The man had served in those places? Then what was he still doing as a private and assigned to Scott? If he'd lasted this long, attrition alone could raise his rank a few notches. Scott should learn more about his driver.

❧

Rachel tuned out their bickering.

"There. Let's try that one." Scott pointed toward a shack that looked like it'd been covered in stucco. The shutters hung at a listless angle, but at least the roof seemed intact. There couldn't be much room in there, but she'd be grateful for any place she could roll out her bedroll and collapse.

After Tyler pulled to a stop, Scott approached the door with his hand on his pistol. A well sitting at the side of the house looked like a few stones had been knocked off but otherwise stood in one piece. Maybe she could sponge off the dust that caked her skin during the drive. Rachel didn't want to think about how hard she'd have to scrub to release its hold.

"All clear." Scott waved from the door. "No one's home. We'll leave a few C rations as payment when we leave."

"Okay." She tugged the bags out with her, annoyance growing as Tyler watched. At least he could have helped.

The inside of the cottage was dim, making it hard to see. The main room served as a combined kitchen and living area with rustic, handmade table and chairs. The stove in the corner dated back to the turn of the century, and the walls were bare of anything but a cross. The faint scent of oregano hung in the air.

"How long do you think it's been abandoned?"

Scott turned her direction from the doorway to another room. "Depends on if they left before the German retreat."

"Why would they leave before?"

"I've heard of atrocities after the Italians surrendered to the Allies. Guess the Germans didn't appreciate their allies switching sides. There were calls for all men of a certain age to turn themselves in for shipment to labor camps. When they didn't, the army either took them or terrorized the families." Scott looked around the room. "Maybe that happened here."

She shuddered. "I hope not."

"Me too." He moved forward and yelped. "Found a shelf. We need a light." In a few minutes he located and lit an oil lamp. The tour took a minute. There was one small bedroom and nothing more. "Guess the facilities are out back."

Rachel held back a grimace. There went any hope of cleaning up. At this point she'd settle for a bowl filled with boiled water since a soaking bath seemed as likely as a scoop of gelato. "Do you know if the army's serving meals?"

"Tyler can check. There are enough troops moving through here, there's got to be a tent somewhere."

These experiences could fill her next dispatch but weren't the same as the average soldier who would hike the distance, carrying his gear and hoping for a place he could start a fire to heat his C rations. She could imagine how tiring cold beans and franks became day after day. "Don't send him. I'm fine here. At least I have a floor under my bedroll."

"Maybe we can find some powdered eggs for breakfast."

"As long as the cook doesn't use powdered water."

Her comment drew a burst of laughter from him. "Didn't see that coming."

"Every once in a while humor slips to the surface."

"You should let that happen more often." His gaze locked with hers, and in the swaying shadows Rachel felt frozen in spot. His gaze roamed over her face, landing on her lips before bouncing back to her eyes. Her fingers itched to brush a wavy hank of his dark hair off his forehead. Every time the tension they lived under released, the pull connecting them surfaced. She couldn't afford to be distracted one moment from her mission, yet she didn't want to look away. The flickering light played across Scott's square jaw, accentuating his strength. Her breath stalled in her chest. She needed space . . . now . . . before she moved toward him.

"Well." Scott stepped back, but it felt like the connection between them continued, maybe lengthened, still a tangible cord holding them together. "I'll check on Tyler." He turned and stumbled through the door, disappearing into the yard, but not before she saw a flash of emotion on his face.

He felt it too.

She sank onto a chair wrestling with the realization he felt attracted to her.

What was she supposed to do with this? Stuff it down deep to a place it couldn't resurface? A distraction. She needed one fast. Now. Yesterday.

She hurried to her bags. Earlier she'd wondered if Private Salmon had taken the liberty to dig through them, but she couldn't check in the jeep. It shouldn't be hard to figure out if someone had pawed through her things. The gear bag looked untouched, though it'd be hard to tell since she'd dumped everything in to make the artificial five-minute deadline to get in and out of her hotel room.

Her personal bag was a different story. She'd prepacked it, knowing she'd leave any moment. She'd slipped the sketchbook and diary in, carefully packed and protected. She tugged the zipper back, the scent of lavender pouring out thanks to the sachet inside. Had anything moved? Maybe. More than she'd expect from a day of starts and stops along the heavily rutted road. She searched the bag. It was possible Tyler had gone through her bag, but that wouldn't explain why.

Her hand grazed the skirt she wrapped around the art journal. She pulled the book free and carried it to the table and light.

"Why was this so important to you, Momma?"

How Rachel wished she could ask her mom that. But V-mail wasn't an option. Not when every military censor could intercept and black out the message. No, she wanted to sit across the table and ask Momma all about the book, her time in Italy, and hope for an answer.

Rachel longed to stroke her momma's hand instead of the journal's cover. To stare into her healthy eyes and read her delight rather than scan sketches one more time for a hint of a clue. Anything that would peel back the layer of mystery. Who was the artist? Did he matter to her momma?

Rachel wanted to believe the artist was her father.

She needed to believe the book could help her find him.

Believing it wouldn't make it so. She knew it, but her heart resisted the knowledge. If she gave up on the slim hope the book would lead her to her father, then she had nothing left. The trail to her father would end before it began.

Chapter 19

THE DAMP EVENING AIR chased Scott back toward the cottage.

After whatever just happened with Rachel, he had to distance himself, think of her as Captain Justice before his thoughts carried him somewhere he couldn't go. How had Rachel Justice woven herself into his very fiber? She gave every indication that she had no idea what she did to him. It wasn't planned or coerced.

No, the tug he felt toward her was too real. Too distracting. He was responsible for her and couldn't get tangled up in imagining more. He would see her through this phase of the war and onto a transport back home in one piece.

There would be life after the war. When it ended, he could look for someone to spend his life with. Right now he had to stay on mission.

When he spied a bucket near the front door, he picked it up, then headed to the well. If they boiled the water, it should be okay to drink. At a minimum he could get enough to clean up. Getting layers of grime off would feel good. After one day in the caravan, he felt like he'd lived through a sandstorm.

He lowered the bucket and waited for it to hit water.

Plunk.

He hauled up on the rope, slowly, smoothly, arm over arm. Water sloshed over the side as he set it on the rim and then unhooked the bucket. It felt good and cold.

In a few steps he was in the cottage. Rachel sat at the table mumbling something as she flipped through her sketchbook, the sort he'd carried around Rome as part of the academy. His instructors lectured they should always carry one because they never knew when inspiration would hit. In a country like Italy, that could happen every moment. He'd never forget his wonder-filled first days and months in country as a recent college graduate who'd been blessed to enter the prestigious academy.

He set the bucket on the floor in front of the fireplace. More water sloshed over the edges. Good thing there wasn't a short supply. "Find anything?"

Rachel startled from her study. "No." Her shoulders slumped a bit. "I'm missing something."

"Want me to look again?"

She stared at him a moment, then gave a small nod. "I wish I knew who the artist was. RMA isn't helpful."

It wouldn't hurt to look at it again, see if he noticed something she missed. As observant as she was, that seemed unlikely. "The jeep wasn't the best place to examine it. Let me try again. Why do you believe the sketches show Italy?"

"The backdrops. They don't remind me of any place on the East Coast. Momma didn't travel after I was born. That narrows the possibilities."

"Why was she here?" He flipped the pages as he waited for her response. Definitely presketches for a painting.

"Why did most Americans come in the twenties? To study art." She tensed. "She had big dreams."

"What happened?"

"I did." Her smile was the saddest he'd seen. "It's hard to rise in the art world while shackled to a child. Children can't survive on the exuberance of creativity. They need bread and milk and shoes."

"Did she ever say that to you?" If so, he'd love to give her momma some parenting advice. What a horrible perspective to saddle on a child.

"Not in that way. But who voluntarily goes from dreams of becoming the next Mary Cassatt to a secretary struggling to make ends meet?" Tears pooled in her eyes, shimmering in the light.

"I bet she didn't. My mom always said kids were a gift."

"My head knows you're right. Momma always wrapped me in love." She reached toward the book he held, but he ignored her.

Scott flipped through the book some more to get an overall impression. Rachel let the silence linger as she watched. After the fresh perusal, he could see why she'd think the sketches were Italian, definitely European. Not a master certainly, but she wasn't claiming the art went back any further than the twenties. "When was your mom here?"

"1920."

"Hmm. So the artist would be somebody who's risen to prominence in the last ten years or so." Mario Armati might have painted in the twenties, but by 1936 he had turned the bulk of his attention to the world of museums. Still in the twenties, he could have been the artist.

"Why?"

"These show the promise of coming greatness, but it's not realized. It's still germinating." Even as he said it, something niggled at him. He should know the artist. "They remind me of something."

"What?"

"Not sure yet, but I'll keep looking." Could it be Renaldo Adamo? He had risen to prominence in the last ten years. In the early twenties his career was nascent but promising, laying the groundwork for today's growing success.

Rachel yawned, then smiled behind her hand. "Long day."

"And it'll be an early morning. Why don't you go ahead and head to bed? You can take the bedroom. Tyler and I will be out here." Maybe his mind would clear, and he could create a list of potential artists without her watchfulness muddying his thoughts.

"Thought he was banished."

"I weakened." He tried to ignore the satisfaction that flooded him at her look of approval. He held up the book. "Mind if I spend more time on this?"

"Be my guest. I understand it's a long shot you'll see anything." Her gaze lingered on the book as if reluctant to leave it behind. "Thank you for trying."

"I promise to take good care of it."

"I feel connected to my mom when I look through it. There's something there. . . ." Her words trailed off, and he waited to see if she'd fill the space. "Well, good night." She disappeared through the doorway, and the room felt emptier.

"Is that her journal?" Tyler stood next to him, looking over his shoulder.

"I don't know." If Scott knew whose it was, he'd know the artist. "I'd like to help Captain Justice." He flipped another page.

Tyler leaned closer, casting a shadow over the page as he did. After a minute he shook his head. "Good luck. It could belong to anybody."

"You're right." Didn't mean Scott didn't want to find something. Especially when it seemed so important to Rachel. He wouldn't mind being her hero.

Rachel unrolled her bedding on top of the firm mattress. Part of her wanted to race back into the kitchen and grab the sketchbook. Why did she turn into such an awkward adolescent around

Scott? He'd agreed to look at it. She needed to accept the reality that he probably couldn't help her search. But she wanted him to. Something about the thought they could find her father, together, made a smile swell inside her.

She snuggled into the blanket, pulling it around her face, and tried to quiet her mind.

If he could find proof she wasn't searching for a mirage, she might have to kiss him. Her cheeks warmed at how much she'd like to do that.

In the morning she awakened to the sounds of someone banging around the next room. Sunlight seeped through a small window above her bed, and Rachel closed her eyes wishing for more sleep. As she lay there, the sound of artillery formed a distant cacophony against the song of birds perched outside the window as they welcomed the morning. She tried to filter out the whine and dull thuds, but they formed an odd accompaniment to the song.

A knock had her tugging the bedroll under her chin.

"Captain Justice, the general wants to see us in twenty." Scott's voice startled the birds, and their song ended midnote while the distance caused by his use of her title soured the morning.

She cleared her throat. "Thank you. I'll be out momentarily." The last thing she needed was Scott barging into the room to make sure she was all right.

"Tyler found some hot food too." There was a pause. "I've set a pot of warm water outside your door. My mom always spends time freshening."

Moisture filled her eyes at his kindness. She got up and opened the door wide enough to slip the cracked bowl inside, a rough cloth resting across the top. She'd have more dirt caked on tomorrow, but she'd gladly wipe a layer off now. She sponged off, then slipped into her freshest uniform. What could the general want with her? Time would tell, but maybe he could help her get film back to her editor in Rome.

A plate of lukewarm eggs and a slice of cheese waited on the table when she exited the bedroom. "Should I repack my bags?"

Scott shrugged. "I'm not sure what the general has in mind. Best to assume we won't be back and be surprised if we are."

"Thanks for breakfast."

"Thank Tyler. He's helpful when he wants to be."

"He drives you."

"True." Scott sat across the table and studied her with intensity.

Rachel looked down at the plate of pale yellow eggs. She took a bite and forced a swallow. The eggs were bland with a desperate need for salt and pepper. The bite stuck in her throat, and she looked for something to drink.

"Here." Scott slid a cracked mug of coffee across the table.

She took a swallow, then forced a smile. "Thanks." She swirled her fork through the eggs, not sure she could take another bite, yet knowing she needed to eat while food was available. Scott let the silence stretch until it reached the point it was uncomfortable. "Everything okay?"

He shook his head, then stopped. "Tell me again how you got the sketchbook."

"I found it in my mom's things. Why? Do you know who the artist is?"

"Why would your mom have it?" His words hung in the space between them, coming so close to an accusation Rachel felt righteousness rising inside her.

"What do you mean?" She placed crossed arms on the table and stared at him.

"Where did this book come from?" Scott placed it on the table. "Do you know the artist?"

"*You* know the artist?"

He jerked slightly. If she'd blinked she would have missed the reaction. "Who is it?"

He didn't answer, and his gaze never left the book. Studying it as if it had great value.

She might not know him well, but the way he refused to look at her telegraphed he withheld information. "I have to find this artist."

"I can't help you yet."

"Why don't I believe that?"

"I'd like to keep this book while I search." He tightened his hold on the edges yet kept his fingers from the sheets themselves.

"No." She reached for it and attempted to tug it from his grasp. "I have to take it back with me." She'd done nothing to give him any reason to believe she'd done anything wrong. "It belongs to my mother."

He snorted. "You haven't told me how you came to hold a book by a contemporary artist. I'm not sure which one yet, but the list is small."

"What do you mean?" She reached for the book. "I have no idea who he is."

His response was a quirked eyebrow and a tightened grip. The nerve!

She gave a final tug and felt a corner of the book's spine give way. Any warm feelings Lieutenant Lindstrom had generated with his offer to help evaporated. He reached for the book, and she swung it behind her, straight into something hard.

"Oof." Tyler rubbed his stomach where the book had landed like a punch. "What's going on here?"

Rachel glared between the two. "Reclaiming what is mine." She stomped to the bedroom, so upset she could hear blood rushing in her ears. "The nerve of that man." She placed the book on the bedroll, then grabbed yesterday's uniform and wadded it into the first bag. She threw her toiletries on top. "He can't keep it from me." She pushed the bag off the bed and rolled up the bedding. Her hands trembled as she tried to form knots.

She sank to the edge of the simple bed. What had happened to her trust in Scott?

"Am I pushing him away for no reason?"

Her whispered words hung in the air.

She didn't like the answer that formed in her heart.

Chapter 20

June 11

SCOTT PUSHED HIS FOOT to the floorboard. If he were driving, they'd be at HQ instead of twenty minutes late. Rachel had slowed everything down with her preparations and then the argument over breakfast. Now the general would be furious when Scott got everyone to headquarters later than the seven o'clock appointment. How was he supposed to gain the general's trust and cooperation when he couldn't get two people organized enough to show up on time? Scott's thoughts raced as the jeep inched toward the church and the general.

Scott could think of two men who could have sketched the drawings. The idea that Rachel had Mario Armati or Renaldo Adamo's sketchbook in her possession had him twisted in all sorts of directions. A corner of his mind admitted it could be someone else's, but he didn't think so.

How on earth had she acquired it? From all he'd picked up, she appreciated art more than the average person, but that didn't explain the book. As he'd studied it into the night, it dawned on him the sketches formed the foundation for a few of the paintings he'd coaxed across the Atlantic for Renaldo's exhibition. Renaldo

171

had hesitated to send those scenes because he insisted they were his favorites.

Did Rachel's mother have something to do with that?

And if the paintings were precious to Renaldo, was the journal also valuable to him? If it was, he wouldn't have parted with it willingly.

Then there was Mario. The man had painted in the modern slashes of color when Scott knew him in Rome. But his style could have evolved since the early twenties. Many painters did over their careers.

The jeep lurched, almost stopping as it sputtered. Scott felt a growl building. "Come on."

"Cool down, Lieutenant." Tyler thrummed a beat against the steering wheel. "I'll get you there in a jiff."

Scott gritted his teeth and pushed harder against the passenger floorboard. If he had the gas pedal and steering wheel, he'd get them there faster than Tyler moved this morning. "We'll still be late."

"You mean, you'll be late. The general didn't ask me."

Scott snorted but kept his mouth shut. In the foul mood he was in, he'd make matters worse. *God, help me. All I can think about is that book. How did she get it?* He needed to be alert as he headed into the meeting.

Would Rachel lie to him about the book? Was it something she found in Naples or her short stop in Rome? Many soldiers and civilians were collecting items to ship home as presents or keep as souvenirs. So why create a story about her mom?

Any way he looked at it, he couldn't shake the idea the sketchbook was Renaldo Adamo's or Mario Armati's. Renaldo had a distinct flair for capturing the feminine form that was clear in the lines of the featured woman. Add in the fact that Scott would vouch on a stack of Bibles that one sketch was made on Armati's family property, and it cinched his conclusion. One or both had connected with Rachel's momma during her year in Italy, if the woman in the drawings was her. Otherwise, there was no good reason for Rachel's momma to acquire the book. And if that wasn't what had happened, then Rachel was lying to him about the origins of the book.

He hated that idea.

"Here you are." Tyler pulled the vehicle to a hard break in front of the church. "I'll wait." Tyler leaned back, tipped his helmet over his face, and crossed his arms.

Scott turned to offer Rachel a hand out of the jeep, but she'd already slipped out.

The MPs on either side of the large doors kept their weapons at the ready. One focused on Scott. "Purpose."

"A meeting with General Tucker." He gave his name.

The silent one opened the door and slipped inside. A minute later he was back and held the door open. "The general's waiting."

Scott waited for Rachel to precede him, then nodded his thanks to the soldier and followed her into the church. The general continued to lean across the impromptu table that held a map. It looked like he hadn't left all night. "Sir."

General Tucker looked up. "You're late."

"Yes, sir. I apologize, sir."

"And this is . . . ?"

"Captain Rachel Justice, sir. Photographer with United Press."

The general examined her closely. "So you're seeing the front?"

"Yes, sir. I've taken photos in Naples and Rome. The action's moved north, so I accepted an assignment to Lieutenant Lindstrom's group."

As the general studied her, Scott had the impression General Tucker didn't miss anything. In fact, Scott was certain the general formed a quick opinion, one that would be dead on. "Is he keeping you safe?" The general pointed at Scott.

"He's trying. A bit difficult in a war zone, sir."

"True. Down to business." The man transitioned so swiftly, Scott had visions of falling off a bicycle as it lurched to a stop. Hopefully, this time he wouldn't break his elbow in the process. "You're the Monuments Man. We've got a problem with troops taking art they find. Some of the losses occur in the villages you've visited."

Scott pulled over a chair and eased onto its hard wooden surface. "What's missing?"

"Small art. Things that disappear in a rucksack. Enough items we're getting complaints. This village, then that village. Each missing something." His gray eyes bored through Scott. "It isn't acceptable, but I can't take it on. My men must focus on winning this unending war. So you'll find the culprit. Whoever they are, I will make an example of them. I will not tolerate my soldiers acting in such a manner."

"I appreciate that, sir, but I need more than a hunch."

"Start with the local priest. What's his name?"

A corporal stepped forward and handed the general a piece of paper. "I've got it on here, sir."

General Tucker accepted the paper. "Right. Father Francesco Gentile. The man has waited hours for someone to care about his problem." The general studied Scott. "That man is you."

Rachel stepped back into the conversation. "I'll look for the priest while you continue meeting." She slipped out of the nave before Scott could stop her. The last thing he needed was something to happen to her.

"She'll be fine, and I'm glad to have a moment." The general stepped around his desk and sat on the corner. "You need to find the thief."

"Sir, I'm supposed to move forward with your men."

"Then find him quickly. We'll move forward. Couple days at most."

"Any other suggestions where to look?"

General Tucker grimaced. "Every soldier could grab some-thing small and tuck it in his rucksack. How'd we know without a search? Many might do it without any idea it's wrong."

A thought whispered across Scott's mind. Had Rachel done that? Picked up the sketchbook as a memento? Now she wanted to know the artist? Who better to ask than the art expert she trav-eled with?

"You still with me, Lieutenant?"

"Yes, sir."

"Get out there. Find the art and the journalist. Can't have anything happen to the press."

"No, sir."

"Locate that thief. Now. Dismissed."

Scott nodded and then hustled after Rachel. Identify a thief? In a sea of soldiers and disillusioned, starving Italians? It was an impossible task. He shook the doubt about the book from his mind. He'd ask Rachel about it at an appropriate moment. Until then he needed to find her and the priest. If he was lucky, she'd be within eyesight when he reached the door. However, after he worked through the crowd separating him from the door, she'd disappeared. All he saw was a sea of soldiers. Some looked ener-gized. As if they couldn't wait to take the fight to the Germans. Others looked like they'd collapse if they could. Instead, they plodded forward, each step moving them closer to battle.

How could the one woman in the military within twenty kilometers disappear?

Maybe if he looked for a black cassock in the crowd of uni-forms, he'd find Rachel. Then he'd accomplish two missions at once. Scott stayed on the top step to see over the heads of those marching past. There. Could that be the priest? Across the court, around the broken fountain, the one with water burbling in a bro-ken mess at the bottom?

Guess there was one way to find out. Follow the robed figure.

The figure turned a corner between a pile of rubble and a still-standing storefront. Scott hurried down the stairs and worked his way through the soldiers. When he reached the corner, the robed man had disappeared. "Come on."

Now he was no closer to the priest or to Rachel. His success—and by extension the Monuments Men—in the eyes of the general depended on how he did.

"Need a ride?" Tyler pulled the jeep alongside him.

"Have you seen Rachel?"

"Nope."

"A priest?"

"Nope." Tyler yawned and crossed his arms. "Why?"

"We've got a new assignment. Find an art thief."

A flicker of some expression flashed on Tyler's face. "Guess our role's expanded."

"Yes."

"Hop in and let's find Rachel."

"I'll travel by foot. Drive around the perimeter of the village. I'll walk around the square and intermediate roads. She's probably shooting photos of the locals." He hoped. After seeing her art journal, he didn't know what she was doing.

❦

"Father?" Rachel hurried to catch the man. She'd needed a mission when she woke up, and finding the priest for Scott seemed easy. The man moved. Fast. What gave him such energy and purpose? She had to learn what he knew about art thieves. Her stomach clenched at the idea someone victimized these people and this country by taking what little they had left. Their heritage, their culture, their art. *"Padre?"*

The man slowed and then turned her direction. *"Sì?"*

"I'm Rachel Justice. With United Press. In the United States."
That had to be meaningless to him.

"Yes?" The word was heavily accented but beautiful English.

"We're supposed to, the soldier I'm traveling with and I, the
general told us to help you find art thieves."

"Thieves?"

"Art. Missing." Rachel groaned. Maybe one word didn't indicate fluency.

"Ah. An image of the Madonna. Very old. Very precious."

He did understand! "We want to help."

"*Bene*." He considered her and looked deep into her soul.
It wasn't as uncomfortable an experience as she'd expect. "This
way."

She waved toward the church. "That way."

"No. Follow me." The priest picked up the pace without a
backward glance. If she wanted to help, he expected her to follow.
Where was Scott? He couldn't be happy she'd disappeared from
the church. But when she saw the priest, she couldn't wait. He was
here, headed away, so she'd follow again. Scott would find her.
After all, the general told him to keep her safe.

Rachel picked up her speed, glad she'd worn boots and trousers. "Where are we going, Father?"

"The location of the taking."

Okay, that made sense, but she looked over her shoulder. Now
would be a wonderful time for Scott to arrive. Especially since the
father led her away from the village toward a row of hills. Away
from the main push of soldiers. She'd be fine for a short distance.
Keep the village in view, the soldiers within screaming distance.

A rumble followed behind her. She turned to see if she
should run away. A shaky laugh escaped when she recognized the
American jeep and the face behind the wheel. Tyler Salmon might
drive her crazy, but she knew him. She waved and waited as he
zipped toward her.

"Scott's looking for you."

"And the priest." Rachel gestured toward the man who had stopped a few yards beyond them. "Let's collect Scott. The priest wants to take us somewhere."

The father studied them, a tightness settling around his eyes as he rubbed his face. He waited for the jeep to approach. "Daughter, come with me."

"After we pick up the soldier charged with protecting art. He will want to come and will know the best way to help." She hoped. Scott would know the right things to say and do to reassure this man who seemed pressed into himself by age and the weight of war waged all around him. She longed to lift part of the burden from his stooped shoulders.

She turned to Tyler. "Where were you meeting Scott?"

"Around."

The one-word answer struck her as absurdly obtuse. "Around?"

"Yeah. He headed the direction he thought the father had taken. I was to circle and see if I could find you. Keep moving and we'll find him. He can't have walked far."

Time crept like molasses slinking from its jar as they circled the small village. A couple times Tyler had to stop to wait for troops moving forward. Each time she could think about how far Scott could walk during the delay. At this rate they might not catch him.

"Private, make this jeep move."

He scowled at her with a look of indifference. "You can't make me run over somebody."

"I outrank you." The words felt ridiculous and petty.

"That's fine and dandy, but you'll have to hold your horses. Scott's a big boy. He's fine."

The father muttered in Italian, Rachel only able to interpret occasional words like *Dio*. As the man prayed, she shielded her eyes and scanned the horizon. To the right she made out the small form of someone walking toward them. "Is that him? Over there?"

Tyler followed her point. "Might as well see." His mumbling didn't have the same reverent tone of the priest's. After skirting holes left by mines and artillery shells and bouncing across the jutted field, Rachel knew she'd break a tooth if he didn't slow down. Tyler finally pulled alongside the soldier.

Rachel leaned out the side. "Need a lift?"

Sweat rolled down the sides of Scott's face as he stumbled toward the jeep. "It's about time I found you."

"Who found who?" Tyler stared straight ahead, only the raising of a cheek muscle indicating his joke.

"I was headed back to the village." Scott climbed into the backseat. "Who do you have with you?"

"This is your neighborhood priest. He's looking for a missing Madonna."

Scott leaned forward to look at the priest. "Father, I'm Lieutenant Scott Lindstrom with the United States Army's Monuments Men. I've come a long way to assist you."

Chapter 21

June 12

THE PRIEST'S IMPASSIONED PLEAS to find the village's relic rang in Scott's ears the following morning. They'd spent the day searching the hills until they'd almost run out of gas and risked a long walk to town through fields the two sides contested. An ME-109 had zipped overhead. Scott had ducked so the landing gear wouldn't brush his hair. Then he'd held his breath as they waited for the plane to circle around and machine-gun them where they sat on the open road. Instead, the plane disappeared over the horizon.

"Mi aiuterebbe." Over and over the father pleaded for help. He'd alternated languages, using English, French, and Italian to ensure Scott understood.

A few times Scott wondered if someone trailed them in a battered car, but when he decided to confront the vehicle, it disappeared.

A day later Scott was no closer to finding the thief than when General Tucker gave him the stolen-art assignment. Today they'd scour more villages, but the father had confirmed much art had disappeared, not all of it under the German army's efforts to "protect" the masterpieces.

"It is worse in Florence. Great paintings are gone. Disappeared. Lost."

Scott didn't want to contemplate which masters those words represented. He wanted to believe the small Madonna—and other pieces—would reappear miraculously. However, the Madonna would tuck in a rucksack as a souvenir. It was possible if a soldier grabbed it, he would have no idea of the painting's worth. Some paintings were valuable because of their age, the centuries they had survived. Others were irreplaceable because of the famous artists who held the paintbrush and chose the colors.

Scott's sleep had been filled with running through a maze. Always moving. Never approaching. Always knowing he had to hurry or lose. Never getting close enough to see the shrouded painting waiting at the end.

Tyler roused Scott from his restless sleep by banging a C-ration kit on the table. In no more than ten minutes, they drove along a road looking for a hiding place the father had mentioned. Rachel had stayed behind with the priest. She said to take photos. He believed it was to help those left in the village however she could, and the jeep felt empty without her riding along.

A break in the cypress trees made Scott sit up. "Turn here."

Tyler complied, and Scott hoped he'd picked the right break to turn into.

He checked behind the jeep but didn't see anyone trailing. Today the roads had been vacant. As long as a slim possibility remained that the painting was stored with others from the region and the priest had forgotten, Scott would continue looking. If the painting had disappeared from the storage facility, it might not be recovered. If he found it, that would raise his status with the father, which could generate goodwill in future towns.

Either way they had to move fast. Track down what he could before General Tucker moved headquarters to another broken village with its own shattered church and square. Down the narrow road between the trails, they reached a deserted village. Each building in the small community suffered damage. As he considered the location, Scott couldn't understand why it would be affected. It didn't hold strategic significance. It didn't house industry or anything that could impact the war's outcome.

"Wonder what happened here." Tyler stopped the jeep and climbed out.

Scott crouched as he kept an eye on the surroundings. The silence was eerie. To the point that it seemed even the birds had abandoned the place. The last thing he needed was some sniper taking a shot at him because he assumed the residents had abandoned the village.

He scanned the second-story windows of one building and hesitated. Could that be a shadow or just the movement of a curtain in the open window? *God, keep us safe.* "Tyler."

The man didn't hear him, so he hissed louder. "Tyler."

"What?"

"I think we need to sweep the buildings. Something isn't right."

"You want me as booby-trap bait? Do I look like a fool?"

"No. But something's wrong."

"Right. This place is abandoned. Empty. Deserted." The man punctuated the words with a sweep of his arm. "Look at it. It's falling apart, so who would stay?"

"I doubt the residents left willingly."

"Great reason to get in and get out. If there's no one to talk to, let's keep moving." Tyler glanced around as if he expected the enemy to show up over his shoulder.

The whistle of a bullet foretold the sharp impact into the driver's-side mirror. The glass shattered, showering over Scott. "Tyler!"

The man dove back in the idling jeep, then shoved it in reverse as another bullet blazed past, this one lodging in a tree they passed.

"Thank God he's a bad shot."

Tyler didn't answer as he swerved the jeep in reverse along the road. The jeep lurched over a crater, then bounced on the other side. Scott landed against the door then the dash.

"Sorry." Tyler gritted out the word.

"Just keep moving."

A couple kilometers outside the village, Tyler pulled to the side and popped the vehicle in park. "What was that?"

"A sniper."

"How'd you know?"

"It was too quiet." Scott shrugged as the adrenaline leached from him. "Glad you were driving."

Tyler kept his gaze on the road. "If it's not a plane, it's a hole I don't see that gets us."

"Don't know if we should sit here. He might not be alone."

"Agree." A moment later Tyler had the jeep moving again.

The broken trees, destroyed houses, and vacant villages they drove past provided constant reminders of the war. It was hard to remember what life had been like before. "What did you do before the war?"

Tyler looked at him for a second before the wheel jerked in his hands. "Worked on a college degree."

"Where?"

"A college you've never heard of."

"Unless it's somewhere like Idaho, I bet I've heard of it."

"Sure. A small liberal arts college for men. I forgot those are all over the place. I'd like to get back and finish what I started."

"We all want to get home."

Shrubs lining the road moved, even though no wind stirred the hot air. "Over there."

"I see it." Tyler gunned the engine but crushed the brake after a shot whistled near the engine. "Think we're stopping, boss."

"Yeah. I'm getting tired of being a target." Scott reached for his pistol and crouched lower behind the windshield. Any protection was better than nothing.

The shrubs rustled again, and a man in a worn red shirt and filthy denim pants edged out. Rifle barrels pointed toward them from behind the man. He eyed their vehicle, then them. "*Americano?*"

"*Sì.*"

The man spoke in rapid, lyrical Italian. Slowly more men fanned around them, their guns held lower, but Scott didn't doubt they'd jump to firing position at the slightest provocation.

"Partisan." The man pointed to his chest, then to his comrades. "*Tutti* partisans."

"Great," Tyler mumbled. "What we gonna do with them?"

"Smile. We're happy to see them." He hoped. No one had advised him how to handle Italian nationals like these. The Tuscan forests overflowed with men hiding from Germans. Guess they weren't hiding from the Allies.

"So?"

"So we radio for advice."

"The general will be delighted." Tyler gestured toward the ragtag group.

"I'm open to suggestions."

Tyler settled back in his seat, arms crossed. "No. You're the lieutenant."

That didn't mean he knew what to do. Give him an artillery-pocked church, and he'd intuit where to add support and how to buttress. Give him malnourished Italians, and he'd dole out extra rations. This was outside his experience. Some of the partisans had heavy work boots while others walked barefoot. Made him wonder how much damage they could do against the well-equipped Germans.

The radio crackled and Scott relayed their situation.

"Tell them we'll send supplies tonight." The disjointed voice confirmed where he'd run into the partisans and signed off.

"How you gonna break the news?" Tyler nudged his chin toward the group. A group that shifted and murmured in low tones. Unhappy tones. "I'm thinking at least one understands English."

Scott could understand enough to know the situation wasn't good, but he didn't want them to know he understood Italian. He stood in the jeep, leaning against the windshield. "Who speaks English?"

The men looked at each other, blank expressions as they shrugged.

"*Inglese*? Who speaks *inglese*?" Scott waited.

"Me." A short, sturdy man stepped forward hampered by a limp. "I help."

Scott conferred with the man, using simple words and lots of gestures to explain supplies were coming. The man nodded, asked a few questions in broken English, then turned to his friends. With much gesticulating and rapid words, he communicated the message. The men disappeared into the shrubs.

"We understand."

"Thank you." What had chased the man into the forest? "Have you heard anything of art stolen from churches?"

The man's expression clouded. "*Sì*. Artifacts disappear."

As Scott questioned him, the man could confirm the rumors and nothing else. "*Grazie*."

Tyler restarted the car. "Daylight's wasting. Let's get while we can."

The last of the men melted into the fields. After a minute Scott wouldn't have known anyone watched if he hadn't noticed where a couple disappeared. Tyler ground the gears, then lurched back to speed. "Wonder if anyone will bring the supplies."

"Why wouldn't they?"

"The battle's that direction. Not here on this side road to nowhere."

～⁂～

Rachel sat in the parish as the priest shuffled to the small stove and slid a full kettle on a burner. She couldn't imagine the sacrifices he'd made to prepare tea for her. At her assertion she didn't require anything, he'd chuckled and continued his work.

"The joy of a guest is the serving."

"I should help."

"Talk with me."

"There's little to share."

He paused in his work and studied her. "You have deep waters, my child. There is much you see as you develop wisdom."

Rachel soaked in his words, accepting the compliment. "You speak English well."

"My brother studied at Oxford. I stayed in Italy. But when he returned, I practiced English." He gestured around the small room. "Here I have few . . ." He looked toward the ceiling as if searching for the word.

"Opportunities?"

"Sì. Few opportunities to practice. Today you bring me pleasure."

She smiled, charmed by his graciousness.

He reached into a small cupboard and pulled out a plate. After he placed a few slices of white cheese on it, he cut an apple. "I don't have much food. The Germans were locusts and took much."

"What was it like?"

The father turned toward her, his gown sweeping the floor. "Like? There was nothing to like. It was tense. Never knowing friend from foe. Who can I trust? Today who like me? Who curse me? Today will a German commander arrive and demand more than I have? What of the Fascists? The Partisans?" He sighed. "I am grateful God holds me in His hand. Many days I needed that knowledge."

Rachel hesitated, caught by something the priest said. "God holds you?"

"Yes, it brings peace in the middle of storms."

Peace. She hadn't experienced that since Momma's diagnosis. The thought of Momma leaving her. . . . Where was God in that? Was he that cruel? And look at the war that gripped the world. She'd seen the devastation, the lost lives, dodged the shells. Surely, if God cared, he could end it. Why would God allow it when he could end the death and destruction? Peace evaded Europe and much of the world. She doubted God cared much at all.

She'd never seen him care for her.

As she studied the priest's face, she saw openness and acceptance. If she couldn't ask him, who could she ask questions about faith? "Why would God care?" She gestured toward the destruction outside the window. "In the midst of everything, does he see one person?"

"Why do you ask?"

"I can't step outside without seeing a destroyed building. It's everywhere. People's lives ended. Where's God? Does he even get involved?" She stilled, waiting for his answer.

The man slid the teakettle from its burner and poured the hot water into two cups. He handed one to her, then settled across from her on a rustic chair. "You have many questions."

"Too many. At least that's what Momma always said." Rachel blinked rapidly, fighting the urge to curl up and cry over the pain her momma's illness caused. The way their relationship had altered as they argued about finding her father. She'd launched from not caring about his absence to desperately needing to find him. All as her momma's body continued to lose its fight and she faced the reality that without a miracle from a distant God, her momma would die. Sooner than she should.

"You are troubled by God's distance?"

"No. Yes. I hear he's personal. Yet he doesn't see me." The words rushed from her. She wouldn't tell the father how she longed to find God. Not too many years ago, he'd been real. Someone she counted as a friend. More than a character in a fable, but a person she knew and longed to know better. Now? Now she didn't know. Could she trust him with her bruised heart? Not when it appeared he had more important things to do than heal her momma and couldn't even do those well.

"May I tell you a brief story? Of a group who felt much like you?"

"Of course."

"Millennia ago, the Israelites, God's chosen, were enslaved. The Bible says they groaned and felt abandoned. Like the God who had spoken to their forefathers had forgotten them. Everything showed God had turned His attention a different direction."

"I've heard the story."

"Yes, yes. But there is an interesting note tucked in the midst of the telling." He leaned forward, eyes alight with joy. "God Himself tells Moses to tell the Israelites He had visited them and seen what was done to them. Even when they felt most alone and forgotten, God was in their midst taking note of everything."

"You believe he still does?"

"Yes."

The simple word resonated with a passion that stirred Rachel.

The father let silence fill the space between them. A silence so deep and sure, she felt it deep inside. She opened her mouth, then closed it, not wanting to disturb the gift. It was tinged with grief, filled with grace. In a world that churned with the machine of war, a moment to pause, to think, felt like the rarest gem.

She walked life alone, always alone.

In that pause she could almost hear a voice whispering her name. So sure, so soft, so full of peace.

She closed her eyes and tried to sort through the peace.

Was it real?

She longed to believe it was. That in God's eyes she was worth seeing and loving. That her lack of a father didn't matter to him.

Could it be possible?

Chapter 22

Tuscany
July 30, 1944

"EVERYTHING OKAY?" SCOTT TURNED to Rachel after she'd spent a morning glancing behind them every ten or fifteen minutes. As the days had slipped by, glances over her shoulder had become more common.

She shook her head, then sighed. "I don't know. I keep thinking a vehicle is following us, but I must be imagining it." She smiled, but it never lit her eyes. "Guess I'm jumpy today."

Tyler exchanged a look with Scott that communicated how little he thought of her nerves.

"Why do you think someone is following?"

"I'm probably paranoid." She shrugged. "In most towns we visit something is missing. Could it be because someone is following us there?"

Tyler snorted. "The problem with that is those in the know miss it before we arrive."

Color swept up her cheeks. "That's why I haven't said anything. I just sense someone watching me. All the time."

"That's just lover boy keeping an eye on you."

Rachel crossed her arms and harrumphed at Tyler's words.

Scott tapped down a grin. Maybe she noticed the way he sought her out more than he'd recognized. Tyler certainly had. "I'll keep an eye out too, Rachel. If anyone's following us, we'll catch them."

She nodded but looked unconvinced as she glanced behind her.

The days slipped by, each filled with visiting one village after another.

In each village Scott led Rachel in a search of churches and other landmarks on his lists. She took careful photos as he examined the structures for damage. Then he'd look for any listed art not at the church. In almost each place Scott was regaled with stories of the lengths the Italian art superintendents and priests had taken to protect the treasures left in their care. Many landholders made their villas available for large deposits of paintings while a large statute or two might fill a stall in a barn. Other times they'd used caves tucked in the hills. Even after all the effort, the Germans had come, seeking and taking what pleased them.

Then there were the items that vanished. In a couple villages the priests or superintendents didn't realize the piece had disappeared until Scott arrived. Could Rachel be right? Did someone follow them and slip ahead of them to take the valuable art?

The list Scott maintained of missing statues, masterpieces, and other artifacts grew piece by piece. The German SS seemed to have a list of their own as they'd moved across Italy making selections. They'd told the local art officials the paintings and statues should be moved north until they reached the Germans' protection.

Had the pieces been moved north for protection? How many of the stolen pieces had been confiscated by the Germans rather than an Allied soldier? Scott couldn't know unless he found a list of art the Germans held. It was possible some pieces had moved north to Florence. Yet the Germans could have used the front lines as an excuse to move the pieces into Austria and Germany.

General Tucker wasn't impressed with his lack of progress. The man didn't realize building relationships with the local church and art superintendents mattered. It would expedite his work as they continued north. The relationships he'd formed in Rome helped, but the local men had to trust him too. Finding a missing piece would go further than shoring up another roof. Scott needed to find something.

"You look like your best friend died." Rachel handed him a mug of coffee.

"The locals believe our soldiers are taking their art just like the Germans did."

"They consider it a souvenir."

"Maybe, but to these villages it's their religious artifact or a piece a Medici gifted."

"I know." She sank beside him, turning to face him.

He took another sip. "I thought I could do something important. Now I wonder."

"You're helping these towns restore what's been damaged. Letting them know they aren't alone, we're here to help."

He wanted to believe her. "When I left, my fiancée returned my ring because she believed I was a fool. I didn't believe her because I knew I could help save Western civilization. Instead, I dodge artillery shells as we move from town to town. Elaine was right. I should have stayed in Philadelphia and continued working my way up the art world."

Rachel reached across and touched his hand. "She was wrong. You're doing something important. The soldiers just don't understand. You can educate them."

"DeWald made booklets for the soldiers in Rome on R & R. That won't work here."

"Find another way to let them know why the art is important.

Your passion will catch. You have to communicate it when you work with the soldiers."

"Look at Tyler. He's traveled with me for weeks and has no greater understanding than the first day. He doesn't care."

"I think he understands more than he lets on." Rachel stared into her cup.

She met his gaze, her chocolate eyes filled with something he couldn't discern. "You don't give the soldiers enough credit. Most recognize beauty. Sometimes they need help understanding it in a new format. Explain what you see in a church that looks like it should be bulldozed."

"You've thought about this."

Rachel nodded, almost dislodging her cap in the process. "I wasn't sure this had a place in the army initially. But spending time with you and with the priests . . . you've changed my mind. I want to help preserve Italy's buildings and art. They will too."

He considered her words. He'd been quick to judge the soldiers. Even Tyler. You'd think driving around, trying to stay alive, would create some type of bond between them. Foxhole if nothing else. Yet the man remained aloof, indifferent, almost as if he schooled himself to behave that way. Maybe it was an act.

Scott poured the balance of his coffee onto the ground. "Time to get back to it."

Despite her brave words as she sat next to Scott, the days that dragged to weeks had attained a monotony of tagging along behind General Tucker's troops in the slow progression north. Each day they'd drive into another small village she couldn't find on a map, and she'd wonder if and when she'd take a photo that would make it onto the front page of a U.S. newspaper. The photos felt the same. One more demolished building. One more broken fountain. One more destroyed village. One more plant poking through the rubble.

Unfortunately the men in the Rome newsroom had nailed it when they said the French landing trumped anything happening in Italy. Without a breathtaking, eye-catching photo, she wouldn't make any extra money to pay medical bills. The good news was each day they inched closer to Florence and Tuscany, but the battle ahead constrained their speed.

She carried the sketchbook with her and showed it to priests, but while they'd been courteous, none had any ideas about the artist. They humored her and said it would take an Italian art expert to identify the artist.

Scott nudged her shoulder, and she startled. "I'll take the cups back. Meet you at the jeep?"

"Sure." Scott handed her the cup, then stood and headed toward the jeep.

After depositing the cups in the mess tent, she returned to the tent she now shared with nurses placed with the hospital at this temporary base. It was an unusual pleasure to have some women around after days spent primarily with Scott and Tyler. Last night she'd developed film in her helmet while they washed clothes in a tub, the group wrapping her into their camaraderie.

When she entered through the flap, the tent was empty of all but a sleeping nurse. Rachel moved as soundlessly as possible as she reclaimed the negatives. She took them to headquarters for dispatch to Rome, then walked by the mail station.

"Letters for you, Captain Justice."

"Glad the mail can find me."

"We do our best." The private handed it over with a grin. "They're getting the system worked out between here and Rome. Expect it more regularly."

She nodded her thanks. No need to tell him letters for her were like snow in July. With the time she had before meeting the guys at the jeep, she settled into a nook of shade to enjoy her letter in peace. Sharp whistles had followed her but she ignored them, background noise to being one of a handful of women surrounded by men. A few tipped their heads as they passed, and she answered with a smile. Her thoughts remained centered on the letters in her hand.

The first was something from her editor. The other V-mail felt thin in her hand, and she wanted to savor it. This was the third letter to reach her in the months since she'd left the States. She wanted to believe others were only lost.

A small, flowering white olive tree sat off the main road adjacent to the field the army had turned into its headquarters for this phase of the approach to Florence. Terraced fields lined with grape vines rose to the north of the tents, but here she'd find a slice of peace away from the watching eyes surrounding her.

She eased to the ground beneath the tree, holding the letters in her hand. The note from her editor said to prepare for a reassignment. If she didn't get fresh photos, he'd have to move her or bring her back to Rome. She refolded the letter and slipped it back in its envelope.

Finding fresh subjects wasn't easy in a region ripped apart by fighting. She shook her head and raised the V-mail to her nose. She longed for one whiff of Momma's lilac perfume. One whiff would feel like a hug, but this copy the army had made from microfiche shipped overseas carried no scent.

The penmanship looked like Momma's, spidery and thin. The wavers through the letters weren't normal. The *t*'s dipped and the *m*'s swooned, nothing like her normal handwriting. Momma always wrote with a strong hand, the hand of an artist.

She let the letter linger another minute, then returned to it. Time to see what news Momma had. The letter was chatty, telling all that was happening in the neighborhood. While Rachel hoped Momma was up and around, visiting her friends and learning their news, it also meant Momma was out of the hospital receiving no treatment.

> *Life continues. It always does though. Calendar pages flip. Months change. Years change. But one thing remains constant. I love you dearly. I will never regret my time in Italy because it gave me you. You are my treasure.*

Tears slipped down Rachel's cheeks. The words felt like a benediction, as if Momma was preparing for a good-bye. Surely Momma hadn't given up. She couldn't. Not while Rachel stayed in Italy, still looking even if it was as hopeless as finding the perfect dress on the battlefield.

"You ready?" Tyler's voice broke into her thoughts.

She wiped her cheeks and took a deep breath. Then turned to watch him approach. He sauntered as if the countryside belonged to him. A lord taking in his estate. "Time already?"

"Scott's waiting by the jeep. He wouldn't interrupt."

Which was why she enjoyed his company more than Tyler's. "I'll be there in a moment." First she needed to slip her letter into the sketchbook. Then it would be safe until she could read it again.

She ignored Tyler's hand and scrambled to her feet. She hurried across the field, back to the shelter of the tent. After she pulled her musette bag from under her cot, she unzipped it and felt around for the sketchbook. Where was it? It wasn't where she'd tucked it.

Frantically she dumped the bag on her bed but didn't see it.

Her heart stuttered at the thought it had disappeared. She'd studied the illustrations until she could probably sketch the outlines herself. However, nothing would replace the ability to turn the pages and see a representation of the woman she believed was her momma during her year in Italy.

She slipped down and looked under the cot. Pulled back her

bedroll. It was gone. Utterly, completely gone. Her breath hitched and her hands shook.

Time slipped as she rammed everything back into her bag, unconcerned with where they went. She didn't care how it was packed. She wanted that book.

Somewhere.

It was here.

It had to be. She hadn't done anything else with it.

"Rachel?" Scott stood in the doorway watching her frantic movements.

"It's gone." She forced the words past the lump in her throat.

"What is?"

"The sketchbook." Her words hiccupped. It had to be here, but she'd looked everywhere. Nobody else would value it, a simple collection of sketches by an unknown artist with the initials RMA. Momma was the one who cared about it, and now Rachel had lost it.

Just like she would lose Momma.

Her thoughts shuddered as her breath caught in her throat. She couldn't cry. Not over this. She'd look hysterical, but the tears came anyway.

"Ah, Rachel." Scott took a step closer. "It's somewhere."

"I've looked. Everywhere." She whispered the words through a tight throat.

"Sure. I've done that too. Certain I'd checked every conceivable place only to find it later. I'll help you search." He took another half step, then must have noticed the resting nurse because he stopped. Still he didn't meet her gaze.

"Why would someone take it?"

"Because it's valuable."

Rachel stared at him. "That book?"

"You'd be surprised." He opened his mouth as if he might say more, and Rachel waited. There had to be more to back up such a crazy claim. However, he kept his peace, then blew out a breath. "Early preparatory works have sold for good prices."

"When the buyer knew the famous artist."

"Someone knows your artist."

"Nobody's seen the book except you and me. Tyler, I don't know who this mystery artist is. Do you?"

"I'm not sure." His face twisted as if he battled with the idea.

"It doesn't matter because it's gone. And I could be reassigned any day. Then I'll never find it." And with it disappeared the one, slim lead she had. Rachel sank onto the edge of her cot, ignoring the squeaking canvas.

"I'm sorry. You're sure you checked everywhere?"

She shoved another pair of socks into her bag. "Yes. How will I explain to Momma?" It had disappeared. Or been stolen. She tried to force back the thought, but with the task General Tucker had given Scott of identifying who was stealing small pieces, it was possible.

She still wondered about Scott's reaction to the book. He acted like it was a treasure, one he couldn't believe someone had entrusted to her. Why wouldn't he tell her who the artist was? Wouldn't most art experts gladly share their superior knowledge on an item? Yet Scott had buttoned up regarding the book. Had he taken it? She shook her head. That seemed as likely as Tyler acquiring it. Neither had a reason.

Scott looked at his watch. "We need to hit the road. Can I help you look tonight? After we get back? Or do you want to stay here?"

A flash of disappointment arched through her. If she left, she admitted the book was gone. Irretrievably lost.

After one last look at her cot, she grabbed her bag and camera. "I'm coming."

Chapter 23

RENALDO'S SKETCHBOOK BURNED A hole through the bag at Scott's feet.

Scott backed his thoughts up. He didn't know for sure it was Renaldo's sketchbook. But he would. It's why he'd done the one thing he would have thought impossible. Then he watched her panicked hunt and said nothing, the whole time feeling like a cad.

Then when she mentioned she could be reassigned, he'd known he did the right thing. Maybe someday she'd understand and in a fairy tale forgive him.

Rachel wasn't interested in cooperating so he'd taken the sketchbook in part to protect it. He had to know who the artist was. Maybe then he'd understand how she had acquired such a valuable item. As interested as she seemed in what he did, she still didn't have the background necessary to identify and preserve the piece of art history. Someday it would matter as a sign of the development of an artist's style and career. Someone with art training would know the sketches were more than doodles.

It could be Renaldo's, Mario's, or someone else's. He hadn't found a clear indication the night Rachel let him examine it. So many men had the initials RMA, and those alone didn't indicate something as vital as nationality. He'd scoured the drawings without finding a name or other clue. Instead, it had been the overall impression and feel he'd acquired as he kept looking at them that made him think Renaldo was the creative genius crafting the sketches. But it could just as easily be Mario. Either way he valued the walk through the pages and the artist's creative genius as he played with ideas.

Rachel stared out the jeep's side, a look of loss cloaking her. He'd done that to her. By taking and keeping the sketchbook, he'd hurt her, the woman he'd allowed to creep into his heart.

When she found out, she would never trust him again.

He couldn't return it. Not yet. First he had to learn whose it was and why she had it.

Now he knew how easy it would be for a soldier to lift a small piece here, another there. Had he become like the thief?

The thought kept his attention as the jeep bounced along roads. Someone was taking art from churches and small repositories. Thieves. Just like him.

He shook off the heaviness.

He was different.

He valued the art. That's why he'd borrowed it.

The thing that aggravated him most with the disappearing art was he had no suspects. It was as if the pieces disappeared into thin air. No one ever had a description of the thief. Instead, they woke up one morning and it would be gone, when the day before it waited in its proper place.

Someone knew enough to pick small items with value.

A warm breeze threatening to take his hat rippled through the jeep as they joined a small convoy of four vehicles headed to the village. It was impossible to tell if anyone trailed them in this crush. Occasionally Tyler lagged behind so he could race over hills, willing the vehicle to fly over each ridge faster than the last. The jeep sailed over another hill, and Rachel gasped when it jolted to the ground.

"Slow down."

Tyler pushed harder on the accelerator. "We're nuts to be out here in a convoy. We're sitting ducks in contested territory."

"General Tucker's staff assured me it's safe."

"Maybe yesterday, Lieutenant. This morning's different."

What did Tyler know? Scott glanced into the backseat. Rachel's face had taken on a shade of green, whether from Tyler's words or his driving Scott couldn't tell. "It can't be that bad or they wouldn't have sent other vehicles."

"You've never been to the front." Tyler scanned the sky, then focused on the road. "Lines don't stay nice and neat. Get on the wrong side and you're dead."

Scott pointed down the road. "There's the village. Let's do what we need to do and head back."

As Tyler slowed a fraction, Scott examined the town. It wasn't large. Maybe forty homes, a few businesses, and a church. To the east of town stood a villa he'd heard served as a collection point for art. He'd need to confirm that gossip. Then he met Rachel's gaze. She was fearless, yet he had to keep her safe. That was his task.

The distant pounding of artillery shells didn't grow closer as they approached the town. "See? Safe and sound."

A barrage of bullets assaulted the vehicles in front of them.

A half-track spun out of control, crashing off the road. A platoon of men swarmed from the back of another canvas-topped truck, using the vehicles as protection as long as possible. Then they fanned along the front of the buildings. Brick by brick, man by man, they worked their way into the buildings.

Time slowed. Crawled. Limped. Scott waited and prayed.

His pistol appeared in his hand without conscious thought. Ineffective as a child's toy, it rested there.

A bullet punctured the windshield, spiderwebbing it before lodging in the backseat.

Rachel screamed and Tyler cursed.

"Get us off the road!" Scott turned to search for Rachel. He couldn't do anything to save her. *God, help us!*

"I'm trying." Tyler took the jeep through curlicues as he tried to turn it around. There was a muffled explosion. "At least we're at the end of this convoy."

Gears ground as the trucks in front tried to get out of the road.

"What is going on?" Rachel's voice was muffled by her crouch, hands over her head holding the helmet in place.

"We got ahead of the lines." Tyler's words strangled at the end as he sent the jeep through another maneuver.

The world seemed to tunnel as Scott glanced through what remained of the windshield.

He saw a glint from the top of a building. "Sniper. Three o'clock."

Tyler grunted. "Right, Sherlock. And he has friends."

Several more soldiers scuttled along the edge of a block of buildings. Each wore the right uniform. So why didn't they find the shooters?

Tyler kept the vehicle moving, watching over his shoulder as he drove.

Whack!

Scott jolted as a blaze of fire burned along his left shoulder. He slumped to the side.

Rachel screamed. "Scott!" She reached for him around the seat.

"Stay down." He gritted the words through his teeth as he clapped a hand over his shoulder. It burned. Man, it burned. Was this his penance for taking the book? "I'm grazed. That's all."

Her wide eyes watched him. "There's blood."

Scott groaned. "Nothing a bandage won't cover."

Tyler rocked the vehicle to a stop beneath a tree. "Had to pick a village without a grove around it." He examined Scott's shoulder. "Looks like you're right. Just grazed. You are one lucky man."

"Protected."

"What?"

Scott forced a grin as he responded to Rachel's strained word. "Protected by God."

He didn't want to think what would have happened if the bullet had strained a few inches to the right and into his chest.

The fighting continued in front of them.

Rachel slipped from the jeep, her camera clutched in front of her, secured around her neck by its strap.

Scott stiffened, fighting the nausea. "Where do you think you're going?"

"To take photos."

Scott and Tyler exchanged a look, and Tyler exited the jeep and grabbed her. "Hope you've got a good lens. This is as close as you're getting." Tyler gripped her shoulders.

She struggled a moment, then turned to Scott. "Tell him to let me go."

"And have you killed? Not a chance." The thought of her this close about stole his breath. He hadn't wanted her anywhere near the fighting, and now they lingered outside the range. The saving grace was that the snipers didn't seem to have anything stronger than a rifle. Otherwise they'd all be dead.

Rachel took a few photographs, then played nurse on his shoulder. He'd been right—the bullet had only grazed him. Didn't mean it didn't hurt like blazes when she used supplies in their first-aid kit to clean the wound. By the time she finished tormenting him with her touch and nursing, he'd flushed hot and cold so many times, he needed a shower and distance . . . lots of it.

"It's quiet now." Her soft words pulled his gaze from her hands messing with the bandage.

Scott listened a minute, then nodded. "You're right. Where's Tyler?"

"Right here, boss." The man reappeared. "They've got the village contained. Medic will take a look at you where he's set up. We were lucky. The lead driver was killed, but nobody else was seriously injured this time."

"Guess we should move out."

They all climbed back in the jeep, and Tyler drove them into town.

Rachel pulled her camera apart so it ballooned in front of her, ready for her to frame and shoot photos. "Glad to see this village is almost intact."

She was right. As Scott glanced around, it was clear the town had avoided most of the harm of war. As they approached the center of town, Tyler slowed and then parked. A few curtains were pushed aside with small faces looking out. Rachel must have noticed as well because she pulled the camera to her eye and took a couple pictures. Then she slipped away to shoot more and he followed. No way he was letting her out of his sight.

She had a gift and used the camera like an artist used a canvas, to paint an image for the public to engage with the personal side of war. To see the individuals, families, and communities impacted. Sometimes that meant a soldier. Other times the civilians left after the battle passed through their backyards and homes.

The medic was involved with injured soldiers, and that was fine with Scott. He'd recover in no time compared to some of the soldiers the man worked to save.

Scott led her to the church. If he found the parish priest, he could soon connect with the art community.

The door to the small edifice stood closed but opened when he pushed a shoulder into the heavy oak door. The engravings on the door captured his attention. A craftsman of high skill had worked intricate details into the figures that graced each of the panes.

"Beautiful, *sì*?" A priest rose from his place in front of a wall of lit candles.

Scott nodded. "Exquisite. Who made them?"

"A humble woodworker graced the church with the story."

In the topmost panel Scott made out a crowd at the foot of a hill, with one man speaking. "Jesus?"

"*Sì*." The priest stepped closer, running his fingers across the carvings. "Hundreds of years later the story still exists for eyes to see." He turned and smiled. "The wisdom of the Messiah has much to teach."

"The Beatitudes?"

"Come. I doubt you came to ask after the door."

"No." But if he'd known to add it to the list of art to check, it would have been reason enough. "I'm with the Allied army."

"So I see." The man waved at his uniform. "Thank you for freeing our village. Why are you here? At my church?"

"I work with local officials and priests to find and repair historic buildings or art."

"Our heritage."

"Yes, Padre."

"Come."

Scott followed the father into the small sanctuary, vaguely aware Rachel continued to take photos. Light filtered through the stained glass in rainbow waves of color. Dust danced in the air, and the faint scent of incense tinged the space. He paused and looked toward the altar and the cross with Christ hanging on it. The image caused him to remember all Christ had suffered on his behalf. So much suffering around him. Did it help them to remember Christ had suffered too?

"It is good to remember, no?"

"Yes, very good." More so on a day he needed to beg for forgiveness. Scott sank onto a pew and waited as the father claimed a chair from behind the altar.

"The pew is hard on my back." The priest adjusted the cushion and then sank onto the chair. "Why here?"

Scott studied his hands a moment. "Men and women in the United States and Britain have created lists. These lists contain items to be preserved if possible. This church is on that list."

"This small place?" The father scoffed. "We treasure it, but there is little for the world to value."

"Someone disagrees. Maybe it's your beautiful doors. Maybe it's the age. I am glad it survived."

"As are we." The priest studied him, curiosity in his eyes as he leaned toward Scott.

"I need to work with local art superintendents. Who fills that role around here?"

The man shrugged. "Most is under Florence. Renaldo Adamo made trips, then the fighting arrived."

"Where can I find Renaldo?"

"I don't know. I'll show you the art."

❧

Rachel sensed Scott's excitement as they headed back to headquarters. Even with an injury and shattered windshield, he looked energized.

"Bring everything tomorrow. Don't leave anything behind."

Tyler thumped the steering wheel. "We heard you the first six times."

"Why?" Rachel leaned forward to make sure she heard his answer against the wind.

"If the father's correct, we won't head back. If we had our things, we wouldn't drive back now." He rubbed his hands with the glee of a child at Christmas. "We're getting close."

"About time," Tyler grumbled. "I'm ready to get this assignment behind us."

"Not sure I can accomplish that, but if we reach the art store-houses, our real work begins. Pray the Germans didn't take anything."

"Waste of breath." Tyler harrumphed and pulled out a ciga-rette. He jammed it between his teeth but didn't light it.

When they returned to headquarters, Tyler dropped Rachel off at her tent. Seeing the heavy canvas ruffled by the wind brought back a heavy sense of loss. She rubbed her upper arms, then forced her steps inside. She needed to face the reality the sketchbook had disappeared.

It was just a book. She'd watched men die today, so this shouldn't upset her. The small battle gave her perspective she'd lacked.

After she pushed through the flap, she approached her cot. Her bags sat on the cot, the bedroll in a neat roll. The other cots held bags and bedrolls too, except for one tucked in a corner. A nurse lay curled up on that one, catching a little shut-eye before her shift.

Rachel's respect and admiration for the women who served as nurses had elevated during her time sharing quarters. Their dedi-cation to their patients humbled her. The conditions they lived and worked in were so far below what they'd find in the States, but they hadn't complained.

Who had packed her things? Did everything look so tidy because the nurses were moving out?

That news would be what Scott wanted. The skirmish and whatever the priest had said had transformed him from the lost man of the morning to one energized.

She sank onto the cot, ignoring the unique squish of the taut canvas stretched on the frame. She pulled out a V-mail letter and drafted a few lines for Momma, her thoughts turning home.

If she found her father, she could finally ask him why he never came. Would his answer fill the hole in her heart? The ache of never having a daddy?

She'd watched other students at her school interact with their fathers. Watched families in their building. Always the outsider.

Always longing to know the hug of a father. Always wondering why she didn't have one.

She imagined her father as a famous painter who'd dislike having a child show up. Without the journal could she find him?

Her eyes closed, and she wondered if she should pray, but she couldn't force any words so she waited. For what she wasn't sure. Maybe for peace. For the thought that her time in this war-torn place wasn't wasted. That in the midst of it all there was purpose and meaning.

God, are you even here? Sometimes I wonder how all of this must grieve your heart. This can't be what you intended.

She slumped to her side across a bag. All this introspection wouldn't change a thing. The tent flapped open, and a group of gals waltzed into the room.

"Keep it down over there." The words came from the nurse who huddled on her cot. "Not all of us feel joy today."

"Come on, Annie. It's a gorgeous day."

"It's just another one."

"Leave her alone." A new nurse nudged Heidi, a bouncy redhead who always smiled. "She lost a patient today."

"At least we're alive and the birds are singing. That makes it glorious." Heidi tugged her fellow nurse up. "Come on. We're moving out in the morning."

Annie flopped back down. "I need to sleep while I can. The wounded don't stop arriving."

Heidi sank next to her. "Fine. I'll join you in your doldrums. Will that make you happy?"

"Sure, honey. Misery loves company." Annie stretched out her lanky form. "Hey, Rachel, ready to move again?"

"As long as it's north and not to the rear." Her editor's note reinforced her need to keep moving with the army.

"I kind of liked it here." Annie harrumphed and sat up.

Heidi nudged Annie and pushed her off balance until the girl slid to the floor. "Ignore her. She's not always this insufferable."

Rachel stifled a laugh at the girls' pointed banter. While it might seem intense, an underlying affection for each other was clear. "Are you sure you didn't know each other before enlisting?"

"Are you kidding?" Heidi poked Annie with her toe. "We'd kill each other if we had history."

"What do you call this?" Annie tugged Heidi's shoe off and tossed it toward Rachel.

"Sisters in arms keeping each other sane."

"I always wanted a sister." On all those long days and nights when Momma worked and Rachel was alone in the small apartment, she'd wondered what little brothers and sisters would be like. Even one annoying sister would have made the loneliness bearable. The neighbors were older with busy lives. While kind, they often forgot she lived there too. "So where are we headed?"

Heidi leaned across the space between the cots and lowered her voice to a whisper. "The medical unit is headed due north about twenty kilometers. I've heard you're headed somewhere different. With a certain handsome escort. You have to tell me how you ended up with a designated assignment versus floating like so many correspondents."

"I wasn't looking for it."

"I would have." Heidi waggled her eyebrows and slipped closer. "Haven't you noticed how easy on the eyes he is?"

"Scott?"

"My, my. Don't you mean Lieutenant Lindstrom?" Annie laughed as she grabbed her shoe. "This is cozy."

"Not really." She hadn't thought her consistent assignment with Scott unique. It was a way for higher-ups to keep her out of the way. It didn't hurt there was something magnetic and compelling about him. Heat traveled up her neck, a color she hoped the girls couldn't see.

"The girl protests too much." Heidi settled back on the cot. "What's he like?"

Rachel shrugged. "There's not much to tell." Except that his kisses could bring her to her knees.

"After all the time you spend together? Not buying it. You've learned something worthwhile."

"He's dedicated to preserving art."

Annie groaned and pantomimed throwing the shoe at Rachel. "You've got something better than that. Who cares about art when they're under attack?"

"Scott does. He gave up curating a museum in Philadelphia to come here."

"You mean Uncle Sam invited him."

"I got the idea he made the first move."

Annie snorted. "Typical man. Creating a better story than reality. Nobody enlists to parade around a war zone and find art."

Rachel had thought that at first. "With him it's different. He's a gentleman committed to his assignment. Even when the general gives him impossible ones like me. He does what's asked."

"The girl is smitten." Annie faked a swoon worthy of a film star and then jumped back to her feet. "Time to eat some of that junk they call grub."

Part of Rachel wanted to deny she was smitten. But the words lodged in her throat, and she knew the larger part of her wanted to accept the words. All that was good in Lieutenant Lindstrom drew her, even when she wanted to resist a relationship. Annie and Heidi had shone a flashlight into the deep corners of her heart and seen something Rachel wouldn't admit.

A tumble of thoughts and emotions coursed through her as she followed the girls to the mess tent. She wasn't hungry, but maybe she'd see Scott's face, and her heart would tell her if the words it whispered were true.

Chapter 24

August 1

THE CHATTER OF THE nurses and zips of their bags woke Rachel the next morning. "Come on, sleepyhead." Annie clapped next to Rachel's head. "I have it on good authority your man is pacing out there, waiting for you. And don't bother denying he's yours."

Rachel tried to open her eyes, but a night of restless dreams with images of the skirmish colliding with Scott left her unprepared to meet the day. Instead, she wouldn't mind being back in Rome or Naples with the comfortable hotels and bed. The opportunity to block out the fact she was preparing to chase the front lines again.

Annie grabbed a tin cup of water and held it over Rachel.

"You wouldn't!"

"Try me." Annie cocked an eyebrow.

Rachel kicked the bedroll away from her feet and tried to stand. Instead, she rolled to the ground and collided with a bag as the bedroll encased her feet. "Okay, you got me."

Annie laughed so hard water tipped from the cup and splattered against the worn grass. "Glad to know that old trick still works. Seriously, the man is creating a path out front."

"I'm half tempted to leave him pacing."

"You could. But the soldiers will be here to tear down this tent in fifteen minutes. You might as well get up."

As they packed, Rachel asked the gals if they'd seen her sketchbook. "I had it in my bag but it disappeared."

Heidi and Annie looked at each other. Heidi frowned. "You don't think we took it?"

"No." That was the last thing Rachel believed. "Have you seen anyone with it?"

Both shook their heads. Annie rolled up a stained pair of trousers and shoved them in her bag. "But when I'm here I tend to sleep like the dead."

Heidi nodded. "Me too. The rest of the time I'm eating or at the hospital."

"That's what I thought."

Ten minutes later Rachel collected her bags and bedroll and said good-bye to Annie and Heidi. She doubted she'd bunk with them at the next stop. Still she'd miss the way they kept her days interesting.

Scott grabbed her bags when she exited. His continued chivalry in the face of war honored her. When they reached the jeep, he set the bags in back, then turned to her. Her mouth dried as he helped her into the vehicle. He held her hand a moment longer than needed, but she didn't want to end the connection. Tyler cleared his throat, and Scott dropped her hand like he'd touched a pot of boiling water.

The kilometers clicked by as they joined another convoy headed north through a fog that settled over the area. A fog that surrounded her inside and out. Rachel scanned the surroundings, imagining the enemy watching and waiting for the perfect shot that had missed her the prior day. The eerie feeling settled along her spine. After they'd driven in silence awhile, Rachel leaned forward. "Where are we headed?"

"A villa. Or castle. It's called Montegufoni, located in the heart of Tuscany about twenty kilometers from Florence. The father told me it's a repository for some of Florence's treasures." Scott stared through the spiderwebbed windshield.

"It can't be good people know where those paintings are."

"Perhaps statues and other antiquities too. I don't like the idea of the knowledge floating around. I doubt there's great security."

The jeep traced a bend in the road. The vista opened and Rachel couldn't stifle a gasp. A beautiful, utterly old castle graced the horizon. With yellow stucco walls soaring stories into the air, it had an imposing tower that stood point over the middle of the building.

"It's beautiful."

The words had slipped out when a plane flew in at great speed and overtook the castle.

"Don't drop anything!" Scott moaned as he rubbed his shoulder.

"Maybe nothing's there." Tyler ground the gears and edged toward the side of the road under the meager protection of a cypress. "We'll wait until the plane's gone."

Scott's mouth opened, then closed. His gaze never left the plane as it soared and then circled back. "Is it coming for us?"

Rachel shuddered. She'd heard stories of pilots on both sides of the fight using their machine guns to strafe those unlucky enough to be on the road when they flew overhead. She didn't want to become a target. Staying in the vehicle would paint a large circle on her in the middle of a shoot-me zone. "We can't stay in the jeep."

She started to climb out but noticed the plane turning around again. "Is it headed for the castle?"

Her heart ached at the thought of that gracious building taking a hit. Forget the art; the building itself was worth preserving.

⚜

"Come on." Scott pushed harder against the floor of the jeep. "Get us there now, Tyler."

"You want to be plane bait? You're nuts."

"I have to be there."

"Then you might want to run. I'm not approaching until the plane disappears."

If Scott had to sit here and watch that plane bomb the villa, he might throttle Tyler. Then he wouldn't need a driver because he'd spend the rest of the war in a cell.

"Tyler, the plane's gone." Rachel's voice soothed him.

Scott searched the sky afraid the plane would circle or come back with friends. After the plane didn't reappear, he thumped the dashboard. "Let's move."

Tyler grunted. "You're explaining to my family if I'm killed."

Scott ignored the comment, instead praying for protection as they approached the estate. The castle didn't grow closer as they drove. The way it sat on a slight rise with a road winding around it lengthened the journey. He couldn't tear his gaze from the ochre tones contrasted against the vibrant grass and pale sky. It looked like the plaster-covered walls were intact. He focused but didn't hear the drone of a plane. Instead, the song of a bird chased by the laughter of children reached him. Children? God help them if they remained when the plane returned.

"Stop the car." Rachel tapped Tyler's back. "Now."

"Why?" The man didn't budge as he steered through a curve.

"I need a framing shot."

"Of course you do."

As soon as he slowed, she hopped out and snapped a couple pictures. Scott caught her glances at the sky. "Okay, I'm done. Thanks."

"Dames."

"Photographers." Scott corrected Tyler.

Tyler grunted. "Now what?"

"I'll see who I can find."

"Know anything about this castle?" Rachel slipped into the backseat, and Tyler pulled back to the road.

"Just what the father told me."

"And that was . . . ?" Tyler looked at him.

"It's owned by an Englishman. He's fighting for the Brits but allowed art to be stored here."

"Sounds about right."

Scott stared at the private. "What do you mean, that sounds right?"

"I make it a practice to know what I can about important people and places."

Scott snorted, then turned away. The man liked to give the illusion he knew more than anyone else, yet he didn't share fresh information. "Spent time at Montegufoni?"

"In the area as a kid. My father dragged us here for a summer. Thought it'd be our version of a Grand Tour. Such an outdated idea. Bored me to tears."

Rachel leaned between them. "You spent a summer in Tuscany?"

"Yep. Aren't you jealous?" The man navigated another turn.

Scott kept his peace as he wondered how much of Tyler's story was true.

"Actually, yes." Rachel sighed from her spot in the back. "I would have loved the opportunity. My summers consisted of a once-a-month trip to the beach if we had money."

"Well, it wasn't so swell being stuck with a bunch of kids who didn't speak a word of English when I didn't know Italian. Got so mad I decided I'd never learn."

"Why not learn as fast as you could?"

"I didn't want it to matter."

"Still, it must have been marvelous. I've always wanted to come." A wistful tone colored her words.

"Why?" Scott turned around to catch her expression as she answered.

"Not Italy so much really." She looked out of the jeep. "I've always wanted to follow my mom's journey." The breeze blew her hair across her face, and she didn't brush it aside like usual. His fingers moved to do it for her, but he pulled back. Her face had closed, and he could feel the wall she'd erected.

With the last turn before the castle, activity on the road increased. It sat on a bit of a raised hill, like a gorgeous peridot set in a ring of deeper emerald hills. Some part of the Allied army had taken residence.

"Tyler, any idea whose military that is?"

"Well, it ain't the Germans."

"That's good, but I'd sure like to know who I'm dealing with." Scott tried to see the flag, but it flapped too much in the wind.

"No one in headquarters gave an indication?"

"Not much more than it was contested but should be in Allied hands when we arrived. Far as they knew, we were the first headed here."

"We came before it was secure?" Rachel stared at him.

Tyler muttered something Scott hoped Rachel didn't catch. "It'd be nice to have good intel once."

"Like you said, this is war." Scott squinted to try to make out who held the approach. "Guess I should have paid attention to flags in school."

"It's British of some sort." Rachel pointed where it flew in front of the castle. "See the Union Jack on the background. Maybe New Zealand."

"Well, boys and girls, I think this is where we stop and hope those folks are friendlies." Tyler halted in front of a couple men standing beside the road, each holding a Lee-Enfield rifle at the ready.

"Papers." The lilt to the voice indicated the man had British ancestors, but an independent tone accented the words too.

Scott pulled them out. "Here you are."

The man took the papers and scanned them while his friend kept his gun at his hip. "Monuments and Fine Arts? You've found the right place. Watch for the Italian."

"What?"

"The chap's into his art and explaining it to whoever stops."

The other soldier nodded. "Passionate fellow."

"Thanks for the warning." Scott looked beyond them to see a milieu of soldiers milling. "Where to now?"

"Wherever you can park. Be on guard. Locals moved into the castle during the fighting. Children are everywhere."

"Thanks."

Tyler launched the jeep into gear, then edged up the incline and parked. A bell hung above the formidable entrance. It bore a slight resemblance to drawings of Texas's Alamo, if you subtracted the desert and added the Tuscan countryside. Imposing yet with the sunshine-colored plaster welcoming.

"Can't leave our stuff in the jeep. Especially if this is a refugee camp."

Scott nodded at Tyler. "Unless you want to stay here while I see what's happening."

"Not on your life." Tyler glanced up the hill.

"All right." The castle drew Scott to it. He had to know if the rumors were true. Did great masters hide inside its walls?

Rachel eyed the steep hill. It wouldn't be easy to schlep her gear up there, but with the guys carrying their own, she'd handle hers.

Soldiers had deployed their tents on a large field next to the castle, the one sign they weren't British being their unique patches and the occasional flag. She grabbed one bag and her bedroll, but Scott grabbed her other bag before she could. She offered him a smile, then headed up the hill, sandwiched between Scott and Tyler.

She was so close to her destination. The last map she'd scoured had shown Montegufoni twenty-five kilometers southwest of Florence. She could almost see the city. Once there among its occupants she'd find someone who remembered her momma. She pressed her lips together and jutted her jaw. It might be impossible, but she would.

She staggered over the top and turned to gaze over the vista. Her breath caught at the rows of hills, some with grapevines, others with fields or lines of trees. It looked like an oasis; yet hints of battle remained. At least it hadn't been as horrible as the fighting around Anzio and Cassino, but to those who lived here, it had been every bit as terrible. To have opposing armies battle for position across your land and home. She forced the image from her mind and tried to memorize what lay before her. A tapestry of immense beauty crafted by an amazing Creator.

A soldier strode toward them, head high and shoulders back. He looked as if he expected to battle them and win as he had over the retreating Germans. "You are?"

"Lieutenant Scott Lindstrom." Scott dropped her bag and snapped a quick salute. "With me are Captain Rachel Justice and Private Tyler Salmon."

Tyler didn't bother with a salute, and the officer's mustache twitched. "I see. I've heard your name. What can I do for you?"

"A place to work, and we'll take care of the rest. Captain Justice is with the United Press, so she may wander around a bit in her capacity."

The officer eyed her, his gaze taking in every centimeter of her. Rachel fought the rising heat in her neck, praying it didn't reach her cheeks where it would be noticeable to the men. Instead, she raised her chin and met his gaze. With a quick jerk of his head, he acknowledged her challenge. "All right. Within reason of course." He turned back to Scott. "My man will show you where you can set up. Study the way there. This place is a maze. Alcoves and such in every direction. I'd suggest you wait in the courtyard for him."

"Thank you." Scott shifted the bags to the ground and stood at ease, even as his fists clenched and released behind his back.

Chapter 25

UNIFORMED MEN MIXED WITH weary civilians in the courtyard. Each bore the effects of war. Filth, fatigue, with the civilians bearing the added look of starvation. Closer to the land, Rachel had assumed they would have a better source of food, but the initial look belied the idea. While Scott and Tyler conversed with their guide in the courtyard entrance, Rachel looked for a corner of unoccupied shade.

She worked into a darkened corner, her locket thumping against her collarbone. The best photo opportunities would arise once everyone had returned to their activities. If they could forget she was there, they'd show her what life looked like at this castle turned into refugee center.

To one side a child wailed, hidden somewhere in the shadows. Several young children kicked around a ball of rags in a version of soccer. Their dirty faces radiated joy as they scrambled. The kind she would see in children back home who were untouched by war. One child kicked the ball in the path of a soldier. He stumbled to get out of the way, and they cowered. He studied them, their frames slumped and eyes hooded. Then he stepped toward the ball, and the boys backed away. What had they experienced that made them fearful?

The sergeant picked up the ball and tucked a loose rag in the wad. He pointed it toward some of his mates. "Want to play?"

One pulled his cap lower over his eyes and crossed his arms, sinking lower to the ground. Another nodded. "Why not?"

In a matter of minutes, the man had rallied a crowd of weary soldiers to participate in a raucous game with the kids. The children lost their fearful expressions, and laughter rang through the courtyard. Rachel edged from the corner and took several photos, praying some captured the spontaneity, joy, and grace.

Scott found her with the sun warming her back as she framed another photo from her spot on the ground.

"We're here until Florence opens. I've found us rooms inside."

She pulled the camera down and eyed him. "I'm sleeping in a castle?"

"We've got two bedrooms. Almost like a suite. It's the best I could wrangle unless you want a corner of the courtyard?"

That held no appeal if there was the possibility of a place to relax in privacy after a full day of jostling over a road. "It has a door?"

"Yes, and I'll even sleep in front of it."

Her smile grew. "I feel like a princess. Lead on, Lieutenant."

⁂

Scott led Rachel to the rooms, wondering if he needed a piece of chalk to mark the way. There were more twists and turns than he could track. And stairs going in all directions. It'd be a miracle if he didn't get lost since his guide had returned to official duties. With each room he passed, Scott ached to open the door and scour it for treasures, many waiting in plain sight from glimpses he'd had. Once the bags were deposited, he'd get to work and Rachel could explore.

The cracked doors they passed hinted at the riches waiting. He might need several notebooks to catalog all hidden here and identify what—if anything—had been removed. A retreating army shouldn't place a premium on moving large paintings, but he didn't understand German interactions with and demands on Italian art superintendents in this region.

He made a last turn, then opened a large, heavy wooden door. "Here we are."

Rachel stepped around him then gasped. The room elicited that kind of response. The frescoes across the walls and ceilings were unlike anything he'd seen in the States.

"It's a museum."

"In many ways. The owner's father purchased it on something of a whim."

"To be able to finance such whims."

"Right." Scott chuckled and led her to an interior door. "Your room is here." She followed him into the smaller space. "Will this work?"

A double bed rested against the wall, with a small dresser carrying a pitcher and bowl next to the bed and a large chest at its foot. "It's fine." She dropped her bag and bedroll on the chest, next to the bag he'd already deposited. "Thanks for getting that here."

"No problem." He glanced around the small room, then at her. The space closed around them. Where could time of peace to court the beautiful Rachel Justice lead? He inhaled and corralled his thoughts. "All right. I need to find this Italian."

"Shouldn't be too hard." She glanced up at him, a soft smile tipping her lips, lips that begged him to tug her close for a time-stopping kiss. "I heard several soldiers mention him. Seems to get around and isn't intimidated by them."

A knock followed her words. Scott hurried back across the main room, grateful for the reason to leave before he did something he shouldn't, like kiss Rachel. When he opened the door, a smallish man with olive complexion waited. A tenuous smile tipped his lips and broadened as he studied Scott.

"Tell me this cannot be true. After all this time. My friend Scott Lindstrom."

"Renaldo! You are well." Scott pulled the man into a bear hug.

"In one piece as of this moment. Of tomorrow I make no promises."

"Neither can I." Scott studied his former mentor. "What brings you to Montegufoni?"

"Similar mission to yours. Protecting my precious arts."

Scott studied his friend, noting the shadows under his eyes, the gauntness of his cheeks. "This has been a hard time."

"A hard time for *Italia*."

Scott nodded. How had the man's experiences melded with his own? He'd seen the devastation after it occurred. How much had Renaldo witnessed? "And your family?"

"Also safe. For the moment." He jangled something in his pocket, a familiar gesture that reminded Scott of so many conversations they'd had in the past. The teacher impatient for the student to catch up. "It is why I left Florence. Walked the long kilometers from the city. With me gone, maybe the Germans will not care about my family."

Maybe, but from what Scott had collected from conversations, the Germans liked to use families as tools to prompt actions they demanded. "So where do we begin?"

"A tour." Renaldo clapped his hands and gestured down the hallway. "This way."

Scott glanced back toward Rachel's room. Should he get her or let her rest? She hadn't slipped from her room, so if he got oriented first, he'd be better prepared to help her. Maybe he could determine whether Renaldo knew of the sketchbook. He followed Renaldo into the hall and down the dark corridor. The amount of filth surprised him. In many of the rooms, it looked as if a previous occupant had smashed the furniture to pieces. "Why?"

"The destruction?" Renaldo shook his head. "Much is beyond repair. But the Germans," he shrugged, "they weren't happy to leave such a fine place alone. Up and down the country it is the same. We hear reports of things taken, others destroyed. There won't be much left when this ends."

"So art was moved here?"

"At one time, fall 1942 should not feel so distant. We thought the valley would be spared. We prayed Firenze would be, but it was prudent to prepare." He walked a few feet in silence as if seeing a terrible vision.

Scott understood. "It was prudent. You did what was needed."

"Until now. Even the owner of Castello di Poppiano returned to Florence, believing it safer."

"Where is Poppiano?"

"Across the valley. You can see it from here. With its villa it hosts the wealth of Florence not stored here." He sighed, a rough, bitter edge making the sound harsh. "You should see the paintings. Six hundred. Crammed into vehicles. Shipped in heaps. We tried to wrap them to protect them. But the war . . ."

"Chaos."

"Yes."

Renaldo led the way down a narrow staircase and then across a small courtyard. "Like all old castles this started as seven small buildings and has grown over hundreds of years."

"A maze. I might need you to guide me back."

"My job is to keep moving. So the soldiers never know where to expect me. Then they will not take even small pieces. I know this *castillo* as well as the owner. Ah, here."

Scott followed the art superintendent through another door. This room took his breath away. Each wall was painted with a mix of cubist or classical harlequins. "What is this?"

"A commissioned room that is art. Severini is the artist."

"Who?"

"An Italian artist who paints under the influence of Picasso. You don't know him?"

"Not yet." Scott walked closer to the south wall and examined the work along it. "Does this represent something?"

Renaldo made a face. "If you can call it art."

Looking from the frescoes then out the windows, the setting for it was Montegufoni. "I wonder if the artist inserted himself into the paintings. Maybe the commissioners too."

"You can ask when this terrible business ends."

"Maybe." Scott would remember the name. See if he could learn more about the man who could bring such fanciful creatures to life on a large scale. "So where is all this art?"

"Hidden in plain sight. A couple local farmers have guarded it. Even so some were used as tables for meals cooked in the same rooms." The man looked like his eyes would roll out of his head at the thought of such perverse use of the art.

"Two years ago this castillo was abandoned. Everything cloth covered and mothballed. Now? Now the farmers moved back. The landowner spent years moving the peasants off the castle, and the war has chased them back. Add in soldiers." The man raised his hands and rubbed his temples. "It is amazing any survive."

"In what condition?"

"Varied." He turned to leave the frescoed room. "This way."

Five minutes of silence passed as they wove their way through refugees and soldiers. A family was tucked in every covered walkway. Many rooms had sheets strewn along the open spaces to make tiny apartments. "Where have you slept?"

"I have not. If I sleep, the art is undefended."

No wonder the man stumbled occasionally. He was exhausted. "When did you arrive?"

"Two days ago. In time to seek shelter from an air raid in the Poppiano's basement." Renaldo gestured to another room. This one was dark, the curtains drawn against the light, furniture absent. Scott had expected grandeur, but the room felt empty, cold. Then his eyes adjusted to the room.

"There you are." Tyler strode into the room. "I've been searching all over this mess of a place looking for you and Rachel. The New Zealanders ignore me."

"Must be your sparkling wit," Scott bit out as he continued to scan the room.

"What have we here?" Tyler marched deeper into the room, toward the stacks of canvases Scott had noticed the moment his eyes adjusted.

Renaldo looked from one to the other.

"This is my driver Private Tyler Salmon."

Tyler waved without turning toward the man. "The treasure trove sure as day." He walked to a stack and flipped through them, causing Renaldo to flinch as Tyler smacked frames together.

"Take care, Private."

With a nod the man kept flipping. "These are fantastic. Look, . . . is this a Giotto?"

Scott strode over, determined to break the man's hands if he didn't take some care with the priceless art. He glanced at the piece, then nodded. "Looks to be." His hands itched to inventory the room and the others in Montegufoni, Poppiano, and the villa. To think there were more repositories, places overflowing with the artistic wealth of Italy. In this case the Medicis' legacy to Florence and the world.

It was a singular thought that could scoop his breath out of his lungs and scatter it.

"It's kind of a cruddy place."

Renaldo stood as tall as his small frame allowed. "This is improvement over others. Montagnana. Such desolation. Art stolen. And others left on the floor like trash. Perugino's *Crucifixion*. Lorenzetti's *Presentation at the Temple*." Renaldo crossed himself and swooned.

Scott steadied him. "We're here to help."

"For that I am grateful. We need assistance."

Tyler pantomimed sitting on a chair. "You're missing a few things."

"That is easy. Many hid valuable furniture. Even in the countryside the elite learned it best to hide anything they did not want destroyed." Renaldo's voice carried with authority. "Have you seen her?"

Tyler straightened and walked over. "Seen who?" His eyes held a curious light for one who moments ago had showcased a knowledge of art.

"The *Venus*."

Chapter 26

A DANK CHILL SEEPED through Rachel as she lay on the bed. She stretched. How long had she allowed herself to relax? It seemed foolhardy when the day before the Germans and Allies hurled artillery at each other around this very place. Yet after the full day it had taken to travel the ninety kilometers, she'd felt jostled to pieces and in desperate need of a moment to rest.

She reached into her bag to pull out the sketchbook. Then stopped. Of course, it wasn't there anymore. She knew better, but this seemed the place to study the drawings. From what she remembered, this was the type of location where the sketches could have been produced. The sweeping hills. The wide-open sky. The feeling the land and buildings had stood for centuries and would continue to. What would it be like to belong to something so lasting, so permanent?

No matter how long she thought, an answer wouldn't come. All she'd known was her small family with Momma. And when Momma died, even that tiny bit ended.

"Stop it." The words echoed toward the high ceiling.

She needed something to distract her. Florence.

The city was so close, she could see it as a dot on the far horizon if she found a tall enough hill to stand on. She grabbed her momma's diary from its spot hidden in her bedroll. Now that someone had gone through her bags, it seemed the best place to protect her remaining treasures.

She held the book a moment, fingers stroking the cover as she longed for her momma. The pages had become as familiar to her as a favorite book. If Momma joined her here, would she finally tell the story of her time in Italy? Would she offer it with a smile, or would a cloud of sadness tinge the story?

Momma's letters spilled onto the bed across Rachel's lap. They'd arrived in trickles, each letter shorter, as if a reflection of failing strength. She leaned against the pillows and headboard, letting the letters feel like an embrace of her momma's love. She closed her eyes, tears slipping down her cheeks unstopped. No one was here to see so she let them flow. After a few minutes she stopped the silent course. Now she'd read the diary.

> *Today I met someone. He has a passion for life that is breathtaking. On the whole I expected to find this in most Italians, but they seem to carry a weight. Left over from the war, perhaps? It's a mystery, but this man has escaped the weight. Instead, he vibrates. Whether teaching a class or escorting me to the next museum, he brings a verve for every situation that must be equal parts exhilarating and exhausting. All I know is I long for that. Or something that will spark me out of this melancholy.*
>
> *I miss home. I miss the wide-open farm country of Pennsylvania. The excitement of our town house in Washington, D.C. Seeing the different sights, walking the Mall to sit on the steps of the brand-new Lincoln Memorial. Here I feel alone with nothing but my dreams. Then I am with him.*

The pen left a squiggly mark as if she had left it there for several moments while she daydreamed or imagined what to write next.

And everything changes.
I am alive.
I feel.
I want more of both.

Rachel released her breath trapped by the passion of the reading. Her momma had hesitated to show such depth of feeling. Instead, she was a steady personality with few passions Rachel had observed. To see this side of her momma unsettled Rachel.

This was a side of her momma that mattered. Without that rush of passion, Rachel would never have breathed. Never discovered the joys and pains of life. Her own existence wouldn't have slipped from the shadowed worlds of potential. The thought could shatter her. Because here she was—fatherless, alone, maybe motherless and unknowing. Her mother had lived with TB for years until it changed to a relentless course. The thought stabbed Rachel.

Who would she be when alone?

Would she return to a world of shadows without someone who loved her?

The thought pained her to the core of her being. There had to be more to life than wavering in and out of lives. Struggling to know and be known. Always holding back from the real fear that if she exposed who she truly was, the rejection would follow in a rush. She would always be the fatherless one others avoided because of Momma's questionable morals.

Rachel had developed a story about her daddy dying, but it wore thin like the lie it was. Explaining sounded weak, like defending the actions of another. Instead, as an adult she'd learned to hold her head high and act the part of one who never cared what others thought and hesitated to share her full story. Then she'd met Scott and wanted to be known.

She turned the pages, hand on Momma's necklace as she read.

Tonight he gave me a heart locket. He said to reflect his great love for me.

Then he took my hand and led me to see the stars.

He said it was to sketch me under a new light. Starlight. To craft a new page in the book that is us. To stroke a pencil across the page as he longed to touch me. Even as I pretended to believe, I knew there was more.

I still can't write his name, as if the very act of doing so will cause him to evaporate like the mist. I can't because when I am with him, I am alive. It is as if I hold my breath until the next moment he is with me. Too long and I feel sick as if I will expire from lack of air.

Tonight there was more.

We were more.

We were complete.

It was beautiful. Fearsome. So much more and less than I'd hoped and imagined.

What it means, I know not. Only that my love for him seems more complete and emptied.

Strange. And wonderful.

He took me to see the stars.

Rachel continued to read, inhaling the prose and wondering why her momma had never written for publication. What had stolen this gift from her?

Today my world shattered. The other girls in class giggled when I walked in. They whispered, telling secrets but saying them loud enough to ensure I heard. I told myself they were merely jealous. Upset that I was chosen while they were not. Then the truth confronted me, exposing me, my foolishness.

Tonight he appeared at the graduation party. With his fiancée.

My world erupted into a thousand pieces. My heart disappearing in the sparkle of her ring.

He had another. But took me.

· I watched, a growing sickness in me. I had done everything my father warned me to avoid.

And now instead of returning with a ring or a husband, I return with a child within. A child the father shall never know.

This I vow.

The last words splotched across the line as if the author had cried even as she etched them on the page.

Rachel shut the book after that last entry. It was as if with penning those words, admitting the depth of her fall, Momma could write no more. As far as Rachel knew, she'd never kept another diary. Instead, her writing ended with that moment.

Momma had been alone for an extended period and influenced by a country known for romance and passion. It wasn't surprising she'd been swept along. Her thoughts turned to Scott and his gentle ways. The way his strength came from seeing people and understanding them beyond a surface level. That drew her to him, made her wonder what a future with him could be like. Add in the crucible of war, the reality that life could end with the next shell, and Rachel could imagine how easy it would be for the loneliness to give way to passion. The desire to be seen and understood sweeping aside the restraints calmer times enforced.

Could she ever love a man with the passion her momma had felt?

For years she'd thought no. She'd always held back, wondering if men saw her or focused on the fallen status of her family.

Then Scott collided with her carefully ordered world. Of course, it happened in Italy. Where else did the Justice women lose their hearts?

With Scott it didn't seem to matter. He hadn't probed, nor had he changed the way he looked at her with the revelation she'd grown up without a father. Instead, compassion had colored his features, and he treated her with even more kindness.

Thrust into a situation where so much of her time was spent with one, very appealing man—she could imagine the direction her emotions would travel if she let them spin unchecked. Instead her momma's life was a cautionary tale. A living example of what happened the moment she lowered her guard.

The sound of singing lured her to a window to seek its source. She stacked the letters inside the diary cover, then wandered to the small window. Standing on the lone chair positioned beneath it, she peeked out. She couldn't see much but heard the dulcet sound of children singing a sweet tune. One she wanted to hear in person. She returned the diary to the bedroll and grabbed her camera. After it was around her neck, she exited the room, closed the door, and pocketed the key that had been in the doorknob.

After a few false turns she made her way back to the courtyard.

Fires circled the courtyard with women leaning over them stirring different pots. The children had been shooed away from danger, but she noticed the curious light in their eyes as they watched her. She eased closer, pointed at her camera, then raised it to her eye and pantomimed clicking a picture. She shrugged as if asking permission, pointing to them then her camera.

The children giggled and nodded in excitement. She gestured for them to squish together, and they did with laughter and the light of children who don't understand anything but war. She snapped a couple shots, then turned to shoot photos of the adults strewn around the court. They carried desolation and fear in place of the children's joy. After several tries she found the perfect shot of a woman standing by the fire, her husband slouched behind her with a couple soldiers speaking in the background. When a ball rolled across the frame as she clicked, she knew it was perfect. It captured the layers of war perfectly.

After taking an extra shot, she turned to walk outside the castle's courtyard to a place where she could watch the sun sink beneath the horizon. A low wall built of rocks extended from the back of the courtyard. She walked along it, fingers brushing the rough surface. The heat cloaked her like a blanket, and the sounds of children mixed with the barks of a couple dogs wrestling under a bush. The faint scent of something sweet drifted from a flowering bush on the other side of the fence.

If she stood right there, eyes closed, she could imagine the war had been a horrible dream rather than a reality that exploded kilometers down the road.

And she could imagine the Tuscany her momma had loved.

❧

Tyler slipped away before a quick gander at *Venus*, and Scott watched Renaldo pace the hall, wavering side to side. The man must be beyond exhausted. The stress, long walk from Florence, and lack of food couldn't have helped. Scott slipped into Italian, a courtesy for the man he respected, one of the men he'd taken the sketchbook for. "Are you sure you shouldn't rest first? *Venus* will wait thirty minutes."

Renaldo spun on his heel and stormed back toward Scott, finger raised and stabbing. "You do not understand. Any moment one can disappear."

"We're here."

"So were the Germans. They assured they safeguarded. The first troops did. Then the SS and paratroopers arrived as the others pulled back. They had no respect. So where is safe? Austria? Germany? For you, the United States?"

Scott stepped back, shocked by Renaldo's passion. "Only for the war."

"So they say too."

"We mean it."

"Words." The man got within a foot of Scott, so close he could smell the garlic of whatever hearty Tuscan dish Renaldo had last eaten, then stopped. "Words mean nothing." He paused and seemed to gather his emotion. "Tell me about the young woman with you."

"Rachel?"

"That is her name?"

"Yes. She's a photographer with newspapers in the States." What should he say? He wanted to understand Rachel, but she hadn't let him in far enough to understand why Renaldo was important.

"Ah, an artist." Renaldo squared his shoulders. "She is beautiful."

"She is." Renaldo continued to stare at him as if seeing into his soul. "She has inner beauty too. But I don't know much about her except she's from Philadelphia and the most amazing woman."

"I see." Renaldo turned from his questions and moved down the hall. "Come."

Guess he would meet *Venus* tonight. "When did you develop the idea for the series we exhibited in January?"

Renaldo's steps hitched but he didn't turn. "The series you protect?"

"Yes." Scott bit the word out, already tired of the recrimination he sensed from Renaldo. Things must be much worse than he imagined for the man to exhibit such bitterness.

"I was young. Maybe twenty-one, twenty-two. This way." He barreled down a hallway that led to darkness and shadows beyond.

"Did anything trigger the inspiration? A person? An idea?"

"Why the questions? All art grows from inspiration."

"What served as yours?"

The man waved an arm toward a closed door on the first floor. An Indian soldier from the Mahratta battalion stood guard and saluted as they approached. "Maybe she remains. Her size precludes easy taking."

Was the man so distracted by his charges he couldn't carry a simple linear conversation, or was it intentional deflection? The Renaldo Adamo he knew and studied under had been open and free with his thoughts and opinions. Had the war altered that part of his character? So far the man dodged certain questions. Maybe because it related to his creative process. Some artists held those thoughts and ideas very close, even after the creation had ended.

Maybe the last months and years of protecting the art, of creating the artful dodge, made it second nature.

"So? Open the door."

Scott nodded. "Of course." It must be an amazing painting if Renaldo was acting this intent about how Scott first viewed it. "Remember I've visited the Uffizi. I've seen her collections."

"Not close. Never like this." Renaldo handed him a large brass key. "You may open it."

Chapter 27

THE GOOD-NIGHT KISS OF the sun lingered on Rachel's skin as she studied the countryside from her perch on the cooling stone. Even the distant rumbles and whistles of the artillery had stilled, maybe in the waning light recognizing the need for a pause. She shook her head. What foolishness to attribute anything so beautiful to a war machine. Both sides remained determined to win, entrenched in their respective positions, one pushing ever northward while the other refused to give way.

Now that she was ahead of headquarters, she didn't know when she'd hear from home. She should send another letter, but what could she say? Another day, another brush with danger and the unknown. Not exactly a message of hope for Momma. Still she should write something when she returned to her room, if for no other reason than to let Momma know she was still well. And then Rachel would develop the rolls of film she'd shot on the drive north and around the castle. The stills of destroyed vehicles and the dead mixed with the children at play under the watchful eyes of parents and soldiers. For now she'd rest another moment. Enjoy the quiet beauty of twilight in Tuscany. Etch it on her mind to take out and enjoy again and again after she returned home.

"Captain." That word sounded so strange when addressed toward her.

A throat cleared behind her, still she faced forward. She'd learned it best not to encourage a soldier. The man started again with clipped, accented words. "Captain, are you in need of a meal?"

She turned and took in the officer's clean appearance. "I haven't eaten. If you're offering more C rations, I'll pass."

"No, I thought you'd enjoy a real meal. The cook does a decent job. The meal's hot and not overcooked yet." He made a show of looking around. "I don't see the men you arrived with. Would you care to join me? Name's Leftenant Alistair Barkley."

"With the Indian regiment?"

"Family moved there in the late eighteen hundreds and stayed. So . . . some food?"

Her stomach rumbled and his grin widened. "My stomach answered for me. Thank you."

"Sometimes the soul needs a spot of beauty more than the stomach needs gruel."

What a beautiful way to phrase it. "Exactly, but my stomach voted." She stood and straightened her cap. "Lead on."

They walked along a side of the castle she hadn't explored, to an open area hosting a collection of tents. "That big 'un over there is the kitchen of sorts. As long as we don't get a repeat of the spring rains, we'll be good."

"Was the fight as awful as the papers said?"

The man nodded, his hands clasped behind his back. "Every bit and another foot. I've never slogged through such hideous streams of mud. Certain we'd all die around Monte Cassino. Lost too many good men. Nothing to compare it to, and I never want to repeat it."

"I'm so sorry." The reporters in Rome had told her stories he'd lived. "Have you been in Italy long?"

"I've walked every step from Sicily, ma'am."

"A terrible thing."

"Part of me wishes we'd arrived earlier. Done more to stop this. But Mussolini enjoyed power a long time."

"That he did."

He allowed her to enter the tent first. The inside smelled of some sort of stew mixed with bread and the aroma of unwashed bodies. The clank of silverware against trays stilled as she walked the line. Lieutenant Barkley flashed an apologetic smile. "The men are a little unaccustomed to seeing women around."

"Nothing I haven't grown used to." An odd thought still, as she wasn't used to stopping all conversation and attracting full attention in the States. Life was so different here.

After the privates in the serving line loaded her tray with an assortment of mystery food, she followed the officer to a long bench. The meal passed quickly. He didn't bother to fill the space with conversation, which suited her fine. Odds were too good they wouldn't cross paths again once the troops moved. However, she appreciated the opportunity to enjoy a hot meal, even with the exotic flavor lacing each bite. The man's attention was flattering too. He seemed nice, but nothing could come of it other than a pleasant hour in the midst of the war. After she finished, he grabbed her tray.

"Thank you for the company." He lifted their trays a bit. "I can't salute, but you were a welcome respite."

"Thank you for rescuing my empty stomach."

"May I escort you back to the grounds?"

She nodded, grateful not to make the trek alone. "Thank you."

The officer stepped closer as they proceeded to the courtyard. "I'm glad your editor asked for someone to check on you."

Rachel felt as if cold water doused over her. "I'm sorry?"

"Your editor contacted us and asked for someone to confirm your status."

"That's why you sought me?"

His eyebrows crinkled as he smiled. "I would have anyway. It was just nice to have an official reason."

She rolled her eyes and started walking again. "That assuages my ego." After a minute of quiet, she turned to him. "Did he do this in other places?"

The lieutenant shrugged. "I don't know but it's likely."

"That would explain things."

"What things?" He watched her intently, with an intelligence that made her want to trust him.

"I've often felt like someone followed just out of sight."

"So they weren't all as bold as me?"

Rachel laughed. "No, they weren't." She glanced around, taking in the way twilight fell in trickles. "This must be what the old writers meant by gloaming."

"Pardon?"

"I've always wondered what that felt like when I'd read the word. This fits."

He paused and turned toward her. "You are a most unique woman."

She dipped her chin. That was one way of putting it. "I've heard that before."

"You act like it's a bad thing." He tipped her chin up, and she caught her breath at the intensity in his eyes. A lock of dark hair fell over one eye, as if it had been too long since his last regulation cut. His attention never wavered as he released her chin and brushed her cheek.

She stepped away from his touch with a nervous chuckle. She did not want a war romance that could go nowhere. She needed someone who would stay.

Even as the thought trailed through her mind, Scott's words chased them. *"God is the Father who is always there. He never leaves us."*

What would that be like? To have a father who cared that much?

Lieutenant Barkley nodded at her. "Until next time."

"Thank you."

"My pleasure." The officer turned on his heel and headed back toward the tents.

She watched him move, frozen by her fears. Annie or Heidi would have prolonged the time with the officer. They would have known the words to say, the ways to move to keep him by their side as long as they wanted. Maybe Rachel didn't know how to interact with men on a romantic level because she'd never had a father to make her feel cherished and loved beyond all capacity to understand.

Could she trust God to love her like that?

The thought left her wanting to hyperventilate. To relinquish that kind of control and trust?

God, are you here? If you are, will you show me? Because I'm not sure I can trust something I can't see.

The sound of families gathered inside the grounds clashed with the soldiers moving around. She should go inside, find her way to the room before it was too dark to navigate the maze. A door stood with the top half open, letting the breeze pass into the villa. Rachel walked toward it. Maybe someone on the other side could help her find her way back to her room. A bevy of activity flowed on the other side. As she looked in, a collection of women bounced off each other as they moved about a kitchen, each focused on cooking, chopping, or other culinary skills.

Rachel grabbed her camera and took a photo. "What is this?"

A startled pause greeted her before the women took to chattering in Italian. Rachel rubbed her forehead wishing she could understand.

A thin woman stumbled forward, pushed by another. "A kitchen." She raised her chin so her dark eyes could search

Rachel's face. Her face looked drawn, pulled down by weariness and fear, yet there was a spark of hope in the way she refused to be intimidated.

"Yes, I know. But so many?"

The woman studied the ground as if searching for words. "We . . ." She looked up and ran her hands around in the air as if spinning something. "We mix together. Share."

"A community kitchen?"

Her head bobbled to the side. "Yes."

Movement toward the back caught Rachel's attention. A thin woman in a worn dress covered by a voluminous apron, one that had once been as white as her cap, gasped something, then turned to the side, her face fading to the color of her apron. Another placed a hand beneath her elbow to steady her.

"Is she okay?"

The woman who interpreted studied the woman, muttered a few words, then paused to listen. She turned back to Rachel. "Not okay. She says you a spirit."

Mutters flowed around her at the word. That must be one word that translated well in both directions.

"Why?"

The woman shrugged but said nothing.

Rachel rubbed her forehead. Wasn't her life complicated enough?

~~~⊰❈⊱~~~

"All right." Scott felt the guard eye him as he inserted the key in the doorknob and twisted. The heavy baroque door eased open, and he stepped into a darkened room. Renaldo strode toward a row of windows and pushed open the curtains.

"With the electricity out, natural light must suffice." With each set of drapes the man opened, more wonders were revealed.

Rows of dusty bookshelves lined a wall of the vaulted hall.

Against those, two or three deep, stood paintings. Rows and rows of them. In the middle of the large space stood a rack, against which more paintings leaned.

Dust played in the faint sunlight streaming into the salon. Faint rays touched an impossibly large piece. It might be larger than some rooms if laid on the floor. Scott inhaled, captivated by the color and figures posed across the canvas. *"Primavera."*

"Yes."

"I thought you had the *Birth of Venus*."

"Elsewhere. I bring you this Venus. No two masterpieces of such caliber from the same artist hide in one place. Too dangerous. Instead, I can show you *Supper at Emmaus* by Pontormo or Rubens's *Nymphs and Satyrs*. There is also Raphael's *Madonna del Baldacchino*. And in another room Ghirlandaio's *Adoration of the Magi*."

Scott stood in front of the massive frame. This was why he had come to Europe. To ensure masters like this had been preserved. Standing in the presence of this painting made everything right. "She's beautiful."

"Sì." Renaldo smiled like a proud papa displaying his treasured daughter.

"You've brought the Uffizi here."

"Yes. I would give my life for these." He turned Scott toward the sweeping work. "This is but one piece. This is what I protect."

Scott stepped closer, drawn by the figure in the middle of the massive canvas. "This is worth protecting."

"They all are." Renaldo stepped back while he absorbed the details.

"And the shelling?"

"It comes and goes, a constant companion since I arrived."

Scott nodded, understanding why the man risked so much as the intermittent, punctuated refrain of artillery whistled around the castle. If an errant shell landed at Montegufoni, better to know only one of Botticelli's life works stood exposed to destruction or harm. "Where is *Venus*?"

The man waved a hand in the air. "Irrelevant at this moment. Enjoy this . . ."

Scott walked to the windows to catch the glory of the setting sun when movement across the way caught his attention. A woman dressed in the American uniform walked next to an Indian officer. Even with her head down and away from his line of sight, he could tell it was Rachel. Who else could it be? No one else could cause his heart to stutter at sight. Nor could anyone cause this surge of protectiveness.

He didn't know the officer. Would he honor Rachel or draw something from her she didn't recognize or anticipate? Scott shut his eyes and clenched his jaw. This was ridiculous. He needed to back from the window and return to why he was here.

"What draws your attention?"

Scott tightened his fists as Rachel and the officer paused. Any other person and Tuscany in the evening light would be perfect for a romantic moment. Instead Rachel was sharing a moment he longed to have.

Now wasn't the time.

It might never come.

Renaldo approached, stood next to Scott, and looked out. Scott swallowed the urge to punch the soldier who touched a strand of Rachel's hair. She slipped a step back and lowered her chin. Yet he felt the pressure of the touch, of the man's forwardness.

Rachel would never be his.

Not while the barrier of her questions and her quest stood between them. Not while he had a niggling doubt about how she had acquired the sketchbook.

Not until some questions were answered. Questions Renaldo might answer.

Scott couldn't deny the way she drew him. Her creativity and the gift she had for seeing the things, the people, everyone else missed. The way she brought a tinge of joy to situations. There were depths to her he hadn't seen in Elaine, yet Rachel held herself aloof like an island. Isolated yet longing to join the fray around her. To do something that mattered.

"She stirs much in you. Women have great power."

Rachel turned and made her way into the courtyard. The officer returned to the sea of tents that lined the field. Good riddance.

"Who is she?"

"She takes photos of the war, sends them to papers in the States."

"Why would a woman do such a thing?"

"Because she is gifted."

"She looks familiar, but it is impossible."

Maybe not as impossible as Renaldo thought. Scott turned to him. "Who does she resemble?"

"An impossibility." Renaldo swept his hands wide. "I have never seen her before you arrived. Yet . . ." He sighed heavily.

"She had a sketchbook of preparatory drawings. For an art series. Paintings."

Renaldo shrugged, a movement Scott could feel. "And?"

"The drawings could lead to the series of your paintings my museum holds."

The man bristled. "On loan."

"Of course." Scott held his hands in front of his chest and took a step back. "Rachel asked me to look at the sketches. See if I could identify the artist."

"Did you tell her?"

"That you were the artist?" Scott shook his head. "I'm not 100 percent certain, and I couldn't think why she would have something so personal."

Renaldo nodded, then turned from the window. A slight hunch shifted his frame forward as he moved toward the painting that consumed the room with its presence.

"If it's yours, why would she have the sketchbook?" Scott kept pace with Renaldo's quick steps. The man moved as if he needed to stay a couple steps ahead of the German SS or *Kunstschutz*.

The man shrugged again, his shoulders rolling in a fluid motion. "How could I know?"

"One of life's mysteries?"

"Maybe."

There was something in the way the man refused to meet his gaze that alerted Scott that something wasn't quite right. "You have a theory."

The man pulled a pipe from his pocket and shoved it in his mouth. He chewed the end, not seeming to mind he had nothing to put in the bowl. "Life is not a straight line."

Scott nodded but remained quiet.

"Life inserts a curve. A stop. That happened with me."

"Makes life more interesting."

"More complicated." The man pulled his pipe out and pointed out the windows at the hills around Montegufoni. "You see there. Farmers have tended that plot for centuries. Maybe at first little grew. Now grapes are trained. They grow in abundance. Our lives are like that. A barren area, one that shows nothing for the work, later it flourishes."

"How does this relate to Rachel's sketchbook?"

"I wish to see it. To be certain."

Scott hesitated a moment. "I have it."

"Why, if it is hers?"

"I wanted to protect it until I could find you, see if my theory was correct."

A storm clouded his features as Renaldo thrust his shoulders back. "It was not yours."

"Nor hers." Scott stopped and inhaled the loamy scent of earth that seeped through the old windows. "It was stolen from your possession?"

The man shifted his head and grimaced. "Not from me."

Scott turned to face Renaldo. "Spit it out."

"I gave it to a woman who formed my heart one summer."

"Who?"

"It does not matter now. At the time it conveyed my love."

"But how did it get to Rachel Justice in the United States?"

The man's skin sallowed under his olive complexion. "Justice?" He took a stumbling step, then moved toward a chair. "That woman? The one out there? Her name is Justice? I'll sit now."

"Are you all right?"

Renaldo held up a hand. "It is much to take in. I have spent months trying to stay alive. Trying to keep my *famiglia* alive. And now this." His hand wavered, then sank to his lap.

Scott eased down beside his mentor, keeping a close eye on him. Maybe all the stress and tension had caught him. That didn't explain why this sketchbook held such power. The fading light filtering through the window did nothing to warm the room. Instead, goose bumps trailed up Scott's arms as he waited for Renaldo to say something. The man seemed spooked beyond what Scott would expect for a conversation about a sketchbook. Yes, it was a piece of his artistic, creative process, but more underlay his sudden pallor and need to sit.

Renaldo cleared his throat. "As a youth I knew an American. Loved her. Cherished her as best I could."

"Many of us had such a love."

"You Americans. Never let a man finish a story."

"You Italians. Always so slow to get to the point." Scott smiled at the memory of the times they'd had such discussions in the past. An answering smile did not grace Renaldo's face. "I'm sorry."

The man waved him off. He took a wavering breath, then seemed to settle something in his mind.

"Her name was Melanie Justice."

Chapter 28

RACHEL STEPPED INSIDE THE castle and walked toward the room with the window where she'd seen Scott's stormy face. One glance had told her she needed to find him and make sure he didn't need her. Then she'd develop today's film. Maybe someone with the Indian and New Zealand troops could transport it to headquarters for her and from there to the press office in Rome and her editor.

It wasn't until she found the right hallway and stepped closer to the salon that she noticed the men deep in conversation somewhere inside the room. She nodded at a sentry and slipped inside, only to return to the hallway before they could see her—the intensity on their faces warned it was more than casual. She'd wait until Scott was done talking to whoever was in there. She caught the occasional word, but she heard enough to stay riveted in place.

One glance in the room had stunned her. The soaring ceiling and the walls lined with art. Could they be discussing the paintings?

She hadn't meant to overhear, but the cavernous ceilings seemed to carry select words her direction. Just enough to leave holes she couldn't comprehend what they discussed. When she heard *Melanie Justice*, she would have rushed into the room if the sentry hadn't stepped in her path.

The soldier sidestepped out of her way quickly, but even though she wanted to rush in, she remained frozen.

How many people knew her mother's name?

It couldn't be many.

She squared her shoulders and stepped into the room.

A man brushed past her, eyes unseeing, feet rushing down the hall and away. A moment later Scott followed, but he seemed more intent on the Italian than on her. She took a step to follow, but the way Scott didn't see her stung. She'd find him later. Ask why they spoke of her mother. She retraced her steps to the room the men had occupied. The guard nodded at her but let her enter, perhaps because the door wasn't locked. Maybe in here she could find the item that launched their conversation.

The large room stood shrouded in gathering shadows. As her eyes adjusted to the dim light, she searched the wall for a switch. When she flipped it, nothing happened. Still her breath caught at what she could see in the growing darkness. So many paintings lined the walls. The treasures of Florence? The room stood empty of most furniture except for an occasional chair. She imagined hours soaking in the beauty of each piece, let alone the combined glory. All in one room. Framed canvasses stacked like cheap reproductions, one after the other in rows.

May she never grow immune to such great works.

Momma had often taken her to museums. That was her way of conveying her affection for art to her child. While Rachel tolerated the visits as a youngster and then longed to end them as she approached adulthood, she now marveled she could move as close as she wanted to each painting. No guard waited inside the room to keep her at an honoring distance from the art.

An amazing painting overtook the wall next to the door, where it rested as if waiting to be hung. It stood over six feet tall and more than ten feet wide. She felt dwarfed by its size and even by the figures painted into the scene. Each felt larger than she was. It was the sort of painting she could spend a lifetime admiring and analyzing and still miss the true story the painter had in mind.

"She is breathtaking, yes?"

She startled and turned to see the Italian had returned. "I didn't hear you."

"I can be . . . stealthy." He grinned at his word choice, revealing straight, yellowed teeth. He stood an inch or two taller than her. She met his gaze as he held a pipe in one hand, clasping the other behind his back. "I forgot to lock the door. So the painting?"

She studied the painting. "It pulls me into its story."

"Botticelli, he had a way with paint."

"Botticelli? But it isn't religious." She remembered her momma showing her several of his works in a book of collected Italian pieces. Each had told the story of a scene in the Bible, all with heavy religious undertones.

The man tsked, even that carrying a melodic Italian sound. "Sandro Botticelli did much more than that alone." He turned to study her rather than the painting. She focused on the figures and details in front of her, unsure what to make of his attention. "Italy creates many things of beauty."

What must it be like to be so comfortable with the masters that the person in front of you was more compelling? At the moment Rachel couldn't imagine as her gaze seemed glued to the scene in front of her. To stand in front of it was to be consumed by the mystery. Why paint a mythical scene? Most of his famous works held spiritual overtones like *The Nativity* or the *Adoration of the Magi*. Had his patron, possibly a member of the Medici family, ordered it?

"Venus in her created glory." The Italian accent colored the English words with a heavy stroke, one that drew her to pay attention to his words. She had the sense she didn't want to miss anything he might say.

"Why Venus?"

"Why anything?" The man stepped closer to the painting. "I have loved this painting since I instructed in Florence. See the detail? The multitude of flora in her garden?"

Rachel nodded. It was impossible to miss the patterns and variety. The central woman captivated her. The red cloth she held draped around her form, not shielding her shy yet knowing smile. Her head cocked as if she gave her full attention to the person standing before the painting. It seemed an invitation to share secrets. Come closer and maybe she'd whisper hers in exchange for learning one or two of yours.

Rachel stepped back, away from the magnetic beauty that begged her to come ever closer, to risk her questions. "It tells a story."

"Much like your camera." He pointed the pipe at her constant companion.

"I suppose." She held the camera up. "May I?"

"Me?"

"With the painting."

The man shrugged, a mix of pleasant smile and shyness warring on his face. He stepped near, then shuffled his feet with one hand on his hip and the pipe held to his mouth.

"Look at her."

"Ah, Venus. She demands attention." The man pivoted a degree toward the painting. "I have known few women with her beauty."

Rachel adjusted her camera, then snapped a shot. Then another. She prayed her editor would see the value in photos of an art superintendent who had worked so hard to save the beauty he now admired. Standing with the fruit of his labor in such an unlikely spot. If only she could send a sound track to accompany the photo, then the world could hear how near the battle trudged to the depositories. Replicate this moment across Italy times the number of pieces saved. It would astound those who saw, but she could capture this image, this man.

She finished, then let the camera hang around her neck. "Why store them here?"

"A way to keep them from the war. Little did anyone anticipate the armies marching through this quiet valley." He shrugged. "We did what we could." He looked past her as if seeing into another place. "There are many more. . . . I wish . . . ah . . ."

"What happened to them?"

"They were scavenged." His features tightened. "Soldiers took what pleased them." He stood in thought, then made that laconic motion again, one that seemed to move his whole frame. "But these I protected." He led her to a chair. "Why did you come?"

"I wanted to be part of this story, but I also have a personal mission."

"Sounds important."

"It is . . . to me." She closed her mouth before she shared too much with the kind man. But her mother's name?

"Have you been successful?"

"It is hard since I seek a man. It was crazy to hope I could find someone during war."

"Who do you seek? Maybe I can help."

"I don't know his name. Only that he was a close friend of my mother's. I had a clue with a sketchbook, but it's disappeared. It was crazy to hope I could find someone based on sketches."

The man studied her with compassion softening his expression. "Crazy keeps us alive in these times."

"I suppose." She smiled at him as he stifled a yawn. "I must let you go."

"Now you are here, I will return to Florence to see what I can save there."

"But the Germans remain."

"As does my wife. If I am gone long, things will not go well for her."

"Of course." She frowned at the thought of the tension he must feel. "Lieutenant Lindstrom will protect these paintings."

"This I know. He is honorable."

"Yes." The man turned to go, but she needed him to wait while she gathered her courage. To ask a question. "Wait."

The man turned sharply at her words.

"One question? Please?"

"I must leave."

"This will only take a moment."

He nodded, then glanced at his watch.

Rachel inhaled, then squared her shoulders. "I don't have the sketchbook, but maybe you can still help. Did you meet an American woman who studied art in Florence in 1920."

"Many study art in Firenze." The man paused as if torn between asking a question of his own and fleeing. "It is rich with heritage and beauty."

"Of course." She tugged together her collapsing courage. If he planned to leave, she must spit it out now. "This woman was sketched by a local artist."

"Often students serve as models too." The man blew out a puff of air, as if his pipe was filled with tobacco and lit. "A name?"

"Melanie Justice. You spoke of her as I arrived. Why?"

"I must leave." He turned on his heel and left.

The walls of the large bedroom pressed against Scott. Quite a feat for a room that could house several refugee families. Tyler hadn't reappeared since they'd arrived. Rachel might as well have evaporated in a mist. He hadn't glimpsed her since he'd seen her through the window.

She could do as she wished, and if that included cheering a soldier, who was he to discourage it?

A small, petty man to feel the flood of jealousy that appeared when the soldier brushed her cheek. Skin so soft his fingers still sensed the smoothness.

Rolls of weariness crested in him. Being ever alert on the drive up had taken exhausting vigilance. Then the arrival contained a mix of excitement to see Renaldo, to know he was fine, that he'd survived the battles so far. That was tempered with the reality the man was tied to Rachel's mother. He should retrieve the sketchbook and take it to Renaldo so his mentor could confirm whether he drew the sketches. Then Scott could figure out how to tell Rachel he had taken it.

"Can't believe I found my way back. Never seen so many sets of stairs that go in different directions. None connected." Tyler strutted into the room, smelling of garlic. "These refugees are quite accommodating. Grateful to have the Americans arrive."

"I wouldn't say the army's arrived."

"But we're here." Tyler slouched against the pillow on his bed. "Any luck finding your art thief?"

"None." Scott sighed. "The person remains a ghost."

"I've got a theory."

"Yeah?" Might as well listen since he didn't have a good one.

"What if it's Rachel?"

Scott bolted upright. He didn't like the direction Tyler's thoughts turned his. "Are you crazy?"

"She has access traveling with you. And who would search her bags?"

"You have the same access."

"Sure, but I'm with the jeep. She always carries a bag too. Do you think it's just her camera?"

"Women carry bags."

"In a war zone?"

"When did women start coming to wars? It's all new."

"I bet if you searched her bags, you'd find something." Tyler shrugged.

Scott didn't like it, but there was a thief. "If it's not Rachel, who could it be?"

"You."

Tyler's short word brought Scott up short, hitting too close to the truth. "Me?"

"You're the expert. You're the one telling us where to go. Why not you?" There was a spark of something dangerous in the man's eyes. Did he know?

"Who else?"

"Every soldier out there. Most don't have a clue what they walk by every day."

"And you do?"

"More than most." Tyler shrugged. "It's your problem. I'm off to find a sweet woman to watch the stars with." He sauntered out of the room.

Scott stared at the door separating his room from Rachel's. He could search her bags, but he didn't want to. What would he do if he found something? And what if she walked in? He groaned as the thought wedged into his mind. He should search Tyler's too, let them search his after he gave the sketchbook to Renaldo. Then they'd all be clear, and he could focus his energy on finding the thief.

One soldier probably took one, another stole a second. None understanding exactly what they liberated. Maybe the only way to clear the lingering doubt about Rachel was to search. Then he'd know one way or another.

He shook off the thoughts. Tonight he'd get paperwork caught up so DeWald knew where Scott was, what he'd found, and could select other MFAA men to join him. And Florence waited around the corner. The twenty or so kilometers had never seemed longer.

He closed his eyes and imagined the narrow, lined streets. The apartments that closed in from above as the roads neared the bridges that crisscrossed the Arno and connected the sides of Florence. His favorite was Ponte Vecchio with its multistoried shops that looked ready to spill from the bridge, which had been in use since medieval times. The bridges were another piece of the artistic glory of the city that shone like a jewel along the Arno.

He pulled out the typewriter DeWald had insisted he bring north from Rome to type reports. Scott groaned when he knocked over the stacked bags as he tugged. One spilled open. Great, now he'd have to clean that up too. Just what he wanted. Especially since it looked like it was Tyler's. Scott set the typewriter on his bed, then moved to the mess. Standard government-issued clothing mixed with personal items. *Better shove it in and get on with things. Let Tyler put it all back just so.*

He thrust things in the bag, then his fist collided with a hard, sharp edge.

He froze. Each person was entitled to privacy even in the close quarters life in the army dictated. But if that was art . . . should he look?

Footsteps echoed in the hallway. *Now or never.* In that moment of hesitation, the door opened.

Scott tugged the item out far enough to see it was a book. Why would Tyler carry a heavy book around if the man never read?

Tyler stepped into the room as Scott pushed another item in the bag. "All the ladies have gone to bed." He looked at Scott and frowned. "Care to explain what you're doing?"

"Must not have zipped your bag."

"Sure." His eyes tapered at the edge reflecting skepticism.

Scott stood, pulling the bag up with him. "Here. You can put it back together."

The man took the bag to his bed in the alcove. "You could have left it on the floor."

"For you to trip on whenever you came back? Thought I'd help you out since it's pretty dim around here. Next time I'll remember to leave it as is."

Tyler turned his back to Scott as he tried to tug the zipper up. Scott kept his gaze glued on the contents. How should he approach this with Tyler?

More footsteps came toward the room, this time the more-pointed tap of Rachel's steps when she wasn't in boots. "Hey, boys."

"Rachel." Scott's word was short and abrupt, but between keeping an eye on Tyler and feeling guilty around her, he was done in.

"Everything all right?" She lingered in the doorway as if uncertain she should enter.

Scott sighed. With both of them here, he'd have to wait until morning to retrieve the sketchbook and show it to Renaldo. "Sure, we're all right. Ready to turn in?"

She worried her lower lip between her teeth as she watched both of them. He wished he could know which one she thought crazier. The guy shoving clothes in a bag while glowering or the guy who bit her head off. At the moment neither of them sounded like a winner.

"It has been a long day."

"Leave her alone, Lindstrom. She's a big girl and doesn't need you to tell her what to do unless you want to look at her bag too." Tyler turned toward her. "Soldier boy here was digging through my bag when I came in. Might want to check yours. Makes me wonder what he's hiding."

Rachel stood taller and her eyes narrowed. "Tell me you weren't in my room."

"I wasn't. I'd never go through your things without permission." Well, except that one time, but he'd had a great reason. One he hoped she'd understand and forgive.

"Guess you get preferential treatment."

"Look, Tyler, your bag fell over. Next time I'm not touching it." Scott took a step toward Rachel. "I promise I didn't dig through your bag." Now he could never ask her to look through it without her knowing he'd lied.

"Do you need to?" Was that hurt lingering in her eyes even as she tipped her chin to meet his gaze?

"No."

"That makes me feel better."

"I'm sorry." Scott backed up a step. "Who knows where we'll be tomorrow, so let's relax and get a good night's rest. In the morning I'll update headquarters and request permission to stay here until we can head to Florence."

"I thought we had permission already." Rachel played with a thread hanging from a jacket sleeve.

"I'll need to update them on what we've found. There are more depositories in this area. I need to alert others and make sure that's taken into account with the planning."

Tyler grunted. "Always taking care of the art. Last I checked it was lifeless."

"But it speaks beauty to the soul. Something we need."

"You're nuts, Lindstrom." Tyler pushed past Rachel and then stomped out of the room.

She stumbled but caught herself. "What's his problem?"

"That is one of life's grand mysteries." Scott stifled a smile at the realization he was finally alone with Rachel, even if she was annoyed with him. His smile faded as the guilt settled across his shoulders.

"Well, good night." Rachel slipped past him and into her room. A moment later the door clicked and the bolt turned in the lock.

He was locked out of more than her room. How many more locks would she add when she realized what he had done?

Chapter 29

August 2

THE SOFT COLORS OF the Tuscan countryside bathed in summer light clashed with the whistling of artillery shells flying overhead. Rachel ducked her chin and tried to pretend the sound came from far over the hills that surrounded Montegufoni. But when the drone of planes added to the underlying crescendo of noise, she ran for the castle's portico.

After the conflict with Scott and Tyler the previous night, Rachel had thought she'd start the day with a quiet morning walk. She'd rather soak in the unique beauty than stumble around the castle, bumping into refugees she couldn't help. The need was so great and overwhelming, tears kept forming in her eyes. She longed for the resources to put shoes on the children's feet and food in their hopeless mothers' hands. Instead she'd slipped to a side of the villa without attracting the attention of either the children with eyes that begged for relief or the soldiers amused that an American woman walked among them.

Something skittered across her path and around her ankles, tripping her up. Rachel fell to her knees, feeling the burn of bruised and abraded skin. The whine of the shells came closer, confirming the Germans had decided to target the castle or at least the nearby artillery. She needed to get up, to move, before the next shell landed beside her, but her limbs had turned lethargic and unresponsive.

Velvety fur brushed her leg, and she looked down to find a black-and-white kitten twining around her feet. "Hello." She picked up the ball of fur. "Where did you come from?"

Rachel needed shelter, but she could imagine the reaction if she brought the kitten with her.

In a time when those in the communal kitchen had inadequate food to provide more than a vegetable-based soup with hearty bread for those seeking shelter, she should leave the little guy on the ground and walk away. But she couldn't. She tucked the kitten under her chin and stroked its soft fur, taking comfort from its quiet rumbles that contrasted with the whines flying across the sky.

The kitten wiggled against her hold, and she eased down to release him. He scampered away as another shell whizzed nearby. He pounced under a lilac bush, batting at a branch. Maybe he had the right idea for shelter. The grounds were filled with people hunting for safety, the screams of scared children, the silent stares of others weary of the barrage. Tucked in one of the castle's corners, the lilac bush might provide limited shelter if a shell landed nearby.

Rachel knelt for a closer look and caught her breath when her gaze collided with dark eyes. "Hello there."

The urchin stared at her without a word.

"Are you all right?"

The child studied her but stuck two fingers in her mouth as if to plug any words. The child appeared fine, no more shaken by the chaos than the kitten. The kitten ran right into the girl's knee and bounced back on his hindquarters, then shook his head. A soft smile blooming across her face, the child reached down and picked up the kitten.

"Well, enjoy the kitten." Rachel sucked in a steadying breath and whispered a prayer.

God would protect the ancient castle, right? If not for the sake of tradition and the hundreds who sought shelter there, then for the priceless art stored inside. Her heart cried at the thought of *Primavera* and all the others hidden inside. The Botticelli stacked next to an Allori. Famed pieces created at the direction of the Medici family over the centuries and now historic pieces of Florentine and Italian art and culture.

If Scott and the superintendant were right, the masters found safety ensconced in the castle. Yet another group of guests that graced the great home through its several hundred-year history.

The rumbles moved beyond the hills she could see.

Too many families sought refuge within the walls of Montegufoni. If anything happened here, the refugees would be set adrift once again to dodge the combating armies. She shuddered at what that would mean for the old men, women, and children. A baby's wail carried on the breeze, a welcome change, but other than that the people remained quiet.

She'd started her walk in front of *Primavera*. The art met a need deep in her soul.

To take an idea and spin it on its axis.

To take a thought and give it dimensions unseen.

To take a musical note and give it visual wings.

The sound of a plane jerked her from her thoughts. This one sounded close, the risk near. She glanced around, frantic. The castle lay too far away to reach the safety of its thick walls. Yet if she stood here, in the open, the machine gun alone could strafe and kill. Shelter, she needed shelter.

Her gaze landed on a small building. Its walls couldn't stop much, but some shelter was better than none, and at least it could hide her from view and provide more protection than the lilac. She rushed toward it, then slowed as she heard a panicked whimper.

She turned back and crawled under the lilac. "Come with me." She tugged on the girl's wrist and gestured. "Hurry. We have to hurry."

The sound of the plane drew closer as she freed the girl's braid from where it had tangled in the bush's branches. She dragged the girl behind her, rushing toward the safety of the shelter. She bounced into the door. Tried the doorknob. It refused to move. She twisted it again and again.

"Please?" *God, I need help. If not for my sake, for this little one. I can't watch another child die.*

There had to be a key somewhere close so it was easy to access the inside. She ran her fingers along the top of the door frame. She grasped metal. The key.

The lock gave as she thrust the key in and twisted. "Come on, sweetie."

The girl didn't move, didn't speak, just stood stiff and frail. Rachel tugged her in and closed the door. "We'll hide here. Shh, we'll be okay."

The girl stared past her, a vacant look in her eyes. Rachel's heart cinched at what the child could have endured that created emptiness where she'd seen such vibrancy minutes earlier. Rachel gathered the child in her arms. The dank space seemed empty of all but cobwebs and debris. A depression sank in the middle of the floor. Had it been a well at one time? She couldn't see much in the dark corners. Rachel edged toward the wall and sank next to it clutching the child, hoping that would be enough to keep her safe.

God, does your heart break for her?

Rachel hoped so. Isn't that what a daddy did? Hold his little girl and keep her safe even when the world fell apart around her? How she needed someone to do that for her.

Violent vibrations tremored through the earth.

How close had that shell landed?

Far enough away that their shack still protected them. The child moaned, a keening sound that pierced Rachel.

"It's all right, darling. It's all right." The words felt hollow. Who was she to make promises?

She needed something to distract the child. She set the girl on the floor and tipped her chin up until she could see her wide eyes. "I'm not leaving. Just looking for something." Rachel had no idea if the child heard and understood, but she'd tried.

The darkness hid the edges of the room, and nothing stood out in the dim light that she could use. The thought of disturbing whatever hid in the corners made Rachel want to fling open the door and run, but until the sound of the plane disappeared, she'd stay with the little girl.

She eased to her feet and dragged one foot along the edge of the building. Maybe her shoes could protect her from anything that might not appreciate a disturbance. She made it along two walls when her foot collided with something. It didn't make noise, so it wasn't a metal box. She knelt in front of the box, then pulled it toward her. It was the size of a hatbox. When she removed the lid, all she found were a pile of papers and some pencils. Would the girl doodle in the dark? Unlikely.

Why would someone tuck a box filled with papers in this abandoned space?

The little girl's wails renewed and accelerated, and Rachel returned to her side. "I wish I could help." She pulled the girl onto her lap and hummed the song her momma had sung over her each time she needed comforting.

"Jesus loves me, this I know."

Her momma's face had always acquired a sheen of peace, relaxation seeping from her to Rachel as she hummed or sung the words. Could Rachel accept the words the song communicated? Did her momma believe or sing? They hadn't darkened many church doors during her childhood, but maybe that had more to do with protecting her from others' reactions to her status than her momma's lack of faith. In fact, Momma had made sure they were at church on what she called the important days: Christmas, Easter, Thanksgiving. Days Momma said they needed to let God know they valued what he had done.

Silence settled. A silence so deep it took Rachel a minute to recognize the planes were gone. Then the sound of life returning sank in.

Rachel should struggle to her feet, but one foot had fallen asleep tucked beneath her other leg. She shifted and waited as her foot prickled to life. Had she taken her momma's protection of her as a lack of faith?

God, I want to believe. I want to know You as my Father. Will You stay with me?

A whisper of hope eased through her. This was something she needed to explore further. It felt like a baby step, but it was a start.

The child relaxed in her arms. It felt like a mirror of what she'd done with God. She smiled as she struggled to stand with the dead weight. Somehow she knew God wouldn't struggle. He'd carry her if she'd let Him.

The door flung open, and Rachel squinted against the surge of brightness that blinded her.

"Rachel, thank God!" Scott's words sounded broken. "I saw you run in here as the attack started. And I couldn't do anything to get here. If something had happened, . . ." The words trailed off as if the thought was too terrible to complete. He moved to her and pulled Rachel close. He kissed her until her thoughts clouded, and she leaned into him as much as she could while holding the girl.

He pulled back and touched his forehead to hers. "Don't ever disappear like that again." He looked around the small space. "Why come here rather than the castle? You would have died. . . ."

"Castle walls wouldn't stop shells. It's just more to be buried under." She swayed under the weight of the girl and her words.

"Who's this?"

"A little girl I found tangled in a lilac bush. She couldn't get free."

"Let's get you both out of here. I'd wager her parents are frantic."

Rachel nodded and let him ease the child from her arms. She sagged under the relief of him lifting the burden. She had to tell him what had happened, but as he barreled out of the building with the girl, she held her tongue. She'd tell him when the moment was right. When he could hear the wonder of the journey she'd restarted.

The rest of the day passed in a daze of evaluating the damage and comforting those she could. She took photos, but her focus remained on the people rather than the images. They'd been fortunate—none of the shells had collided with a building. Instead, cypress trees had been uprooted and a few tents destroyed. Guess the dirty tents had been too tempting a target for the pilot. A few soldiers had been injured, but the group had escaped largely unharmed. The little girl's parents had scooped her from Scott's grasp and disappeared with her in a flurry of grateful Italian and relieved tears.

Later that evening things settled down, and Rachel's thoughts returned to the box in the corner of the small building. In the middle of the attack, she'd noticed sketches along the outside of the box that reminded her of those in her sketchbook. She returned to the courtyard, determined to find the little girl, to see for herself that the child was fine. However, the child and her parents had disappeared.

Rachel wandered, drawn back to that small shack. Had it been a well house at some point? Now it was a dilapidated structure that had provided shelter when she needed. She tried the door but someone had locked it. She still had a key in her pocket, where she'd thrust it earlier.

She stood in front of the door, inhaling deeply, then releasing the air in a slow exhale. The battle had shifted, but as she stood there, she heard a sound track of plane engines and whistling artillery.

"Either do this or go back inside." She muttered the words, waiting for courage to flood her or at least enough self-embarrassment to get her moving. She stuck the key in the hole, twisted the knob, and reentered her sanctuary. The box had been in the far corner, and she knelt in front of it. She tried to examine the box, and then shuffled through the papers as best she could in the near darkness. To learn more she'd have to carry the box to her room. She grabbed it and stood, then made her way to the castle, walking like she had every right to the box.

As she stepped through the French doors, she collided with someone. She gripped the box hard to keep from dropping it but was startled when the woman started yelling in Italian. Rachel examined the woman—the cook who'd acted so odd the prior night. Now she placed a hand over her heart, pointing at the box with the other hand as she backed away from Rachel.

"Ma'am? Can I help you?"

The woman shrieked and raced back toward the kitchen.

Chapter 30

FROM THE MOMENT HE woke up, the day was utter chaos mixed with uncertainty. At Montegufoni the evidence of why Scott had given up his comfortable job and his future with Elaine lay stacked around multiple rooms. He'd felt a fresh aliveness from the moment Renaldo had shown him *Primavera* and known with certainty he was here for important work.

The air raid brought the war to the castle's door. The German plane had swooped back and forth for no more than five or ten minutes. It had probably been a short lark to break up an otherwise boring flight for the pilot. But Scott had stood paralyzed in fear the moment he realized the plane was shooting while Rachel was outside.

The near miss still shook him as he paced. It had taken determination to let Rachel walk around the castle without hovering. She'd insisted she should check on the girl and wanted to do it alone.

He pulled the sketchbook from his bag. He wanted to take one more look before handing it to Renaldo for his verdict. If only the man hadn't left for Florence. The way the artist had drawn the woman indicated an attention born of love. Perhaps the kind Renaldo had spoken of in relation to Melanie Justice.

Since her mother had been in Italy and had the sketchbook, she had to be the one Renaldo had loved—if he was the artist. If that was correct, it led to one conclusion.

Renaldo Adamo was Rachel's father. The man she'd come to Italy to find.

Against all common sense she'd found him.

Yet she didn't know because of his deception.

~~~

Tyler's heavy footsteps ricocheted as he whistled a hollow tune that echoed in the hallway. Scott grimaced as he took a seat in the lone comfortable chair in the room, setting the sketchbook behind him. The last thing he needed was Tyler seeing the journal and jumping to conclusions. Tyler continued down the hallway without entering the room. Scott stood and hurried to the door. When he reached the hallway, Tyler turned the corner. Something about the glimpse Scott got, the way the man carried himself, made him think it hadn't been Tyler after all.

Scott clenched his jaw as he returned to the room and settled back into the chair. The walls felt like they were closing in, but he needed to wait in the one place he knew he could find Tyler and Rachel. Both had to return to sleep in their beds.

The first half of the book held peaceful images of the haunting woman in the Tuscan countryside, but near the end of the book were images that could be early sketches of the paintings Scott had brought to the States for the exhibit. They were dark, filled with the terror of trench warfare during the Great War. Scott didn't remember Renaldo serving, but maybe he had. The quick pencil strokes conveyed emotion that even in rough form forced him inside the scene.

The sound of the door squeaking on its hinges caused him to

jerk. The book slid from his lap to the floor. He scrambled upright and was groping for the book when he heard a gasp.

"Scott? You took my book?"

He straightened, looking from Rachel to the sketchbook and back. His mouth moved, but he couldn't form words. She considered him, posture stiff, and he could feel her anger.

"Come here, and I'll tell you what I've learned."

"Okay."

He vacated the chair and offered to take the dusty box she carried, but she clutched it close. "What's in there?"

"Papers of some sort." She sank onto the chair.

"Where did you find it?"

"In the well house." She studied him until he wanted to squirm like a child caught misbehaving. "Why do you have my sketchbook?"

"It's not yours."

Color climbed her throat, and her hands tightened to fists on the sides of the box. "Excuse me?"

"I just meant you didn't draw the sketches."

"I never claimed I did."

This book mattered immensely to her. "I took this to try to figure out why you had it."

"Why?" Her face paled, and the edges of her mouth trembled. "You had no right."

"I can't understand why your mother would have a book of this importance."

"It was a gift. I don't know why."

"But who is she? Why would she have a sketchbook from an Italian artist?"

Rachel took the lid off the hatbox and focused her attention on the contents before looking at him, disappointment flooding her eyes. "All you had to do was ask. I trusted you."

Her hurt sliced through him. What had he damaged with his betrayal? "I'm sorry."

"You're a thief." Her voice shuddered. "You stole something precious from me and then let me think it was gone." She set the box down and launched to her feet. "I trusted you!"

Rachel snatched the book from his hands and seemed to grab her heart back with the same move. Scott edged toward her, but she held up a hand. "Stop."

"Rachel, . . ."

"I can't believe you did this. I thought you were different. That you might care about me. I should have known it was all about the art."

Her words pushed him back, a barrier of truth in the face of his deception. "You're right." He'd let his hunger to know the story get in the way of his good sense. "I knew better. All I can say is I'm sorry, Rachel."

She shuddered as she held the book against her chest. "This is the best link I have to my father, and I'm not even certain it's his. I have to find him though. Without medical treatment my mom will die. Even a little money could make the difference in her living and dying. We have no family, so the hope he would help is all I have."

"Most artists are penniless."

"Not all. This one needs money and a caring heart." She shrugged. "As far as I know, my mom never asked anything of him. I will." Her face fell. "If I can find him."

Scott sorted through the information. Should he get word to Renaldo? He'd seen Rachel and Renaldo leave the storage room, so Renaldo must have figured out Rachel was his daughter. If not, should he?

The problem was, he'd caught a fleeting glance of Renaldo that morning but had not talked to him. He hadn't found the man in the chaos after the attack. Only heard he'd left.

An uncomfortable silence filled the room as Rachel picked up the hatbox and sketchbook. She moved toward her room, and Scott didn't know how to stop her and make it better. He'd messed up. Royally.

She stopped in the doorway. "This morning I prayed. I think I believe. I'm at least trying. I can imagine God as a father now. And I hated the idea of that . . . before we started talking." Her gaze collided with his. "All I could think this morning was that you were the one person I wanted to tell. I thought you'd celebrate with me. Now I don't know if you're who I thought you were."

Scott grinned, one that grew from the joy in his heart and exploded on his face, even as her last words stung. "I'm so glad, though I'm sorry I've hurt you."

"Thank you." She studied her hands. "I know enough to know I need to forgive you, but I can't. Not yet."

"Every faith journey starts with a small step." He wanted to pull her into a celebratory hug but restrained himself considering how he'd betrayed her. "We'll find you a Bible. Get you introduced to Jesus. Do you know much about Him?"

"I know His song."

"His song?" Which one would she consider His?

"'Jesus Loves Me.' And I remember things from Sunday school."

"That's a great beginning."

She eased back on the bed and removed the lid from the hatbox, the hooded expression still on her face. "When will we move?"

"It depends on the front. Hopefully it won't stall between here and Florence." The box remained open but untouched. "Will you examine what's in the box?"

He watched the light ebb from her face as if scrubbed away by the memories. "Tomorrow. Right now I'm ready for a new day." She replaced the lid. "Do you think I'm crazy to believe the artist is my father?"

"No." Where was Renaldo? "I think you should show it to the art superintendent."

"Renaldo Adamo?"

"Yes. He might recognize it."

"I think you're right."

Fear filled her expression. "What if he doesn't want me?"

"Then you'll still be an amazing woman." He wanted to step forward, to comfort her, but the reality of where they were, alone in a bedroom, kept him frozen in place. One step in that direction would be dangerous based on the way he longed to wrap her in his arms and never let go.

~~≈~~

The small bedroom stifled Rachel like a prison as she sat on her bed. Her ears were hyperattuned to every sound on the other side of the wall. The good news was the walls were thick enough to prevent much from reaching her.

The art superintendent had filtered in and out of her thoughts. Now she wanted to find him, but not with Scott. She feared what he would say or do when he saw the sketchbook. Her heart still smarted from his betrayal. He probably believed his reasons for taking the sketchbook were honorable, but it hurt to know he'd done it, seen her distress over its loss, and never said anything until she caught him with it.

The box sat next to her, the sketchbook on top. Rachel fingered the binding, aching from Scott's deceit. Her belief he was more honorable than other men had shattered the moment she saw him with the book. She closed her eyes and tried to remember the peace she'd felt, the presence that had seemed to settle next to her in that small building.

God, You're real, right? I haven't suddenly started talking to my imagination, have I?

A calm overwhelmed her, and she wanted to cry with relief. She wanted to learn to walk in this peace. Her journey truly had just begun.

Help me forgive Scott. He's hurt me, but I don't want to hold it close.

The hatbox teased her. The flickering candle on her bedside table cast enough light to see inside. She could open it and evaluate the contents. She moved the sketchbook and pulled off the top. A set of charcoal pencils and a nubby eraser sat on a stack of thick sketching paper. She removed the pencils and eraser. Next she examined the stack of papers. The first few didn't look more impressive than what she could draw with effort and focus.

Then she flipped to another page, and her fingers trembled. This drawing had details and a style that mirrored one she knew well from the sketchbook. To confirm, Rachel flipped to the page. While not identical, the symmetry struck her. Could the artist be the same and here at Montegufoni?

The next sketch had a contemporary style, the sweeping landscape of the prior sketch abandoned for a reckless still life that was all harsh lines and angles. Incomplete sketches of a woman's features followed that. Here an eye, there a chin, and on another page a sensuous mouth. Whoever she was, the artist had endeavored to capture the minutiae of the woman's every line and shadow, yet her sketchbook just revealed a shadowed profile.

Rachel sat back after examining each sketch. They all reflected the talent of the artist. A couple even bore a scratched *R* and *A*.

Why would a box of collected sketches and scribbles be hidden in an outbuilding at Montegufoni?

Maybe she was getting ahead of herself. Scott would be better positioned to tell her how her insights matched an art expert's. Would he bother to help her after the way they'd separated? She swallowed her pride and approached the door separating their rooms. She'd heard no movement for a while. Maybe he'd turned in for the night.

She tapped the door, loud enough to be heard but quiet enough to avoid waking him unless he was a light sleeper.

A moment later someone approached the door. "Yes?"

"Do you have a minute?" She swallowed around the sudden cotton in her throat. "I'd like your opinion."

There was a moment of silence, then the door opened revealing Scott, still dressed in his uniform. He eyed her cautiously. "How can I help?"

She glanced behind him. "Is Tyler back?"

"No." Scott's expression clouded. "I have no idea where he is or when he'll return. Better be soon since he has the jeep keys."

"I need an art expert and you're here. Unless Renaldo would be a better choice."

"He left for Florence." At her frown he shrugged. "Earlier he told his sister he needed to protect its art. Must have left after the attack."

"And his wife." Echoes of their conversation flowed into her memory.

Scott leaned against the door frame. "How can I help?"

She held up a couple sketches. "The hatbox is filled with drawings. Some struck me as similar to the sketchbook. Could the same artist have created them?"

"Anything's possible."

"What do you think?"

He studied her a moment, then nodded. "Let me see."

She handed over two sketches that seemed most similar to the book. She bit her lip to keep from giving more of an opinion. Better to let him examine them and see if he reached the same conclusion.

"Can I see the sketchbook?"

She hesitated a moment.

"I promise I'll return it." His tipped grin softened her concerns.

"Here."

He studied them a minute, flipping back and forth. "Why do you think the same artist drew these?"

"There's a sketch in there." She reclaimed the book and flipped it open. "This one. See how the view is so similar? And the woman's profile looks identical?"

"Maybe." His gaze bounced between the two, but he didn't say anything more.

After a few minutes the silence annoyed her. "What do you think?"

"I don't know." He handed the book and drawings back to her. "There are similarities, and if Renaldo is the artist, it's likely he drew both. But if it's another man, he's in Rome and wouldn't come to Montegufoni. I don't want to disappoint you."

"That's gallant." Especially after what he'd done. She sighed. *Forgiveness, Rachel.* She took a breath, then spoke. "I don't need you to protect me from disappointment. Did you notice the initials on the loose drawings?"

He squinted at the two sketches. "I see that. An *R* and an *A.*" He held them back to her. "If I'm right—" he held up a hand as she opened her mouth, "Renaldo drew these. But someone else could have. The way to know for sure is to show them to him."

Rachel felt the blood drain from her head as she hurried to her feet. "He knew who I was." The truth hit her . . . hard. "He knew and he still left."

"You may be right."

Rachel grabbed the sketches and stumbled back to her room.

Chapter 31

August 2

SCOTT SANK ONTO HIS bed. His body told him it was late, that he needed a long installment of rest after the adrenaline-laced day. Why would Renaldo hide sketches like those at Montegufoni?

It bothered him almost as much as Renaldo leaving. His mentor had left, taking off without warning or a good-bye. It felt like the man ran to the Germans in his effort to run away from something . . . or someone . . . else.

Had Scott's mention of Rachel caused Renaldo's sudden return to Florence? Or had it been his subsequent visit with Rachel?

Whatever the cause, Scott wanted to know.

Scott tossed and turned all night and spent the early morning updating reports and inventorying the castle. Renaldo had provided a detailed list of everything that left Florence. It could take a week to explore the castle's rooms and match the art he found with those listed. *Primavera* was easy to identify; some of the others were much lesser known works.

Scott grabbed the list and his attaché case, then knocked on Rachel's door. If she helped, the work could progress faster. Especially since Private Salmon hadn't appeared.

After a minute he knocked again, this time hearing movement.

"Yes?" Rachel had dark circles under her eyes and her hair stuck out at funny angles, but she still looked beautiful.

"I'm getting ready to tackle an inventory of the art. Would you help?"

Rachel rubbed her face and then looked up at him, a face so appealing he longed to pull her close for a kiss that would remove any doubt or fear of him from her mind. "I can be ready in a minute."

"I'd appreciate it."

She turned, then looked over her shoulder at him. "Wait for me?"

"Yes." The words he'd-wait-the-rest-of-his-days-if-she'd-ask almost slipped past his lips. What had gotten into him? He needed a tighter rein on his attraction. Rachel was an amazing woman who pulled the best from him . . . when he wasn't stealing from her. He slumped against the wall with a groan. Someday she'd understand, and he'd forgive himself. He'd wanted to protect her, be her hero in the midst of the chaos of war, but had failed.

A minute later she breezed out.

"How do you do that?"

"Do what?"

"Get ready so fast. My mom would take twenty minutes even when we had nowhere to go."

She played with the silver chain around her neck. "There's not much use primping here." Even so, soft color painted her cheeks. Maybe she was glad he'd noticed.

"I thought we'd start in the salon. With Renaldo gone, we'll have to be careful we don't miss anything."

Rachel remained quiet as they worked their way downstairs. "Do you think there's an attic where they'd hide valuable paintings?"

Scott thought about it. "Maybe. I need to find the caretakers Renaldo assigned."

"Who?"

"Renaldo didn't leave the paintings unguarded. A couple farmers have the task. Maybe they can give us guidance." He looked out a window, taking in the view. "Let's explore what's around us and track where we've been."

Maybe he could keep her out of trouble. And maybe the Germans would pull out of Florence without a fight.

❧

August 3

The salon's erratic collection felt like a mad art collector's home. The paintings sat in an odd assortment of frames—some so elaborate they overwhelmed the painting, others so simple they looked like something her momma would have purchased at a five-and-dime. Each was a different size and contained different subjects. She couldn't discern a pattern. Thirteenth-century masters were stacked next to those of the sixteenth century. Then brightly colored, gold-leaved altarpieces leaned next to small landscapes next to portraits. The altarpieces were a variety of tri-folds that would be wall mounted and smaller pieces that would sit on a table. There was even a collection of crucifixes on the floor. A truly eclectic collection that made her appreciate her mother's lectures in Philadelphia's various museums.

She walked toward the crosses, noting the pained expressions on Christ's face. "Why would He do that?"

"What?" Scott looked up from the stack of paper he held.

"Allow them to hang Him on the cross. If He's truly God's Son, why not force His way down?"

"It was the only way to restore our relationship with God."

A powerful God would allow that to be done to His child? "If God is the best Father, wouldn't He protect His Son at all costs?"

Scott nodded. "That's exactly what He did. He sacrificed His Son so the rest of us would have the opportunity to become His children. Sin creates a barrier of separation Jesus' death destroyed. Now the barrier's gone, and the choice is ours. To approach God out of gratefulness for what Jesus did and offer our lives to Him or to remain behind a broken barrier." Scott set the inventory aside. "The best news is that though Jesus died, He rose from the dead. So while the crucifix shows Him on the cross, Christians know He's no longer there or in the grave."

"I'm glad I don't have to grasp it all today."

"Ask God to open your eyes and help you understand. He loves to do that."

Rachel stepped away from the crosses, though the image stayed with her. "This could take a while."

Scott strode to the middle of the room, an oddly open space when you considered paintings lined the walls. "Let's get started." He handed her a packet of papers. "This is the inventory. I'm not sure how it's organized. Mark which room each painting is in so we can find it later if needed. We'll also note the day and time we identify the painting. Just in case it disappears later." He grimaced. "The Indian troops will leave soon, so I've radioed a request for standing guards."

The morning melted into afternoon as Rachel watched Scott examine each painting. He'd say a title and artist, then she'd scan the list until she found the painting and checked it off. On occasion he'd dictate a note she added. As they worked their way around the room, the scope of his knowledge impressed her. At the rare times he didn't recognize a painting, he'd scan the list until he could narrow it down.

"All right. That was the last one here." Scott stood and dusted his hands off.

"Now where?"

"We'll check each room. Hopefully the next will go faster."

She followed him down to the door and inhaled as they walked in. "These must be by the same artist."

"You're right." Scott seemed surprised by what was in the room. "I didn't think he'd store his work here."

Rachel turned toward him. "Renaldo? It looks like the drawings in my sketchbook."

"I didn't know they were here."

What would it have been like to see this with her father? One painting might be sufficient to provide the money for the medical treatment Momma needed. *One piece.* Her fingers itched to hold one, to take it and sell it as fast as she could.

"I need food." Rachel spun and left the room. She needed time away from the art. Time to think. She rushed through the maze, not caring if Scott followed. Yet after a minute, the soft thud of his steps followed behind her.

"Where are you going?"

She pushed into her room, throwing his inventory on the bed. She grabbed the sketchbook. "Look at this." She pointed at the sketch of the woman staring into the distance. "This painting was in that room. It could fund the treatment Momma needs. Right now, I understand how someone could take one. One painting nobody would miss."

"Why should Renaldo give you a painting?"

"Momma contracted tuberculosis here in the twenties." Her breath wavered but she plowed on. "The doctors say it's waited, dormant, for years. Now it's roaring through her with a vengeance. The doctors did all they could with the little money we had. Until I can raise more funds, she has to wait in a small room friends gave her. She can't work; she can't breathe." Her words hiccupped on a sob.

"I'm sorry, Rachel." Scott reached out, and when she didn't step away, he pulled her into an embrace.

"I wouldn't have left her, but there was no other way to find money. I'm crazy to try to find a man I'd never heard of that she forbad me to find. A man whose name I didn't suspect until yesterday. He's gone again."

"Then we'll get to Florence as soon as it's safe. Track down Renaldo. I promise."

"But it could all be too late. I hear from Momma rarely. The war slows down our letters. Maybe she's already dead, and I should have stayed home. Maybe she died alone because I was too determined to save her." Sobs racked through her. She wanted to hide, to prevent him from seeing her pain.

As Scott rubbed her back and murmured soft sounds, she felt sheltered.

She felt like she'd come home at long last. Even after what he'd done.

If she didn't move away now, she'd stay forever. "I'm sorry."

She pushed away from him and hurried downstairs. Somehow she made her way through the maze of the castle's halls and around the refugees who had pushed into the building and the few soldiers mixed with the crowd. At the door to the kitchen, Scott caught up and spun her around. He pulled her to him.

Then before she could move, he claimed her with a kiss.

A kiss that sent sparks spiraling through her.

A kiss that had her wrapping her arms around his neck or else her knees would collapse.

A woman cleared her throat, and Scott jerked away. Rachel almost groaned at the sudden emptiness.

The woman who thought Rachel was a spirit stood next to the stove, gaze locked on her. She clucked and returned to stirring whatever was in the large pot. Was this woman related to Renaldo? Did that explain the intense reaction she had each time she saw Rachel?

Scott pulled her back to his side and gave a slow exhale. "Would you stop running?"

"I can't. My father was here. Now he isn't, and I don't know where to find him. I have carried that sketchbook across an ocean and through a war and he's gone."

"We don't know yet that he's your father. Just that he's probably the sketch artist."

Rachel puffed out a breath. "The woman in the painting upstairs looks like my mother in her early twenties."

"She looks like you."

"No." Rachel had never carried her mother's easy grace and elegant beauty.

"Yes, Rachel. I see so much in you."

"Upstairs?" The cook's voice penetrated the fog Scott's words created.

"Yes."

"*Grande?*" The woman held her arms out to reflect a large painting.

"Yes." Could this woman be the key? Could she help?

The woman's round face split with a smile. "My brother paint."

"Your brother?" Rachel staggered against Scott at the idea. "Where is he?"

She waved a flour-covered hand. "Gone."

"Please, where is he?"

The woman backed away, an invisible wall settling on her features. Rachel followed her.

"Please help me. If I'm his daughter, you're my aunt." Rachel knew she was babbling, and the woman couldn't understand, but that didn't slow her words.

Scott spoke a couple quick words in Italian, listened, then nodded, and steered Rachel from the kitchen.

"What are you doing?"

"Preventing you from scaring the woman. She thinks you're a ghost."

Scott led Rachel to the inner courtyard and settled on a bench, then patted the seat next to him. She joined him but stared at a rosebush climbing the far wall. The cascade of blossoms colored the air with sweetness, a scent she'd noticed before, a picture tinged with the brush of hope.

~⚬~

Scott slipped an arm around Rachel's shoulders and nudged her closer. He'd almost allowed the kiss to get out of control in the kitchen. He wanted to be her hero. He wanted to be the one who provided the money she needed to get treatment for her mom.

But he thought of the pittance in his bank account. It was an impractical idea. Was Renaldo the solution?

"I need a little time alone." Rachel edged away from him and stood. "Thank you for listening."

"We'll find Renaldo, Rachel. I promise we will."

"I hope so." Her smile didn't reach her eyes as it trembled on her lips.

Scott remained on the bench to honor her request for privacy, even as he felt the rejection that he wasn't enough for her. Who was he kidding?

Elaine had left him in New York because his vision of the future hadn't been enough for her. Now he couldn't be enough for Rachel.

After his betrayal he should be grateful she stayed here.

He looked at the sky, a clear cerulean with hardly a wispy cloud dotting it. A flock of birds cawed overhead as they circled and danced in the drafts. What would it be like to be that free of other's expectations?

That's what I want for you. The words echoed in his soul, as clearly as if someone had sat down next to him and spoken them.

A verse from Galatians came to him: "For do I now seek the favor of men, or God?"

He'd allowed his focus to switch to what men—and women—thought of him. In the past—before Elaine—he'd felt such freedom. But that came when his eyes and focus rested squarely on God and what He wanted from him. Scott sat on the bench praying and meditating on the Galatians verse until his stomach growled. Then he headed into the kitchen, which was filled with women doing their communal cooking. He stood a moment watching the bevy of activity, until Renaldo's sister approached.

"Signor?" She offered him a roll.

"Grazie." He took a bite and enjoyed the way it melted in his mouth. How could she create such delicacies with limited supplies?

He left the kitchen and stopped by his room. Tyler's bed was a mess, like someone had decided to sleep in it. Had he come and left again? Scott looked around for a note but didn't find one. Guess he was an adult and would reappear when they needed him.

Scott moved on to the room storing Renaldo's art. The door stood cracked and a muffled voice reached him.

"Is this my father's? Or am I crazy? God, I don't know what to do or think." The last came out like a prayer, but in a rush as if she wasn't sure about speaking it out loud.

Scott pushed the door open and whistled a few bars of "I'll Be Seeing You" in an effort to let her know she wasn't alone. She startled and stepped from the painting. It was one of Renaldo's disturbing, realistic portrayals of the Great War. Scott was certain those paintings would escalate in value thanks to the current war, but Rachel didn't understand that.

He joined her, close enough to see the sparks in her brown eyes. "He's an amazing artist."

"He is."

"It's easy to tell you're his daughter because you create art with your camera."

Chapter 32

SCOTT'S WORDS WATERED HER soul.

With all his education and credentials, he thought she had talent. He stepped closer and cupped her cheek. His touch turned her thoughts to jelly. She forced herself to step away.

"Will he help? Do you think Renaldo will understand?"

Scott shrugged. "If he's half the man I knew, he'll find a way."

Rachel felt a tightness in her back relax. "When can we leave for Florence?"

"As soon as the army clears us and Tyler returns with the jeep. We have a lot to inventory while we wait."

The next hours passed in a blur as Rachel tried to keep up with Scott. He was a man consumed by a mission, identifying each piece lining the walls of the great castle. Rachel tried to focus on the beauty surrounding her but found her thoughts adrift between uncertainty at being so close to the end of her journey and intrigued as she listened to Scott explain what made the different works meaningful. If only they had the time for him to properly introduce her to the paintings. She could imagine spending unhurried days wandering the halls of the world's great museums with this man who saw beauty in the paint strokes and the stories of the artists.

Someday.

Her world was a collection of somedays and maybes.

By the time they finished inventorying the second floor, Scott had seen an abundance of art, most of it in good condition. Some frames were broken. A few removed from their frames, but at least no canvases had been slashed or otherwise damaged. Rachel had taken a few photos saying someday people would want the story about what happened to the rich artistic heritage of Italy. Now though, she yawned as she rubbed her back.

"Time for a break. We'll finish the rest tomorrow."

Once Tyler reappeared, Scott would take the jeep and drive to the castle at Poppiano and inventory the art there. If Tyler didn't show up soon, Scott would walk. It couldn't be more than a few kilometers since he could see Poppiano and its accompanying villa from Montegufoni. Maybe when he was done with that castle and villa, they'd receive the green light to travel to Florence. He should radio Lake Trasimeno where the division headquarters had set up, see what the other MFAA officers were hearing about their ETAs to the great city since the troops of the first battalion didn't know more than he did.

Rachel stretched her lower back and moved to a long window. "The troops are ready to move."

"All packed up?" Scott joined her.

"Even most of the tents are down." She pointed to the empty-ing field. "Tyler's back."

"Really?"

"At least the jeep is down there." She turned toward Scott. "Where has he been?"

"That's one question I'll ask." Now, if only he could find the slippery man. He took Rachel's hand, stroking her fingers. They were so delicate and smooth. "Let's get you downstairs so you can eat before the cook closes the kitchen."

A few minutes later Rachel sat at the table in the corner with a slice of warm bread and a bowl of vegetable soup. They had stopped by their rooms, but Tyler hadn't been there. His bags looked like someone had rummaged through them. "I'll find Tyler while you enjoy your supper."

Rachel's gaze studied him, warm with concern. "You should eat too."

"Later. Hearing what Tyler's been doing is more important."

She could use the time to probe the cook about her brother, something Rachel could do more easily without him.

Where to locate Private Salmon? He'd start with the jeep. In the growing gloom of twilight, he walked to the jeep. The vehicle was covered with mud as if it had forded its share of streams, but otherwise it was in good shape. He couldn't find anything that indicated where Tyler had disappeared.

Scott stepped back from the vehicle and scanned the horizon. About a hundred yards in front, a man slipped around the castle. Looked like an American uniform, so Scott headed that direction. When he turned the corner, he'd closed the distance and could tell it was Tyler.

Scott paused a moment, then decided to keep trailing, see what he could learn before alerting Tyler to his presence. When the man glanced around, Scott dropped behind a tree trunk. Tyler seemed satisfied he was alone because he approached the well house and pulled a key from his pocket. After he unlocked the door, he slipped into the building.

Why would the man go in there?

Scott couldn't imagine any valid reason. Rachel had told him the small space was empty after she took the hatbox. Guess it was time to see for himself.

Scott approached the building. From inside he heard a grunt followed by creaking. Scott paused. Entering was the only way to know what was happening.

Scott took a breath, then eased around the side of the building. The door stood cracked to let the fading sunlight enter. He couldn't see anything through the crack, placing Tyler behind it.

Releasing his breath in a trickle, Scott squared his shoulders, feeling a surge of alertness.

God, help me.

It was past time to confront the man. Tyler was up to something.

Scott eased toward the door. Tried to squeeze through the opening.

Instead, his shoulder brushed into the door, and the door groaned.

"What the . . . ?" Tyler's startled words were followed by a growl. "Scott. Mr. Goody Two-shoes. Mr. I'm-Here-to-Save-the-Art-World." The man pushed his weight into the door, squeezing Scott between the door and the frame.

Scott huffed and pushed back.

"I'm not letting you in."

The man must not understand that throwing a challenge like that made Scott more determined to get inside. He shoved against the door.

Tyler grunted and the door shifted.

It wasn't enough.

If he couldn't force Tyler to move, Scott would never get in the room.

One.

Two.

Three.

He shoved against the door with everything in him.

The door shifted.

He thrust his full weight against the door.

The door flung open.

Tyler must have moved.

Scott lowered into a stance he'd seen boxers use when preparing to absorb blows.

In the middle of the floor, a trapdoor was pulled up revealing a gaping hole. Could that be a former well? The next moment Tyler launched at him. Scott fought to stay on his feet as Tyler's head connected with his stomach. Air whooshed from Scott's lungs.

His feet grappled across the floor, fighting for purchase, as Tyler pushed.

"I am tired of you and your superiority." Tyler spit out the words through gritted teeth. "You're not the only one with an art degree."

Tyler pushed harder, and Scott felt himself falling. He had to stop this movement. But he couldn't breathe. "What?"

"You underestimated me. I took a painting here. Another there." The man grimaced as Scott swung an elbow into his gut.

"Why?"

"I'm not returning home without a retirement plan. If I have to be here, I can take care of myself."

Scott's heel caught on a dip and he lost his balance, falling to the ground.

The action threw Tyler off balance and he staggered. Scott thrust a foot out and tripped Tyler. The man landed with an *ooff*. He groaned as Scott struggled to his feet.

Scott's gaze searched the room.

He had to find something to disable Tyler long enough to get help. Nothing.

There was nothing he could use.

"Why here?" Scott panted as Tyler stood.

"Remember that summer of mine in Italy? I played in here. This was my place, one everyone else forgot. The cellar is the perfect place to hide things. No one else will find it. I'll return after the war and collect my reward. As long as your girl doesn't do more exploring."

Red clouded Scott's vision at the thought Tyler would harm Rachel.

Tyler moved, lumbering like a bear. An angry bear based on the fire in his eyes.

Scott pulled air into his shaky lungs and settled back into the boxer's stance. It hadn't worked so well before, but he didn't know what else to do.

Tyler's lips curled into a snarl, and he launched at Scott.

In the moment he had to respond, Scott threw himself to the side. He kicked out again. Tyler stumbled and fell into the upright door.

His head caught the corner, and he slumped to the floor.

Scott approached with caution. When Tyler didn't move again, Scott leaned over him and felt for a pulse. He kept breathing but didn't stir.

A soldier edged into the building. "What's going on?"

"Do you have any military police here?"

"No, sir."

Scott blew out a breath. "Then go get somebody to help. I need to see what's down there."

The soldier eyed him uncertainly. Scott struggled to stand as upright as he could with his screaming ribs.

"Private Salmon attacked me and told me he's stolen and stashed something there. I need someone to make sure the private doesn't escape."

Rachel dipped the bread into the soup and felt warmed. The broth was rich, and she was grateful for something fresh that wasn't army fare. As she ate, she could feel the cook's gaze on her. The small woman had an intensity about her that drew Rachel's attention.

She pushed the bowl back and smiled. "That was good. Grazie."

The woman nodded. "You are her."

The broken English surprised and delighted Rachel. "Her?"

"She stole heart." The woman looked away and frowned. A moment later she seemed to find the word. "Beautiful."

Rachel stared at the woman, mystified. "My mother?"

"Mel-a-nie." Each syllable acquired a musical tone as she strung them out. "Renaldo." She shrugged. "He change."

"How?"

"He loved Mel-a-nie. More than others."

"Momma loved him too. So much she never married."

"Renaldo has wife."

Rachel's heart quivered at the thought. She'd imagined her father as in love with her momma as she adored him. It was impossible to think their love had been unrequited on both sides, but it had somehow made the separation bearable. Now she sat across the table from her aunt, a woman who knew her father and seemed willing to talk.

Slowly she pulled details from the cook. The man was an artist of growing fame. Occasionally he would speak of Melanie and their year together, but family pressure had dictated he marry a woman from the right Italian family. He had been content. Then the war came.

"All so difficult."

In the struggle to survive, he'd taken a post with the government. Assistant art superintendent.

"Why bring his art here?"

"Safe. Protected." The woman puckered her lips and rubbed her forehead. "Is okay."

Rachel nodded. "Can you tell me where he is in Florence?"

The woman shrugged. "Always moving." She gestured in the air as if writing. "Make list."

"Thank you." Rachel stood. Should she hug the woman? She didn't feel like family really, but the woman had accepted Rachel wasn't a spirit. That was an improvement.

In the end the woman decided for her by turning around and sticking her hands in dishwater. Rachel slipped into the courtyard, mind spinning. Her father worked with the German Kunstschutz in Florence. Maybe he had no choice, but the thought made her a little sick to her stomach. Yet he'd kept much of the art safe here.

Rachel glanced at the twilight settling over the courtyard's activity. Scott hadn't come back yet, which worried her. She'd expected him to return after he found Tyler.

The families had settled in, and she paused when a sweet Italian ballad reached her. The haunting melody sounded like a benediction over those assembled in their makeshift shelters under the sky. The last note of the song rose to the sky, and she stirred. She'd never find Scott standing here. She walked from the courtyard toward the area surrounding the castle. As the stars twinkled overhead, she imagined what it would be like to walk across the fields hand in hand with the man she loved. A line from her momma's diary returned to her.

Tonight he took me to see the stars.

If the sky had been like this one, she could understand how her momma was swept away in the passion of the moment. *Protect my heart, God. I don't want to repeat my momma's mistakes.*

A muffled scuffle pulled her toward the well house. A subdued curse carried on the evening air; then she heard silence. That didn't sound good. A soldier hurried away from the structure. What if Scott was in there? She couldn't leave him.

The door stood open, and a form stretched across the front. A sound rustled beneath a hole that gaped in the floor. "Scott?"

The rustling stopped, but the form stirred and reached for a pistol stuck in the back of his pants. Tyler? There was only one person she could think of he would fight.

She couldn't stand by and watch him shoot Scott.

She scanned the ground. She needed something she could use as a weapon. Something that would make Tyler believe she could hurt him.

"Come on." The whispered words slipped out. She couldn't see anything useful. A rock. A board. Anything would work. There had to be something.

Her limbs trembled at the thought she would lose someone she loved if something happened to Scott. In that moment she was confronted by the truth that she wanted more than friendship with Scott. Much, much more. She wanted him to be the man she could build the rest of her life with.

There!

She spied a rock. She hefted it in her hand, the weight heavy, but the heavier the better.

"I've had enough of your interference, Lindstrom." Tyler stood to his feet, gun held unflinching in front of him.

"You don't want to do anything drastic." Scott's voice sounded hollow as it rose from below. "If something happens to me, they'll hunt you down."

"No, they won't. I'll leave you there with the art. You'll disappear, and they'll assume you wandered off and got killed. Especially when I bring them the sob story about you taking the jeep and heading to Florence alone. Too bad a shell got you. Left nothing to collect and send home. Another man destroyed by this war."

Rachel eased closer as he blabbered on. The man was so sure of himself, he never noticed. She cocked her arm and threw the rock at his head.

The rock bounced off. He growled and spun on her. "You." He grabbed her arm. "You couldn't leave this alone, could you?"

She whimpered against the pain.

"You just became my insurance." He pointed the gun at her. "Come after me, Lindstrom, and I'll kill her."

Scott caught her eye and mouthed a message. *I will find you. I won't let him hurt you.*

She struggled against Tyler, tried to find his face, scratched, twisted, kicked.

Tyler cursed yet pulled her toward the jeep.

Somebody had to help her. She screamed and thrashed, but the refugees slipped into the shadows. "Help me!"

Tears poured down her cheeks as she realized no one was coming unless Scott did. Still she fought.

She wouldn't give up.

Not now.

Chapter 33

SCOTT GATHERED HIMSELF. PAIN coursed through his ribs, and his lungs still refused to grab and hold a full breath, but it didn't matter. He couldn't let Tyler hurt Rachel.

Stealth was impossible. At any moment Tyler would get her in the jeep and carry her out of range. Then anything could happen, and he might never see Rachel again. A wave of anger surged through him. He couldn't let that happen. He would fight for her, and he would win. The alternative . . . wasn't an option.

When he got outside, he saw Rachel twisting and screaming. She couldn't fight harder if she tried. She placed a solid elbow into his side, but Tyler twisted her arm ferociously.

Scott clenched his fist and picked up speed. There weren't many places to hide. So he'd replace stealth with speed. *God, I need an idea.* Tyler had a gun and he didn't.

He worked his way until he was about ten feet behind them.

Tyler spun around, hand clamped around Rachel's arm. "You're as stealthy as a herd of buffalo."

"You can't take her." Scott wished he had his pistol. Even that would help even the fight.

"I have the gun. Since you don't have your pistol out, I assume you forgot yours. The one with the gun wins." The gun wavered, Tyler taking turns pointing at each of them. "So move back."

Scott took a shuffle step back.

"Not far enough." When Scott took another step, Tyler nodded. "Keep going that direction. If you follow, I will kill her." The hard look in the man's eyes convinced Scott he was serious.

Where was the soldier he'd sent for help? Why hadn't he returned? He must have expected Tyler to remain unconscious. Instead Tyler would get away, taking Rachel with him.

Scott eased back another step, then watched as Tyler edged Rachel to the jeep. Her eyes pleaded with him to do something.

His mind raced, trying to concoct a plan.

The problem was, his brain refused to work. He wasn't a real soldier. He was here to work with art, not subdue the enemy. This time the enemy wore his country's uniform, and he felt inept.

Rachel's life depended on him doing something heroic.

If things continued on this course, he'd fail.

He had to think. Tyler pushed Rachel into the jeep, then forced her to slide across. In that moment his attention was on her instead of Scott. This might be his only chance.

Scott launched at the vehicle, putting every ounce of effort into driving his legs as hard as he could. His feet pounded, and he covered the distance before Tyler turned around.

One more step.

Then he jumped on top of the man who'd turned toward him. In that moment he pinned Tyler's gun arm. "Run, Rachel! Get away from here."

She stared at him a moment, then scrambled out the other side of the jeep and ran screaming for help. Maybe one of the remaining light infantry men would finally come.

Tyler threw an elbow at him.

Not again.

Scott didn't want to repeat the well-house fight.

He pressed all his weight onto Tyler and pulled back his right arm for a punch.

He put all he had into it and it smashed Tyler's cheek. The man grunted but acted like it hadn't hurt more than a bee sting.

Tyler kicked, throwing Scott off balance.

His hold on Tyler's gun arm wavered.

Scott gritted his teeth and reached inside for the force to push back. "You can't have her."

"Then neither can you." Tyler jerked his head forward, catching Scott in the nose. A flood of warmth flowed down his face.

Scott slammed Tyler away through a haze of pain that made his eyes water. He rolled to the side with all his weight, pulling Tyler out of the jeep.

They crashed to the ground, Scott rolling until Tyler was under him again.

Tyler gasped but pulled nothing in, his mouth opening and closing like a fish out of water.

"What's going on?" The accent had never sounded better, but Scott didn't tear his gaze from Tyler to see who went with the Indian tone.

"This man has stolen art from the Italians, abducted a captain in the American army, and attacked an officer." Scott grunted as Tyler shifted sharply. Then he stilled as the barrel of a rifle came alongside his face.

"Then it seems you should give your gun to me." The rifle shifted closer to Tyler. "Now."

Tyler's features tightened into a mask of anger. The gun dropped from his fingers. Scott knocked it to the side, then shifted away.

"We'll take it from here, sir."

"Thank you."

The soldier prodded Tyler to his feet.

"I'll take the keys to the jeep." Scott waited for Tyler to do something, but the man remained rigid. "May I?" After a moment the Indian nodded. "Thank you." Scott patted down Tyler's pockets until he retrieved the keys. "I'll come find you in a few minutes to give you my statement." First, he had to find Rachel and see for himself that she was okay.

He wanted to hold her and say aloud the words he was no longer afraid to say. Only then would he secure the paintings from the well house.

∼⤙⤚∼

Rachel paced back and forth in the courtyard, trying to stay out of sight, but her stomach tightened in knots as she prayed Scott would be okay. Tyler had transformed into someone she barely recognized. The anger and bitterness seemed deep set, and he had scared her as he shoved her toward the jeep. She hadn't known what he would do. And no one came to her aid. No one except Scott.

Then Scott had told her to run.

She should have stayed and helped. Instead she'd abandoned him. She braced to hear a gunshot at any moment but prayed it never happened.

She couldn't wait like a schoolgirl who was afraid of her own shadow. She could do something even if it was throwing more rocks.

Rachel looked around the courtyard for something she could use. An old rake leaned against the wall. That would do. She grabbed it and started back toward the jeep, keeping to the shadows as she moved.

A man came toward her. He staggered a bit and wore a uniform. Blood leaked from his nose, down his chin, onto his shirt.

Could it be Tyler coming after her? She stepped deeper into the shadows, then braced the rake to bring it down on the man's head.

"Rachel?"

The word had to be the sweetest she'd ever heard.

"Scott?" She dropped the rake, and it clattered against the ground and his foot.

"Ouch." He jumped back, then held his arms open. "You're okay?"

She raced into his embrace, feeling sheltered and protected as he wrapped her in a hug. She nestled into his chest, listening to his racing heartbeat slow. "Thank you."

"For what?" He stroked her hair in a soothing motion.

"For coming for me."

"There was no way I'd let him drive away with you." Scott sighed. "I'm sorry I didn't do a better job of protecting you."

She pulled back enough to see his eyes in the faint light coming from the kitchen windows. "Shhh. You're my hero. Without you I don't know what back road Tyler would have me on or where I'd end up. Thank you."

His gaze skimmed her face like a feathery touch that sent shivers down her spine. Her breath caught with anticipation. The moment stretched as if he couldn't decide whether to lean down. She lifted onto her toes, bringing her face closer to his. His breath brushed her cheek, and she ached to know the feel of his lips on hers.

"I don't want to react to the moment." His words breathed against her nose.

She tipped his chin, brushed a dribble of blood away. Then she cupped his cheeks. "I do."

He leaned closer, and the moment their lips touched, she felt the sensation of coming home. This was where she was supposed to be. Lost in his embrace, sheltered by this man.

The moment the kiss ended, Scott placed his forehead against hers. "I love you, Rachel Justice."

She reached toward him, and he sealed his declaration with another kiss.

Chapter 34

August 4

RACHEL LANGUISHED IN BED the next morning. Her dreams had been filled with thoughts of Scott. She'd feared nightmares filled with Tyler, but Scott's kiss and his promise had filled her slumber with sweet things.

A brisk knock startled her from her introspection.

"Just a minute." She scrambled from the bed and started grabbing clothes and the other things she would need to get ready for the day.

"Meet you in the kitchen in five minutes?"

Scott's voice warmed her, and she was grateful he stayed on the other side of the door. "Give me ten."

As she dressed, Rachel wondered what Scott wanted. She hadn't heard him after he escorted her back to her room. He'd checked it thoroughly, then said he still had much to do. It had been a relief in one way, even as another part of her had felt keen disappointment when he walked away. She'd known he had a list of things to do, not the least of which was offering testimony that would keep Tyler far away.

When she reached the kitchen, he waited at the table with an empty plate in front of him and a full plate for her. "We leave as soon as you give your testimony to the Indian CO. We've got other deposits to check."

"What about Tyler?"

"I've alerted General Tucker. He's asked the Indian Division to accept responsibility for transporting Tyler back to him. All they need is your account. So pack. We might return tonight but better to be prepared. While you give your account, I'll ready the jeep."

Within the hour they were on the road.

"What did you do with the paintings?"

Her question seemed to startle him as he looked at her before turning back to the road. "Where?"

"Those in the well house."

"Brought them back to the castle and inventoried them. They'll be safe here until we can identify where they belong."

Rachel swiped a clump of hair out of her face. "Where are we headed today?"

"No permission to travel to Florence yet, so we'll stick close to Montegufoni." Scott sounded disappointed but shook it off. "At least I've got time with you."

Rachel blushed and settled in the passenger seat. She'd wondered how she'd feel alone with Scott, but his declaration of love hadn't made things uncomfortable. If anything she felt complete, like being together was enough. Without Tyler around she relaxed into the rhythm of time with Scott.

Several days passed as they inventoried the art secreted at Poppiano. She took photos and helped Scott as he identified the collections stored in the villa and castle. The collected art wealth of the two castles and villa was staggering. Scott explained as much as he could about the pieces, helping her see the details that made them irreplaceable. At night she sent developed film back to Rome, each time with the vague hope an image would be radioed to the States.

Then a couple days after the incident with Tyler, a return package from her editor included the film and chemicals she needed. But it also contained a stack of papers with a note:

NY office thought you might want to see some of the places your photos have been published. Checks going to your mom as requested.

An amount was scribbled next to Dick's signature. Rachel covered her mouth to control the gasp that pushed against her lips.

"Everything all right?" Scott touched her hand, his eyes soft with compassion.

Rachel nodded. It took a moment for her to clear the lump from her throat. "Yes." She handed him the note, then gestured to the stack of newspaper pages. "I had no idea so many papers had picked up my photos."

Scott flipped through them, a growing grin stretching his face. "I remember when you shot most of these." He handed the papers back. "Does this mean your mom can afford treatment?"

"I don't know." Rachel's hands trembled as she collected the clippings into a pile. "It should. There's certainly enough money there."

"Then trust she is."

"I have to."

"Does this change your need to reconnect with Renaldo?"

She shook her head. "The treatment will be ongoing. This just means she could restart. Without that the doctors offered no hope. Maybe now . . ." Tears welled, and she turned into Scott's arms and sobbed.

He stroked her back, making no attempt to stop her. He murmured quiet words, words she recognized as prayers.

Eventually she pulled back, dabbing at her face with her sleeve. "Thank you."

"We'll find him again, Rachel. I'll do all I can to make that happen."

"I know." As she clutched the clippings, knowing her momma could start treatment was as important as finding her father and praying he would help with the next piece.

The days morphed into a week filled with checking art deposits in surrounding communities while they waited for permission to approach Florence. Grassina, Castel Oliveto, Montagnana. Each day was filled with nervous travel on winding roads followed by unexpected delights and treasures at their destinations. At night they backtracked to Montegufoni for soft beds and a warm meal. A small British guard replaced the Mahratta battalion that moved closer to Florence.

With each day Rachel reminded herself she had a once-in-a-lifetime opportunity to explore the byroads of Tuscany, but her gaze traveled to the horizon where, if she squinted hard, she imagined the outlines of Florence.

Finally, on August 12, Scott acquired permission to slip into Florence. The city remained under attack, even though the Germans had pulled back to the northern parts of the city on the eighth.

"Are you sure you want to come?" Scott eyed her with a palpable concern that she hoped wouldn't translate to a refusal to let her come. "I can find him and then bring him to you."

"No. I've driven everywhere else with you." After all this time she would finally see the city that had fueled her dreams of coming to Italy. "I can't risk getting stranded."

"All right. We'll leave at first light." He tugged her close, planting a quick kiss on her cheek. "I love you, Rachel Justice."

She smiled. "I know."

"So?"

"What?"

"Aren't you going to say it back to me?"

Rachel couldn't control the smile that erupted from deep within her. "I love you, Scott Lindstrom."

Rachel repacked her bags and settled into a restless sleep. What would morning bring? Only God knew, and she tried to rest in that knowledge.

The next morning as they traveled the road, a tight, winding, narrow passage, she could hear the intermittent shelling. It had become such a constant undertone to her days. She barely noticed it other than to determine the shells fell out of range.

Scott's knuckles turned white as he gripped the steering wheel. "Watch for mines. A farmer warned me the Germans were active along here as they left."

Her eyes soon tired as she kept a close watch on the road. As soon as she pointed a spot out, Scott swerved to avoid it. Destroyed tanks and other military vehicles lined the road. One overturned as if tipped by a giant. Another exploded into a pile of tank parts. Rachel imagined the area had overflowed with chaos and confusion, and her heart broke when she saw a child's pram splintered in the mix. What pain for that family unless it had trundled treasures rather than a child.

She turned away. "What is Florence like?"

"It was a magical city when I was there in '36." Scott steered the jeep around a crater, and even that jarred Rachel. The roads were like an old-fashioned washboard, rutted down to the quick with nothing left to soften the trip. "It's like stepping back to when the Medicis ruled."

"With modern touches?"

"A few. But the best part is the area around the Arno, where you can sense the generations of history. Families have lived in the same place for centuries."

Rachel tried to conjure up images but didn't have much to draw on. "So it's like Naples and Rome?"

"No, it's Florence." Scott shifted into a new gear. "You'll understand when we crest the right hill and you see it rising in front of you."

Like so many drives, this one took hours longer than it should have. Montegufoni sat a mere twenty-five kilometers from Florence, but the drive took all morning rather than a relatively quick forty-five minutes. The closer they moved, the slower the approach. The roads clogged with military transports crawling toward the city.

The artillery barrage continued in the distance, growing closer as they entered the valley, which reverberated with shell fire.

Scott pounded the steering wheel. "They weren't supposed to fight in Florence. It's supposed to be open with the armies honoring its status. It was declared an open city!"

Rachel stayed silent. It was clear he loved Florence, and as she watched it grow across the horizon, she sensed its magic.

The jeep inched forward. At this point walking would transport them faster. Maybe they'd need the jeep when they arrived, but otherwise she'd abandon it to others. "Where are we going when we reach the city?"

"Headquarters. The tried-and-true destination. It's supposed to be located in the Giardino Torrigiani. The army's using a villa there."

Rachel had no idea where that was, but Scott would manage to find it like he did everything else.

"MFAA officer Captain Ellis got into Florence a couple days ago. The Allies are bottled up on this side of the Arno while the Germans dug in on the far side. Ellis reported the destruction is horrific." Scott's jaw hardened and he swallowed. "But we can enter the city to interview the chief personnel of the superintendency. Then we'll leave. There's conflicting information about the status of deposits and the monuments in Florence, and I'm to sort through it and create a plan. Even though I can't see anything."

"Why you?"

"I want to help you find Renaldo." His knuckles were white, he clutched the steering wheel so tightly. "I'm too late to help much with the monuments. The Germans blew the bridges. Monuments that have stood since medieval times."

~~❦~~

As they reached the outskirts of Florence, the buzz of artillery never eased. Somewhere in this madness the Seventy-First Garrison had set up an interim headquarters at the Giardino Torrigiani. The problem was, Scott didn't know how best to work his way through the mess of Florence. People on the streets were drawn, pale, and terribly thin from the weeks of siege. Where the Florence streets of his memory rang with vibrancy, shell-shocked silence and quick movements stirred now. Men were scarce. Why?

"Are we getting close?" Rachel's voice sounded tight and tired as she snapped a photo.

"As long as we find the Seventy-First, we'll find someone who can help us."

The Porta Romana roundabout came into view, and Scott relaxed. They would make it to the villa. The intensity of driving with never knowing where the next shot would come from or if the jeep would hold together long enough to get them off the road had left him with rock-hard shoulders.

A hurly-burly collection of jeeps, trucks, officers, soldiers, and Italian citizens filled the gardens, making it hard to penetrate the space to find the villa. "Let's park here."

Rachel nodded and he found a spot.

Inside the villa finally, the provisional commissioner for American Military Government hailed Scott. "Lindstrom, you're finally here."

"Yes, my orders came for a quick trip."

"Forget quick. There's too much work. I want you in the northern part of the city immediately. Cross the Arno, but first you'll need to get travel passes for the Italian superintendency personnel so they can guide you."

"Yes, sir."

"My aide can find you a spot to work." The man reached across the table he used as a desk. "Good to have you here."

"Thank you."

A corporal materialized at his elbow. "Right this way." Scott followed him through a maze of people working, hoping Rachel could keep up. "Here are the forms you'll need. Complete them carefully, and I'll get you on your way. You'll find the staff on the grounds. Before you leave though," the corporal handed Scott a message, "this arrived a couple hours ago."

Scott accepted the folded piece of paper. "Who delivered it?"

"I didn't see but was told a child."

"Thanks." Scott edged away from the stream of people wanting a piece of the corporal. Only one person would know to look for him attached to the AMG. Renaldo Adamo.

Could he finally introduce the man to his daughter?

He scanned the note.

I have news of great import. Meet me at the Ponte Vecchio at 9:00 p.m. I will come each evening until you arrive. I pray this finds you quickly.

Rachel came alongside him. "Good news?"

Scott slipped the note into his jacket pocket. Should he get her hopes up?

"My father?"

He smiled. She was too intuitive sometimes. "Yes. He wants to meet."

Rachel studied him. "When?"

"Tonight. He gives a fixed location at the Ponte Vecchio bridge."

"So what do we do until then?"

"Get this paperwork complete and cross the Arno. We'll stay for the meeting tonight."

She glanced at her watch. "Okay. Give me an hour to connect with the United Press office. I've got film to turn in. Surely one's an award winner." Her smile was bright but not enough to reach her eyes. Would finding her father remove the last trace of shadows?

Scott finished the passes, a mind-numbing labyrinth of getting just the right information and the right approvals. Then he worked through materials that had been brought up from the other MFAA officers. They'd arrive in Florence soon, but for now he remained a solo endeavor since Ellis had been forced to leave. It would be good to have the help of other experts. What he'd seen on the drive indicated Florence would be filled with damage inflicted by the fighting. Why hadn't the Germans withdrawn as they had in Rome?

After completing the run around with the paperwork and a meal of C rations under a garden pine tree, it was time to head out and assess the damage. While he'd found several of the local art experts, he hadn't located Rachel. Finding her in the pool of people closed into the gardens seemed an impossible task. Too bad smoke signals or some other form of communication couldn't be used to let her know where he'd set up.

"Looking for someone?" Her sweet voice came from behind him.

"You're here."

"It wasn't easy, but perseverance paid off. Now where?"

"The Piazza Pitti. The *palazzo* is a monument of great importance."

"And one you will not recognize." A man stepped near, dapper in a worn suit, bow tie, and fedora. He'd made an effort to be presentable in a city with no electricity, working sewer, or running water, another gift to the city from the retreating Germans.

"Lieutenant Lindstrom at your service."

The man bowed slightly at the waist. "I am Professor Berti. I shall guide you to the others. The Pitti is our center."

They reclaimed the jeep, then used it to work through the crowds. The professor wove a story of the people who lived along the Arno being told to evacuate. Then of the Pitti that offered sanctuary to many of the displaced. "It is worse than any slum you can imagine. But what choice is there?" The man shrugged in a smooth motion of pain and explanation. "War changes things."

As they approached the beautiful Boboli Gardens, Scott couldn't believe the sight. "How many refugees are here?"

"Rough guess only. More than five thousand. The gardens are the facilities, and the water supply is taxed."

Rachel wrinkled her nose in a way that only emphasized her pale beauty. "I don't think I wanted to know that."

"It is reality."

Scott maneuvered to a spot where he hoped the jeep would wait when they returned. Before he pulled the brake, a crowd surrounded the vehicle.

"My colleagues." In short order the professor introduced him to at least a dozen people. Their names swam in a quagmire in his mind.

One superintendent clapped. "This way. We meet now." He led the way to a conference room that stood in a frescoed hall of the palace. Once all were settled, the man turned to Scott. "Please explain the process."

"My pleasure." Scott fought for patience as he worked through the MFAA structure and how it would interface with the local superintendency to reclaim and restore the art and monuments of Florence. "That's the plan."

The man snapped and an assistant presented a document.

"This contains information on the deposits that remain occupied by the Germans and their locations."

"This will help us know where to avoid shelling."

"Yes. The shells are too destructive."

All around the table murmurs of assent erupted.

"This meeting has been productive." Scott eased his chair back and stood. "But now I must see the bridges."

Professor Berti nodded. "You will need a guide. I will take you."

Chapter 35

August 13

THE DAY'S SUN SHONE too bright, rays colliding off the mounds of rubble that marred the beautiful city. If she tried hard, Rachel could imagine how the streets must have looked, striking her as a romantic escape. Today her combat boots formed an essential part of her wardrobe. Without them she would have fallen or stumbled in the debris of stones splintered from buildings by shells and bombs.

"How much of this was done as the Germans moved out?"

The professor hobbled along, his gait hesitant and his gaze darting as they neared the edge of the palazzo. His shoulders hunched up to his ears until he looked like a turtle unwilling to stick his head out of the shell. "They were active. The partisans remain so."

Rachel sidled closer to Scott. "Should we be worried?"

"It's an active war zone."

Right. And she hadn't already considered that. Rachel waited as he moved closer to the professor and bit back her frustration. She pulled her camera out and raised it to her eye, scanning for a shot. If Scott was one of the first nonessential AMG officers in, then she might be one of the first photojournalists. She patted the pass he'd given her.

"Oh my." Rachel stopped in her approach. A mound of debris at least thirty-feet high stood at the edge of the Piazza Pitti. She raised her camera and took several pictures.

"We cannot pass here." The professor glanced at her with an apologetic air. "I wanted you to see."

Scott's jaw worked and his hands fisted as he took in the scene. "The Arno is a couple blocks away. No more than a five- or ten-minute walk."

"If you are very slow."

Scott matched the professor's weary smile. "True. Are we barred from approaching?"

"There is a way." The professor waved them back toward the Giardino di Boboli.

Scott spoke in a muffled tone to Professor Berti. Rachel tuned them out as she kept looking for a shot that would be different from another photographer's. Their circuit took them along the edge of the gardens and in range of the rubble and a few standing buildings. She slowed her circuit as she scanned to the right. Sunlight glinted off something metallic. "Scott?"

"What?"

"Something is shining in that window."

Professor Berti dove behind a pile of rubble that barely stood tall enough to protect his head. Scott tugged her down. She kept her camera up and snapped a shot.

"What are you doing?" Scott yanked her down again, and she tumbled onto the debris. Her palms scraped against the jagged rocks, and her camera banged against the ground. He crouched beside her.

"Scott?"

"If that's a sniper, the sun can glint off your lens and draw attention to you. It would become a clear target."

"There are many who shoot as cowards but kill at will." The professor wiped his brow with a handkerchief from his position behind a pile of broken cement blocks.

She examined her camera, then folded it up with shaking fingers. "I . . . I didn't think."

"Just keep your helmet secured." Scott tapped it, even as he searched beyond the piled broken rocks to the windows overlooking the street.

"Shooters keep us full of nerves." The professor's gaze shuttled over the building, never settling, always moving. Professor Berti glanced over his shoulder. "All is clear."

"You are sure?" Scott asked.

"A friend cleared the building and signaled me." The man stood but remained stooped. "We must hurry. The dark brings danger." Berti studied the road, then glanced back. "It is not easy from here. The Germans destroyed much along Ponte Vecchio."

"Yet spared the bridge."

"Yes."

The destruction was so complete, Rachel could hardly capture the utter and absolute nature of it through her viewfinder. Nothing was left inhabitable within a couple blocks of the bridge.

The professor narrated as he led them to a ladder. "The Germans told the residents to leave on 29 July. They had short hours' notice. The Jewel of Europe was attacked by former friends. General Alexander's proclamations that dropped from the sky over Rome made things worse. By the thirty-first no one could cross the bridges. We feared the worst, but the Germans made us wait three days. The night of 3 August rang with the artillery of your advancing army but worse with the destructive German mines." The man teared up. "Follow me."

He started up the ladder. Rachel examined it before trusting it to climb up out of the gardens into the blast zone. "Where did my father want to meet?"

"Along the Ponte Vecchio." Scott's breath sounded ragged. "This corridor used to connect the palace and the Uffizi, the famous museum. Is it open?"

Professor Berti tipped his head to the side in that universal sign that he didn't know. "It will take us to the Santa Felicita."

Quiet minutes followed as they traversed the distance.

Scott took her hand to help her over a pile that had once been a house wall and then kept his hold. His warmth enveloped her, and she rested in the sense of protection. As the corridor came to an end, she was grateful to have him next to her. "There's nothing left."

Scott closed his eyes, then reopened them. "This is criminal. There was no reason to destroy this ancient section of the city."

"Rome was their reason." The professor knelt in front of a shattered cross. "Your army moved through Rome too quickly. Our bridges paid the price." He crossed himself and stood. "We must move on."

Rachel held her nose against a smell that took her breath and shoved it back down her throat.

"The sewers." Professor Berti said no more.

They joined a flood of civilians picking their way across the Ponte Vecchio. "Be careful. The mines are plentiful."

Rachel had to agree as she noticed the liberality with which the Germans had strewn the mines along the bridge. Even with the low level of the river, walking the bridge was better than fording the Arno with some dangers hidden and others visible.

"There's the Uffizi." Scott pointed. "How damaged is she?"

The professor shrugged. "Much broken glass and plaster. The art was removed." He paused and looked at Scott. "Your friend will meet you there?"

"Renaldo? He said the bridge later tonight."

"He sent me to bring you here."

Scott nodded. "All right. Let's be quick. We'll need to return to our quarters before dark." He swatted at a mosquito.

"You mean to the castle?" Rachel tried to keep the enthusiasm from her voice. So many were trapped in desperate circumstances, yet if they could leave, it would mean less strain on the limited resources.

"Yes. It's a better location to regroup than here. With our passes we can come and go freely."

The shelling picked up again. Rachel kept an eye on the sky as the professor ignored the constant whine and whistles.

"If this keeps up, Florence will be pulverized." Scott helped Rachel over another compilation of rubble that left her scrambling like a mountain goat to get to the other side.

"We can only pray." The professor's stoic words matched his resigned expression.

Rachel wished there was more she could do, but at the moment taking photos and praying seemed all that was left to her. She hoped it was enough to stave the hand of destruction.

⚯

He should have left Rachel at the gardens or the palazzo. As she slipped and slid over another mound of rubble, he hurried to her side. She grimaced whenever her hands touched the rocks. Her palms must sting. They had to use care as they picked their way across. A mine could hide anywhere in this mess, and there was little he could do. Still, she was with him, and he had to get to the Uffizi and find Renaldo somewhere in the maze of the palatial museum.

Rachel reached the top of yet another mound and snapped a series of photos, starting with a backward glance at the Arno River and the utter destruction around the Ponte Vecchio before continuing to the disaster in front of them.

Time ticked as he waited for her to finish her shooting. Time in which another sniper could site on her. "Are you ready to move?"

She shook her head yet began closing her camera. "I could take photos for a week and never capture the absolute destruction." She sighed. "It's such a waste."

A bullet whistled past, and she dropped to the ground. Scott army-crawled toward her. "Can we get out of here?"

"The shooter is too far away to harm us."

"That didn't feel far." Scott waited five minutes, then nodded at Rachel. She crouched as the professor led them on to the Uffizi.

The slight man remained silent as he led the way until a ripple of applause reached them. Scott stopped and looked for the source, humbled when he saw a small group of Florentine residents with half-empty baskets resting at their feet. "They wish to say thank you."

Heat charged up his neck into his face. Snipers mixed with celebrations. What a crazy circumstance. "I'm the wrong one to say grazie to."

"You are here."

The solemn words settled over Scott. Professor Berti was right. Scott and Rachel were the only ones wearing American uniforms. So they received the thanks that belonged to the soldiers who had fought their way up Italy and now across Florence. Rachel had reopened her camera and snapped another photo as Scott bowed his head to acknowledge the quiet applause that ended after a look from their guide.

"Follow me." The professor led them into the building and up a glass-strewn staircase to the top floor of the Uffizi. There, in the loggia that ran around the top of the building, windows and their frames were destroyed. Roof tiles were displaced, but in the shadows stood the figure of a man, looking out over the Arno.

The professor turned to Rachel. "Captain Justice, a roof tour of Florence?"

Rachel glanced at Scott, then accepted the professor's proffered arm. "Thank you."

Scott waited until Professor Berti led her in the opposite direction before approaching Renaldo. The man reached out to grasp him with a strong hug and kissed both of his cheeks. "You made it to Florence."

"Yes." Scott slipped into Italian. "I am saddened at what I see."

"Hearts have broken." Renaldo stepped back and turned to stare in the direction of the Pitti. "Now that you are here, I can provide more information. Where the Germans have taken art. Much are tales, but you are better positioned to locate the truth than I."

"I will do what I can." He checked the progress of the professor and Rachel. "We have another matter to discuss."

"*Sì*." The man bowed his head. "I think I know of what you speak."

"She has come a long way to find you. To know you as her father."

His mentor looked as if he had aged a decade in the short days since he'd left Montegufoni. Could Rachel be the reason? Or was it the destruction of historic Florence? Scott waited, giving his friend the freedom to direct the conversation.

"I did not expect her." The man held his hands up in a small gesture. "When Melanie left, . . ." he groaned, "she took my heart with her. I did not know she carried a child. If I had, I would have followed. Somehow." He walked away, head bowed. "How do I help Rachel understand?"

Scott considered his words carefully. The man needed hope almost as much as Rachel needed her father to acknowledge her. "God has her on a journey of opening her heart. But you should also know she comes seeking something."

"This I expected." The man turned to Scott, an intensity burning in his eyes. "I must meet her. Officially. Where she knows who I am."

Scott looked out the windows, noting the time. "Do you want to meet her now? Or come with us to Montegufoni for the night?"

"Now. We shall see about the rest."

"Wait here." Scott left the man leaning against a broken window, his head bowed as if in prayer. Rachel turned toward Scott as if she'd waited, keenly in tune with his every move. She held her breath until he took her hands and stroked them, feeling a faint tremble in hers. He waited until she lifted glistening eyes to his. "Your father would like to officially meet you."

"Really?" He could hear the ache that edged her words.

"Yes. Are you ready?"

"No." She shook her head. "Yes. I don't know."

"He doesn't want to wait." Another shell whistled overhead, punctuating the wisdom of that sentiment.

Rachel squared her shoulders and lifted her chin. "He's why I came."

"There's my spitfire. Let's go." He looked for the professor, but the man had melted into the background. "Where did Professor Berti go?"

"I don't know. He said something about needing to get someone else."

"Well, let's go see Renaldo."

While her words had been eager, her steps faltered as Rachel followed Scott across the gallery. He kept his fingers laced with hers, lending his support and strength as he led her to the man who was her father.

"Renaldo, may I introduce your daughter, Rachel Justice. Rachel, Renaldo Adamo, your father."

Chapter 36

YOUR FATHER.

The words sounded sweet to her ears, blotting out the reality of where she stood. All that mattered was that the man in front of her was her father. From their conversation at Montegufoni, she knew he had a compassionate heart. Now he was here.

She studied him through a mist of tears that threatened to erupt into sobs if she couldn't hold them in check. He didn't stand much taller than she did, but as she studied the planes of his face, she could see the remnants of a handsome man who had swept her momma or any woman off her feet. He gave her the same studious examination, one she submitted to in hopes he would see traces of her momma.

"You are as beautiful as Melanie." The accented English was musical and tentative.

"Thank you." Rachel swallowed against the sudden dryness in her mouth. "I wish I knew more about you."

"A grief for us both."

"One we can fix."

He shrugged in a languid motion. "If we are blessed. Tell me about Melanie."

"She is sick, dying." Rachel bit down before she said too much, too quickly.

"This I am sorry to hear."

"Thank you."

"But why come find me now? In a war?"

How to make him understand how truly desperate she had been? "We have no money and the hospital could do no more without it. All I knew was my father was somewhere in Italy near Florence. It wasn't much, but Momma is everything to me. I had to try. Here I could take photos to sell to newspapers. And I could find you." Her breath shuddered.

"Can she be cured? She was always so alive."

"She has tuberculosis. The doctors think it's been dormant since she lived here."

"But how?"

"It can hide for years. In her case it did. Then it came and went. Now it stays."

"Why not remain with her?" His question made sense. Her momma was the only one who never asked it. Others had and hadn't understood.

"I had to find you. Find help."

Scott stepped forward. Other than his hand on her shoulder, she'd forgotten he remained. Later she could think about how odd and wonderful it was that she could share her pain and this moment with this man her heart adored.

"We can't stay much longer. Renaldo, come with us."

The man shook his head. "I need to collect more information. Return tomorrow, about noon. I will have something for you both." He stepped to her, tentatively touched her cheek. "Your momma captured my heart. Now you have."

Rachel turned to Scott. "Please, can we stay a few minutes?"

"I'm sorry, Rachel, but it'll be tricky crossing the bridge. We need light to avoid the mines."

He was right. She didn't have to like it, but she would acknowledge it. "Renaldo?" What to call this man? "You promise? You'll return tomorrow?"

His smile was slow, like a sunrise, and it lit his face. "I will do all in my power. If not here, I will find you at the gardens." He turned to Scott. "Keep her safe. I have much to learn from my daughter." Then he faded into the shadows.

Rachel felt a tremor work from her heart to her toes. "I can't let him leave."

"You can't stay. It's too dangerous." Scott tugged her toward the staircase. "Renaldo will be here tomorrow. You'll see."

The next day she paced the glass-littered gallery again. Had she made a fatal mistake in following Scott across the Ponte Vecchio, to the jeep, and back to Montegufoni? The return trip to Florence this morning had left her harried, always waiting for a misplaced shell to land on top of them and then stepping around a poor civilian who'd been shot by a sniper and left where he'd fallen in the ultimate indignity. Killed by a countryman.

And now her father hadn't returned.

"He'll be here."

She brushed aside Scott's assurances. "What if he stepped on a mine last night? We'd never know."

The sound of steps shifting through the glass had Scott pushing her into the shadows. "We stay here until we're sure it's Renaldo."

She nodded, pressing as far as possible into a nook along the wall. She hadn't made it this far to die because she was too stubborn to take precautions. Still, she sagged against the wall when her father's small frame came into view.

"Scott? Rachel?" His whispers carried through the space, held by the walls that used to hold the artistic heritage of the Medicis and Florence.

"Over here." Scott stepped around a pillar, letting Renaldo

see him. Her heart swelled at the way he continued to protect her. "You are alone?"

"*Sì*. Who would come? Where is my daughter?"

"I'm here."

Renaldo walked to her as if he carried a burden too heavy for him. "I made a decision last night. May it be in time to assist Melanie. The art I entrusted to Scott you may have. Sell it, keep it, do as you please. My wife may have what is in our flat and Montegufoni."

"Thank you."

He smiled weakly. "It is little but what I can do. I wish we'd had time to know each other. You are an adult. I wish to have known you as a baby, a child." He traced a hand down Rachel's cheek. "You have her eyes. They drew me to her in the first moment and never let me go. Even many years after she left." He reached into a pocket and pulled out an envelope he handed to her. "This has what you will need to take ownership of the paintings. Scott will help with the details."

Rachel took the envelope and slipped it into her rucksack. "Thank you."

"Thank you for finding me. If God smiles on us, we will spend hours together. I long for that."

He shook his head and turned to Scott. "For you I also bring a gift. Information on where the art is hidden. More recent and detailed than you had. Any information I could compile."

"Locating the art is a high priority."

"Long we have questioned the Germans' purposes. But when they destroyed the bridges. When they destroyed the Ponte Santa Trinita taking the four seasons with it, . . ."—the man's sigh ripped from his soul—"their dishonorable intentions became clear."

There was something about the way he said it that sounded worn by worry and life. This time her father—the words sounded funny—reached into a valise she hadn't noticed. He pulled out a sheaf of papers, the writing tiny yet very legible. "What I know from watching and listening is here."

Scott accepted the rubber-banded papers with a nod. "Thank you."

"Maybe when you Americans have pushed the Germans far from my city, I will enjoy moments with you, Rachel." His look was so intense, so knowing yet scarred, that Rachel wanted to walk away yet felt compelled to stay. Was he memorizing her features, the details that made her unique or the ones that reminded him of her mother? Would she someday find herself painted onto one of his canvases?

"Do I have any siblings?"

He shook his head. "My wife and I were not blessed. You and my paintings are what I leave."

Such an odd way to say something. Almost as if he thought he had a foot already in the grave, which as another series of shells whizzed by might be true of everyone near Florence.

Glass crunched in the distance. Scott jerked toward Renaldo. "Did you expect anyone?"

"No, but the building is not closed. Anyone can enter."

"It's on my list of items to fix immediately."

Rachel had seen his list, seen the innumerable items that filled it. But with soldiers not allowed into the area except for essential AMG officers, the chance of getting guards for a building, no matter how historic and significant, remained small.

Scott pushed her behind him. "Stay in this nave until we know who's coming and hang on to these papers for me." She nodded and he leaned toward her. "Promise me."

"Yes, Scott."

He leaned closer, and her pulse picked up its pace. He stopped when they were nose to nose. "I love you, Rachel Justice." He swooped in for a kiss, then turned to leave before she could respond.

I love you. The words reverberated through her as the men

moved from the niche she'd slipped into. She longed to shout a response back to him. Whisper the words. Anything to let him know she felt the same.

This was wrong. Very wrong. Scott couldn't shake the tightness in his gut as he moved away from Rachel. From the moment Renaldo had arrived speaking cryptically as if his demise was imminent, Scott hadn't liked the situation. Now that at least one someone was joining their party, he liked it less. It felt like a setup, but he didn't think Renaldo had arranged it. Why would the man give paintings to Rachel if he never expected her to collect? Unless he wanted to get rid of a woman who claimed to be his daughter. Scott shook the thoughts from his head.

The man longed for time with Rachel.

If he and his wife couldn't have children, Scott understood why learning he had a daughter would be a powerful, moving moment.

Now Renaldo walked in front of him, not shifting from hiding spot to hiding spot. He strode toward whatever approached, occasionally stepping in the middle of glass with its accompanying crunch.

A moment later the noise near the stairs ended. Scott slid farther behind a short wall that provided a limited barrier between him and the stairwell and slipped his small pistol from his waistband. He doubted the gun would be much help in a fight, but it was all he had. Having Tyler with his rifle would be an asset at the moment, though who knew if Tyler would have fired first and asked questions later. Either way Tyler had shown himself a traitor, and Scott had no backup.

Rough German reached his ears, and Scott tried to pick out a word. German? Here? He'd heard there was the possibility of a few Germans remaining behind in this part of Florence to stir up ongoing chaos, but he hadn't expected to run into one. He'd have left Rachel behind if he'd had to tie her to a chair to keep her there rather than bring her to the enemy. How could he keep her safe now? Warn her of the danger?

Renaldo's voice reached him, soft, placating, words obscured. What was the man doing?

Another voice answered, this one in Italian. Who? The professor? Surely the man couldn't be part of this conversation. Scott hadn't seen him since he disappeared the prior night.

Scott inched toward the passage. He had to get a glimpse of what happened on the other side of the wall. He edged closer until he could slip around just enough to eyeball the scene.

Renaldo's back faced him as the man walked toward two men. One had the bearing of a soldier, the rigid attention and sneer of one of Germany's elite. Next to him stood Professor Berti, who mangled his fedora in his grasp.

The muffled German and Italian mixed into a smorgasbord of indecipherable sound. After watching for a moment, Scott edged back around the corner. If a German was here, in territory the Allies supposedly held, this situation had escalated to a level Scott couldn't manage.

Light poured through the shattered windows, limiting the shadows. How could he help Renaldo without understanding what they discussed? Maybe this was a planned meeting after all.

The snarl on the German's face didn't make it seem like one between equals, though.

Scott jerked when he felt warm breath on his neck. He spun and grasped Rachel's shoulders to keep her from falling. "What are you doing?"

"Checking on you." Her voice was low but dangerous if anyone heard. "Where's Renaldo?"

"Out there. You promised you'd stay back and guard those papers."

"No one's coming from that direction, and the silence made me nervous."

The voices rose on the other side of the room, and Scott put a finger to his lips. Rachel nodded but settled next to him.

"Why would you consult with the Americans?" The words were startlingly clear. The German must have switched to Italian and walked closer to Renaldo.

"They came to me."

Scott frowned. The answer was partly correct. At Montegufoni they had found him, but he had sought them in Florence, brought them to the Uffizi.

The professor spoke up. "He sent a message to them."

"What are they saying?"

Scott placed a hand over Rachel's mouth before she revealed their location.

"You are no longer a friend of the Reich?" The clip of the man's boot heels neared their location. "What shall we do about that?"

The sound of a slide being pulled back captured Scott's attention. He inched back around the corner in time to see the German extend his Luger.

"Where is the art?" The man pointed the pistol at the professor. "I will kill him if you do not tell me."

"There is none to move." Renaldo tipped his chin, clutching his hat. "It was too dangerous to bring any back from the castle. And without transport . . ." The man shrugged. "What could I do?"

Was the man trying to buy time? "We need to go." Scott pointed toward the other direction.

Rachel nodded, edging back toward the nave and the other door.

Renaldo turned their direction, a mask of horror distorting his features. The German pulled the trigger, and Professor Berti collapsed without a sound. A pool of red seeped from his head onto the floor.

Scott pulled out his gun, but before he could do anything, Renaldo pulled a small firearm from his jacket. The barrel wavered slightly as he pointed it at the German officer. "Run." The word fell from Renaldo's lips before a puff escaped his gun, and he collapsed to the side.

The German growled and moved toward them, his arm hanging at his side.

Rachel screamed and reached for her father as Scott pulled her back.

He shook her. "He did that for you. Come now. Don't let it be in vain."

She looked at him, eyes hollow.

"Do you hear me?"

She gave a slow nod, then tightened her grip on his hand. He tugged her after him, and they sprinted to the next wall. A spray of bullets followed them. When they reached the wall, Scott sucked in a breath. "I counted eight bullets. He'll have to reload. Run!"

Chapter 37

RACHEL SOBBED AS SHE ran back to the niche, the wrong direction from where her father must lie. She scooped up her father's bag and kept moving. Scott led her through a maze of small rooms and chambers. Her stomach wanted to revolt at the image of Professor Berti dead and her father falling.

She trembled as Scott dragged her into another room. This one had a half wall he hunkered behind. "We'll catch our breath here."

The silence was as deafening as the gunshots. Where was the German? Could he creep up on them? "Should we keep moving?"

"I need a moment to think how to get out." Scott cupped her face, made her look at him. Lines etched his face. "Your father planned for this. He had a gun."

She nodded, sinking into the feel of him with her. Would she escape this building? Glass crunched somewhere and she jerked.

Scott eased up, then back down. "I can't see the soldier. We have to get out of here, get you to safety, send someone for Renaldo." His words rambled as if he was talking to himself as much as to her. Of course he was. He'd known her father for years.

"All right."

"Pray we pulled the German away in time." He released her and fisted his hands. "We can't stay here, but we have to be smart. Stay close, and we'll make it back to the other side of the Arno."

They slipped through the vast maze of the Uffizi. As they ran down a staircase, Rachel froze when she saw the German skirt around the corner. Scott tugged on her arm, but she refused to budge. She could never find her way back to her father without Scott. She'd be lost in a hopeless circle, but if the soldier had left, was it safe to go back?

He gave his life for me. She choked on the words. Why would a father who didn't know her sacrifice himself? Had he mirrored Christ in that moment? Was that the way God loved her? Sacrificially? So much more than she could ever hope to deserve . . . yet He'd given His all for her.

Scott tugged her forward again. "We can't stop. Not yet."

The heat pushed against her as he led her out of the building. "As soon as I get you back to the gardens, I'll come back. Check on your father."

"It will be too late." She turned to go back in. She couldn't leave him after she'd just found him.

He yanked her back. "You can't go in."

"Please. The soldier left, and I just found my father." Tears started anew and she hung her head.

Scott pulled her back into the sheltering walls of the Uffizi, then into his arms, his solid embrace that offered sanctuary. He opened his mouth, then closed it. "I will give you fifteen minutes. If there is the faintest noise, I will rush you out of here."

In a flurry of action, he swung her through a reverse course, retracing their steps to the main floor. Nothing stirred except for a bird that flew in one window and then raced out another. When they reached the top floor, he set her in the niche. "Do not move from this spot unless I tell you. Understand?"

She nodded, afraid to trust her voice. Long minutes passed as she waited. Finally Scott returned. "Come quickly."

When she saw her father, she cried out. Red covered his chest and shoulder. She rushed to his side and fell next to him. "I am so sorry," she sobbed. "I should have stayed back."

Her father's dark eyes fluttered open, then closed.

"Stay with me. Please."

"Daughter." The word was a benediction on his lips. A balm to her aching heart. "You are worth this." He shuddered, then was still.

"Papa!" She rubbed his shoulder, looked for breath, any sign of movement. "Scott, help me. Help." She could feel her panic rising in the face of his utter stillness.

She couldn't lose him, not when he'd tried so hard to protect her.

Scott pulled her back. "I'm sorry."

She twisted away from him, feeling emptied inside, like every emotion had been scooped up and thrown across a canvas. A smattering of color and form but an absence of depth. She'd wanted to know him, learn more about him, but now she couldn't.

You can know Me. The words resounded through her heart. An invitation to come closer. How she wanted to.

"We have to leave."

Rachel stood. "Thank you for the paintings, Renaldo." Sobs edged her words. Then she turned and followed Scott from the Uffizi. The weight of what had happened followed her.

She pulled into herself and searched her heart as Scott led her back to the gardens and then back to Montegufoni. Over the next days Scott spent more and more time in Florence, and she spent time in her room or in the baroque gardens at Montegufoni. She read the Bible Scott had found and pondered what her father had done. Most of all she sought peace. That elusive feeling.

The days passed in a blur—trips into the city, wrestling with the AMG for more passes, the miles of paperwork that never ended. Visits to different buildings and monuments in the heart of Florence in an effort to get repairs launched led to more paperwork. A never-ending cycle of paper and red tape. Some days Scott felt caught between the church, the art superintendents, and the battle that still raged too close to the city.

At night he escaped to Montegufoni. Rachel had stopped traveling with him. Had she worked out a break from her editor? He didn't push. Instead he did what he could to ease the way for her to sell one of Renaldo's paintings. His assistant curator back in Philadelphia assured him multiple buyers were interested. But each day felt like a delay that could make Renaldo's sacrifice meaningless.

Through it all Rachel had pulled inside herself, and he'd sit next to her praying for God to reach her heart.

She had captured his, and it killed him to wait, not knowing how to smooth the process or speed it along.

Three weeks after that day in Florence, he drove back to Montegufoni with a letter in his pocket. A radio from his assistant sat next to it. He prayed the letter held news as good as the radio message. He jerked the trusty jeep into park and hurried toward the courtyard. The bite in the evening air made him wonder what fall would be like in the Tuscan countryside. The rain was already intermittent but always threatening. It looked like another fall and winter of slogging through the Italian countryside waited for the poor grunts.

Scott shook a couple lingering raindrops from his jacket and looked for the bench Rachel often occupied. Most evenings he'd find her there even in a light drizzle, waiting for him. If it was dry, the sketchbook would sit in her lap, her momma's letters next to her. A time or two she'd even had her camera, though it wasn't quite the automatic attachment it had been.

Today she wasn't on the bench, so he headed to the kitchen. Only a few refugees remained. As the fight had moved north of Florence, the families had left determined to rebuild. He'd grab a glass of water before he started looking for her.

Soft voices greeted him as he reached the half door. Rachel laughed softly, and he looked through to see her wiping tears from her cheeks. He raised a hand as she found his eyes.

A shy smile graced her face, and his heartbeat quickened. She had to be the most beautiful woman God had created.

As he studied her face, he imagined a life with her. Growing old. Having children, then watching them parent grandchildren. It sounded like the perfect life. One he would be content to know and live.

"Enter." Renaldo's sister welcomed him with flour-covered hands. "Your Rachel makes pasta."

Rachel grimaced and shook her hands over the table. "I'm pretty terrible at it."

"You will improve."

"I doubt it. I never could make bread either. Guess I should leave the cooking to others." She turned toward Scott. "Your day was . . . ?"

"More of the same until I left." He pulled out the letter, studied the address a moment, then handed it over. "A letter for you."

She accepted it, holding it against her. "Your day couldn't have been that routine."

"Close. I've got more news."

She swallowed. "They're moving you north?"

"No, I'll be here. Is that all right?"

"I don't want you to leave."

He nodded. "I don't want to leave you either. At some point we'll get separated."

"Not yet." She shuddered. "I couldn't stand it. Being alone."

Her hand rested on the table between them. He grasped it, trying to infuse her with his strength. "I have to trust that God sees us and knows our desires." Renaldo's sister had moved away, giving them an illusion of privacy. He'd bet she still heard every word. "I heard from Philadelphia."

Rachel inhaled sharply. "Is there a buyer?"

"Yes, and it'll be a substantial sum. This particular art investor wants to increase his holdings. He liked the exhibit and has offered several thousand for one painting."

"Is that okay? Or is he overpaying?"

Scott clamped down a laugh. "It's a bit high, but I agree with his assessment that Renaldo Adamo will become a name many know and appreciate. Rachel, your father created works that speak to people. As we leave this war behind us, his paintings will be in demand. I wouldn't be surprised if the man is able to resell the painting in a couple years for much more."

"So I should keep it? Wait until it appreciates?"

"No. You need the money now for your mom's care. Renaldo knew that, and I have a feeling he'd approve."

Rachel's eyes misted and she nodded. "Then sell it." She dipped her chin again. "Thank you."

"You're welcome." He would do so much more for her if she asked. He was grateful to do anything to relieve her burdens. He tapped the envelope where it rested in her hands. "Gonna read it?"

"I'm afraid. The next letter could tell me Momma's passed and I was here." Her fingers tightened on the paper. "Before I met Renaldo, I accepted I'd be alone. Now . . ." Her voice trailed off. "I get so sad to think of that day."

"I can leave if it's easier to read it alone."

She grabbed his hand. "Please. Stay."

He settled onto a wicker-back chair next to her and let the silence settle as Rachel played with the envelope. After a few minutes she gingerly opened the V-mail. The paper shook as her gaze trailed down the page.

"Everything okay?"

"Yes. They've seen a couple of photos they're sure are mine in the paper. Momma appears headed to remission. If we can get her the treatment, the prognosis is much improved."

"Then let's get that painting sold."

"Thank you again, Scott. For everything. For helping me find my father." Her fingers played with the locket at her neck. He fought to keep his attention focused on her face. "For loving me."

His heart thundered to a stop at her words.

A flicker of emotion flashed across Scott's face, too fast for Rachel to decipher.

"I'm sorry. I didn't mean . . ."

He placed a finger on her lips, stilling her frantic attempt to make things right. "Shhh."

"I love you, Scott Lindstrom."

"Shhh." He leaned closer until she could feel his breath against her cheek. As the area cleared of refugees, leaving just a few men in the security detail and a few who came and went as their work allowed, she'd tried to prevent them from having time alone. Now she wanted to give in to the longing that surged through her to feel his arms wrapped around her, holding her close enough to feel his heart. Instead he teased her by lingering in the space right above her.

"Scott . . ."

"Shhh." He leaned close until his breath mingled with hers.

Then his lips claimed hers, and she sighed.

A moment later he pulled back, searching her eyes. "Rachel, I want to spend the rest of my life getting to know you. Even in that time I know I will barely plumb the depths of who you are. But I want to know and love you the rest of my days."

Her mouth fell open. With conscious thought she closed it and searched for words. "Is that a proposal, fine sir?"

His eyes tightened and then he relaxed. "Yes, if you will have me."

She leaned toward him and matched her lips to his.

A minute later he pulled back, and she looked breathlessly at him. "That was a yes?"

She nodded. "You are my home, Scott."

As she rested in the circle of Scott's arms, she understood the way God had shadowed her life with His grace, even when she didn't know to look for Him. He'd provided an opportunity for her to work in Italy. Then He'd sent Scott to work with her and keep her safe. He'd even led her to her earthly father if only for a few days. In the process He'd reaffirmed His deep love for her.

Peace settled over her, and tension leached from her muscles.

She could rest in God's care. And she could rest in Scott's love.

Rachel smiled as Scott's arms tightened around her.

She'd found her home in the storm of war.

Author Note

A story is rarely created in a vacuum. For me the process often starts with the spark of a historical hook. For this book that spark ignited when I found Robert M. Edsell's book *Monuments Men* at the library the summer of 2010. From my first glance at the cover with its photo of World War II soldiers carrying paintings, I was hooked. While his book focuses primarily on France and Germany, it created a passion to learn more. That led me to other books including *The Venus Fixers* by Ilaria Dagnini Brey and *The Rape of Europa* by Lynn Nicholas and its accompanying documentary. While Robert Edsell had a book on the Italy art campaign release in May 2013, I'd already completed this novel. I look forward to reading it in the future. My deepest appreciation to the men and women who do the research to write the books that bring history to life.

However, the book that was key to knowing the time line and challenges of the Monuments Men as they approached Florence was *Florentine Art under Fire* by Frederick Hartt. He served as a Monuments Man in Italy and wrote the book in 1949. I relied heavily on portions of his book to capture how the Monuments Men responded to the devastation and challenges in Florence.

When I wanted to get a sense for life in Tuscany during the war, I stumbled upon a wonderful diary: *War in Val D'Orica* by

Iris Origo. You can imagine the thrill when she talked about the Monuments Men in the pages of her journal. *The Day of Battle* by Rick Atkinson provided key information and framework for the aftermath in Naples as well as the fighting around Florence. *Where the Action Was* by Penny Coleman and *The Women Who Wrote the War* by Nancy Caldwell Sorrel were two of the resources that helped me understand what it was like to be a woman journalist during the war. *Assignment to Hell* by Timothy M. Gay gave me invaluable information about the campaign up Italy from a reporter's perspective. The tidbit about how the Rome newsroom reacted to the news of D-Day came from that fascinating look at four reporters during World War II.

The history is so important to me that I do all I can to get the details correct. However, any mistakes are mine alone.

Thank you for joining me on this journey into a little told story of World War II and the battle to save the treasures of Western civilization in the face of aerial warfare.

Acknowledgments

I couldn't have written this book without Julie Gwinn's enthusiasm. From the first moment I mentioned the idea at ACFW in 2010, she has been a staunch supporter of this idea and the story. Karen Solem, my agent, has been a constant source of encouragement about my World War II books. Thank you, Karen, for reinforcing my desire to write stories about the Greatest Generation. Julee Schwarzburg has a reputation for being one of the elite editors in the Christian book world. For this book I had the supreme privilege of working with her. Thank you for your care with my characters, the story, and the history. I learned so much!

Many thanks also to Dave Schroeder and Kim Stanford. Dave, your vision for this book and passion for getting the word out has been a huge blessing. It's been a true pleasure to work with you. Jennifer Lyell, thank you for your support.

I have also been blessed with a host of first readers. My daughter Abigail was the first person to read this book. Thank you for sharing your excitement as you read. Casey Herringshaw, Robin Miller, Sue Lyzenga, and Ashley Clark are stalwart first readers. Not only are these women talented writers, but they each bring a different skill they lovingly apply to my stories before my editors see them. Sue, thank you for your attention to detail and getting the words right. Robin, thanks for making the sacrifice of reading a hysterical. And Casey and Ashley, I so appreciate your sharing your talents with me and can't wait to someday hold your first novels!

When this book was complete, my cousin Beth Hraban graciously read it for accuracy on Italy. She and her husband, Matt, had taken a vacation of a lifetime in Italy and spent time in Tuscany and Florence. Not only did she read it for details, but she also shared her photos with me. Someday I'll get to Florence. Until then, thanks for sharing your experiences and making sure Rachel's matched!

My husband, Eric, is an immense support to me. He is quick to research when I need help and a great sounding board when I need to test an idea. He is also my loudest cheerleader. Thank you for always believing in me.

Discussion Questions

If you would like to have me participate in your book club, please go to my website at http://caraputman.com and contact me. I'd love to join you by phone if in person doesn't work.

1. Rachel Justice is on an impossible journey. Have you ever been thrust on a journey where success seemed impossible?

2. Rachel's mother tells her to leave her father alone, but Rachel can't. Have you ever faced a situation where you chose to directly go against a parent's instruction? How did it affect your relationship?

3. Rachel travels to Italy during World War II for the love of a parent. Do you think she made the right decision? Why or why not?

4. Many of us have experienced abandonment and pain at the hands of those who should love us. How do you recover from that?

5. Rachel has a hard time seeing God as a Father who loves her and would lay down His life for her. Do you think our image of God is affected when a parent is absent in our lives?

6. Scott is a man on a mission. Do you think his mission (saving Western civilization) was a valid one in a time of war?

7. Which character did you find yourself relating to more: Rachel or Scott? What drew you to that character?

8. Scott and Rachel find each other during a high-stress, adrenaline-laced time in their lives. In your experience is that a good time to form a relationship? Should they take any precautions? If so, how would you advise Rachel to proceed?

9. Which of the characters would you like to get to know better? Why?